"A refreshingly different hero, in a splendid coming-of-age tale of assassins set to track down another assassin, with a dash of intrigue, magic, skulduggery . . . I'll warn you now, this is one of those books that I'll pester you mercilessly about"
Espresso Coco

"With an original, immersive world that wouldn't let me go and a pair of assassins worth rooting for, *Age of Assassins* is a pleasure to read. I can't wait for more!"
Melissa Caruso, author of *The Tethered Mage*

"Leaves you wanting more from Girton . . . phenomenal"
The Tattooed Book Geek

By RJ Barker

The Wounded Kingdom
Age of Assassins
Blood of Assassins

Blood of Assassins

PRAISE FOR THIS SERIES:

"Outstanding. Beautifully written, perfectly paced and assured. Kept me reading well into the early hours of the morning. A wonderful first book – a wonderful book, period – that should be at the very top of your to-read list"
James Islington, author of *The Shadow of What Was Lost*

"A poison-store of fantasy and murder-mystery, with a pinch of coming of age. I wholly agree with the recommendation 'for fans of Brent Weeks and Robin Hobb', but it's clear RJ Barker has his own distinctive style, voice and brand, and that main character Girton Club-foot stands on his own two feet, club foot or not"
Fantasy Faction

"A dark-humoured game of cat and mouse between assassins, with traitors on all sides"
David Dalglish, author of the Shadowdance series

"Simply unputdownable . . . the perfect mix of fantasy and mystery"
Fantasy Book Review

"Dead gods, dread magic, and a lead that feels like a breath of fresh air. Great fun"
Peter Newman, author of *The Vagrant*

"A riveting tale that never fails to disappoint. I'm calling it now – if you're a fantasy fan, then RJ Barker is an author you need to be paying serious attention to"
The Eloquent Page

"Often poignant and always intriguing, *Age of Assassins* reveals its mysteries with the style of a magic show and the artful grace of a gifted storyteller"
Nicholas Eames, author of *Kings of the Wyld*

"Readers will appreciate Barker's complex mythology and smoothly flowing plot"
Publishers Weekly

"Both a coming of age story and a tale of twisty intrigue, *Age of Assassins* builds a compelling fantasy world and peoples it with characters you can care about. Riddled with intrigue and dangerous magic, this is a hugely enjoyable debut"
Jen Williams, author of *The Copper Promise*

"A combination of swords-and-sorcery fantasy, *Assassin's Creed* and an Agatha Christie murder mystery. This is well worth a go for fans of the genre"
British Fantasy Society

"*Age of Assassins* is a beguiling story of action and intrigue combined with a poignancy and humour that are as sharp as any blade"
Jon Skovron, author of *Hope and Red*

Blood of Assassins

RJ Barker

www.orbitbooks.net

ORBIT

First published in Great Britain in 2018 by Orbit

All characters and events in this publication, other than those clearly in the public domain, are fictitious and any resemblance to real persons, living or dead, is purely coincidental.

A CIP catalogue record for this book is available from the British Library.

ISBN 978-0-356-50857-3

Typeset in Apollo MT by Palimpsest Book Production Limited, Falkirk, Stirlingshire

Printed and bound in Great Britain by CPI Group (UK) Ltd, Croydon CR0 4YY

Papers used by Orbit are from well-managed forests and other responsible sources.

Orbit
An imprint of
Little, Brown Book Group
Carmelite House
50 Victoria Embankment
London EC4Y 0DZ

An Hachette UK Company
www.hachette.co.uk

www.orbitbooks.net

For Mum, Dad and John

Chapter 1

A ground mist was rising. The sun brushed the dew-soaked grass, and after days walking through the stink and dirt of the eastern sourlands the riotous excitement of yearsbirth made me drunk on the scent of early-morning blossom. Far over the horizon the Birthstorm swelled, towering pillows of dark cloud that heralded the giant storm which told us yearsbirth was truly here.

It felt like a weight on my back.

The mercenaries came upon us in that moment when the world seemed unreal – poised between outgoing night and incoming day. Six attacked, four men and two women of the Glynti, a hard and relentless people from the arid mountains far across the Taut Sea, where water was as valuable as bread and those who could not prove their worth were killed out of hand. If our attackers had been men of Maniyadoc they would have come for me first, seeing a man in armour as more of a danger than a woman, but they were not. The Glynti tribes kept to the old ways, and besides, if they hunted us they knew who we were. They knew my master was the real danger.

Four went for her, two for me. They had roarers, long sticks that sent out shards of sharp metal in a cough of smoke and fire; as weapons they are as ugly and as poor at killing as most Glynti. One exploded, killing its bearer and wounding the woman with him. The other made a horrendous noise and shredded a small bush by my side.

My master and I were tired, we fought in silence.

The Glynti are fierce but rely on numbers and savagery. I had spent five years as a mercenary, stood in shieldwalls facing down charging mounts and wasn't scared of a few men and women in animal skins, no matter how hard they fought.

"I'll skin you alive, boy," hissed the huge Glynti, the first to approach me. His long beard was dyed with a blue stripe and his blond hair was tied in braids which snaked out from underneath a rusted helmet. In one hand he held a heavy sword and in the other he twirled a skinning knife, laughing all the while. "I'll carve the skin from your bones, child," he said, his mouth an unkempt wall of missing teeth.

I have lain back in silence while my master carves magical glyphs which twitch and move of their own accord into my flesh.

I am not afraid of pain.

"In truth, I've never been comfortable in this skin." I smiled at him, and for a moment he was confused, but only a moment. He feinted with his knife. I ignored it. Then he brought his sword over and let its weight bring it down on me. I angled my large shield, taken in single combat from a Loridyan champion and painted with a bleeding eye, and his blade slid away on it and bit into the earth as I brought the beaked warhammer, taken from a man I had killed in vengeance, round in a swing which punched a neat hole in his helmet and felled him.

I glanced over at my master. She fought with two stab-swords, dancing lithely in and out of the flashing blades of her attackers as if they did not exist. For a moment her skill stole my breath away, and then the second Glynti was on me. This one was far more careful and held a long spear – a better weapon against an armoured man with a shield – but like his fellow he was too used to ferocity winning his battles. His only skill lay in attack and he lacked the warrior's greatest ally – patience. He came in, jabbing his spear against my shield with a teeth-grating screech of metal on metal. As he jabbed again I put all my strength into a forward push of the shield. I felt the strength of his blow in the jarring of my shoulder joint. He felt it in his hands and though he did not drop the spear his control of it lapsed for long enough to let me in close. The warhammer rose and fell, rose and fell, rose and fell until his head was a pulpy mush of grey brains, white bone and bright red blood.

"Girton –" my master's soft voice behind me "– they are done." Blood dripped from a cut on her arm. It ran down her hand, along the hilt of her stabsword to mingle with the Glynti blood that stained her blade. It was only when she spoke that I heard myself, heard the noise that I was making, the screaming of an animal. I dropped my weapon in the mud. The warhammer was heavy.

"One still lives," I said, and pointed at the woman who had been felled when the roarer exploded. I walked towards her, unsheathing the black metal stabsword I kept on my left hip.

"Wait, Girton."

"Why?" I continued towards the woman, she was burned down one side but had no killing wounds. "She will only tell others where we are."

"Wait!" My master jumped over a corpse and ran to me, grabbing my arm just as I was about to kneel down and slit the wounded woman's throat. "There are better ways." I stared at my master, the muscles of my arm tight against her grip.

"So you say." I brushed her hand from my arm and sat back on bloodied grass.

The burned woman watched all this with eyes as bright as those of the black birds of Xus the unseen, god of death.

"Your lover is fierce even though he's mage-bent, Merela Karn," croaked the woman to my master. If she had ever had beauty for the burns to spoil it had long since fled.

"He is not my lover," said my master.

"Are you one who prefers women, then? He is young, strong . . ."

"Quiet!" My master grabbed the woman's face with her hand, breaking the burned skin around her mouth and leaving a raw fingerprint that had the woman hissing in pain. "What tribe are you?"

The Glynti woman had eyes like a hunting lizard, as blue as the sky they dived from and full of the same scorn for life.

"Geirsti." she said, the name of her tribe distorted by my master's hold on her face and the pain of her burns.

"And your name?"

"Als."

"Well, Als of the Geirsti. Listen to me. I am Merela Karn and my companion is Girton Club-Foot. We have killed many Glynti as we travelled back to Maniyadoc. Seventeen of the Corust, twelve of the Jei-Nihl and fourteen of the Dhustu. By my reckoning that means if you head back to your mountains the Geirsti will outnumber the other tribes. Take this information to your leader, conquer new lands and send no more of your young to die in search of the price on our heads."

The Glynti woman stared at my master. Before she replied we were interrupted by a grunt from behind us. I turned, the first man I had hit with the hammer was convulsing.

"My man," said the tribeswoman. "He fought well. Let your boy give him a good death, and I will consider what you say." I looked to my master and she gave me a nod so I walked over and slit the man's throat with my black blade. By the time I returned the Glynti woman was on her feet. "I will give your message to our clanwoman."

"My master told you to stop sending people after us . . ." angry steps towards her, blade in my hand, but my master held me back once more.

"Thank you, Als of the Geirsti," she said. "Leave here and die well."

The woman staggered away into the ground mist, turning at that moment when wisps of thickened air made her look like a ghost.

"I will die well," she said, "but you won't, Merela Karn. No, you won't. You will die hard." The moist air swallowed her figure, leaving only laughter behind.

"She did not promise to leave us alone," I said. "You should have made her promise to leave us alone, or killed her."

"One more Glynti won't make a difference in the great scheme of things. Girton, but if I can convince them to start a tribal war they'll be too busy killing each other to come after us. The Geirsti are the biggest tribe, and . . ." Her voice tailed away and when I turned to her she looked stricken, her dark skin grey with shock "Geirsti," she said, and stared at the cut on her arm. "Dark Ungar's stolen breath," she hissed, "the Geirsti are poisoners." As she spoke she was pulling the rawhide cord from the neck of her jerkin and wrapping it around the top of her arm. "Girton, start a fire, hot as you can get it. Quickly."

"Yes, Master." A cold fell upon me, far deeper than could be explained by the yearsbirth morning chill, and it froze the simmering resentment that had been my companion for the years of our exile. I was running almost before I was aware of it. Wood is sparse in the Tired Lands, especially so near the border of the sourlands, but I found a derelict haystack, sodden with dew on the outside, and I burrowed within to pull dry grass from it. Beyond the haystack was a field where cows had been kept, and dry circles of dung punctuated the grass. When I returned my master had wrapped the cord so tightly around her bicep that her forearm had ballooned up and gone corpse blue.

"Quickly, Girton." My hand shook as I struck flint to steel. The flame refused to catch, as if the morning mist sought to foil me by sucking away the sparks. Finally I got an ember and set the grass to crackling, but I could see impatience on my master's face and knew the fire would not be hot enough quickly enough. "Give me your Conwy blade," she hissed.

"Why?" I asked. Stupid, time-wasting words.

"Because mine have crossed with the Geirsti's weapons and yours never leaves its scabbard," she spat. "Give me it." Her hand flashed out. I pulled the blade from the scabbard at my back and handed it to her; she gave me hers. "Stick this in the fire, Girton, get it hot, you know what to do." I nodded. "The poison acts quickly. I don't have time to wait for mine to heat so I will lose a lot of blood. Be ready."

"Wait, Master." And I was scared, like a child. "I should check the bodies for an antidote."

"You would know it how?"

I stood, my hands trembling, fear chasing anger in circles like a mad dog after its tail.

"I could go after the woman."

My master shook her head. "I'd be dead before you got back." She gritted her teeth against a spasm of pain. "No. It must be this way and we must be swift – I do not want to lose my hand. Give me your belt." Her teeth were chattering as I slipped the thick leather belt from my skirts and passed it to her. She paused before folding the leather double and forcing it into her mouth so she could bite down on it. Then she stared into my eyes, removed the belt for a second. "If I pass out, Girton, you must finish this."

"Yes, Master." Fear returned: fear of losing her, fear of being alone. She gave me a small smile, bit down on the leather and started taking short deep breaths through her nose. Then she nodded to me and pushed my knife into her wounded left arm.

She screamed against the leather belt, more in fury than pain, when she pushed the razor edge into her flesh three fingers' breadth above the wound. Then she forced the sharp metal down into her arm and along the bone, growling and moaning like an animal all the while. With a sound like a rotten apple being squashed underfoot the blade came out of her, taking a chunk of flesh as long as my fingers with it. Her hand convulsed, and my Conwy stabsword fell from it as she slumped forward, unconscious. I dived for her, grabbing her hand and pulling it into the air with one arm and using my other to cradle her limp body against me. Thick blood poured over my arm as I lay her down on the damp grass and pushed a cloth hard against the wound, the muscles in my arms straining and sweat starting from my forehead as I worked to keep up the pressure. I willed the knife in the fire to speed its way to glowing cherry red. *"Don't die, don't die,"* going round and round in my head like a ride at Festival. The thicket of scars on my chest that kept the magic in check writhed as the dark flow within tried to rise up and take advantage of my fear.

When the blade was hot enough I cauterised the wound in my master's arm – I doubted she would ever have the same skill with a blade after this – then I covered her in blankets from our packs. There was nothing else I could do past that so I sat, miserable, in front of the fire and tried not to think of the agony she had just put herself through or of how much mental discipline was required to cut out such a large piece of yourself.

I could not have done it.

The sun burned away the mist and winged lizards trilled a welcome to yearsbirth, flowers opened their colourful eyes in search of the sun, but I was as blind to them as they were to me. Somewhere, far in the distance, thunder rumbled.

Chapter 2

One foot in front of the other.

The rope straps of the travois bit into my shoulders and my master moaned and sweated. I had watched for a day and a night as the poison raged within her but had never crossed from my side of the fire to go to her. I had wanted to, but even as she fought with death there was a gulf between us – one scored out by the knives she had used to cut progressively deeper sigils in my flesh – and though I understood, had even asked for them, it was still hard not to resent her for it. There had been a moment, in the darkest part of the night while the moon hid her face behind silver clouds, when I had thought her battle over – lost.

Breathe out.

The mixture of poison and blood loss had weakened her– her breathing stopped – and there was silence. The fire cracked and popped in the darkness and the flames rose like a hedging come to catch a lost spirit. With our gods dead there would be no return to the land for my master. She would reside quiet in the dark palace of Xus the unseen, god of death, until the world was made again and the hedgings threw themselves into the sea from where the gods would be reborn.

But maybe the fire was not a hedging, maybe the heat was a wall that held her spirit prisoner.

Breathe in.

As the light of the sun returned to the land so the light

of life returned to her. She was not strong and her eyes did not open, but her breathing took on a regularity it had lacked in the night and it was as if I was released from a spell. Only then could I move, stiff and aching, to go find fuel for our dying fire. As I searched in the weak light I became convinced I was watched. I would catch movements from the corner of my eye – the Glynti. It was unlikely anyone from Maniyadoc would come this near to the sour-lands, and as the Glynti woman knew my master had been poisoned it made sense for her to wait rather than attack. Maybe she had more warriors with her or maybe she waited for more to come. Either way, I did not feel safe going beyond where I could see my master, and eventually I had made the travois by lashing together the Glynti roarers, spears, my shield and sacrificing my long bow. Then I began the long trek towards Maniyadoc where I hoped to find Rufra, the king, and my only friend.

One foot in front of the other. Sometimes it is the only thought you can allow yourself. When your muscles ache, when your master moans, when your back itches like a target for unseen weapons, when you are sure you are followed and that attack is inevitable.

One foot in front of the other.

One foot in front of the other as the ropes bite into your flesh. If Fitchgrass himself had jumped from the fields – a twisted mass of prickles, burrs and sly promises in the shape of a man – I would have sold my spirit to it for rest and my master's health.

But it did not, and there was only one foot in front of another.

Maniyadoc had changed in the five years I had been away, selling my sword and my morals to the highest bidder while trying to stay ahead of the Open Circle's assassins. I had seen much of war: we had spent half a year with the Ilstoi of the far seas, they believed that if you angered the land it would form itself into a giant and smash all you owned and loved, replacing it with a carpet of green. It looked like one of these Ilstoi giants had been loosed in Maniyadoc. I trudged past farm buildings collapsed in on themselves and thick with grasses and small trees. Only when you looked more closely did you see the black scars of fire on timbers and the unnaturally straight cut marks of swords and axes. In other places the grass grew strange and thick, and when I put down the travois to forage along the sides of the roads for water I found bleached bones among the lush growth. I was not surprised. War had been my business for five years and it raged nowhere fiercer than in Maniyadoc where the three kings, Tomas, Aydor and my friend Rufra, warred for supremacy and access to the scant resources of a land scarred by the actions of ancient sorcerers.

Sorcerer. That word still sent a shudder through me, despite, or maybe because, I am one. As always when I thought of magic my mind slid away to other memories, replacing fear of what was in me with hate or anger.

The face of my lover, Drusl, in the stable, as she cut her throat to return her magic to the land.

A pain in my chest so fierce I had to stop. There had been other women, and men, since Drusl, but only one I had become close to, and even then it had not been love. The secrets inside me had killed Drusl and I held them close. Who I am and what I am could never be aired. I could not let myself get close to anyone, not truly close, and so I had not.

I walked on, one foot in front of the other, past fields overrun with weeds. In one place the road was verged with blood gibbets. I counted twenty, each one marked with the parched branch and tattered flag of a white tree on a green background that belonged to the Landsmen. Once, the blood gibbet, with its tortuous machinery of windmills and blades, had been solely for magic users, but above many of these were wooden plaques with "TRAITOR" burned into them. Some had no sign above them, but all contained bodies in various states of decay, many wearing the red and black I knew Rufra had taken for his colours. It seemed the war had allowed the Landsmen to run rampant with their cruel punishments, and they had gone beyond their usual search for magic users. This close to the sourlands the stink of putrefaction was barely discernible.

In the last of the blood gibbets was a man, young, emaciated and crack-skinned. He croaked something, whether begging for water or food I do not know. He wore the yellow and black that showed he was one of Aydor's men. I had tangled with Aydor before and had been instrumental in putting Rufra on his throne. He had been a cruel, stupid boy who killed for his own amusement; I had nothing but hate in me for the old king's heir. No doubt he had grown into a cruel and stupid leader. I walked on, leaving the man to his fate.

One foot in front of the other.

I kept my eye open for signs of assassins, the subtle signposts of the Open Circle – knotted grass, a scratched post, an arrangement of flower petals, but though death was everywhere signs of assassins were curiously absent. Occasionally I found a bit of scratch, but the requests were either struck through as fulfilled or so worn as to be clearly years old. My master had said that the Open Circle generally avoided war; our skills were wasted in the shieldwall. When I questioned why we were fighting in them she would not answer. But still, it appeared the Open Circle were not active in Maniyadoc, and that made me a feel a little safer.

As the midday sun burned away the last of the morning chill the Glynti made their move. I was passing through a steep-sided gulley, a place where it seemed a massive axe had scored a furrow in the middle of a wooded copse, and the branches, late to leaf, were a skeletal lacework of black against blue sky. A voice rang out and stilled the singing of the winged lizards.

"Stay still, boy. Stay or we shoot."

The voice of the woman we had let go. I put down the travois and slowly unstrapped the warhammer from my thigh. It was a crude and vicious weapon, a hardwood staff topped with a head made of glittering stone. One side was beaked for punching through armour and the other rounded for breaking limbs. I itched for my shield, but it was too securely worked into the travois for me to get at.

"I knew I should have killed you," I shouted into the wood, emboldened by the weight of the hammer in my hand.

"You should have," rang the reply, bouncing from tree to tree and robbing itself of direction and distance as it worked its way down the steep and mossy slopes. "But as my life was spared I will give you one chance. The woman is dead already, you must know that. The poison cannot be stopped. Leave her there and walk away. Do that and we will not shoot you down."

"I wanted you dead, woman – you owe me no favours," I shouted back. "I think you bluff, I think there is only you and you wish me to walk away so you do not have to face me."

The woman laughed, a rich and hearty sound, and then she let out a piercing whistle. Glynti appeared from behind trees – only for the briefest second. I counted five but heard more behind me. I felt no fear, only an ache in my arms from the weight of the warhammer.

"We have numbers, boy."

"Then why let me live?"

A pause. Almost long enough for the timid winged lizards to begin their disturbed song again.

"You killed my man, maybe I want you as a replacement, eh? I'm giving you a chance to live, mage-bent boy. Take it."

She thought me a boy as I am small. Many make that mistake and it is their last.

"I will not leave my master." I spread my arms. "Shoot your arrows if you have them."

My breath came slowly and the world took on a rare clarity: branches bobbed, the fuzzy promise of life in their buds, grass waved and the sun warmed my skin.

No arrows came.

The wood rang again with the woman's laughter.

"You're a brave one, I'll give you that." She let out a piercing whistle and the Glynti appeared from behind the trees. Twelve of them, eight men and four women, including her. "You can't stand against us all, child." They pushed through knee-high bracken, treading carefully as they came down the steep slope. Eight stopped in front of me and the rest took up positions to my rear. A calm fell on me. It was like this before most battles – a time for readying yourself, for checking weapons and armour, preparing your mind for the moment to come when you took a life or lost your own. The Glynti hefted their weapons. The eight were going to rush me; the other four were there purely to make sure I did not escape.

"Come, boy," said the woman. "This is your last chance. Your master is dead in all but flesh. Walk away. I will still allow it." She picked a scab from one of the burns on her face and flicked it away. "We are not a greedy people; another can have your price."

"No."

"Walk away, boy."

"No."

"I will not ask again."

"Good. I am tired of talking."

She shrugged, and the men around her organised themselves into a rough shieldwall; their circular shields had been polished to a sheen and reflected distorted trees back at me.

As I readied myself, choosing how I would die on their charge and which Glynti I would take with me to Xus's dark palace, an argument broke out. A tall warrior with long, dyed-red braids was shouting at the woman in Glynti, a language I didn't understand. She shouted back at him and occasionally they would point at me.

"Brank would avenge his brother, boy." she shrugged. "But I have seen you fight and do not want to lose another bedmate."

"Then you and your people may walk away," I said, then added, "I will allow it."

She chuckled, shaking her head and looking at the ground.

"It is a pity you will die, I would have enjoyed you. You have spirit." She motioned Brank forward.

The warrior came on at a crouch with his shield raised and his curved sword held high. I waited for him to come near and thought that, had he been less of a fool, he would have brought a spear. He launched a swing at me with his sword and I jumped back, avoiding the blade. He brought his shield up, an instinctive reflex but the wrong one. The hammer came down, with all my strength behind it, on the shield – and like all Glynti shields it was a flimsy thing, thin metal over wood, and it shattered, as did the bones in the arm that held it. With a scream Brank launched himself at me, swinging his sword overarm. I grabbed the haft of the warhammer, one hand at the hilt, the other below the head, and blocked his blade .

Even though he was one-handed and in pain it was a jarring blow, and he followed it up with another and another, forcing me back until I tripped over a rut in the path. Brank aimed another blow and I twisted the hammer so his blade hit the stone end, shattering the sword's poor-quality metal. Then I brought round the pommel, crowned with the claw of some fearsome beast, and ripped the man's stomach open. I started to push myself up, thinking him beaten, but he threw himself at me, his entrails looping around our bodies as he knocked me back to the ground. As we rolled in the dirt in his blood and shit he managed to get one huge hand around my throat, squeezing the life out of me even as the life drained from him.

Breath hissed in and out of his teeth. I could smell the tang of his last meal and the badly cured hides he wore as armour. Through the trees behind him I thought I saw Xus the unseen fluttering though the shafts of sunlight. Reaching up I grabbed Brank's head, pushing my thumbs into his eyes and forcing a scream out of his mouth. Even blinded he kept his hand clamped around my throat, his thirst for vengeance overwhelming his pain.

My hand scrabbled at my side, looking for my stabsword. My vision began to swim and all feeling fled from my body. Did I have the blade? I didn't know. Time was running out. Above the Glynti hovered a figure of shadow and sadness. With all my strength I thrust my arm forward. It seemed every scar etched into my chest convulsed, grasping my body far tighter than Brank's hand around my neck, thrusting blades into my flesh. And then I was breathing, coughing and choking on the air, and the weight of the Glynti was gone from my chest.

I lived, for what it was worth.

The remaining Glynti had gathered around while I fought, standing in a ring, swords and spears extended towards me and faces twisted in disgust and horror. The body before me had a smoking hole where his throat should be and my blood sang a sweet and sickly song in my ears.

"Sorcerer," hissed the woman. "Maniyadoc's filth." She drew back her blade for a killing stroke and I did not have the strength to stop her.

The arrow took her though the throat and she fell, coughing, to her knees. The remaining Glynti turned as archers emerged from the undergrowth and the air filled with the thunder of mounted troops. Another round of arrows felled more Glynti and then three huge mounts charged in, heads down, lethal antlers sweeping from side to side to cut down anyone in their way with razor-sharp gildings. In moments the Glynti were dead and I was surrounded by armoured soldiers. They wore no colours and flew no loyalty flags, only stared down at me – suspicious eyes behind grimacing faceplates.

"Who are you?" asked their leader, a thin man. He was familiar but I could not place him. My mind was shattered, twisted and confused by what had happened. I had used magic – had it been that long since the Landsmen's Leash was cut into me to hold the magic at bay?

"Girton ap Gwynr," I said. Like a fool I used the name I had been known by in Maniyadoc when my master and I had brought down Queen Adran and her odious son, Aydor. All the prospective kings of Maniyadoc would know that name and only one would welcome hearing it.

"Girton ap Gwynr, eh?" said the Rider. "Well, my king will want to meet you." He lashed out with his boot, catching me on the side of my head, and I fell into a darkness I had been secretly longing for.

Chapter 3

A sacking hood was the walls of my cell. My head ached and I stank of old blood. When I tried to move I found I had been trussed like a hog for the spit, and I could barely tense my muscles without pain. Below the stink of the blood on my clothes the air was heavy with other scents: mud, mounts, mouldering grass and the rancid fat used to grease armour. Wind whispered across canvas and my skin was patched with cold by the touch of a breeze.

This was a battle camp, and an ill kept one at that. I froze so the hiss of my clothes against the groundsheet did not interfere with my hearing. Breathing. Someone else was in the tent with me.

"Master?" The scratch of leather on canvas as I moved. "Master?"

No reply, but whoever was there turned towards me. I heard the creak of leather and an infinitesimal increase in the volume of their breath.

"My master, where is she?"

No answer.

"Please, she was dying. Is she still alive?"

Still no answer, and it left me feeling angry, ashamed and weak at the begging tone in my voice. I resolved to say nothing more. Instead I fell back on counting out the seconds.

One, my master.

Two, my master.

And every second I counted was a reminder of her sweating and moaning as the Glynti poison sucked at her life. I approached fifteen "my-masters" before whoever shared the tent with me left.

I was taken from the tent some hours later. They cut the straps around my legs and lifted me to my feet while blood rushed back in a painful wave. I could have escaped, but the thought of facing the world without my master terrified me, the cuts she made were all that stood between me and the magic, and all that magic ever brought with it was destruction and death.

"Come on." I did not know the voice, a man of indeterminate age, and there was neither friendship not scorn in his it. He led me over slippery mud by my elbow.

He was not rough – maybe someone wanted me unharmed, the better to endure the torture. Part of me hoped that this was one of Rufra's camps but I knew it was unlikely. From the way I was being treated it was more likely to belong to Tomas or, even worse, Aydor, who had always delighted in casual cruelty and throwing around his considerable weight. Whoever it belonged to I felt sure that, at best, my neck would be meeting the chopping block before the end of the day. But if it was Aydor who held me that was unlikely; he would delight in my death, it would be long and agonising.

I did not bother to count the steps or work out the direction we walked from the feel of the yearsbirth sun on my skin. What point? I had run the world over to escape death and still ended up in this place with my master poisoned and myself captured by armed men and on the way to meet my fate. I was tired, tired of fighting, tired of pain, and I let them lead me as if I were a prize boar ready for slaughter.

We entered a large tent, the fierce heat of braziers warmed my face even through the sacking. A hand on my shoulder forced me to my knees. "The prisoner, sire."

Some communication must have passed, as the bag was pulled from my head. My vision swam. So many candles had been lit that their brightness dazzled me, a thousand stars shining in a smoky firmament.

The fug cleared. Focus returned. A chill settled in my stomach.

Leaning forward to scrutinise me from a raised chair was Aydor ap Mennix, formerly heir to Maniyadoc and the Long Tides. He was bigger now than he had been five years ago, weightier than he had been. A fool would have called him fat and underestimated him for it, but I had been among armies and I recognised a fighter, and I knew him for one. On the field he was the sort I would be wary of because size generally meant strength even if did not mean skill.

Aydor wore his brown hair long, falling around his shoulders, down his chest and catching on the bright yellow enamelling of his armour. The scar his mother had given him bisected his face and when he smiled I could see half his teeth were missing.

If nothing else, at least his breath would not be as rotten as before. Dead gods grant us such small mercies.

"Girton ap Gwynr," he said, "if that was ever your name."

"It wasn't," I said. "I call myself Girton Club-Foot."

"Girton Club-Foot." He chewed on the name thoughtfully for a while. "Is that not an insult, to be called Club-Foot?"

"Not if I am the one to choose it."

He nodded to himself.

"They call me the Fat Bear behind my back." I heard the guards around me stiffen – a jingling and chinking of armour. "They think I don't know they do it but I do. I quite like it if I'm honest, the bear part anyway." He looked up from me to the man by my side. "Cut Girton Club-Foot loose, Captain Thian. And give him back his weapons."

"Sire?"

"Do as I say," said Aydor, his voice sharp and used to command.

I was too shocked to speak. Then, as my bonds were cut

and my blades and the warhammer dropped by me, I wondered if he meant to fight me and if I cared enough to beat him. I stared at the weapons on the floor, wary that reaching for them may be the trigger that sprang the jaws of a trap.

Aydor stood, tottering slightly, and I realised he was drunk. He took a step forward and, using a hand to steady himself, sat on the low stage his wooden throne had been set upon.

"It's not a trick," he said, pointing at the weapons.

"Where is my master?" The words sprang from my mouth before I was aware they were even being formed.

"You mean the woman you were with?" He frowned as if confused; it was almost comical. "She's with my healer. He is foreign like her and he knows poisons."

"She lives?"

"For now. Mastal says he has halted the poison's advance but a cure confounds him. He says the Glynti are clever with poisons." He nodded to himself then pointed at me with a thick finger. "You killed my mother."

"Tomas's great-grandfather, Daana ap Glyndier, killed your mother," I said. It was true, though, to be fair, my master and I had put into motion the series of events that led to her death and put my friend Rufra on the throne. All in all, if I were to die here for that it would be worth my life.

"Maybe he did, but you had a hand in it." I nodded. He had been there after all. "You would have killed me too, given a chance." I nodded again and Aydor stood, carefully clambering back onto his throne, treating it as if it were an unruly mount that was likely to rear and send him sprawling onto the floor. When he finally settled he stared at me for a long time before speaking. "I forgive you," he said.

I could not have been more shocked if he had sprouted antlers and asked me to ride him around the tent.

"Sorry?"

"I have a child now, Girton Club-Foot." He tried to smile but it was as if thoughts of his child brought as much pain as pleasure. "A daughter. She's called Hessely and you have never seen a child as golden and beautiful as her." His smile broadened and he was no longer looking at me; his gaze rested far from the tent we were in.

"Congratulations?" I said, confused and unable to reconcile the man before me with the spiteful young man I'd known five years previously.

"They took her away from me, of course." He stared at the floor and then looked up. His gaze locked with mine, his blue eyes clear as ice. "I didn't meet my mother until I was seven, Girton, you know that? Seven. Before then I'd only ever known my nurse. First thing Mother did when she met me wasn't hold me, or even talk to me. She took away my favourite toy. She was a complete stranger who took away my toy and give me a sword. 'Kings don't have stuffed mounts,' she said." Aydor shook his head. "He was called Dorlay, my toy mount. She burned it and made me watch. Said it would harden me. Said kings need to be hard."

"She was a hard woman."

"She was a cruel woman!" he shouted, standing and dashing his goblet from the table by his throne with a gauntleted hand. Then he spoke more quietly, "And if we tell the truth, the Tired Lands are probably better off with her dead and myself nowhere near a throne. But still, I loved her." His hand briefly touched the scar on his face she had given him and then came to rest on the hilt of his stabsword. I glanced at the weapons lying before me.

"I do not blame you for wanting vengeance," I said. He stared at me as if I were a madman then shrugged, the leather beneath his armour creaking.

"I was telling you about Hessely," he said quietly and bent over, swaying slightly as he picked up his dented cup. "My Hessely . . . Her mother hated me. She died in childbirth and the nurse told me I had a daughter over her corpse. She looked frightened, the nurse, small and frightened, holding out this tiny bloody body and almost apologising for not handing me a son." He filled his cup from a barrel of perry on the other side of his throne. "But when I held Hessely, when her skin touched mine . . ." He drifted away again, then took a drink. "Everything changed. Nothing else mattered. The politics? The fighting? Thrones? They were all my mother's dreams, all her wants and needs, not mine. After that it was the priest Neander who talked me towards power." At Aydor's mention of the priest my ears pricked up a little. He had been the shadow behind so much at Maniyadoc, including the death of my lover, and thoughts of vengeance had kept me going through hardship and long, cold nights.

"Neander is here?"

Aydor stared at me as if I were an idiot and shook his head.

"I realised all I wanted was for Hessely to be safe, and from the moment I held her there was no other thought in my mind. Is that not strange? She could not talk, or even smile. But . . ." His voice tailed off and a tear ran down his cheek.

"Why are you telling me this, Aydor?"

"I want you to understand, of course." His brow furrowed in puzzlement again. "You need to understand. I made some very bad decisions you see, Girton Club-Foot, and I cannot put them right, not alone."

"And this is to do with your daughter?" I said haltingly. "You said they had your daughter, who are they?" He frowned as if I had missed something obvious. "Tomas and Neander of course."

Suddenly I felt like I understood where this was heading.

"You want me to get your daughter back?"

Aydor stared at me.

"Yellower's piss, no. She's quite safe. She carries the blood of kings and they want to marry her to Tomas's son, Diron, and besides, Celot guards her."

"Celot has left you?" It seemed impossible. The Heartblade had been utterly loyal to Aydor in his own childlike way.

"Celot? Left me? No, I sent him to her, to keep her safe. If anyone can, he can." He sat down again, a sadness falling over his scarred face. "I did send him away once. I called him a fool, you know? I called him a fool and sent him away."

"To guard Hessely."

"No, before that. Of course I was the fool. I have been such a fool. Thankfully Celot did not leave me. He hid in the woods outside the camp and when Neander decided to have me killed Celot was there. Fighting like a god. Saved me."

"Why did Neander want you dead?" In his alcoholic fuzz Aydor was hopping from subject to subject and I was finding his tale difficult to follow.

"Wait," he said. He emptied his goblet onto the floor and went over to a water butt in the far corner of the tent. He filled his cup from it and drank the contents in one gulp, then did it again and again. Once he had drunk his fill he stuck his head into the cold water. When he emerged, water streaming down his armour from the soaked ropes of his hair, his eyes seemed a little clearer. He glanced at the guards. "You can go." When they hesitated he roared, "Go!" He watched them leave and returned to his throne, filling his cup from the perry barrel before letting out a small noise that could have been a laugh or a cough. "So many times I dreamed of having you before me, you know? All the things I said I would do to you. Now that I actually have you here all I want to do is ask for your help. I'll beg, if needs be."

"Why, Aydor?"

He lifted his cup and stared at the hunting scenes chased into the gold.

"After Hessely was born, Girton, I saw it was wrong. All of it. The way I'd been raised, the lust for power. The constant wars. Wrong. I wanted it to stop. I told Neander that and we met with Tomas to discuss an alliance to finish Rufra and end the war."

"But?"

"I wanted Neander to meet with Rufra also. He wouldn't. I pressed him. At some point I think Neander realised his desire for power could be better served with Tomas than with me."

"What of Neander's sorcerers?" I whispered the words, unsure who knew about the plot that had brought down Aydor's mother.

"He told me they were dead."

"And you believed him."

"Girton," he sighed, "until Hessely was born I did not even think to question him. After she was born I no longer believed a word he said. A gulf grew between us and when I insisted on meeting Rufra I think that was the last straw. If Celot had not been as loyal as a hunting dog I would be dead now and Neander could carry on with his plans unopposed." He put his cup down. "But I am not dead."

"Why did you want to meet with Rufra? You hate him."

"Aye. I did. Maybe I saw in him something I could never be and that is why I loathed him." He picked up his cup again and laughed quietly. "Sometimes you only see truth through the crystal of hindsight." He stared at the floor, his huge shoulders rising and falling as he breathed. When he spoke again he spoke quietly. "Anyone can be a king, Girton, anyone. And anyone can find followers if they have money and power, but there are very few people who troops actually want to follow." He looked up, wet lips working at his few teeth. "I fought Rufra all across Maniyadoc." He sucked on his lips. "Sometimes I even won." Aydor sat back in his throne and took a drink from his goblet then let out a laugh. "More often I lost." He leaned forward. "I lost even when I should have won, Girton. His people always fought far harder than mine, and Rufra was always there when I lost, always in the thick of it, always."

"And you?"

"I watched from my mount. Too valuable to risk, as

Neander put it. I did fight of course – I led my cavalry – but Rufra mostly fought in the shieldwall."

"He was always reckless."

"Mad, Neander said, fighting next to the thankful, but when he was there those thankful fought like Riders." He took another drink. "Like Riders! He inspired them, see. Even when we outnumbered him it seemed to mean nothing. So I thought I should try it, fighting with the commoners. But Neander would not allow me to fight in the shieldwall no matter how I tried to reason with him. One day he let me take out a patrol, a patrol of living men and women of course – there were no thankful fighting in our army."

"How did that go then? Badly?" I could not keep the sneer out of my voice. It was not hard to imagine how the high-handed arrogant heir I had known would rub his troops up the wrong way.

"Yes, it went badly, but not in the way you think."

"Did you put many to death?"

He pointed at me casually with the hand holding his drink, as if I had not spoken. "I liked the troops. Got on with them. Had ten with me, good men and women all. But . . ." He let the word tail off and stared into the air. Outside I heard a mount whistle and men and women laugh.

"But?"

"I misread the map, never paid much attention to such things in my lessons. What sort of king has to read a map, eh?" He took another drink. "We got turned around, went the wrong way. Got ourselves too near Rufra's lines. By the time I realised that it was too late. He had us."

"Rufra?"

"Himself, aye. Caught us in a valley. My heart still jumps at the thought of him on that hunger-cursed white mount." Aydor squinted at me as if he was having trouble focusing – it may have been the drink but his eyesight had always been bad. "He had twenty of those pissing mount archers with him. On the other hill forty heavy cavalry, and there was me with ten, all on foot. Well, Aydor, I thought, this is it. Your time is over and you'll never see your daughter again, but you know what?" He took another drink, spilling half of it down his armour. "Part of me was glad the fight was over. I'm tired of war."

"But he didn't kill you."

"No." Aydor shook his damp head. "He didn't. Tomas would have. Tomas would have laughed and set his heavy cavalry on me. Probably had me taken prisoner so he could execute me himself."

"But not Rufra."

"No." He put down his goblet. "Not Rufra. Do you know what he did, Girton?" I shrugged, though I had a fair idea. "He took out his sword and saluted me. He saluted me and then he waved his cavalry away so we could return to our lines. He could have killed me but he didn't. His honour would not have been tarnished. He had found his enemy on the field; he only needed to bring me to battle."

"Rufra does not care about honour," I said, "he only cares about—"

"What is right." Aydor nodded slowly to himself. "He only cares about what is right." He raised his head and pushed his straggly fringe out of the way so I could see his eyes. "Walking back to my camp I found myself thinking, 'I could follow a man like that.' What sort of thought is that for a king, eh?" He laughed quietly to himself. "But the thought wouldn't leave. This was way before Neander took Hessely, by the way. Maybe it was when the fracture started between us. I don't know. But I couldn't lose that thought. I started to see that from the moment my mother burned Dorlay all I've ever done is follow. Followed what my mother wanted at the castle, followed what Neander wanted since then. Dead gods, Girton." He sat back in his throne. "I'd make an awful king, awful. But we both know that." Then he stared at me, his eyes as sharp as any flying lizard's. "I want you to go to Rufra for me and—"

"Offer an alliance?" I sneered. "From you? He'll never accept that."

Aydor stared at me for a while. His hand strayed towards his goblet, seemingly of its own accord. He picked his drink up and then looked at it as if surprised at what he held. He put the cup down.

"I think, Girton," he said quietly, "we both know Rufra better than that."

He was right: I did. Rufra was an idealist. He'd put aside his own hatred of Aydor if he thought an alliance could shorten the war. At least the Rufra I had known would, and from his actions on the field he did not seem to have changed much. I looked away.

Aydor chuckled. "I'm not a fool, Girton. Rufra's Triangle Council would never accept me on nothing but my word. That's why I'm telling you all this – about my daughter, about my weakness. But there's something else. Something he needs to know, whether his council accepts me or not."

"And what's that?"

"It's why I am glad to have found you, Girton Club-Foot." He leaned forward. "You solve puzzles and see more than others. There is a puzzle in Rufra's camp that needs to be solved."

"Which is?"

"Someone close to him is a traitor, Girton, and they plan to kill him when he finally faces Tomas. That is my gift to King Rufra. It is not the few troops I have still loyal, it is that information."

"Your gift is to sow dissent among his people?"

Aydor stood, his armour clanking as he heaved his huge bulk up from his throne. He paced backwards and forwards. When he stopped anger burned in his eye.

"I knew you would think this" he shouted. At the sound

of raised voices two guards ran into the tent. "Get out!" he screamed at them and then grabbed his long hair in his hands. For a moment I thought he would tear it out but when he spoke again he was calm, though breathing heavily. "Neander has long crowed about his source in Rufra's Triangle Council. And he knew things – he knows things – and I have no doubt his traitor is real. If Rufra wants proof ask him about the battle of Goldenson Copse. He'll understand." He stood close to me, and for a moment I thought he would fall to his knees. "Some time soon Tomas will bring his full force against Rufra. He's never going to be stronger than he is now and he intends to destroy Rufra and his army totally. The best way for that to happen is on the battlefield. That is when the traitor will strike, and you know what happens when a king falls on the field."

"Yes."

"Then you are free to go, Girton. And your master too. My healer says she will need care over the next weeks so I will send him with you. I will also send some of my guards with you. The Long Tides are safe for no one and you are a hunted man."

"You mean you'll send a spy with me and some of your men to escort me to Rufra's lines to make sure I deliver your message?"

He returned to his throne, sat back and let out a sigh.

"No. Go where you will, Girton Club-Foot, and send the healer away if you feel you cannot trust him. What you do next is your choice. I'm done with ordering men about. I will offer myself to Rufra whether you go to him or not." He picked up his goblet. "Now, I have a wish to drink myself into oblivion. Maybe one day we will share a goblet, Girton Club-Foot. I had hoped that day would be today but it is not. Leave when you wish. Go where you wish. I will not order you to do anything."

I watched him drink and wondered what game he played.

Chapter 4

The same man who had kicked me in the head, a captain named Thian, led our little convoy away from Aydor's small encampment. Aydor had no more than twenty Riders and a few hundred troops. Everything about his encampment was bedraggled and careworn, a ragged collection of patched tents festooned with yellow and purple pennants which hung impotently in the still air. Four mounted men headed our column and six on foot brought up the rear. The troops walking with us were subdued and edgy, whether this was because we would walk into enemy territory or because they were men and women who knew they were on the losing side I had no idea, but it did not make me feel any more comfortable with the situation. At some point I would have to make a decision about where we headed and talk to the man who led us, but for now there was only one road to follow and I would choose my fork when I found it. For the moment I maintained a sullen silence and plodded along with the draymount, worrying about my master and dwelling on all the harsh words that had passed between us since we were last in Maniyadoc.

I glanced at the healer who cared for my master. I could not hear her breathing and only the occasional soft groan told me she still lived. When he caught my eye I looked away, though more than anything I wanted to ask how she was, but at the same time I was frightened of the answer he may give. When I finally approached him he raised his face to me, dark skin and deep brown eyes under a sharp, intelligent brow. I wondered if he came from the same faraway lands as my master.

"How is she?"

"Ill, very ill," he said, "and the cart does not help."

"Oh . . ." I began and the cart hit a rut, making my master moan as if she were stuck in a nightmare and he turned back to her. I waited but he did not look back to me, his entire attention focused on her in a way that made me uncomfortable. When next I looked his way he had returned to the mortar he was grinding strong-smelling spices in, and I thought it best to leave him to his work.

Even though yearsbirth brought her green cloak to Maniyadoc it felt like a very different place to the one I had left five years ago. Entire villages had been reduced to a few blackened poles, and green shoots forced their way through the rotted remains of ungathered crops. We passed stumps where copses of trees had been struggling on their way to becoming woods before they were cut down to make siege machines. An hour later the machines themselves came into view. The slender towers of catapult arms rose above the grassland like the necks of the huge herbivores I had seen in lands far away where sorcerers' wars had not bitten as deep and people did not even know of the Tired Lands or care for its horrors – mostly because they had invented their own.

"Where do we go, Girton Club-Foot?" asked Thian.

"Wha . . . ?" I had been lost in my own world. Travelling my own dark road.

"We'll be at the bonefields soon, where the four roads meet. You'll need to make a decision as to which way we go." I looked up into the thin captain's face. I recognised him from somewhere but couldn't place him.

"If I don't decide will you kick me in the head again?"

He smiled and it transformed him. It was as if his armour and weapons sloughed away and I saw a man of middle age, amused by a joke on himself as much as anything.

"I hope not to, and I only did that as I've seen you fight before. I wasn't going to risk any of my men. To be honest, I was surprised you were so easily taken."

It was true, I had been easily taken. I had been shocked by the magic sneaking its way past the wards carved into my flesh and worried about my master. And I had been tired, I was still tired.

"Where did you see me fight?"

He slowed his mount so it walked by me and I was enveloped in the comfortable warm smell of the animal. "Maniyadoc. I was guard to the queen when you took her to the king's quarters. I've never seen anyone fight like you and the woman." He nodded at my master on the cart. "The men thought you were hedgings come for their souls."

"Not you?"

"No. I thought you were well trained and decided to keep out of your way." He gave me a grin. We walked on for a few minutes.

"What are the bonefields?" I knew Maniyadoc well but had never heard of them.

"They used to call it Four Roads," he stared at the pommel of his saddle, "before the war. You'll see when we get there." He spurred his mount on up the road and I watched him ride away.

Hedgescares remained, that part of the landscape had not changed. Maniyadoc was a land of hedgescares, the ragged sentinels of the fields. Sometimes they were wooden effigies clothed in rags and sometimes they were statues, painted to be lifelike. Other times I would think I saw a hedgescare and it would turn out to be a person, nearly always alone and hurrying away from our convoy. Where anything grew that was strong enough to bear their weight were hobbys, the little straw good-luck dolls made to keep away the hedgings. Largely they were the rag-clothed and bloodied type for quieting yellowers, the fell spirits of the sourings that brought strife and disease. Most of the hobbys were old and falling apart, but some were fresh.

At one point in our journey a shiver ran through me when I thought I saw the black-robed form of Xus the unseen chaperoning lost souls across the fields to his dark palace. When I blinked the image away I saw it was a woman with a baby strapped to her back and a small flock of children flowing around her feet as they ran in search of safety. The children, instead of shrieking and laughing like normal children, did not make a sound. I think that was one of the most terrible things I saw that morning.

Until we reached the bonefields.

Lush patches of grass, far more green and healthy than the scrubby yellow shoots struggling out of the earth around them, were the first sign. Then I started to see the pigs. The occasional lone animal to begin with, then in groups of two and three that scurried and squealed away when we approached. As the day wore on their numbers swelled until there were huge herds flowing across the land. A vast boar stood upon a hill and stared at us as we passed, grunting out a challenge, "What are you, to enter my domain?" None of the men or women in our group challenged him back and, even more strangely, none took up a bow. Pigs were a staple food of Maniyadoc and the Long Tides. When we passed another patch of long grass I made a detour and found what I expected: bones, white, clean and covered in the marks of gnawing teeth. I counted four skulls, all broken open by hungry mouths. The corpses still had mail, armour and weapons, which struck me as odd as such things were valuable and the people of Maniyadoc were poor and ever given to scavenging.

"Captain Thian," I shouted.

"Aye?"

"Will you not have one of your men take down a hog for us? So we can eat tonight?"

He shook his head and slowed his mount, all the time

keeping his eye on the massive silhouette of the boar on his hillock far behind.

"No, not here. The pigs have got a taste for human flesh and have lost all fear of us, even if we are armed. We'll be fine as long as we're out of the bonefields before nightfall. But if we kill one of them they'll follow us and overrun us as soon as we camp." He turned to look at me, his face taut with horror. "They remember."

"You jest," I said. "They are only pigs."

He remained as cold and serious as a blood gibbet.

"Five years you've been away, Girton Club-Foot, and we've created our own dark land in that time. The wild pigs are animals, they can at least be understood. Pray we meet no Nonmen." He glanced up at a sky streaked with grey and black. "Not far to the crossroads now." He clicked his mount on.

The crossroads once known as Four Roads was situated right in the centre of Maniyadoc and the Long Tides coast, near the delta of Adallada's River. There had once been a temple to the dead gods here but now it was another burned-out skeleton. It looked like someone had made an attempt to fortify it but they had not done a good job, probably priests trying to save themselves – priests make poor warriors. Now the tallest structures at the crossroads were the blood gibbets swinging slowly in the breeze.

Thian walked his mount towards me.

"Well, Girton Club-Foot, now's the time to make your choice . . ." His voice tailed off as he looked over my shoulder. I turned. Not far from us, maybe two arrow shots distant, was a man on a mount. He was dressed in boiled leather and a kilt, on his head he wore a boar's skull. He stared intently at us. His face was painted with red crosses. "Be ready, troops," said Thian quietly, "but don't be too obvious about it. He's probably only curious."

"You know him?" I asked. The man continued to stare from his hill, he radiated threat.

"The Boarlord, Chirol. He rode with Aydor for a while but he liked killing too much to make a good soldier. Then he left to ride with Tomas. Now he rules the Nonmen."

"Nonmen?"

"Those who love to kill, or those sent mad by doing it, who knows? Whatever they are, I would rather not tangle with them."

"You think they'll attack?"

Thian spat on the floor.

"Probably not, but you can never tell. Nonmen prefer an ambush or to pick off stragglers, when they're not attacking defenceless villages. On the other hand, if he knows who you are and he has the numbers he might take a risk. Tomas will pay well for your head."

"I thought he didn't run with Tomas any more?"

"Not officially." Thian brought his mount round to block the man from my sight and pointed along the road we had travelled. "Back east leads to Aydor's camp, no point you going that way. South leads to Tomas so you'll want to avoid that. West is through the marshlands and to Rufra. And north will lead you deep into the delta, maybe you can find a ship to take you out of Maniyadoc." He let his mount walk forward a step so I could see Chirol. "My men and I are going west towards Rufra, whether you are or not."

"So," I said, gazing at Chirol, "this is Aydor's idea of letting me go where I wish? To leave me at the mercy of the man on that hill?"

Thian shook his head.

"No. Believe what you want about Aydor but he meant you to choose your own way as soon as you left camp. This is all my doing."

My hand tightened around the haft of the warhammer at my hip.

"You mean me to die then, Captain Thian."

"No," he said, and raised his hands so I could see he held

no weapon. His mount sensed the tension between us and let out a low whistle. "Aydor is not the man you knew, Girton; he has changed and I owe him my life. He came back for me when I was wounded, he could have left me."

"That doesn't sound like Aydor."

"No. As I said, he's not who you think." He leaned forward in his saddle and spoke urgently. "You have to go west, Girton. Rufra is the only hope for peace in Maniyadoc. Tomas remembers slights and will pay them all back in blood if he comes to power."

"If all I do is sow dissent among Rufra's advisers, what will that do to your hope?"

"Just keep Rufra alive," he whispered, making sure only I could hear him. "Listen, come with us as far as the border of Rufra's territory. Make your mind up then."

"It looks like I have no choice."

Thian sat straight on his saddle again. "No," he said, "and I am genuinely sorry for it."

It did not matter. I had intended to go on to Rufra anyway but I did not want to give Thian the satisfaction of knowing that. I would let him sweat a bit and feel guilty. I do not like to be pushed around.

We walked on in silence, trailed by the man on the mount. As we left the bonefields Thian took us off the main path and down a shallow incline into the tidal flats where the air was heavy with the scents of salt water and rotting vegetation.

"Where are we going?" I asked.

"Chirol the Boarlord is following us. We can't make Rufra's lands tonight so I thought I'd take us into the tidal flats to camp. If we stop among the causeways it will limit the routes of attack in case Chirol decides to try something."

"Very well," I said. I couldn't fault his tactics. I had been watching Thian with his troops. They had an easy camaraderie; clearly they trusted the man. We continued walking until twilight, by which time we were deep into the wetlands that made up the tidal flats, a series of islands linked by causeways. When the tide was out the water was replaced by black, sucking mud.

We stopped to camp and Thian's troops took wooden stakes from where they had been slung under my master's cart and set up quick defences facing outwards on the four causeways connecting our small island to the others. When Thian had decided we were safe a fire was lit and a pot of stew put on. I sat by my master's cart as the healer worked on her. Occasionally he would give me a smile but it was forced and he rarely turned his attention from my master, mopping her brow or feeding her a mush of herbs.

"How long have you been with her?" asked the healer.

"Fourteen years." I reached out and touched her forehead; she was hot to the touch.

"And how long was she here before that?"

I turned to him. He was staring at me intently, eyes bright.

"Why do you ask?"

"I am merely curious." He shrugged and I took my hand from her forehead.

"You should be trying to bring down the heat in her," I said, "not quizzing me about things that have no bearing on her health." I left him to his duties.

The air in the flatlands was thick with ozone and heavy with the weight of the Birthstorm. Sometimes it broke early and the weather would be good for growing crops, but sometimes it held off for weeks and the air would become stagnant and oppressive, unable to decide whether to be cold or hot, wet or dry. I wished the storm would come, smash us with water and wind to blow away the burden on the air.

When darkness fell the screaming started.

Some trick of the land made it difficult to know where the screams came from. All I knew was that they were coming from close to us and it was someone in terrible pain. Thian looked up at the first scream and did a quick headcount of our group. Finding everyone present he threw another log onto the fire and sat staring into it, bunching his hands into fists. The screams continued. Loud, harsh screams of agony followed by the sound of a man begging for help, then they would start again, each time reaching higher and more agonised crescendos.

The healer left my master and crouched by me, muddy brown robes puddling on the floor around his feet.

"Your master sleeps. Now I must go out there." He pointed out into the darkness, in the direction of the screaming.

"No." My hand clamped around his arm.

"It is intolerable."

"If you leave this camp you will die."

"You threaten me?" His hand came down on mine, trying to prise my fingers away as Thian interrupted.

"He doesn't mean he will kill you," said Thian, though I did. "That man out there is bait – he is being tortured to lure us out."

"Something must be done."

"They're Nonmen," said Thian. "He's probably one of their own."

"How can you be sure?" I asked.

"Can't," said Thian. Something collapsed in the fire with a loud crackle and, as if in answer, another lingering scream filled the still night. "I have known the Nonmen do this before," he said quietly, "and I lost men for my compassion. I will not lose any more, and definitely not a healer."

"Get me a bow," I said.

"A bow?"

"He's there." I pointed out into the night. I had been listening to his screams, carefully tilting my head until I finally had a good idea of where the sounds originated from. Now I fancied I could feel the tortured man's presence, a red throbbing against the black mud of the landscape. "I can end this."

"If you kill him," said Thian, "they'll only start on another. They prey on weakness even among themselves."

Another scream.

"Then what do we do?" asked the healer.

"Wait," said Thian, "and tell yourself it is Blue Watta trying to lure you out into the channels to drown. Those who do not have to keep watch can stuff their ears with grass, it may help or it may not."

I did not sleep that night, and while I tossed and turned on the damp ground I tried to comfort myself with the fact that at least I was more comfortable than the man whose screams kept me awake.

Chapter 5

Sunlight crawled over our camp, diamond fingers dewed the grass and made it as beautiful as the low whimpering coming from outside was ugly. As the sun pushed night further into Maniyadoc I took up my bow and waited at the edge of the camp while the troops got busy packing it away. My club foot throbbed painfully with the cold.

A tortured figure was tied spreadeagled on a slope just outside what most would consider bowshot. Where the body should have had eyes, nose, mouth, fingers, toes and groin there were only bleeding wounds, and I could no longer tell if it had been male or female. It was almost impossible to believe it was still alive, but I could see the figure struggling weakly, whether against its bindings or against the pain I did not know, though it could escape neither. At the figure's head stood Chirol, the Boarlord, in his bestial headdress; he wore a small leather shield on one arm and in the other held a knife which dripped blood onto the grass. I could not make out his features apart from the glint of teeth when he smiled. I felt sure that his smile was meant for me.

I nocked an arrow and drew the bow back. The Boarlord watched intently. Aiming high I waited for a lull in the salty breeze blowing in off the water and let the arrow fly. I lowered the bow and watched the arrow's course. Chirol watched it too, and it seemed to stay airborne for an impossibly long time. Flying lizards sang circular songs and I heard a fish jump from the water and land with a splash. I shielded my eyes, looking for the arrow against the glare of the sun and the man opposite me did the same, as if we were mirrors of one another. Then he brought up his buckler, so fast it seemed a blur, and I heard the *"thunk"* of the arrow hitting the hardened leather. The Boarlord lifted his buckler, looked at the arrow sticking out of it then let out a throaty chuckle and worked the arrow backwards and forwards until it came loose. Bending his knees and keeping his body straight, he slowly pushed it into the eye socket of the tortured body below him. When his victim finally stopped moving he turned and walked away as if he cared nothing for the bow in my hands.

"He won't forget you," said Thian from behind me.

"Good. You think he will attack us?"

Thian shrugged. "Depends on his numbers, but if he had the men I think he would have come in the night." He watched Chirol's retreating back. "We'll be within Rufra's borders by midday," he said, "so we'll know before then."

We recommenced our walk through the countryside, gradually coming up out of the tidal flats and leaving behind the stink of ozone and rotting fish. Out of the flats the landscape of Maniyadoc was long undulating hills punctuated with burned-out farms and blood gibbets, though these were mostly empty. I walked by the side of the cart my master rode in, and when the healer sat back from the work he had been intent on his gaze settled on me. A night of listening to a man being tortured had aged him and there were puffy circles under his eyes, his cheekbones protruded, creating hollows in his face. In the early light I almost thought I recognised him and was about to ask if we had met over the seas somewhere when I realised we had not. What I had seen as familiar in him was only echoes of my master in his face, echoes of her nose in his slightly longer one, echoes of her delicate arched eyebrows in his bushier ones, echoes of her hard gaze in his unblinking stare.

"How is she?" I asked.

"She lives but she is in great pain. I think I have the

poison removed from her and then it rallies again. I have never come across anything like it." He gave me that smile, the one I didn't quite believe, and added, "I will her to live. She is strong. She fights."

"She always has." He nodded at me, as if he knew her. "What is your name?"

"Mastal," he said and glanced away.

"You have no family name?"

"Not any more."

"Why?"

He tapped a long finger on his worn leather herb pouch. "You are very forward."

"You hold my master's life in your hands and you work for my enemy." He shrugged as if it meant nothing. "Are you a criminal?"

He shook his head. "No. I am not. I have no family name for the reason most would not."

"You don't know your family?" I said.

"No." He looked puzzled and then closed his eyes slightly, realising I spoke of myself. "When I was a younger man I fell out with my father. He thought I should do things one way and I thought I should do them another – it is common enough between sons and fathers." I nodded as if I understood. "We fell out," he said again, this time more quietly.

"Do you regret it?"

"Your tongue is as brutal as your choice of weapon, boy." He nodded at the warhammer and I covered the hilt with the palm of my hand as if the weapon were a guilty secret I had to hide. "But I shall answer you, in a fashion. Yes, I do. Often. I lost my honour though I still think I was right."

"It is lost for ever?"

"Unless I carry out some great and charitable task." My master coughed and he glanced at where she lay, keeping his eyes on her for long enough to make me worry. Then he turned back to me. "But now I am older I understand—"

"Riders!"

Mastal climbed back onto the cart to check on my master as I took up my bow. The troops around me formed a loose circle with their pikes.

"It's those hedge-cursed mount archers," hissed a woman by me.

"Shields up," shouted Thian. Then he slipped from his mount as did the three other mounted men and they all joined the circle. "Make no move to attack."

The men and women around me crouched behind their teardrop-shaped shields, and I grabbed my own as the Riders thundered in. They were like no troops I had seen before, neither heavy cavalry nor simple mounted troops like Thian. They wore light armour of boiled leather rather than the usual colourfully enamelled heavy armour of Tired Lands cavalry. They all had swords sheathed by their saddles but made no move to draw them, instead they carried curiously small bows, bent like the gentle curve of a courtesan's painted lip. They circled us, twice, and then darted away – they were extraordinarily skilled in the handling of their mounts. If this was how the Nonmen rode I knew we were dead; even small bows, like theirs could wound and wear us down over time. The Riders drew up out of bow range and their leader, a tall man whose wide helm was topped with a silvery flying lizard, trotted towards us.

"Thian ap Myrrvin," he shouted, "you are a long way from your king's lands, if he still has any." I felt I knew the voice but five years is a long time and the name escaped me.

"Are these Nonmen, Thian?" I asked.

"No, these men are far more dangerous, they are Rufra's mount archers."

I glanced back at the Rider, and it was only then that I noticed his mount. No, not his, it was mine, I was sure of it, and something soared within me at the sight of him, while at the same time an anger rumbled within that another should ride him. I had not seen Xus for five years. I had missed him.

"Xus!" I shouted and expected the animal to rear and throw off the interloper on his back, but the mount ignored me. It felt like a spear in my guts.

"Girton?" shouted the Rider. "Girton, called ap Gwynr, is that you?"

"Aye," I shouted back.

The Rider pulled off his helmet. Once I would have been shocked by what I saw but I had seen many injuries and the scars they left. This Rider had taken a blow from an axe, or maybe a warhammer like the one I carried, and it had caved in one side of his face, taking most of the flesh with it. He had blond hair, shorn short on one side, and when his skull-face smiled it looked like he was in agony – though from the laugh he gave he was clearly not.

"You are lucky we found you, Girton. I don't know what Captain Thian has told you but he bares his throat to the pretender, Aydor. I am sure he is someone you would rather avoid."

"We come from Aydor with a message," shouted Thian.

"Really?" He sounded amused. "I doubt that. Give us Girton or—"

"It's true," I shouted. "Aydor seeks terms and has freed me to carry a message to Rufra."

"Then tell them to give up their arms, Girton."

"I cannot. I do not—"

"Disarm!" shouted Thian to his men, and he lay his shield and spear on the ground. "I hope you are as trustworthy as the man you call king, Boros ap Loflaar."

"Boros?" I said, remembering the beautiful youth who had sided with a young Rufra, and his identical twin who had not.

"You did not recognise me . . ." The man on the mount laughed and pointed at his face. "Of course you didn't. This was a gift from my brother – people find us much easier to tell apart now."

"I hope you paid him back in kind."

"He escaped before I could, but I will, don't doubt that." A feral anger burned in his eye. "And when I do I'll make his death last." His mount had picked up his anger and was straining at the bit. It looked so much like Xus and yet it had not recognised me. Boros wheeled it round, having to fight to get control of the animal back. "You have my word, Captain Thian. Neither you nor your troops will be hurt, but I cannot let you loose in Rufra's lands with weapons. You must give them up to me and then you may go back to your master."

"No," I said.

"No?" Boros's scarred face twisted and all levity fled. "You are giving me orders, Girton?"

"I do not mean to, Boros. On our way we were followed by one of the Nonmen."

"Which one?"

"The Boarlord, Chirol," said Thian. "If you send us away without weapons we are dead."

Boros stared down, looking for all the world like one of the shatter-spirits, the fierce and angry ghosts of those who have given in to the worst of the hedgings and are cursed to share their gnawing hunger for evermore.

"Many of my men have died at your hand, Thian."

"And many of mine on the arrows of your archers, ap Loflaar." The two men locked gazes for a count of twenty and then Thian stepped forward. "Take me prisoner, or send me out alone at the mercy of Chirol, but don't let the Nonmen take my troops simply because they obeyed their king's orders."

Boros snorted.

"Pick up your weapons," he said. "Tell me, while you were wandering the roads did you find a girl by name of Fara? Or a corpse that could be her. Darvin, one of our priests, has lost her."

"You think I would have left a girl alone with the Nonmen out there?" said Thian. "No, no corpses either, except one killed at the hands of the Boarlord, and I swear it was a man he tortured. He made him suffer too – he screamed us awake all throughout the night. Dead gods know I'd like to get Chirol on the end of my lance."

"Thian," said Boros with mock seriousness, "please don't say any more. I'm discovering common ground with you and if I have to respect you it will make it harder to kill you in the field."

I saw Thian smile as he bent to pick up his shield and spear. He saluted Boros in the old way, raising his head and offering his throat. Boros nodded to him.

"Come, Girton," said Boros. "We'll chaperone you the rest of the way to Rufra's camp, and you can see what it's like to ride with real troops." He turned to a Rider at his shoulder. "Hran, take fifteen and see if you can catch Chirol – maybe he's strayed too near chasing Thian. I want him alive though, you understand?" There was a real fierceness in his voice.

The Rider nodded and spurred his mount, and fifteen Riders followed. I marvelled at their discipline and wondered how they had known who was to follow and who was to stay with Boros.

"The cart comes with me," I said, "and the two on it."

Boros shrugged. "Fine." I stepped through Thian's line and put out a hand towards the muzzle of Xus, still barely able to believe the great mount didn't recognise me. "No!" shouted Boros and reined the mount back. "Galadan is war trained, he'll take your arm unless he knows you." I stood still as a statue with my hand poised in the air midway between me and the animal.

"Galadan?" I said. "But I thought . . ."

"Oh," laughed Boros, "you thought it was Xus? Dead gods,

I like my life too much to try and ride that one. No one can ride that animal. Rufra decided that at least he could be of some use and put him to stud. Galadan is Xus's son, one of many fine children by him."

"Life always goes on," I said, my voice dropping to a whisper. "I must see to the cart and my master." I turned, thinking about how much the land had changed in the five years I had been away and wondering if, when I met Rufra, he would still be the person I remembered. As I said my farewell to Thian and his men the captain clasped my arm.

"Don't be a slave to old hatreds, Girton. People change, remember that. Forgiveness is its own reward."

I stared into his eyes and the warhammer on my belt felt like it took on an extra weight. I nodded, even though I did not believe him. We are cursed to be the sum of our deeds, black as they may be. They are like an arrow: once the shot is made, there is no escaping the consequences.

Chapter 6

I thought I saw blood, but then it turned into flowers. There was a spattering of red, like the pattern sprayed on a wall when a limb is severed, which resolved into a colourful garden around a small house. In a land that had been at war for five years it was incongruous, and the closer we came to the house the more out of place it looked.

"Boros, what is that?"

He grinned down at me from his mount. "That is the house of Magar the Thankful."

"How does it stand in the midst of war?"

"It stands, Girton," said Boros, "because King Rufra commands it."

"Why? It is just a house."

"I thought so," said Boros, "but this was the main road taken by those fleeing Tomas, Aydor and the Nonmen, and that house hides a well. The first thing those fleeing to Rufra see when they enter his territory is a garden, and then they are offered water and food by one of the thankful."

The perfume of the garden wrapped itself around me and I felt my spirits lift.

"Is Magar there, Boros?"

"No, there is no such person as Magar; Rufra invented her."

"Why?"

"Sergeant Beyish, Rider ap Garl," he shouted, and two of his Riders trotted their mounts over. "Ap Garl, tell my friend where you are from."

"I am the son of the ap Garls and our house is in the far north. We claim marriage kinship with the ap Glyndier and the ap Mennix."

"Sergeant Beyish," said Boros, "tell my friend where you are from."

The sergeant shrugged. "Little village called Haarn. My father was a cobbler."

"He's scum," said ap Garl, but he smiled when he said it.

"That's Sergeant Scum to you, ap Garl," replied Beyish, and the two rode off laughing.

"You see?" said Boros.

I gaped, unable to hide my shock. Rufra had always been an idealist, but to have one of the living class in charge of one of the blessed was to turn the way the Tired Lands had existed ever since the gods died on its head.

"It is a symbol of Rufra's new ways?"

"Exactly."

"I cannot believe Tomas approves of this place. I cannot believe he lets it stand."

"Oh he hates it," said Boros with a laugh. "He used to destroy it regularly, and each time we would rebuild it. Tomas got bored before we did, or, to be more truthful, he realised the cost of men was not worth the insult to his blessed ego."

We passed through Magar's garden, a riot of flowers, and I saw a woman, young and beautiful, sitting by a well with a golden cup in her hand. She smiled at me and I turned away.

"Where are the refugees, Boros?"

"It has been five years, Girton. Magar's garden has been undisturbed for three because the refugees are gone. Those who think Rufra denies the gods and undoes the way the world should be went to Aydor or Tomas. The rest came to us, and those who made no decision, well . . ." his voice tailed off ". . . many died."

"How many?"

"I don't know," said Boros, but his words were so quiet I heard them the way one feels an old scar hidden deep beneath the skin. "Too many."

We journeyed for half a day in silence and I saw the country around me change. It was not healthy, the Tired Lands had never been healthy, but at least what I saw here was a familiar sickness, not the ravaging plague of war. At twilight I saw the unmistakable shape of Castle Maniyadoc rising on its hill above the plain, but to my surprise we did not head towards it. I was glad of that; it held nothing but memories of pain.

"Where do we go, Boros?"

"I go to Rufra's war camp, but you stay here with Beyish." He leaned in close. "No one here knows who you are for now, Girton ap Gwynr, or what you are, and it may be Rufra wishes it to stay that way. Mind what you say around the campfire."

I avoided the troops he had left and bedded down with the healer and my master. She did not wake, and the man did not speak. He seemed to be in some sort of trance as he put his hand on her forehead and felt her temperature or tasted her spit and blood. He worried me, and I wondered what he would report to Aydor.

I slept in a blanket, wrapped tightly against the night. I did not sleep well. Since my master had started scoring the Landsman's Leash into my flesh to control the magic within me I had stopped dreaming in anything but odd, disturbing snippets and it felt like my mind wormed around subjects the way the leash wormed its way over my skin.

I was pulled struggling from sleep's dark mud by the sound of claws drumming on the ground. Two Riders entered the camp: Boros and another I did not know, he rode a brown mount with four-point antlers, an unassuming-looking beast, and was dressed in battered and dull armour. He must have been from Rufra's heavy cavalry as he was armed with a lance, unmarked shield and twin swords scabbarded by his saddle. His visor, blank apart from eyeslits and holes to breathe through, was down to hide his face.

"You!" Boros pointed at me using his bow. "Follow this Rider. He will take you where you need to go."

"But the cart—" I began.

"We will deal with the cart," said Boros. There was none of the levity in his voice that had been there the day before and I wondered what had changed while he had been at Rufra's camp. I wondered what Rufra had heard of me, if he knew of the things I had done as a mercenary.

The Rider turned his mount and started walking it away. I followed, trying to make conversation with him but he ignored me so I studied his mount instead. It was a dull animal, the sort of mount a down-on-his-luck blessed may own, and I wondered at that. Perhaps I was a little insulted because I had expected my friend to come in person, but I tried to put my disappointment aside. We passed through a stand of trees, small, silvery moonwood saplings with plenty of sparsely grassed ground between them, and the Rider spurred his mount on and then turned it towards me about fifty paces away. He lifted his visor to expose the face underneath, a face I knew.

"Rufra!" I shouted, a grin on my face, but it soon fell away. Rufra's face was hard; there was still the boy I had known there but the man had emerged now. A shadow of stubble covered his jaw and upper lip, his thick brows covered bright, alert, green eyes, and I saw no signs of friendship in him, only the cold hauteur of a ruler.

"I should have known you would come," he growled. "It was only a matter of time." He lowered his lance.

"Time?" A shiver ran through me.

"Girton Club-Foot, the only assassin they thought could get close to me."

"No, Rufra. I am not—"

"Defend yourself, assassin," he sneered and put spurs to his mount.

I was so shocked I made no attempt to reach for the warhammer at my side, or even to dodge the rapidly closing point of the lance. At the last moment the mount jinked to one side, thundering past and the weapon fell to the ground.

I heard a strange sound from behind me, as if someone were choking. I turned. Rufra was no longer holding the reins of his animal and a moment later he fell from the saddle and crashed to the ground, his arms wrapped around his stomach. He made a sound I could only describe as howling. I scanned the treeline for archers before glancing back at Rufra, who had rolled onto his back. There was no sign of an arrow or bolt in him and as he propped himself up I saw tears streaming down his face. He was laughing as he pointed a gauntleted hand at me.

"Your face!" he choked out. "Oh Girton, you should have seen your face!"

"My face?" I stared at him. "That was a trick?"

He nodded. "Yes." More tears of laughter. "Oh I am sorry. My life is so serious now and I could not resist, could not." I stumped over to him as he pulled himself to his feet.

"That was your idea of a joke? I thought you were going to kill me!" He started laughing again and I punched the fishscale of his upper arm.

Immediately, all levity fled and his face hardened. When he spoke his words came out in a hard monotone.

"You dare to raise your hand against your king, Girton Club-Foot?" His gloved hand fell to his sword hilt. "Such an act is punishable by death."

I stared at him, at that serious, ugly face, and something happened, something so alien and long forgotten to me that I did not recognise the strange sound that burst from my gut. First it was small, small like clouds on a sunny day, and then, like rainclouds swelling the Birthstorm, it grew until it was unstoppable.

And I laughed.

I laughed, and Rufra, seeing he could not trick me twice, laughed as well, and soon we were leaning on each other for support. I had found my friend once again, and the world did not seem so bleak – its colours felt a little brighter and the air a little warmer.

"I have missed you, Girton," said Rufra. "It is lonely being a king."

"I cannot believe a king is ever alone."

"One need not be alone to feel lonely."

"I know that well."

"You travel with your master – you are never lonely."

My flesh itched and writhed.

"A master is not a friend."

"True." He picked a blade of grass and idly chewed on it. "I heard you have travelled. I know you passed over the Taut Sea but heard nothing after. I knew you would not be dead though."

"Came near a few times."

"So have I."

"War is hard," I said.

"You still carry your Conwy?" He lifted the sword I had gifted him from its scabbard so I could see the shining steel of the blade. I nodded and drew the stabsword that was brother to his longer blade from the sheath on my back, so he knew I had not abandoned it, and then let it fall back into its prison. "And yet you use that." He nodded at the warhammer. I touched the claw that topped its hilt.

"There was a girl. She died. I took it from the man who killed her."

"You once told me a warhammer was a weapon for an animal."

I took my hand from its hilt.

"It is," I said.

He nodded but did not speak, not immediately, nor did he press me further.

"Boros tells me you come with a message but do not tell me it, not yet. Nywulf will come looking for me soon enough, and then I will have to be a king again. Let us only be friends for a while longer." I nodded, and he climbed onto his mount, offering me his arm and lifting me up behind him.

As we rode we spoke of inconsequential things, of the weather and our memories of time spent as squires at Maniyadoc.

An hour later I saw a Rider approaching, leading a second mount. Even from far away I recognised the squat figure of Nywulf, the man who had been squiremaster last time I visited Maniyadoc and now acted as Rufra's Heartblade, the warrior tasked with keeping him safe from assassins, like me. Rufra brought his mount to a halt and we slid off the animal.

"We will wait here for Nywulf. I am in no hurry to be told off."

"Told off? But Rufra, you are king."

"You would not know it from the way Nywulf treats me." He gave me a lopsided grin and shrugged his shoulders before going to his pack and taking out food for us. We ate in companionable silence while we watched Nywulf wind his way to us through the sparse trees.

"Maybe a hedging will jump out of a tree and carry Nywulf off," said Rufra through a mouthful of bread.

"I do not think it would dare," I replied. "Even Black Ungar would run from Nywulf."

When he finally entered our clearing Nywulf made no attempt to get down from his mount, only looked us over from his vantage point.

"So it is true," he said. "Your playmate has returned." He turned his predator's gaze on me, "Welcome back, Girton," and he may have bared his throat in salute but the movement was so small it was difficult to tell. Then he turned back to Rufra.

"I told you it was safe—" began Rufra.

"Being right in fact does not mean you were right to slip out of camp without me, Neliu or Crast," growled Nywulf. "You are a king. You must act like a king. Guard yourself like—"

"A king. I know." Rufra stood. "And if I am a king then maybe you should show me the respect due a king and get off your mount before addressing me?"

"Very well," said Nywulf and left a long gap before adding, "my king," and sliding from the saddle. "I brought Girton a mount." He pointed at the animal behind him.

"Not Xus?" I said, unable to hide my disappointment.

"I may owe you a debt, Girton," said Nywulf, "but I'm not willing to lose my hand just to bring you your beast." He smiled then, a fleeting and rare thing.

"Girton brings word from Aydor," said Rufra, his pique forgotten.

"He wants to join us?" said Nywulf.

"Yes," I said.

"Well, we knew it was coming. What will you do, Rufra?"

Rufra rested his hand on the hilt of his blade before speaking.

"Take him in. I know it will not be popular, but it is right and it will shorten the war; it may even bring Tomas out to battle."

Nywulf nodded.

"He had more to say," I added.

Rufra shot me a venomous look. "It can wait, Girton."

"He says there are spies?" Nywulf raised an eyebrow, but before I could speak Rufra interrupted.

"Of course there are spies, there are always spies, Nywulf," he said, "but my council is loyal. I do not doubt any of them."

"You should," growled Nywulf.

"Nywulf –" Rufra spoke through gritted teeth "– I am not having this conversation again. The Triangle Council are men and women beloved and trusted by me and—"

"Even Arnst and the Landsman?"

A shiver ran through me at the thought of the Landsmen, the men who hunted sorcerers. "The Landsmen have no love for me," scowled Rufra, "but they are not foolish enough to betray me either, and Karrick is the best of them. There is no spy in my council, Nywulf."

"Arnst?"

"The priest is utterly loyal," said Rufra through gritted teeth, "as you know."

It pained me to speak – I could see how fervently Rufra wanted to believe in those who followed him and I hated the idea of Aydor being right – but Nywulf was no fool and so I spoke before the argument readying its wings took full flight.

"Aydor said to ask you about Goldenson Copse."

My words stopped the flow of conversation dead, and for a moment I thought Rufra would draw his blade on me in seriousness. Instead he turned on his heel and walked away, his steps quick, as if he needed to carry away the anger within him before it burst out. He didn't stop walking until he was at the edge of the clearing, where he found a shattered tree trunk and kicked it, twice, before sitting down on it with his back to us and his head in his hands. I was about to go after him, to apologise for whatever it was I had said that had made him so furious, when Nywulf's hand closed around my arm.

"Leave him. He won't thank you for approaching him now. He will want to talk later."

"What did I say, Nywulf?"

"Nothing I haven't. He just doesn't want to hear it."

"What happened at Goldenson Copse?"

"We nearly lost the war when we should have won.

Happened about a year and a half ago now. Rufra had been chasing Tomas down since the start of the war, despite Tomas having the bigger army. We knew Tomas had divided his forces to protect his supply lines and that he marched with a smaller force than usual. We planned a surprise attack at Goldenson Copse near the old bridge over Adallada's River, but it was us who was surprised. We caught Tomas all right, but he was with his full army. As he had his back to the river we had a tactical advantage so we pressed the attack anyway. We would have won, but Aydor came up on our rear and we didn't have the troops to fight on two fronts."

"I bet Rufra thought about it though."

"Oh aye, he did, and he still does. Rufra has a tactics table in his tent, and each night he plays through different strategies for Goldenson Copse. Never seeing he couldn't have won. The boy saved a lot of lives by withdrawing when he did, even though it pains him."

"Then why is he . . ."

"So angry? Because he thinks Tomas beat him that day because he was careless. He blames himself for those who died and all those who have died since. I've been telling him we have a spy in the council for three years – no one else knew about our plans for Goldenson Copse – but he wouldn't believe me. Maybe he will now."

"And if I do believe you?" said Rufra. He had walked up behind me so quietly I had not heard him. He sounded tired. "What then, Nywulf? Do I set my advisers at each other's throats when we are so close to bringing Tomas and Neander to the blade again?"

"Sometimes," said Nywulf, "even dead gods send gifts." He pointed at me.

"Girton?" said Rufra.

"Death's Jester," said Nywulf. "The jester can go anywhere, and no one questions."

"No." Suddenly my throat constricted and there were tears

in my eyes. "My master lies in a cart back at camp and Xus stands by her side. She cannot dance."

"Oh Girton –" Rufra's face was full of concern "– I have healers. Whatever can be done for her will be—"

Nywulf stepped in front of him.

"What is to stop you wearing the motley, Girton?" I had dreamed of taking the Death's Jester motley for a long time, but I had cast away the dream in childish anger the day I picked up the warhammer. "It is just a costume, after all."

"No, it is . . ." I searched for the word ". . . a calling. It is to say you are a master, that no other can surpass you, and—"

"Your master lies ill," said Nywulf, "and we will tell no one, if you are worried about what she may think. Give her back the motley when she is well."

"I . . ." my mouth dried, my brow sweated ". . . I am not ready."

"Girton," said Nywulf, "Tomas has an army twice the size of ours. We can beat him, but with a spy reporting our strategies back to Neander, or worse, with Rufra dead, we don't stand a chance." He put his hand on my shoulder. "I suggest you become ready. I suggest you become ready now."

Chapter 7

Rufra left me on a hill overlooking his war camp – a city of brightly coloured tents. It was not quite as big as Festival, the great caravan that orbited the Tired Lands, but was impressive in its own way. It had a sense of purpose that Festival, with all its multicoloured anarchy, lacked.

In the centre was a pair of the big two-storey carts more commonly used by the Festival Lords, and around them had been built a fence of wooden spikes designed to stop a cavalry charge. Around that was a semicircle of neat rows of military tents, each round tent covered in colourful waxed felt. Smoke from fires gently seeped from the edges of their roofs. The other half of the semicircle around Rufra's command tents consisted of paddocks for the cavalry mounts, and I could hear their keening wails as they called to one another. The Landsmen had set up a stockade between the paddocks and the centre of the camp; their flag – the white tree – flew above rows of pristine green tents. Further out was the chaotic, muddy village of the camp followers where the night and day markets were situated, and further out still, and protected by a simple thorn fence, was the smith's' village, kept well away from the main camp to avoid the risk of fire. I estimated Rufra had a force of about a thousand men, a huge number. Generally an army's strength was in infantry and about a tenth were cavalry, but from the number of mounts it seemed Rufra had skewed that balance and I wondered whether this was to do with his mount archers. I had never seen warriors like them before and was annoyed with myself for not asking him about them.

I sat by my loaned mount, a docile enough creature, and watched his camp for hours. I watched the mounts in their paddocks until I picked out one I was sure was Xus, named for the god of death. There was no mistaking him, huge and proud, his massive antlers dominating the other mounts around him. I wondered if he knew I was here – doubtful – or if he had missed me at all – even more doubtful. Then I wondered how he would react if my master died – there was a bond between them that could not be denied. In battle I had seen the huge creature put himself between her and danger or gallop with little thought to his own safety to get us away from pursuers. If she died I was sure his great heart would break and I could not let that happen, could not. Whatever was needed I would do to make sure my master, and her mount, survived.

Even if it meant taking on the motley of Death's Jester?

Could I do that? In my anger at my master I had cast aside my training, forsaken the precise iterations of the assassin's bladework for the brute power of the warhammer. I had stopped practising the dances and tumbles I once loved, telling my master that the scars she cut into me made it too painful, though it was a lie and one we were both aware of. I did it to punish her. I did it so I could claim some sort of independence, even if it was one where I gave up what I loved the most. I did it because I was a fool, and not the sort that wore a motley.

"Girton?" I jumped, shocked out of my reverie and turned to see Boros. "Rufra sent me with these." He threw down a soldier's tabard in red and black. "Your master has been taken to the healers and your packs moved to Rufra's tent. If you come in with me dressed as a guard no one will look twice at you. I think Rufra would like to keep your presence quiet for now." He was clearly waiting for me to change, but

I could not do it in front of him as my body was criss-crossed with the scars of the Landsman's Leash, and though I doubted he would know what they were I did not want him to see them. I did not want anyone to see them. So I sat staring at him. "What? Is there some oath you have taken that means you cannot change clothes in front of another?" I nodded and he shrugged. "Very well, I shall wait further down the track for you."

"I am sorry, Boros. I do not mean to appear rude." It felt strange. Manners were something I had seldom needed in our travels. My weapons had always spoken for me.

Boros waved my concern away with a hand. "Do not bother yourself, Girton, we all have our hungers to suffer." He pulled down his visor to cover his scarred face and trotted his mount down the track.

I waited until Boros was out of sight and pulled off my harlequin armour, feeling the web of scars pull on my skin, the way it subtly changed the shape of my body and the way I moved. To those who can read that scars I am an illustrated man, the story of my shame told in the increasingly deep lines and whorls of the Landsman's Leash across the wiry muscles of my chest. Unlike normal wounds these scars did not heal into white ridges, but into lines of clear skin that gather the sunlight, radiating it round my body and turning me into something strange and unworldly. I could let no one see me unclothed, and Landsmen, the green-armoured guardians of the land, would know me for what I was immediately, but even those who did not recognise the symbols could not help but see something strange in me. They would cry sorcerer and I would be dragged away to be questioned before ending up in a blood gibbet, my life used to feed the land.

Years ago my lover Drusl had met me under the eaves of Castle Maniyadoc where there was no light. I had thought this was for modesty but learned later it was to hide similar scars that covered her body, and just like it is for me the scars could not hold in her power. She died by her own hand rather than live to threaten the land. And me? I am not so brave. I keep my secret close, not even able to tell Rufra, the only true friend I have. For all his admirable qualities he still fears sorcerers as much as any other.

With my guard's uniform on, Boros led me down the shallow incline of the hill to Rufra's war camp.

"When you turned up, Boros, one of Captain Thian's troops called you mount archers."

"Is that all he said?" He lifted his visor to expose his ravaged face.

"Well, she called you hedge-cursed mount archers."

"That's more like it." Boros gave me a grin that, on his scarred face, made him look like a strange and fierce hedging spirit of war. "They fear us even more than Cearis's heavy cavalry."

"With those bows?" I pointed at the small weapon, and he laughed then pulled his mount to a halt and slid down from the saddle. He gave me his bow.

"This bow –" he took my shield from me "– is why we will win against Tomas." He walked away with the shield and leaned it against the trunk of a tree and then returned. Taking an arrow from his saddle he passed it to me. "Loose an arrow at the shield."

"But this is your bow, you should . . ."

He shook his head and pointed at his face. "I was not only scarred but blinded in one eye. My troops pretend I still shoot well but it is a lie. Shoot the bow, Girton; do not force me to make a fool of myself."

I nocked the arrow. The bow felt strange, lighter than the longbows I was used to, and unlike them it was not made of a single piece of wood but of many pieces layered together. The tips bent back on themselves and when I drew on the string I was surprised to find it had the same pull as a longbow twice its length. Boros smiled at the look on my face but I ignored his hideous grin and aimed my arrow at the shield. The string stung my fingers as I let go, its release far quicker than I was used to and the arrow flew faster too. I had expected such a small bow to be weak, but instead of bouncing off the shield the arrow pierced it with a loud *crack*. I walked over to see the damage. The arrow had passed straight through the centre of the bloodied eye and buried itself to the length of my thumb in the bole of the tree.

"It's as powerful as—" I began.

"A crossbow, but not as unwieldy. And because they're smaller we can fire them from mountback."

"It's amazing. Where did it come from?"

"A hillsman travelling with Festival brought it to Rufra, said he was the last of his people and the last to know the secrets of the hornbow."

"Hornbow?"

"That is what we call it, as it is made from wood and horn. There's not a draymount in our herd still has its horns now." I offered him the bow back and he shook his head. "Keep it, a gift to you. I have another."

"Thank you, Boros. It is a great gift."

"Bowmaster Varn says you know a man by his gifts –" he smiled his awful smile again "– so if anyone asks you can say that I am a great man."

We entered the camp and Boros rode away, saying he would only attract attention and telling me to make my own way.

Nywulf met me at the palisade, ushering me into the central camp in a way that I was sure would appear suspicious to anyone looking – though no one was. The camp was busy, the air ringing with the sound of metal on metal from the smiths and the chatter of men and women as they went about their business. It was washing day, and wherever I looked people were arm deep in water, clothes hanging everywhere, and the air was full of the fresh scent of the herbs used to clean them. There was singing too, and though it sounded tuneless to me because the leash carved into my flesh dulled my senses, still there was no denying the joy in it. This was different to the war camps I had been in as a mercenary, they had all been tense places, full of violent men and women looking for excuses to show their prowess. There was little sign of that here, though I noted that all the soldiers I passed seemed alert, and the blades of their spears and pikes were bright and sharp. But still, there was a cheery atmosphere in Rufra's war camp.

We walked past the two huge double-storey caravans towards an equally huge round tent. It was covered with skins and brightly coloured material, strung with flags and hobby dolls of many different colours, and above the entrance was a bonemount, the symbol of war – a mount's skull attached to a construction of skins and streamers that flapped in the wind and made it appear to have bright legs of flapping material. The skull had one antler much shorter than the other and I knew it must be Imbalance, Rufra's childhood mount killed during an attack on him when we were young. An attack I had foiled and put at the feet of Aydor or Tomas, though I had never proved which.

I was gazing at the bonemount when my attention was drawn from it by a movement in the corner of my eye, a woman leaving a tent. She did no more than glance at me but it was like I was struck. Her face was finely boned, and long hair the black of the valuable darkwoods that grew slowly in the south fell in tight ringlets over the shoulders of her green gown. As soon as she saw me return her glance she looked away and quickly vanished into one of the huge caravans.

"Through here, Girton," said Nywulf, pushing me forward, "and stop staring after Areth." He shoved me into a tent guarded by a boy and a girl with the brightest red hair I had ever seen. The boy winked at me as I passed and Nywulf cuffed him. "You guard the king, Crast. Act like it." The boy nodded sheepishly and the girl stared resolutely ahead, ignoring us as we passed into the tent.

"Who was she?" I could not keep the wonder out of my voice. It is rare to see a woman so beautiful that you are stopped by a simple glance from her. Nywulf could hear the effect she had had on me in my voice but, being Nywulf, chose to ignore it.

"Neliu. And the boy is Crast. I train them to replace me."

"I didn't mean her. I meant Areth."

"Don't get any ideas about her, boy, she is Rufra's wife."

"Rufra is married?"

"Aye, married a serving girl of the living, a sign to all that the old rules no longer apply."

"I would have thought he would marry into a blessed family, to cement alliances."

"At the beginning of his rule they did not want him, and now it is too late for them. Besides, Areth is good for him." There was something behind his words, some mystery I itched to pick at, or was that just a desire to get close to the woman I had seen? I put it aside. She was Rufra's wife and I was his mage-bent friend. I would never betray him even if the opportunity arose – which it would not. "Rufra is in session with the Triangle Council. We can watch through the curtain and I can tell you who they are."

He led me through the back room of a heavy tent kitted out for war. There were maps on the walls, weapons and armour on stands and a large table in the centre with a map made of clay that depicted all of Maniyadoc and the Long Tides. On a smaller table to the side was a paper map showing a bend in the river and a broken bridge, on it were small wooden horses and men. One of the king pieces lay on its side and I noticed a crack running down the edge of the figure, as though it had been hit or thrown. "Leave that,

Girton," said Nywulf, pulling gently on my arm. He led me over to where a pair of weighted curtains led into the next room and gently moved aside part of the curtain and turned to me, a smile on his face. "See what he has done?"

For a moment I did not understand. In front of me was a tented chamber like many others. A fire burned in one corner and loyalty flags lined the walls, some of which I recognised, like Rufra's red and black flying lizard, while others were new to me. In the centre of the room was a table, a huge equilateral triangle, with men and women sitting around it, three to each side. Rufra sat with his back to me between a man and a woman. Nearly all of them wore similar clothes – well worn, not overly fine – and unless you knew the Tired Lands well you would not have seen the differences between them. But I did, and though I had been told already what Rufra had done I had barely believed it.

"He really has made them equal, blessed and living, they share the royal table."

"Aye," said Nywulf, and I could hear his pride.

"The thankful are absent though," I said, and could not keep the disappointment from my voice. I had been raised a slave but had been saved from that short hard life by my master.

"Yes the thankful are absent from here, and there are still resentments and feuds over class, but mostly it is working. Rufra has no slaves in his camp and there are thankful squads in his army."

"But not on his council."

"No, change takes time, Girton. He is trying."

I felt like I had let Nywulf down somehow.

"Who are they? If you want me to find a traitor I will need to know them." I nodded my head towards the table in the other room.

"You will do it, then? You will take up the motley?"

I waited, time moved on.

One, my master.

Two, my master.

Three, my master.

Four, my master.

"Who are they?" I said again, and Nywulf stared at me, his ice-chip eyes seeming to measure me. I broke his gaze, afraid that I may be found wanting.

"With their backs to us are Cearis ap Vthyr—"

"Rufra's aunt?"

"Yes, her flag is the purple with the ap Vthyr lizard in the left corner. She leads his heavy cavalry and acts as his right hand."

"Not you?" I was surprised.

"No, I am his Heartblade, and tradition dictates I cannot sit on my king's council."

"Rufra doesn't strike me as a traditionalist."

"No, he isn't," again I could hear the pride in Nywulf's voice, "and he discusses most things with me, but if I was his right hand some would whisper I controlled him the same way they say Neander puppeted Aydor and now Tomas. I have been with Rufra since he was a child, it is better he is seen to be his own man." I nodded. "On the other side of Rufra is the bowmaster . . ."

"Varn?" I stared at the back of the man's head. He had extremely long straight black hair that fell over the back of his chair.

"Yes. His flag is the green and black check with the black bow. Varn acts as quartermaster for Rufra's army, when he is not making bows, which he prefers to do. On the left of Varn is—"

"A Landsman." It felt like a kick in the stomach, almost a betrayal to see one of the Tired Lands sorcerer hunters there, though of course Rufra did not know what I was and the Landsmen were a power in the Tired Lands. He would struggle to rule without them on his side.

"Aye, Karrick Thessan of the stricken mountains. His flag is the green and tree, obviously."

"Rufra should rid himself of the Landsmen."

"They are necessary, Girton," said Nywulf, "and he builds with what material he has."

My gaze moved along the table and once more a frisson of fear shot through me. I had been concentrating so hard on the Landsman I had not looked at the figure next to him. Clad entirely in black was a priest of the dead gods, but black was worn only by the hermit priests of Xus, and they had no allegiance; they wandered, living off what could be begged. The last time I had been in Maniyadoc there had been such a priest – except only I had seen him, even when others stared straight at him, and more and more I had wondered if he was not a man at all, but something more, Xus the unseen, god of death. Then the priest turned, and he was only a man. He did not even wear the mocking porcelain mask of a priest of Xus or the blank masks worn by the priests of the dead gods. Nonetheless, my unease remained.

"Who is that priest?"

"Arnst the Lost. He has no flag of course, and I believe he sits next to Karrick purely because he enjoys annoying the man. He says Xus is the only true god and all the others should be forgotten."

"I am surprised he does not decorate a blood gibbet."

"Aye, Karrick would like nothing more, as would the other priests. But they squabbled among themselves so much Rufra appointed Arnst to spite them, and now they must go through him, which they hate. He is a trouble causer, but Rufra chose him and now we must live with it." I heard disapproval in his voice. "The last of the three is Bediri Outlander – her flag is the green and gold check." The woman sat quietly at the table, listening to the priest and the Landsman argue about some minute piece of camp politics. Her skin was almost pure white, as was her intricately braided hair, and she wore cleverly worked leather armour. A scar ran down her face from her forehead, cutting a furrow through her nose and lips. "She heads Rufra's archers and is Varn's wife."

"Does that not advantage Varn, if his wife is in the council?"

"Anything but. Bediri seems to take great joy in opposing her husband and he in being opposed." Nywulf sounded bemused. "Bediri and Arnst together also speak for the common people of the camp, though positions in Rufra's council are fluid." He took a breath. "But Bediri and Varn are unlikely spies as they have only sat on the council for a year and Varn's knowledge of weapons could make him more than spying ever could." I nodded again. "Now, across the table from Bediri sits Boros ap Loflaar, who you know, and his flag is the yellow with the half draymount's head. The curling horns on his flag are the only ones you'll see in the camp; the rest have been shorn to make bows. Next to him is Gabran the Smith. His flag is the blue with the hammer and—"

"He represents the smiths?"

"No, he leads Rufra's infantry."

I turned my gaze back on Gabran, who was small for an infantryman and thin for a smith. Like them all he wore his hair long, though it was so thin as to be little more than wisps around his sharp face. He had the look of a rat but it was a fool who judged a man by his features. I had a club foot but it did not stop me being a killer.

"He does not look like a soldier," I said.

"He isn't, or says he wasn't. But he fights like a hedging and seems to know no fear. He is also fiercely protective of his infantry, though in truth he is a hard man to know. Again, I think him an unlikely spy."

"And the man on the end?" Of them all he was the only one I would have been able to identify as blessed without prior knowledge – from the slightly finer quality of his clothing, the smoothness of the skin and the slight plumpness of his body, a rarity in the Tired Lands where even the rich often went hungry. He had a round face which would have been jovial if he did not look as if he believed everyone else around the table was in sore need of a bath. He had pushed himself slightly away from the table, as if to distance himself from what was being done there, and hardbread hobby dolls were woven into his hair so they danced whenever he moved.

"That is Lort ap Garron. He is there to represent the blessed." There was no mistaking the distaste in Nywulf's voice, though whether it was for Lort or the blessed in general he gave no clue.

"He looks unhappy to be there."

"Yes, but it is all a front put on so the more stuck-in-their ways blessed trust him. He has been a supporter of Rufra's from the start and stands to lose everything if he falls." Nywulf paused before speaking again. "I do not like him, but he is trustworthy. Tomas killed his entire family and revenge is all he dreams of. There, Girton, now you know the names of the people who have access to Rufra's plans, which one looks like a spy to you?"

"I do not know, Nywulf," I said, and I did not for if there is one thing I have learned it is that a good spy is like a good assassin: they never look like what they are.

Chapter 8

As Nywulf finished pointing out the men and women of Rufra's council the meeting broke up; an agreement had been reached. When Rufra stood his body was tight with tension and I retreated from the curtain, I did not want it to appear like I was spying on him. Rufra swept through the curtain, pulling off his armour and throwing it into a corner then throwing himself into a camp chair that creaked alarmingly as his weight hit it. He sat, staring to one side, his hand idly coming up to his mouth as if he was about to bite on his nails before he noticed what he was doing and sat straighter, clamping his hands onto the wooden arms of the chair.

"You did not get your way then?" said Nywulf.

"They will stop Aydor coming?" I said.

"No, they saw the sense in Aydor joining us readily enough," said Rufra, "Messengers will be sent." I felt sick at his words. "But they turned down my other plan and now people will die."

"Such is war," said Nywulf.

"It need not be," said Rufra. "I am sure that my plan—"

"You should not let Aydor come," I said.

"I would rather have him with me than with Tomas."

"He says he cannot go to Tomas as he and Neander tried to have him killed. You should let the land have Aydor – send him out with the desolate to be bled."

"They tried to kill him?" Rufra leaned forward, interested, and his chair creaked again. "All the more reason to have Aydor with me then, if he has a score to settle."

"Have you forgotten what he was like at Castle Maniyadoc? He was a monster and—"

"People change," said Rufra quietly. "Events change us all."

"They do not." My nails were digging into the palms of my hands as my fingers curled into tight fists. "We only become more of what we are. Tomas has his daughter too. Aydor will—"

"Not have to worry about her," said Nywulf. "As the last Mennix she is too precious to waste."

"So you agree with him." I stared at Nywulf.

"In this, yes," he said, "in his other plan, no."

"And what is that plan?" I asked, glad to get away from the subject of Aydor.

Rufra looked glad of the change of subject too. "I'll show you, Girton. Maybe you will see that I am right and help me find some way to convince the others." He sprang up from his chair and went over to the big map table in the centre of the room. "See the red lines?" There were lines of red material pinned on the map, which looped around Maniyadoc, taking in the river's delta and most of the coast, in the centre bulging out to meet the western sourlands. "That is the land we control. The blue lines show Tomas's land, and in between no one rules and Nonmen raid."

"So it is also Tomas's land," said Nywulf.

"We do not know that Tomas has anything to do with the Nonmen – I am sure he is better than that," said Rufra.

Nywulf let out a quiet laugh and shook his head.

"Tomas rules a lot more land than you," I said.

"Yes, he does." But instead of looking downcast about this Rufra was grinning; his whole face and body had become far more animated. "But all this –" he gestured towards Tomas's land on the map "– does not mean he is winning. Most of it I have ceded without a fight."

"The more land he has, the further he must stretch his forces," I said.

"Exactly. We control less land but we hold it more tightly. We also control more fertile land than Tomas, and we have both Demis and Hart, the deepwater ports. So Tomas may have more troops than we do but he has to stretch them more thinly, and he also has trouble feeding them as his land is mostly sourings."

"Knowing this," said Nywulf, "makes me wonder why you cannot see the same problems in your pet obsession that the rest of us do."

"Ignore Nywulf, he thinks this is to do with Goldenson Copse."

"It isn't?"

"No, Nywulf. It isn't." There was a hardness in Rufra's voice, and Nywulf stiffened at the sound of it.

"I should go to Neliu and Crast, King Rufra. They require training, and I am sure you are safe with Girton by you," said Nywulf. He gave a formal bow but Rufra had already turned back to the map. Nywulf gave me a quick shake of his head. "See if you can talk sense into him, Girton."

"Are Neliu and Crast good?" I asked when Nywulf had gone.

"The new Heartblades? They should be, the amount of time Nywulf has spent training them. You will meet them later – you will like them," he said distractedly as he stared at the map. "Now, Girton, see these four villages here?" He pointed at four flags on the map to the south east of Maniyadoc sitting near a huge bend in the river.

"Yes."

"They are Belder's Mill, Fludmere, Goldenson Copse and the largest is Gwyre. I wish to bring them all under my protection."

"And your council do not?" I could see why: they were far from the red lines that marked Rufra's territory and would cause him exactly the same problems he seemed delighted Tomas had caused himself.

"No, they say we are too near a final battle, that soon

Tomas must fight me or starve and garrisoning these places is a waste of troops."

"It must be hard, having to tell the people of these villages that."

"Yes," said Rufra and he looked away, suddenly finding the small model of Maniyadoc far more interesting for some reason.

"They have asked for your help, Rufra?"

"Well," he still didn't look at me, "they say they are independent, but it is only a matter of time now until Tomas hits them, him or the Nonmen. But we can protect them." I glanced across the map.

"They are over a day's ride away, Rufra. You would have to garrison the villages and feed your troops."

"You sound like my council."

"Maybe they are right?"

"Girton, there are children there. You cannot know how sick I am of seeing dead children."

"Children die, Rufra, the Tired Lands are cruel."

For a moment his face was stricken, as if a storm had blown in behind his eyes, and I knew he had no magic in him, because if he had lightning would have reached out and fired the room. He blinked. "Your master is in the infirmary tent, Girton," he said. "You should go and see her."

"Rufra, have I upset—"

"You are probably worried about her, Girton. Go. We will speak later." I realised he was dismissing me and wondered if I had made the right decision in coming here. A long time ago an old man had told me you could never be friends with a king, not really, and I had not believed him. Maybe he was right. On the other hand it was to Rufra's credit that he was so concerned about casualties despite having been at war for five years. I had seen dead children too, many of them, but they did not haunt me.

Though maybe they should.

*

The infirmary was in one of the two huge double-storey caravans. Inside it smelled strongly of pine, but that could not hide the high, sweet and unnerving, smell of rotting flesh. There were not many beds, maybe twenty, and only half of them were filled as most wounds taken in battle were either quickly fatal or quickly recovered from. It was seen as unlucky to cross the path of the healer-priests of Anwith; after all, the god had been unable to heal himself. Those who had to remain in the infirmary were the unlucky ones, those whose wounds had taken on the sickness of the land and sourings spread across their flesh, landscapes of mocking green that were fertile only for maggots. The white sheets of the beds were stained with pus and filth from leaking wounds and as soon as I entered my greatest wish was to get out again.

Aydor's healer, Mastal, stood by my master's bed in animated conversation with one of Rufra's grey-robed healers; they paused in their conversation as I approached. Between them lay my master as still as the dead, looking smaller and thinner than she had the day before.

"Girton," said Mastal as I approached, "this is Tarris, priest of Anlith, your god of healing."

"The god is called Anwith," snapped Tarris.

"My apologies. Anwith, god of healing. Tarris and I discuss how best to treat your master." She lay in a clean bed, her black hair damp with sweat and her face sallow – dark skin fading to grey.

"It is usual, in cases of poisons, to bleed the patient and purge the body of the hedge spirit's taint." The priest had pushed up his porcelain mask and his face was lined with age, and not a little concern.

"But I disagree with Tarris," said Mastal. "The woman has bled quite enough from the wound she took to try and remove the poison. To lose more blood will take strength from her she sorely needs."

Tarris turned to me. He was an old man, the sort I have

seen many times. One who has lived long enough to wear such a rut in life that he is unable to see over it, never mind leave the path he has carved.

"Mastal says you are a friend of the king?" he said to me. "Well, then the treatment of your companion must be decided by you, as I would not gainsay a friend of the king. So, young man, do we bleed her, as all good sense says, or do you wish to take the advice of this –" he paused as if he smelled something bad "– foreigner, who does not even know the names of our gods?"

I thought for a moment. It seemed a yellower's choice. Trust a man who was Aydor's creature or let this old man, whose infirmary smelled of death, treat my master.

"Priest Tarris," I said, "thank you for your concern and for letting my companion rest in your infirmary, but in my experience it seems men and women more often die for want of blood than for having too much." The priest looked like he may be about to explode and I tried to soften the blow a little. "And although I respect your learning, the poison that afflicts my companion is a foreign one, so maybe it is best treated by a foreigner?"

"I suppose this should be expected from a follower of the king's new ways." He pulled down his mask and his voice settled into the inflectionless tone common to the priests of the dead gods. "You will have to move her, of course. I cannot have a foreigner in here upsetting my charges, and her poison may infect others."

"But she is comfortable," said Mastal, "for the first time in days."

"I am sorry," said the priest and turned away.

"I will find out where I am quartered," I said. "I am sure Rufra will have arranged for me to have my own tent." Especially if I was to spy for him. "She can be put in there."

Mastal nodded. "She will probably be disturbed less with you, so it may even be for the best."

I left the infirmary, annoyed with the intractable old man who ran it, annoyed that I must trust Aydor's healer and suddenly aware how difficult Rufra's task truly was. People did not like change. The priests of the dead gods told us change was impossible, that when the gods died the world had been cast like molten metal dropped into water. The blessed would be blessed, the living would remain the living, and the thankful would stay just that, thankful for whatever small pickings they could get. But Rufra was turning this on its head. It would not surprise me to find resentment in the buried chapels, where people chanted over books of names and signed them so that in the future the reincarnated gods would know they had kept faith.

Curse Nywulf and Rufra. Meddling in Maniyadoc's politics had come close to getting me killed once before, and here I was, already letting curiosity's dangerous tendrils worm themselves into my mind. I could not do this, not again; I should stay out of it and concentrate on making my master well. I had been wrong to come here, wrong to think we could be safe. Maybe I was wrong to doubt myself, but my master had solved our previous mystery, not me. I had wandered blithely past what was important.

A roar distracted me. I had arrived back at Rufra's black and red tent just as he left it, and a cheer of approval had come from the men and women around it.

Rufra gave a wave to the crowd, almost slipped in some mud and then laughed at himself, causing others, common and council alike, to laugh too. By him the jester, Gusteffa the Dwarf, mimicked his slip to even more hilarity. Then a second roar went up, "King Rufra!" followed by a cheer. For a moment I was blinded by a shaft of sunlight reflecting off a shield, and in the shadow on my retina I saw a dark figure, Xus, the god of death, among the smiling crowd. He stood, black-robed and frightening, and appeared to have one arm raised, one pale finger pointing as if to single out one person in the crowd.

I followed his pointing finger. Nwyulf moved to one side and exposed Rufra. Xus was not solid, not there entirely, his form ghostly as if he warned of what may be, and as he faded into nothing I knew I could not walk away, not if it might mean the death of my friend. I had to try and help.

Rufra stood with Boros and their mounts were brought to them, huge proud animals with antlers gilded in sharpened steel. Soldiers created a corridor through the crowd which they rode through to meet another group of Riders.

I decided to find my own mount, Xus, and headed towards the paddocks. As I wended my way through the camp past the day markets – people everywhere, stalls selling food, butchers cutting meat and pedlars selling trinkets – I found myself drawn towards the sound of weapons drills. The crowds thinned and I entered what was clearly a training ground. A group of soldiers lounged against a fence, watching a practice fight going on within and I sidled over, listening as bets were exchanged between the troops.

"Crast 'as 'er this time, my friend," said one soldier. "Half a bit says he 'as Neliu on 'er back this round." I expected some sort of ribald comment in answer to that but none came; instead there was a considered silence before her friend answered.

"Nah. He's getting better but she still 'as 'is measure. Be a pity to take your money, Anill."

"I'd be 'appy to take yo— Dead gods! She got 'im again."

I went to join the soldiers by the fence and watched Crast, who could be no more than seventeen, getting to his feet with a silly grin on his face as he brushed sawdust from his skirts and picked up the two wooden practice knives he had dropped. His opponent was similar to him in features, though a little older, slight of build with blue eyes and the same bright red hair, like polished copper. Nywulf stood behind the two.

"Swap weapons," he said. "Crast, take the longsword and

stabsword, Neliu, take the knives." They swapped and fell into ready positions and then Nywulf shouted, "Start!"

The two trainee Heartblades were quick and, almost with a sense of longing, I watched them spar. Nywulf stalked around the two young warriors, occasionally correcting footwork with a stick he carried, sometimes shouting out instructions to one or the other, but it was make-work really; the two were ferociously skilled. What's more they clearly enjoyed the work, though the soldier who had refused his friend's bet was right: the girl was quicker than the boy – though maybe not enough to guarantee her a win every time.

She slipped on something, regaining her balance in a flash, but the boy was in, his longsword coming over in a powerful strike. The third iteration, a Meeting of Hands, she brought her knives together to block it, but he lunged with his stabsword to catch her in the stomach, pulling the strike at the last minute so he did not hurt her too much. But it did not matter – she was already gone – and by the time his stabsword was fully extended she was in close with her blade at his throat. The fall had been a trick. The soldiers watching started to applaud, as did I, and Nywulf stood back with a smile on his face.

"Girton," he said quietly, "would you care to show my pupils how it is done?"

I suddenly felt self-conscious. I had not used paired knives or a sword for two years or more.

"Another day, maybe, Nywulf," I said, and he nodded, though there was an odd look in his eye, something calculating. "I have come to find out where I am staying." A horn sounded somewhere in the camp.

"I will have Crast take you." He pointed at the boy. "Neliu, Rufra is to ride out on patrol with Boros. You will have his back today."

"Yes, Nywulf."

The boy looked disappointed at not getting to ride with

his king, and Nywulf placed his hand on the back of his neck and pushed him gently forward. "Do not be down-hearted, Crast. You are tasked with the protection of Girton. Were it not for him Rufra would not even be a king, but that is a secret and you must tell no one."

"I do not want or need a nursemaid," I said, though Nywulf paid no attention.

"Oh." The boy's face lit up. "You are that Girton?"

"How many other Girtons do you think I would let refuse my request to fight?" said Nywulf.

"I do not know, Nywulf," said Crast with a look full of mischief. "I have never met another Girton."

"Get on," said Nywulf, "before I bruise your arse for such cheek." Crast gave me a grin as he joined me, wiping sweat from his face with his palms and I found myself annoyed at Nywulf for telling the boy who I was, though it was foolish of me. As Heartblades they would find out about me soon enough. "Take him to Varn and refer to him only as Rufra's guest. Find out where he is to be quartered."

"I will need two beds," I said.

"Got plans, have you?" said Crast, giving me a wink.

"My master is ill; the second bed is for her."

"Oh." He blushed, unsure of what to say, but Nywulf saved him from further embarrassment.

"That makes things easier actually. Tell Varn that Girton is with the ambassador from the Lean Isles and have three cots provided for them."

"Three?" I said.

"One for the healer, or should the ambassador's healer sleep on the floor?" said Nywulf. "The fact that they are both dark-skinned and new to camp will make the lie more believable." I had not thought Mastal would share with us, and I was not sure I liked the idea of him being there.

"Why the Lean Isles?" I asked and he shrugged.

"Why not?"

We walked away, and when Nywulf was out of earshot I said to Crast,

"You should watch your sister's feet."

"She is not my sister," he said quickly, but he avoided my eye and for a moment I wondered if he lied, but it seemed a foolish lie to tell if it was. More likely he had a crush on the older girl and was embarrassed by it.

"Well, whatever she is, you should still watch her feet. No one moves without their feet giving warning."

"Nywulf says the same." Crast shrugged. "But he says to watch her eyes too, and he also says I must never take my gaze from her blade."

I laughed.

"Well, he is right in all those things."

"I will need more eyes, I think," he said glumly, but he was good-humoured and could not keep up the pretence of misery.

"I will train with you when I can, if you wish," I said. "Help you a bit."

"With that?" He pointed at my warhammer. "Hard to pull a blow with such weight."

"I would use a blade," I said

"I would like that. Nywulf says he has rarely seen your equal."

Crast and I continued to chatter about inconsequential things as he led me back into the camp and towards a group of tents that, rather than being fat and round, were long and triangular, their lengths shot through with black poles which made them look like spiny caterpillars. Above them Varn's green and black flag cracked in the wind. For a warrior sworn to give his life to save his king Crast was strangely carefree, and I felt myself envying him. Occasionally a child would run in front of us, screaming as it played or brandishing a wooden sword, and a shadow would pass across Crast's face, as if he were suddenly struck by how much responsibility he had, but it was gone as quickly as it arrived. I wondered how much combat he had seen – not much, I imagined – but then I remembered how quickly I had been to shrug off the deaths I had caused as a child, and I hoped that Rufra brought a lasting peace before Crast became more like me.

"Varn," shouted Crast, slapping his hand against a tent. "Varn, you are needed. We need a tent for the Lean Isles ambassador." The tent flap was pushed aside and Varn appeared in a cloud of narcotic smoke. He was a small man, old and almost entirely naked. Behind him stood his wife, Bediri, and she was entirely naked. The smoke leaving their tent wrapped me in intoxicating tendrils, and I imagined I could smell sex in the air.

"I was busy," said Varn.

"King's business," said Crast. He did his best not to look at Bediri, though he kept glancing at her body and had no choice but to raise his head to her when she spoke.

"You would think the king would know better than to disturb me when I am taking my man to bed," she said.

Varn frowned. He had a round face with a wide nose that had been broken many times. His teeth had been filed into points, and his skin was so white it was almost translucent.

"I am no woman's man," he said.

"Then possibly I should find a man who is not ashamed to be mine," said Bediri, and though they both sounded fierce there was a playfulness about them that made me smile. Crast's face turned almost puce with embarrassment.

"Few men are that brave," said Varn.

Bediri shrugged. "Then I am stuck with you. Go about your king's business, husband, and if you are lucky I may still be waiting when you return." She turned and vanished into the dark of the tent. A moment later some clothes came flying out. "And dress. Remember these people are odd about such things."

Varn laughed quietly to himself as he dressed.

"I think she forgets that, here, we are the odd ones."

"Where are you from?"

"Oh, a long way off, a place that no longer exists and you will never heard of."

"I have heard of many places," I said, but Varn ignored me. Instead he led me away from his tent, pointing out how the camp was constructed as a giant circle to make it easier to navigate. As I walked I noticed large wooden boxes at the end of each row of tents.

"What are those?"

"Latrines."

"Do you not just use the river?"

"No. Rufra insists the troops use the latrines and each night a cart comes and collects the night soil, taking it to join the mount dung to be spread on the land for crops."

"That must be an unpopular job."

"It is, but it is a good one for enforcing discipline." He sounded happy and had a quality that made him instantly likeable, useful for a military man. I was glad Nywulf thought him an unlikely traitor. "Here is your tent," he said. We had stopped in front of the two huge caravans in the same clearing I had seen Rufra acclaimed in. Now he had gone it was much quieter, and I wondered if the cheering been engineered for morale, or if the people knew their king would be leaving at that time and had just wanted to see him." Around the clearing was a circle of round tents and it was one of those that he pointed at, a grander tent than I had ever had before. I noticed another tent of a strange design, it hung between the two caravans, more a collection of tautly strung sheets than any tent I had ever seen.

"What is that?"

"Rufra's court tent. It will be in session in the morning, so no doubt you will see his justice enacted."

"Is it good justice?' The bowman shrugged. "He is soft, for a king, but he will learn with time."

"You speak very freely," I said.

"That is why the king likes me." He pulled back the flap on the front of my tent and I noticed an intricate interlacing of scars on his inner arm. They were not like mine – though the marks were not random either, they had purpose. When he noticed me looking at them he moved his arm so they were hidden. "You should make yourself comfortable and set up the beds. You will find everything you need. I will send Crast to get the ambassador and her healer."

With that he left and I walked into the gloom of the tent. Finally alone, I felt crushed by the unfamiliar darkness.

Chapter 9

With lamps lit the tent was slightly less foreboding, though still gloomy and overly warm. As Mastal the healer settled my master in her bed I went outside to find Crast guarding the tent.

"I can look after my master," I said. It irked me that Nywulf felt we needed guarding.

"But Nywulf said—"

"Well tell Nywulf I said otherwise, and if he thinks differently he is to take it up with me. Crast looked miserable. "He'll be like a man with two hangovers over this, you know. I'll have to hide from him for a week to avoid lectures on who I am meant to be obeying."

I palmed two bits and slipped them into his hand. "Listen. I know what Nywulf can be like. Drown your sorrows afterwards." He grinned as he took the money and I wondered if I had been played as he skipped off merrily enough. When I turned, the healer had set about pinning back some of the tent flaps.

"To keep the air moving," he said. "The breeze will take away the bad air from her lungs." He pulled a small table over to her bed and started to take a selection of murky bottles from his satchel and set them out. "This wound she has, tell me more of it."

"We were caught by a group of Glynti coming out of the sourlands. She took a glancing blow. Barely a scratch, really."

"And she cut the poison out straight away?" His brow furrowed, turning his eyebrows into a dark "V" of puzzlement.

"No, she did not know they were poisoners, not until she had spoken to one. It was a few minutes, five at most."

He turned back to my master, stroking his small beard. "I must find some herbs. Will you sit with her?" I nodded. "When I return I will give you some unguent for your foot. I see it pains you." He slipped out of the tent and I sat by my master, a sudden ache running up from my club foot and through my leg to my chest. Curse the man. I had almost forgotten about the constant pain in my foot until he had mentioned it.

"Master?" I said, and felt foolish. It was obvious, even to the untrained eye, that she was far away, drifting on the currents of the wine-dark sea somewhere between life and Xus the unseen's black palace. Despite this I began to talk, telling her of what I had seen, who I had seen and how Nywulf wanted me to become Rufra's spy to find a spy. "I cannot do this," I said. "He thinks I saved Rufra before, but it was you, not I, who saw the web and cut the strings. You must wake, Master – I need you."

But she did not wake, and so I sat, listening to the ebb and flow of her breath, remembering the long hours of training – breathe out, breathe in – and instead of the deaths I had wrought I remembered the joy I had felt when I had been dancing stories and tumbling as a jester. As I watched her I knew that I could not do what Nywulf wished: I could not become Death's Jester for him. Not simply because I was not good enough, but because as long as she lived she was Death's Jester, and to take on her role would be the same as admitting she was never coming back.

My veins itched, and to take my mind from the discomfort I found paper and made notes on the people I had seen. When that was done I sketched the scars I had seen on the inner arm of Bowmaster Varn. With that done I looked around for more to do. I found Mastal's bags and went through them. They were packed carefully, full of strange bottles and odd herbs. In one I found papers covered in writing that made no sense to me. It was set out in columns, with some words underlined. It may have been code or it may have been the language of the place he was from. I committed it to memory, put everything away and then wrote it out on another piece of parchment and turned back to my master.

"How is she?"

I looked up, trying not to look guilty as I expected the healer, but it was Rufra. I let go of my master's hand, only half aware I had been holding it, then swiftly covered the papers.

"She sleeps."

"That is good. Sleep is good for wounds."

"I cannot be the Death's Jester for you, Rufra. I am sorry."

"Do not worry for my sake. Despite what Nywulf says there is no traitor here. I suspect Aydor unknowingly spreads another's discord – it is exactly the sort of trick Neander would play."

"Neander's only faith is himself and what power he can get." Neander had been priest of Heissal, god of the day, in Maniyadoc, and though my lover Drusl had taken her own life it was Neander who had forced her into the path of the blade.

"True, and it is working for him. He is high priest of the Long Tides now."

"And you allow his priests into your camp? They could all be reporting back to him."

"I cannot ask people to give up their faith. Besides, Neander is not popular among his own and the priests do not sit on the Triangle. They do not know my real plans or get near enough to do me harm. Nywulf sets too much importance on what happened at Goldenson Copse, but the truth is I was overconfident. The error there was mine, not some traitor's."

For a king it seemed he remained as naive as he had been as a boy.

"Rufra," I said hesitantly. I did not doubt he genuinely believed his council would not betray him, but I have never been one to trust blindly. "Nywulf introduced me as assistant to the ambassador of the Lean Isles, and as the ambassador is ill people would expect me to take over her duties."

"And?"

"It would allow me to question the people close to you."

"There is no traitor, Girton."

"Think of it this way, Rufra: if you do not let me look into this you will never hear the end of it from Nywulf." He was about to argue with me – I could see it in the set of his jaw and wished he would simply be reasonable – then a smile crept onto his face, one I did not much like the look of.

"Very well, but if I let you do that you will have to let me assign either Crast or Neliu to watch over your master."

"I told you, I do not need a nursemaid. I—"

"And what of her?" He pointed at my master. "You say you are still both under sentence of death for betraying your calling. Tomas has also put a price on your head. If an assassin comes and you are not here, do you expect a healer to save her?"

I stood, anger rising within me at the idea I could not look after my master, but I tamped it down. This was not Rufra's fault; it was no doubt Nywulf's doing. He was a clever one, and this way he had me looking after Rufra and ensured I would not be too distracted by worrying about my master.

"Very well, Rufra." I shook my head.

"I am glad you are not going to be stubborn about this."

"Me? You are the stubborn one."

He opened his mouth to argue but then instead grinned and clasped my arm. "Maybe we are both stubborn on occasion." I nodded, laughing quietly.

"Aye, maybe."

"But you more so," he added quickly, a glint in his eye.

I shook my head but argued no further as I did not want to prove him right.

"Did Nywulf suggest having his apprentices guard us?"

"He did." Rufra gave me a sheepish smile. "He said you would not like it. He always seems to be one move ahead of me. Nywulf tells me his only wish is to retire, but he organises my life even when I am unaware of it, and now he has taken on responsibility for you as well."

"To be Nywulf's responsibility is a terrifying thing."

"Aye, imagine how Crast and Neliu feel. He practically lives in their pockets."

"They fight well. Where are they from?"

"A village called Amherd, right at the beginning of the war. The villagers were packing up to move into my protection when Nonmen hit it. They were the only two to survive, including the soldiers I had sent to help. Crast and Neliu hid in a haystack. They were terrified when they came. Gusteffa took them under her wing first and then they passed to Nywulf."

"Captain Thian said Nonmen did not attack defended targets."

"They don't usually, but they are unpredictable."

"Or when they are doing Tomas's dirty work for him."

"I do not want to believe that, but yes, it often seems that way and most believe it."

"But not you?"

"I try not to. I want him to be better than that, but . . ."

"It seems unlikely?"

"He is badly advised."

"And he has created two more young people who want to kill him."

"Aye, that is part of the reason Nywulf took them on. Hate is a powerful motivator, though I wish it were not the case. Life would be easier if people hated less and loved more."

A soft sadness had descended on the tent and Rufra seemed to draw himself up, pulling out of the encroaching melancholy. "But that is not why I am here. There is still a little light left, and I thought you may want to see Xus before night falls."

"I would love to, if he remembers me."

"Dead gods, I hope he does." Rufra grimaced. "There is no one here who can control him. I was hoping your arrival may give my mountmasters some respite."

He took me through the camp just as twilight was pushing the light away. Torches were being lit and a misty stillness had settled on the camp; work had ceased for the day, and all was quiet apart from the occasional calls of sentries letting each other know they were still at post.

"Why are you camped here, Rufra, rather than in Maniyadoc?" In the haze of last light I could make out the huge castle on the horizon. "Surely your army would be safer behind its walls."

"Much safer," he said. "Too safe. I want Tomas to fight me, and he is not so badly advised that he would attack Maniyadoc. If I hide behind its walls Tomas will never come against me and the land will remain ravaged by war." He stooped, plucking a long stalk of grass from the verge. "He has more troops than we do and I hoped a camp might tempt him across the river."

"But it hasn't?

"No." He whipped at the ground with the grass. "He sits in his camps or behind the walls of his keeps and hopes disease will strike my army and do his work for him, though of course he takes the same risk. But he must come soon, Girton, he must, or he will run out of food. I am slowly starving his army."

"If there is a spy or an assassin in your council you will need them uncovered before you fight Tomas."

"If there is." He turned, a half-smile on his face, he looked young and lost – overwhelmed. Then he brightened. "Look, my herds." He pointed ahead of us at the paddocks, where massive mounds of hay stood like giant hives. Around them were clustered the mounts of his army, huge and finely antlered. Even among all the great beasts I could easily spot my Xus. Rufra grinned at me as he saw my eyes lock on the mount. "I may be King of Maniyadoc and the Long Tides, Girton, but there is only one king of the paddocks, and he answers to none, not even me."

"Xus!" I shouted, and if I had expected some show of joy at my return I would have been sorely disappointed. I had not of course – I knew Xus better than that. He raised his long slim head at the sound of my voice and I saw him in silhouette, huge spreading antlers blackened by the falling sun, then he lazily trotted across the paddock towards me, occasionally pausing to nibble something on the ground with an air of insouciance. He stopped his own body length away from the fence Rufra and I leaned on. His small black eyes stared over my shoulder and his ears twitched as if he was unsure whether to deign to recognise my voice.

"Our master is sick, Xus," I said. The words came out as a whisper. Rufra briefly put a hand on my arm and then stood back so I could speak without being overheard. "She is sick, and she would be here if she could be. You will have to do with me for now. I will bring her when she is able. The sight of you will be a balm to her." The huge animal lifted his head and considered this for a moment, blowing air noisily in and out of his nostrils, and then his whole body shivered – I noticed he had not been brushed in a long time – and he stepped forward until he was towering over me. Then he lowered his head so his neck lay on my shoulder and his great head, with those heavy antlers, rested against my back. I put my arms around him, losing myself in the smell of him, the bristles of his yearsdeath coat just starting to moult and the softness of the yearsbirth coat beneath.

"She will come, Xus," I said, "she will." I do not know how long I stood like that with him, but it was a long time, time enough for twilight to finish her retreat, and all that time Rufra stood quietly behind me, giving me the space I needed.

"He has missed you," he said when I finally let go of the animal. "Tomorrow I ride out. You should bring him, give him a run."

"I would like that."

"But first you should tour the drinking holes tonight and tell people you intend to ride Xus, put on some bets. You could become a rich man."

"He is that feared?"

Rufra nodded.

"It became quite the sport for a while, to try and ride Xus. Eventually I had to put a stop to it as I was losing more Riders to injury from falling off him than I was to the blade." He laughed, and I joined with him. I had missed this: I had missed Xus and I had missed my friend.

"I will take him to the stables," I said. "He needs a brush and attention paid to his claws – they are ragged."

"That is because all my stable hands are terrified of him. You should introduce Xus to one of them, Girton. It would do them good to see he is not a hedging that accidentally wandered into my paddocks." With that he clapped me on the shoulder and pointed out the stable tents before walking away into the night.

I watched him, feeling strangely out of sorts and alone. Despite my friend being here, despite my mount being here, I was still wondering if I would ever find a place that really felt like home.

Chapter 10

I woke before dawn the next day. The chill of the years-birth night still clung to the ground and misty kisses had left a rime of frost on the short grass, it crackled under my boots as I limped along. My master had slept right through the night without disturbing me for the first time since she was poisoned. That morning I had not heard her breathing and panicked that she had died in the night. I got up too quickly while half asleep and ended up tangled in my blanket and nearly overturning Mastal's table of medicines.

"Enough, Girton. She rests," said Mastal, and he passed me a bowl of hot porridge. From the bags under his eyes I suspected he had been awake all night. I took the porridge and quickly spooned it down while he bent to pick up the papers which I had knocked to the floor. I froze, worried he would spot my copy of his own papers, but he only paused at the sheet showing the scarring on Varn's arm. "I did not know you understood Tak, Girton."

"Tak?" I said and took the other papers, folding them away into my jerkin before sitting back down to my porridge.

"This." He shook the sheet at me. "One of the old languages."

"I only saw it somewhere is all," I said, glad he had not noticed the copy of his papers and of something to take my mind from the tasteless lumpy slop I was forcing down my gullet. Food in Maniyadoc had not changed. "What does it say?"

"I do not know much Tak," said Mastal. "I only learned enough to read their medical texts, but this seems to be a vow, 'I swear revenge on those who destroyed my people.' But that is approximate. Is it important?"

"It might be," I said, putting down my empty bowl and taking back the sheet. I placed it along with the rest at the bottom of my pack and left the tent, deep in thought.

Outside, Neliu stood guard. She was similar in many ways to Crast, but where he had an easy demeanour and ready smile she offered only a scowl. Her thin body looked carved of wiry muscle and tendon and she looked me over the way a warrior looks over a prospective opponent. I do not think she found me too impressive and I, in turn, saw the ghost of my own cocky youth in her.

"You stood guard all night?"

"Someone has to look after the sickly and the mage-bent," she said, and then turned away as if I were of no import, leaving me both angry and impotent to act upon my anger with a sharp reply. I walked away, the scars on my body fizzing as if a million biting midges had landed on my skin to feast.

"Girton Club-Foot."

My name from another's mouth, but I could not place where it came from. The voice seemed to echo around me, coming from all directions at once, and I half expected Xus the unseen to walk out of the morning shadows.

"Who is that?"

"How soon the youth forget," said the voice, and I heard someone approach, though who it was I could not fathom. The pattern of footsteps and sound was wrong for someone walking or running. Out of the night came Gusteffa the dwarf, cartwheeling along the ground until she flipped herself up into the air in a perfect handspring and landed in front of me. Her face was painted pure white with small red lips and red dots on the cheeks.

"Gusteffa!" I said, and to see her brought me some small joy. "I am glad Rufra kept you on."

"Well –" the jester smiled "– unlike King Doran, King Rufra even pays attention to me on occasion. Though not enough, of course." She performed a mocking bow.

"You're an artist, Gusteffa. Rufra would not be such a fool as to throw away a treasure."

She bowed low again, I suspect to hide the pleasure on her face from my praise. "So, Girton Club-Foot, do you come to jester for your friend? Is my time here over?"

"Not at all, Gusteffa. My master is ill. We came here for safety is all."

"A funny place to look for safety, in a camp at the edge of war. And do not forget it is ill luck for a king to have two jesters.'"

"But I am not here to be his jester, Gusteffa. I would never push you out." She made the gesture of surprise, her startlingly ugly face framed by her hands.

"And your other friend, Death's Jester, where is she?"

"In our tent and ill, gravely ill."

"I am sorry for that," she said, bowing her head. "She is an artist, as you could be. But not with this." And she was tumbling away from me with my warhammer in her hand, though I had no idea how she slid it from my belt without me noticing.

"I no longer tumble," I said. Gusteffa balanced the warhammer in the mud and pretended to walk away from it, acting like it was so heavy it kept pulling her back.

"No wonder, it is as heavy as Castle Maniyadoc." She mimed trying and failing to lift the warhammer. I walked forward to reclaim it but she flipped away, the weapon whirling around her as if it weighed nothing, and then, with a series of cartwheels, she vanished into the gloom.

"Gusteffa!" I shouted, and out of the darkness my

warhammer came sailing back to land at my feet, making me jump back.

"We choose our own paths and burdens, Girton Club-Foot," came a voice from the mist, "so choose them wisely, for once the path is chosen the way is set. You should leave, find yourself a blessed and pledge to do their bidding no matter what. Just as I did. You could live a happy life." I stared at the hammer, leaning slightly to one side where it had landed in the mud.

"I am not sure I am meant to be happy, Gusteffa," I said into the mist. She came cartwheeling out, landing in front of me on her hands.

"We choose what to be, what we are, what to do, who may have our loyalty." She flipped backwards onto her feet. "Lay your weapons down, Girton Club-Foot. You could walk away and leave them. Some other would take them up. Your king is safe – no assassin works during the war."

"How do you know?"

"The kings came to an accord, it is common knowledge."

I stepped forward and picked up the warhammer, hooking it back on my belt. Gusteffa watched me sadly. Then she walked up to me and stood on tiptoe so she could whisper to me.

"No one ever told me I could be anything else, and now it is too late. My path is set. You still have a choice." Then she flipped away into the mist.

I waited for her to return or speak again but there was only mist, and I found myself annoyed with the little woman, this world in general and Rufra for not telling me about this accord. I felt suddenly self-conscious about the warhammer at my hip. I was in Rufra's war camp, not a hostile wilderness, and was probably as safe as I could ever be. I returned to the tent, slipping in. Mastal started guiltily as I entered, thrusting papers back into his bag and moving across to my master without looking at me. I ignored him, placing the hammer carefully among my belongings before leaving again. Mastal was up to something, I was sure. Aydor's work, no doubt.

I stalked through a camp just waking. The sun rose behind the massive colourful tents and painted long shadows on the grass. It had rained during the night and in places standing water had gathered and naked children were running through puddles, laughing as they were pursued by harried parents eager to dress them for the signing ceremonies held by the priests. It was to the signing ceremonies I was headed. Neander's treachery under the rule of Queen Adran Mennix had cemented a deep mistrust of priests within me. There could be no question that Rufra's decision to elevate Arnst, a renegade, to his council would have annoyed the priesthood, so I would attend the signing ceremonies and listen to what they said and who they said it to. While there, maybe I could find someone who knew enough about Bowmaster Varn to tell me a little more about him and the vow carved into his arm.

A mother shouted, and I caught her child as it ran past me. The thing squealed with laughter as I held it away from me, unwilling to touch it – not just because it was muddy but also because children made me uncomfortable.

"Thank you, Blessed," a young mother clothed in the drab rags of the thankful said as she took the child back from me. "Children are a trial, but the king and queen are a reminder that they should be treasured. Even when, like Collis here, they are nothing but trouble." Ever like Rufra, I thought. Such sentimentality was what made him easy for people to love.

"Who are the priests for the camp?"

"Priests?" She looked at me like I had emerged from the earth. "Thought you looked funny. You an outlander?" I nodded. "Well, we 'ad plenty of priests but a fair few left when the king made Arnst one of 'is council." I could not tell whether she approved or disapproved. "Now we only have the three, and that Arnst of course." This time when she mentioned Arnst I was more sure the woman had no love for him. "There is Tarris, priest of Anwith, but he don't preach as all know it's bad luck to talk with a healer if you aren't with the sick. I go to Inla, priest of Mayel, now, she is good with the children, keeps her speeches short as she knows what it is like to be a mother. Used to go to Darvin, priest of Lessiah, but what do I need the goddess of the night for, eh? His words won't help me sleep more soundly, and it's not the whisperings of Black Ungar that keep me awake, it's Collis screaming for his da. Besides, he don't half go on at you – you should avoid him."

"And Arnst's sermons?"

"He stirs up problems like a stone in a pond brings up dirt. We had poisonings."

"Poisonings?"

"Oh aye. Twice we've had the wells poisoned. Course, only the lazy go to the well; most go to the river so we didn't lose as many as we could."

"And the poisoners were caught?"

She nodded.

"Arnst's man, the Meredari warrior, found 'em – spies sent in by Tomas with the incomers. They died on his blade rather than be caught." She leaned in close to whisper. "I been with the king since the start, but many come in 'ere late and only cos it's safe. You can't trust 'em. I bet most of 'em are spies for Tomas, and I'd throw 'em all out for the hedgings or put 'em among the desolate if it were up to me."

"It seems you have really caught the spirit of the times," I said. She scowled, but before she could walk away I added, "If Arnst's man caught the poisoners, why don't you like him?" She looked at me, confusion on her face until she replaced it with a look of annoyance.

"He stirs up trouble, don't he? He shouldn't be here. I

don't like him being here, and it ain't your business anyway is it, incomer? Where you from anyway? You speak funny." She hugged her child closer and balanced it on her hip so she could use her other hand to point away from me. "We don't have buried chapels here, us being a camp and all, so the priests' tents are all down there. Arnst's is in the other direction, near the paddocks." With that she walked away, leaving me feeling like I had upset her without meaning to.

I made my way through rows of tents and, although the camp looked grand at first, the poverty of Maniyadoc and the Long Tides showed through. In the soldiers' camp there was a good selection of spears and wooden shields on display, though there were very few swords; most soldiers carried a dagger and some also had a club. All had helmets made of boiled leather, though there were many different designs, and the most usual form of armour was padded cloth sewn with odd patches of leather or metal. Boiled-leather armour was quite common, though most of it was tatty and well used. Only occasionally did I see expensive armours made of many little enamelled metal plates sewn together, and that was mostly harlequin armour like my own, made from discarded pieces of other armours. Some soldiers had no armour at all, only a spear, but there was a sense of good cheer and camaraderie among them. I heard hand bells ringing, and those men and women who were not outfitting themselves for duty of some sort were heading towards the priests' tents. Soldiers were accompanied by their families, and it felt more like a day of celebration than another day in a martial camp.

The priests' tents stood in a clearing and there had obviously been more than the two before me. I counted five patches of dead grass where tents had stood around the purple tent of Lessiah and the red tent of Mayel. I chose red first as the woman had said the sermons in Mayel's tent tended to be shorter. I hoped I would be able to listen to her priest preach, then catch the priest of Lessiah at the end when he should be working himself up to the climax of his sermon and any traitorous ideas were more likely to slip through. Then I would have to hurry over to the paddocks to catch some of Arnst the Lost's sermon. I was most curious about what the renegade priest of Xus would say.

The woman had been right: Inla's sermon was blessedly short and reassuringly dull enough to make her small group of followers feel safe in a changing and unsafe world. As they queued up for her book she left an acolyte to oversee the signing and went over to a place in her tent that had been set aside for the children and sat with them, involving them in a game that caused much hilarity. She struck me as an unlikely rebel.

Darvin, the priest of Lessiah, across the way, was far more of a firebrand. Even though he spoke in the carefully modulated tones of the masked priesthood I could feel his commitment to the corpse of his god and his belief it would one day rise again. His tent was almost bursting with worshippers. All the seats were full, and I had to stand at the back. Darvin did not rail against Rufra – in fact he was full of praise for those who did what was right no matter what society said – and when he made dark allusions to worshippers of hedgings hiding in plain sight and misleading the just, I wondered if he referred to Arnst. At the end of his sermon, while his acolyte took the signatures or the marks of those who could not write, I made my way over to him. He had not lifted his mask and was easy to find, the pure white mask and purple robe standing out among the rags of his congregation like a frilled lizard in a stable. Behind him I saw a simple bed and a pack leaning against the canvas by it. Darvin stooped, moving his pack out of the way of one of his assistants, and I thought how rare it was to see a priest who kept to their vow of poverty. The man clearly lived in his tent when he could have had much better lodgings.

The priest saw me as I approached and broke off a conversation with one of his congregation, pointing at me as he did, which bothered me. I had hoped to keep a low profile the better to blend in and search out secrets.

"You are Girton?" Away from his lectern Darvin's voice was surprisingly gentle. "Friend of the king and assistant to the ambassador of the Lean Isles?"

"Yes. I was not aware I was so well known."

"I heard your name from the healer Tarris. He described you as 'mage-bent but full of vanity, carries himself like a warrior'." I winced at "mage-bent". "Tarris is not subtle in his conversation or forgiving of those who pass over his ministrations." He leaned in close. "Though I suspect you made the right decision."

He seemed friendly enough, so I decided to play the outlander, as it was the part I had been given – though something in me was saddened by the fact I had become so estranged from the place I had grown up in that I could carry off the ruse without trying.

"What did you mean by 'the hedging's followers hiding in plain sight'?"

"Well." As he steered me to the edge of the tent so we were out of the way of his bustling congregation, I noticed he had a pronounced limp. "In times such as these, when men and women let down their guard or give in to strife, the land spirits, remnants of the power of our gods, rise up to tempt them. These hedgings prey on the misdeeds of men and lead them to darkness, trick them into trading their lives for power until eventually they consume them or, even worse, turn them into sorcerers to devour the land." I dug my fingernails into my palms at the mention of sorcerers and in annoyance that he trotted out the standard sermon.

"You mean like Nonmen?"

"A symptom –" was there a hint of fear in his voice? "– of

a sickness in the land. King Rufra strives to do good, but even kings sometimes make the wrong choices."

"Arnst?" I said.

"That man would destroy everything we are" An edge of real vehemence had crept into his voice.

"Is that so bad? Is it fair that the thankful starve because of their birth?"

"Some change is to be applauded of course," he said, "but to throw everything away, to burn our history as men like Arnst would? It is a terrible thing to do, and it frightens people. They make poor choices out of fear. No doubt, where you come from, they have their beliefs –" I suddenly realised I knew nothing of the Lean Isles and became wary, but Darvin was lost in his soliloquy "– but how would you feel if the land you stood on was suddenly pulled from beneath your feet? If what you love was taken from you, destroyed? Rufra has dreams, but dreams are nebulous. He must have a solid foundation to build on or his dreams will crumble and people will be hurt."

I found myself nodding – it was hard not to having seen the chaos outside the camp.

"So you would have everyone cursed to live whatever life they were born to."

"It is not a curse to know your place. I had an assistant, Fara . . ." He looked away. "She dreamed of becoming something she could never be and I told her it was not our place to question the dead gods, ways."

"And what happened to her?" I had heard her name before, I was sure, but could not place it.

"She vanished, taken by hedgings." He turned back to me, forcing a smile onto his face and I remembered where I had heard the name – the girl Boros had been searching for when I first met him. "But on the other hand, the gods have not been reborn yet," he said, "so maybe we are doing something wrong; maybe some action is needed. We are only men and women, struggling to understand our gods. That they were and shall be again is as true as the fact that Xus walks among us, but the way to bring them back? Who really knows? Maybe we do need a strong arm, ready to sweep away the darkness in blood." For a moment he seemed to be talking more to himself than me but it was always difficult to tell with a masked priest. "Maybe that is what is needed – a true sacrifice. We must all do what we can, must we not? We must all root out darkness and magic whereever it is found."

My mouth became dry.

"I have to go," I said, uncomfortable. "I ride out with the king this morning and will need to find my mount."

"If you find a woman alone on your travels, ask if it is Fara. She is lost."

"I will."

"Blessings of Lessiah on you, boy."

"I don't need your blessing." It was automatic, leaping from my mouth.

"Really?" He took a stumbling step closer, peering into my face from behind his mask. "I was a warrior once, until I took a wound to my leg. I did not sleep well, not for years. I would see the faces of those whose lives I had taken. Only within the teachings of Lessiah did I find solace and peace." He paused and it felt like his whole being focused on me. "You do not look like you sleep well."

"I slept well last night."

"But was it the sleep of the exhausted, which does not bring rest? Or was it the sleep of the just?" He let a moment's silence pass. "Do hedgings whisper of dark deeds to you, boy? Lessiah can stop their voices. Lessiah can bring you a dreamless sleep if you only give yourself to her, take up her quest . . ."

"I no longer dream." He stared at me as if he could sense I did not tell the whole truth, dark eyes sparkling in the shadows of his mask. "And I must go, Darvin; I have to meet the king."

"Go then, Girton." He gave me a small bow of his head. "If you cut behind the tents and over the stream you will find a path that is a short cut to the paddocks."

I thanked the priest and left his tent, glad to be away. The fervour of the religious made me uncomfortable, though it was good that he seemed to understand the need for change. I considered going back to my tent for my weapons and armour but as I would be meeting Rufra by his caravans and my tent was next door it seemed foolish to traipse all the way back there so I took the short cut that the priest had mentioned, passing over a stream and through a small copse of pine trees. Sunlight squeezed through swaying branches to dance on the muddy ground.

That is where they tried to kill me.

Had my attacker not made the mistake of coming at me from behind so the sun threw the shadow of a raised arm over me they may have been successful. Instead, as the club came down I dived to the side, throwing myself into the mud and rolling to my feet, legs wide apart, eating knife in my hand and a curse at leaving my warhammer behind on my lips. My assailant wore a soldier's armour, leather chest piece, chained skirt and a helmet that covered the face.

"Walk away," I said, keeping my voice calm and my breathing shallow. "Your life is not worth the price on my head." I glanced around looking for another; there are always two in an assassin's sorrowing. So much for Gusteffa's talk of an "accord".

"A price?" she said. "Then your death is doubly worth my time."

Not an assassin after my master and I then. Was this simply a robbery?

She thrust with her stabsword. I slid to the side. She followed the thrust with a swing of her club that caught me on the shoulder, numbing my arm and making me swear.

"I 'ad heard you were a bladesman. Seems it is a lie." As

she spoke I backed up, placing my feet carefully in the mud and moving so I was further into a pool of standing water, feeling the slime beneath trying to trick my feet, glad I wore good boots where my attacker only wore sandals.

"Give me a blade," I said, "and I will show you who is a bladesman."

She laughed, coming forward and making small swings with her club to force me further back. She was not particularly skilled, but fully armoured and against a man with only an eating knife she did not need to be. As I retreated my feet found what I had hoped would be there, a tree root under the mud. I made a thrust with my knife and she stepped back, quickly returning the strike and pushing me further back with a few sharp thrusts of her stabsword. When she had taken a step past the root I thrust again and she stepped back again, the sole of her sandal catching on the root, and in the moment she was off balance I moved.

Did I resort to an assassin's trick? Did I move with the Speed-that-Defies-the-Eye? Did the lacework of scars on my flesh come alive for just the slightest hint of a fraction of time?

Then I was on her, hitting her in the stomach and pushing her to the ground. I slid an arm around her neck, and as she struggled I managed to position myself at her back with my arm across her throat.

"Who sent you?" I said, tightening my chokehold.

"I'm only after what you 'ave," she gasped out.

"Who sent you!"

She stretched out a hand, blindly feeling for her fallen stabsword and I rolled us both away from it, covering us in mud, only then realising my mistake as she struggled harder, now slippery as an eel.

"Who sent you?" I shouted into her ear.

"Piss on you, mage-bent." More bravado in her voice now as she was working her way out of my grip. In the struggle to hold her my knife slid from my hand, and rather than let her go so she could retrieve her weapons I rolled us again until we came up against the side of the track and I had a little leverage. Then I let go, and as she tried to rise I grabbed the chinguard of her helmet with one hand and the back with the other, the rough metal giving me a good grip, and I broke her neck using her own rising momentum.

Lying back. Breathing heavily. Her warm corpse draped over my legs. To a passing observer we would have looked like sated lovers lounging in the dappled wood.

"Just a bandit," I said to myself. "You should have walked away." Breath, coming heavily, out and in my lungs. I waited until my heart had stopped hammering, considered taking her head but the corpse would not be going anywhere, and the track was clearly little travelled or would not have been used for an attack. Had she been following me as an easy mark or had the priest set me up? She had seemed to know about me, but not about the price on my head. Had it really been a robbery? That was possible, but no, she had said she'd heard I was a bladesman. She knew something of me. Had Aydor sent her? Had she sneaked into the camp. Maybe she had been with Captain Thian's band and slipped away when they neared Rufra's camp? It seemed likely. I stood, then lifted her visor. I did not recognise her as one of those who had left Aydor's camp with me. I took my attacker's stabsword, putting it under my belt and retrieving my eating blade from the path. I returned to the stream I had crossed and washed my face and hands. I had scraped my face on a rock so cleaned the wound too. Then I made my way to the paddocks, hoping to find a guard I could send to retrieve the corpse. Rufra needed to know about this.

I expected people to comment on my muddy clothes and cut face as I passed through the camp, but no one did. Maybe fights were common. Nearer the paddocks I could hear the sound of a large crowd. Occasionally there was a shout and then I would hear another voice. As I approached I could make out words, It seemed Arnst was still speaking.

". . . and can there be new ways with old gods?"

A loud shout of "No!" came in return. The crowd was large, filling a hollow in the land and not all of them were shouting their support. Plenty were simply standing with their arms crossed, watching, waiting and assessing his words.

"Of course not! There cannot! The old ways must become as dead as the gods they represent. If we need gods at all, perhaps there are better ones, eh? Look at the souring of our land, look where your dull priests have led you!"

I could feel a buzz in the air, the same feeling of impending violence there was at a lizard or mount fight when the betting really started and the animals were brought out. It was then I noticed how many soldiers were stationed around the crowd, all armed and ready, crossbows loaded and held ostentatiously to make sure they were seen. I saw a group of men being marched away, at least one of whom had blood all over his clothes. The crowd was restive; there was a feeling of disquiet unusual at a religious gathering. Arnst clearly had a core of followers who believed what he said, far more of the crowd were uncomfortable with his exhortation to "tear down the old ways". Darvin had been right. I guessed maybe a quarter of the crowd were there to support Arnst; another half were there to hear his words and the remainder to cause trouble. I passed a man who had a club hidden beneath his tunic and another who held his eating knife as if ready to stab the the man in front of him in the back. I was not the only one who had spotted these potential troublemakers. Soldiers quietly moved in to separate them from the crowd. The knifeman went quietly, the one with the club tried to fight back and was swiftly clubbed to the ground by an efficient-looking women with the red feather of a sergeant on her wide helm.

"Come to enjoy the riot, Girton?" I turned to see Boros's ruined face. He sounded amused but it was hard to tell. "Or have you already had your own?" He pointed at my face.

"I am here to get Xus," I said. "Someone tried to jump me in the copse back there." I said the words calmly though my heart hammered at the thought of how close I had come to death. "You'll find her corpse by the path."

"I'll have someone attend to it. We drive the robbers from the camp, but they always come back." He looked more deeply into me. "Or was this aimed at you specifically?"

"I don't know." Why did I lie? Or had lying simply become second nature to me? "Maybe she was sent by Aydor and had been waiting for her moment."

"Why would he do that?" he said.

"Well . . ."

"If Aydor wanted rid of you he could have had you killed and dumped you in the marshes and none would ever have been the wiser."

"You defend him?"

He shrugged.

"I state the obvious."

"He needed me to –" I stopped before telling him about the spy – after all, I did not really know Boros "– to bring his message of surrender."

"He could have sent Thian. Rufra would have seen him."

I looked away, annoyed with Boros for poking holes in what I thought was clear.

"I should get Xus," I said. "I ride with Rufra today."

"Good. I will see you on the ride, Girton; now I must break up this crowd or Arnst will rant all day." Boros moved forward with a group of soldiers dressed identically in leather armour and tight-fitting metal coifs. They used shields and cudgels to muscle their way through the crowd and Boros lifted a lance with Rufra's black and red lizard flag on it and shouted for the sermon to be over. I thought the crowd may turn on them, but when Arnst saw Rufra's flag he acquiesced, quickly bringing his speech to an end and calling for all to embrace the inevitability of Xus.

I wondered if he would think the same if someone had just tried to kill him in a wood.

Before Arnst left the stage, he stared out into the crowd and there was something wistful on his face, as if he regretted having to let go of the power he had held only a moment before.

Boros's soldiers ensured those who had shouted loudest for Arnst were forced to take a different route away from the hollow to those who had simply come to watch. I let myself be carried along with the ragged crowd. The mood was merry enough: some were happily scandalised by what Arnst had been saying, some were appalled and revelling in their own piety, though there were others who walked alone, clearly giving Arnst's words deep thought.

I was one of them.

I did not think he was right – maybe our gods were dead, although Xus the unseen still lived, I was sure of that. But to put aside the dead gods was divisive and I was surprised Rufra let him spread his ideas, surprised he had given him a place on his council, and even more surprised he did not see that Arnst was a man who enjoyed power far more than he should.

I was brought out of my reverie when I walked into the chest of a man.

"You are the ambassador." It was a statement not a question and it came from the kind of man who you built your shieldwall around; he was huge. He wore skirts and a leather jerkin, and had the bearing, and scars, of a soldier. Thick black diagonal lines of face paint ran from his jawline and up over his eyes to meet in a point at his hairline, making his blue eyes all the more startling. Curling blond hair framed an oblong face covered in thickly caked white make-up peeling away from his forehead and cheeks, the skin underneath worn red and rough by wind and sun. I recognised him as one of the Meredari, the people who lived around the huge lakes in the southlands and made their living from fishing and raiding the lands around them. I had passed through the Meredari lands and seen a souring at the edge of a lake, it looked like a splash of paint, as if a god had tripped on their way to paint the sun. In the clear blue of the water there were tentacles of sickly yellow, like Meredari hair waving in the current. When I swept my hand through the yellow in the water I met no resistance and it did not dissipate or mingle with the water around it, like it was a dream of colour polluting the placid lake.

"I am the ambassador's assistant, not the ambassador," I said.

He looked at me as if I spoke in an unfamiliar language. "Arnst wishes to see you," he said.

"I am afraid I have other business."

"Arnst wishes to see you," he said again as if he had not understood my words. I wondered what a Meredari was doing in Maniyadoc. Maybe his tribe had thrown him out; they prized intelligence in their warriors.

"I am on the king's business."

"Arnst wishes to see you." I had the distinct feeling that he was prepared to pick me up and carry me if, as he clearly saw it, I continued to be unreasonable. I ached from my struggle in the woods and had no wish to pit myself against the mound of muscle before me. He took a step forward and he seemed to move very slowly, in the way of immensely strong men, but that did not mean he would be slow when he acted. Without thinking I fell into the position of readiness, legs slightly apart, one foot in front of the other, arms loose at my side. It was always the way: though I tried to reject what I had been moulded into, my body did not forget as easily.

"Danfoth!" The Meredari paused in the act of moving his gigantic body. It was like an avalanche suddenly had second thoughts about rolling down a hill. "I said extend the ambassador an invitation, not drag him to me." Arnst appeared from within the shadow cast by his servant. He was a large man too, only appearing small because he was with Danfoth. Up close he had a thin face, clear skin that almost glowed with health, while his beard and moustache were peppered with grey, as were his eyebrows which accentuated the greenest eyes I had ever seen. But there was something of the Festival hypnotist about him, something that made me wary.

"My apologies, Ambassador," said Arnst. "Danfoth can be a little more literal with my instructions than I intend, but he is loyal to a fault and such loyalty is rare." He smiled at me. Arnst had a strangely high-pitched voice when speaking normally, very different to the voice he had used for the crowd.

"As I was telling your friend, I am not the ambassador, merely her assistant."

"But, and forgive my forthrightness, I have heard you are dealing with her duties while she is unable to act, so surely this makes you the ambassador?" I did not like the implied flattery and thought it said a lot about the man, that he should believe I would like to be promoted over my master while she lay sick.

"No," I said.

"Ah, well –" he seemed flustered "– you are still an important man, to come all the way from the Lean Isles. They are not a place I know much of, and I would like to learn more. Maybe we could take a cup of perry together and you could tell me." Inwardly I cursed Nywulf. I had travelled to many places in the Tired Lands but the Lean Isles was not one of them. I wanted to know more about Arnst but I could not talk to him now for risk of tripping myself up due to lack of knowledge.

"I would enjoy talking to you, truly," I forced the words out in a pleasant suitably ambassadorial tone, "but for now I am on the king's business and cannot stop. Another time possibly?"

"Of course." He raised his throat to me in the way of the old Tired Lands salute. "Xus's blessing on you."

"In my experience the blessings of Xus are generally the last one ever receives."

He narrowed his eyes, reassessing me, and from behind him Danfoth skewered me with a hard stare.

"But," said Arnst, "in his dark palace there is no death, is that not the greatest blessing of all?" Before I could reply he turned away, saying, "Come, Danfoth," and he left me to carry on my way.

Chapter 11

I found Xus and rode him around Rufra's camp to get a better idea of the size of it, stopping off for food and being surprised to find that Rufra fed all of his camp for free. It was simple fare, pork and bread, but good. Then I returned to my tent for my weapons and armour. I warned a gaggle of children playing in the mud to stay away from Xus, and they eyed the huge mount with big solemn eyes. I hoped to the dead gods they listened to me or they would lose fingers.

There was no sign of Neliu outside the tent, and I heard no noise from inside. For a moment I wondered if the worst had happened and as I stepped into the gloom I experienced a moment of fear while my eyes adjusted to the darkness.

"Master? Healer? Where is the guard?"

"I sent her to get clean water," said Mastal, looking up from where he was bowed over my master. "She did not like being an errand girl, but she acquiesced in the end. I have a knife of my own and we are surely safe in the centre of Rufra's camp."

"You are a fool if you think we are safe here." My shoulder ached still from the attack in the woods.

"Come over here," said Mastal quietly.

I ignored him, picking up my harlequin armour and turning my back on the healer as I slid it over my head, feeling the cold of the metal slither down my tunic. I strapped the warhammer and stabsword to my waist before approaching him.

"What?"

He stared up from his seat, an odd smile on his face.

"Look, Girton." He gestured to my master. She did not move, only remained twisted up in her blankets. I could smell the sweat on them, and her. Then her eyes opened, not wide, only a crack, but they opened and I fell to my knees, grasping her hand.

"Master!"

"Shhh, shh," said Mastal and he put a hand on my shoulder. "She cannot speak, not yet, but we have turned a corner. I think we have the poison in retreat."

I wondered if she could hear or understand us, and leaned in close to her.

"I am sorry, Master," I whispered, "so sorry."

Mastal continued to speak, but his words existed only on the periphery of my mind as I searched my master's face for some sign of forgiveness, though I was unsure what I wanted her to forgive me for. A million things and nothing, a hundred thousand moments of childish anger in the face of her patience that I had never apologised for, things she would not expect apologies for and other things which she would. I wanted her to live, and the smallest, most infinitesimal squeeze of my hand that she gave me felt like a gift.

"She needs rest, Girton."

"Of course," I said, letting go of her hand and standing. I still mistrusted the man but at least he seemed to be helping my master to get well. "Thank you, Mastal."

"Your face is cut and you have bruises coming, I have some unguent that—"

"It is nothing, Mastal – a fall, that is all." I do not think he believed me. "And I cannot stop as I must ride out with Rufra." Outside the tent, I found Xus standing quietly and with great forbearance as a group of giggling children clambered all over his noble frame. As soon as they saw me the children jumped off the mount and ran, screaming and laughing into the streets of tents. I stood by the mount and fed him a scrap of pork I had saved.

"Aren't you full of surprises?" He let out a low whistle as I pulled myself up into the saddle.

I met Rufra outside his tent. He waved at me from the back of his white mount, Balance. Unlike Xus she was fully kitted out for war, engraved leather panels protecting the animal's neck and flanks, shining spurs covering the claws on her feet and her antlers lengthened with razor-sharp gildings. Rufra sat on her back in plain armour and a red and black loyalty pennant, cut in such a way that when it flapped in the wind it made the flying lizard on it appear to run, hung limp above his head in the still air. Balance hissed at Xus and in turn he tried to bite her, making Rufra laugh.

"You would think they had just met, rather than having had four offspring together."

"Boros rides one. I saw him."

"Yes, Galadan. The son is the image of his father." Rufra's voice faded away and he looked uncomfortable. Maybe he mistrusted Boros – not that he would say so, even to me, not unless I pushed it, and our friendship was too newly rejoined for me to probe. It felt like the pink skin under a healing wound and I worried it may rip if treated too roughly.

"Life is a little different for you now, Rufra," I said, looking round at all the tents.

"Aye." He sounded a little sad. "I almost miss being chased round Maniyadoc by Tomas and his cronies. Life was simpler then."

"If no less dangerous."

"I do not think I was aware of the danger, not truly. Now . . ." His voice tailed off and he stared into the distance, I imagined he looked to where Tomas's army waited.

"What are these mount archers I keep hearing about?"

"Oh." He brightened. "They are an idea Varn brought

with him from his people – lightly armoured Riders with powerful bows. They are hit-and-run troops, mostly, though they double as cavalry if needed. I have one hundred of them under Boros, and Tomas's men fear them like they are Black Ungar himself. He has no answer to them."

"Is that why he does not give battle?"

"No, not really. He has the advantage in numbers."

"But he has not brought you to the blade yet?"

"He knows my men are better than his. It is the Nonmen I worry about."

"Why?"

"Many of my troops think they are in league with hedgings and sorcerers. They believe them to be magical beings who can curse their spirits, leave them locked and starving in the sourlands. I am not sure of their numbers, but Nywulf reckons them enough to tip the tide, especially with the fear they bring."

"Does Tomas know the Nonmen scare your troops?"

"Of course, there are many spies in each camp. Tomas is a good commander but at heart a timid one." Rufra gave me a wicked grin. "Even with the Nonmen, I will still beat him, you know."

"I do," I said, and I did not doubt it.

"I have tried to catch the Nonmen in the field but they rarely gather in large numbers." I could see the frustration, his face took on an ugly cast. "I just want the battle to come, Girton; it is the waiting that is hard. I have even challenged Tomas to a battle of kings in the old way: he and I fight and the winner becomes king."

"And?"

"He has not replied of course. I told you, he is timid and thinks he can crush me with numbers when the time comes. For now he hides and hopes sickness will strike my camp before the year is up and he must fight me in person or forfeit the crown."

"Or he waits for his spy to strike you down," I said.

"My council are loyal, Girton. I do not doubt it, and, besides, Tomas will want to kill me on the battlefield so he can claim he beat me fairly. I intend to use the time he gives me to draw out the Nonmen somehow, but I do not yet know how. If I can break them, the army I take against Tomas will know no fear and I will destroy him." He shifted in his saddle and stared up into the sun. Despite the steadiness of his voice I sensed he was worried. "How many troops does Aydor bring? You were in his camp, you must have seen."

"Most of the time I had a bag over my head, but I did a quick count on the way out. He has maybe two hundred, mostly infantry." I stared at the sky, dark clouds scudding through blue, hurrying to find the Birthstorm. "You should not trust him."

"I have no choice, Girton. I need his men." Rufra pointed into the distance. "Look, there is Cearis with our escort." He glanced across, grinned and shouted, "Race me, Girton!" He put Balance to the spur, swiftly followed by me on Xus.

"You cheated," I shouted into the wind as Xus stretched to catch up. "You cheated!"

"Kings cannot cheat." Rufra laughed and I laughed too. It seemed in the years I had been away the serious side of him had almost entirely taken over as he planned and schemed against his enemies. I wanted him to laugh.

I wanted him to be safe.

A troop of about a hundred foot soldiers waited for us to ride out. They were all armoured like the men I had seen watching Arnst's sermon by the paddocks. With them were twenty mount archers and ten heavy cavalry, headed by Cearis. All the mounts sported brightly coloured loyalty flags, and at the head of the troops more flags flew. I noticed some of Rufra's council also waited: Nywulf on a shaggy-looking white mount, Cearis riding a spectacular black mount that gleamed in the sunlight and seemed entirely aware of what a fine animal it was. She also carried Rufra's bonemount, topped by a flying lizard flag, its wings spread and teeth bared. By her was Karrick Thessan the Landsman, in his green armour on a mount of patched brown and deep red, under the white-tree-on-green flag of the Landsmen. By him and looking uncomfortable on the back of a mount of red, traditionally the most common and least popular colour among the blessed, sat Gabran the Smith.

"You are late," said Nywulf.

"Kings are never late, Nywulf." Rufra smiled, and those around him, even the Landsman, did the same.

"Then you have made us all early, my king. Apologies for our rudeness," said Nywulf, and some, including Rufra, laughed.

"We should set off then. Let us not tarry here as we have a long way to go."

I had intended to ride with Rufra, but it was not so simple. Cearis rode on one side – as head of his heavy cavalry and carrier of the bonemount she was required to be with her king – while on the other rode Nywulf; as Heartblade his place was also next to the king. So I let Xus drop back, which he did with much ill will, growling and hissing at the mounts around him until I found a place in the procession next to Crast, Nywulf's trainee.

"Good day, Girton," he said, looking away to wave at those lining the track.

"And to you, Crast. Does Rufra always ride out on patrol with such numbers?"

"No." He smiled, rocking gently with the motion of his mount. "There is to be a prisoner exchange. I am to guard the prisoners, though I doubt they will run. Akirin might try, as he rides only to his death, but he is bound to his mount and will not get far with his wounds anyway." He used his thumb to point over his shoulder. It was only then I realised that what I had thought was heavy cavalry was nothing of the sort, five of them were not armed, and one, who must be Akirin, was tied onto his mount, his head bowed and a dirty bandage around his leg. Around them rode five armed cavalrymen, though they seemed relaxed about their charges.

"What have they done?"

"The four who are unbound took arms against Rufra and are to be returned to Tomas in exchange for ransom."

"Rufra gives Tomas his soldiers back?"

"For a price, and they must give their word never to fight Rufra or his soldiers again."

"And Rufra believes them?"

"Yes."

"He should put traitors to death," I said. "Sometimes I wonder if Rufra's mind is a little mage-bent." I smiled at Crast, but he gave me a strange look, as if he did not know how he should react and I half expected him to draw his blade, then he laughed. "I forgot you were friends with him before he was king, but you should be careful how you talk of Rufra around others, Girton. His people are loyal, fiercely loyal."

"You included, it seems." I nodded to his hand, which was clutched around the hilt of his blade.

Crast let go of the sword with a shrug. The resemblance between him and Neliu was remarkable for two who said they were not related, but that was common in the Tired Lands, a place of small and insular communities.

"Without King Rufra, Nell and I would be dead, food for the wild herds at best, at worst toys for the Nonmen –" he shuddered "– and I would wish that on no one."

"Do they keep their word, those that Rufra frees?" I asked, glancing at the men behind me, who looked both miserable and thoughtful.

"Some do; some decide to stay with Rufra; others go straight back to Tomas and pick up their swords."

"What happens to them if they are taken again?"

"They die, Girton, that is what happens to them." He glanced back at Akirin. "They die."

"But their death is given purpose." I turned, having to guard my expression as I found myself face to face with the speaker: Karrick the Landsman. I was glad he spoke to me while we rode, part of the way Landsmen tracked down sorcerers was by scent. Those who were unschooled could not mask it – honey and pepper, sweet-sharp and alluring – though once I had found it cloying and sickly. My master had taught me not to wash too often, to use too much animal fat to grease my armour so its rancid stink overwhelmed any other scent, and lastly exercises to hold the magic within. I saw the scent as an extension of magic, a slow, misty emanation of darkness from the roiling sea within me. If I had to talk to a Landsman there was no better place than in among a group of armed Riders, where the smell of mounts and armour was almost overwhelming.

"I thought the land would not accept a traitor's blood?" I sneered the words at him; I could not help it.

"Neander, the high priest, has decreed it is no longer so."

"Really?" I said. "I did not know the priest was a lover of irony." The Landsman looked puzzled. "Never mind. I am only surprised the Landsmen trust Neander. I thought you would have had him in a blood gibbet."

Karrick laughed. "Ah, you talk of the business at Maniyadoc? No, it became quite plain he had been used as a scapegoat by the queen." He had been no such thing but I kept my face straight. "He was entirely exonerated and now he heads the priests of the Long Tides."

"And gives the Landsmen more bodies for your engines of pain. That must please you."

Karrick looked surprised at my words and my barely suppressed snarl. He was a handsome man, riding with a stiff upright posture that showed off the way his armour hung from his muscular frame. His face was tanned almost as dark as my master's, and he had a full, dark beard, which I suspect he grew to try and hide the fact he had several teeth missing.

"You mean the blood gibbets?" I did not answer. "I have no love for them myself and can understand how they may appear barbaric to an outsider. A swift death should be our gift – we are servants of the dead gods after all and it is in our remit to be merciful – but with the war we cannot march the desolate into the sourlands as we should, and our elders tell us the blood gibbet is also a warning . . ."

"And the leash?" He looked surprised, then puzzled, and I knew I had said too much. The Landsman's Leash was one of their secrets, a system of scars and special knives used to smother a sorcerer's power. He studied me as if I were a puzzle to be unravelled and I cursed myself for letting my temper speak instead of my wit.

"It seems you are well informed for one from as far away as the Lean Isles."

"I fought with your men on the far borders. I have seen what passes for justice among you."

"The far borders are wild. We seek only to stop sorcerers rising there, their beliefs are often close to hedging worship."

"That is what the man I fought for said as well. He was never too choosy about who he killed."

"Girton Club-Foot, wait until we have stopped at Grandon's Souring and seen the work of sorcerers, then see how quick you are to judge me and mine." He spurred his mount on, for which I was glad.

"Do you always make friends so easily?" asked Crast, raising an eyebrow. I ignored him. I was no longer in the mood for levity and although the sun shone in a sky as clear and blue as deep ice, I felt as if the Birthstorm hovered over me as I rode.

We travelled for most of the day, and as the heat and exhaustion took its toll all conversation died away. We left the infantry behind us; even going at their easiest the mounts could not walk as slowly as troops laden with weapons and packs. Nywulf dropped his mount back to guard the prisoners and Crast moved up to ride by Rufra just as my nostrils started to twitch, picking up the rank smell of a souring on the air.

"I still think you should have taken the motley, Girton," whispered Nywulf, "but ambassador is not a bad cover for you, eh?"

"I know nothing about the Lean Isles," I hissed.

"Neither does anyone else."

I glanced up the column, to the gently swaying back of Karrick.

"Why is he here? Surely Karrick reports everything to the Landsmen at Ceadoc? And from there it can be carried to Tomas."

"Karrick is not so bad. In a lot of things he supports Rufra, often in ways that surprise me. And he is not allowed into the war councils, something he accepts with good grace though he could have made a fuss and pushed his way in if he desired."

"You are trying to tell me he is a good man?"

"Maybe, but it may be the balancing power of Cearis that causes him to be so reasonable."

"Rufra's aunt has power? Last I heard she fled her home and had to hide at Festival until Rufra took her in."

"Cearis speaks for Festival on the council, though she has not the power to bring it back to Maniyadoc while war rages."

Festival was the huge travelling trade caravan that traversed the Tired Lands in an endless circle, bringing trade and merriment wherever it went. It was also the Tired Lands' largest city and a power in its own right.

"Festival does not come to Maniyadoc any more?"

"No, it has not since the war started."

"It has its own soldiers. I cannot imagine anyone would be foolish enough to attack it."

"They wouldn't, but we have nothing to trade at the moment so it has no reason to come here until either Rufra or Tomas win."

"They have not picked a side then?"

"Well, Festival have not picked Rufra in the same way the Landsmen have not picked Tomas. They do nothing overt to prop him up, nothing that would offend the other side too much should they win, but there is support in small ways."

"I spoke to Arnst as well."

"Arnst," said Nywulf with a sigh. "Rufra will never admit it, but he made a mistake there."

"I did not like him, and I did not like the atmosphere at his sermon either."

"Aye, Rufra lost his temper and acted in haste. He took a small man and gave him power, and he has used that power. If ever I saw a man who has given his spirit to the hedge-hungers it is Arnst."

"What does he believe?" I said. "I missed the beginning of his sermon. I know he says the gods are dead and gone apart from Xus, but I did not hear much else."

"He changes his beliefs daily, Girton. He was a priest once, but a bad one from what I gather. He likes women, and the vows did not suit him. I think has been weak all his life, flitting from one thing to another, failing and failing again because he does not truly apply himself."

"But he is a success now."

"No, Rufra is a success. Arnst only had a few followers when he arrived, but more came – more weak men and women attracted by the small amount of power Arnst seemed to have gained by being part of the Triangle Council. That attracted more followers, and now he has a power base of his own and it makes me uncomfortable."

"And Rufra ?"

"It makes him uncomfortable too, though he will not admit

it. He is as stubborn as he ever was." Nywulf spoke with a mixture of irritation and fierce pride in his protégé.

"Arnst sounds a little like Neander," I said, thoughts of the traitorous priest from Castle Maniyadoc making the scars on my flesh shiver.

"I suspect they would have much in common and as such hate each other with a passion. Maybe we should introduce them to each other –" he bared his teeth "– leave them in a locked room with a couple of knives. To be honest I am surprised Arnst is not with us today. He has a strange curiosity about the sourlands, though he is nervous around the Landsmen so that may be why he stays away."

"You think he is a sorcerer?" I said.

"No." Nywulf shook his head. "If I thought that he would be dead already. I think he is curious about things that no good can come from. It will look bad for Rufra if one of his council even dabbles at the edges of magic." I stared down at the dirt of the path as Nywulf spoke. "In truth, Girton, life would be far easier if someone were to scratch the name of that turbulent priest on a wall for an assassin to read."

"If that is a hint, Nywulf, I am no longer in that line of work." I tapped the warhammer at my side.

"I am surprised you can even lift that thing," he said, "but it was not a hint, not really. If Arnst were to die, his followers would be trouble for Rufra. No, we have soured that land now and must sow our wheat around it." He stopped speaking, pursing his lips. I glanced over my shoulder to see Karrick was behind us. I wondered how much of our conversation he had heard.

"Grandon's Souring is over the next rise," said Karrick, and he turned to the prisoner Akirin. "You should prepare yourself," he said gently, but the man paid him no mind, only continuing to stare at his saddle.

I had been ignoring the souring, ignoring the stink and the glowering yellow sky to the east. Yet something in the sourings spoke to the magic inside me whether I wanted to listen or not, and it was not a comfortable conversation. The sourings were places where life had been stolen from the land to feed a sorcerer's great working. It felt like eating food that was too rich for your body: you longed for it but it made you sick to the stomach. I could feel the heady remnants of what had been done here – *a thousand screaming voices, a woman begging to be freed, the ache of turning away* – but the magic in me was repelled by the lack of life. It died when I travelled through the sourlands, and something of me died with it. As we crested a gentle rise I saw the souring for the first time and Xus let out a low growl. It was not big as sourings went. It did not vanish into the horizon like the western souring near Maniyadoc; instead it spread across the land like a lake of sulphur, stinking of death, its banks punctuated by the black wooden and metal skeletons of empty blood gibbets. The grass ran right up to it. There was no gradation of land as you would see with sand dunes on a shore; here the grass simply stopped in clearly demarcated lines, on one side life and on the other death. A flock of Xus's black birds lifted from the blood gibbets, harsh voices calling out in worship of their master as they became rags against the blue. On the edge of my vision I thought I caught the flicker of a black robe shivering in the light breeze, but when I turned I saw only a hedgescare dressed in sacking, its head broken off and replaced with a crude face cut into the dried skin of a vegetable.

Gabran the Smith trotted back past us, looking uncomfortable and miserable in the saddle of his mount.

"Where do you go, Gabran?" asked Nywulf.

"Back to my troops," he said. "Seeing this will do nothing for their morale."

"They do not approve of the king's justice?" I asked.

Gabran shook his head. "They love the king's justice, would like to see more of it if anything. But the souring?

No one wishes to see that – it makes me sick to be this near." I understood what he meant. I felt the same nausea everyone else was feeling but I thought the souring also had its own austere beauty. It was like bones lying in grass: it made the life around it somehow more vibrant and real. "Rufra has said I may take the troops directly to the camp. With any luck we will all arrive together." He glanced at me. "Before I go I'd like a word with the ambassador, if that's all right?"

Nywulf shrugged. "Be my guest."

"Come with me, Ambassador," he said, and there was something in his voice I couldn't place as he led me aside. Once we were away from the body of the patrol he leaned towards me. "No need to lie to me," he said, "and if you're lying to Nywulf I'd come clean or he'll like as not gut you like a fish." I started to speak but he cut me off. "Listen, don't flap your mouth. If you're the ambassador for the Lean Isles my balls are a boat."

"I don't know what you—"

"Enough," he sneered. "I saw you at Maniyadoc all those years ago, I know what you are." My hand was at the warhammer though he made no move to stop me. "If I wanted you dead, assassin, I'd not do it here before Rufra or warn you I was going to do it." My hand tightened around the hilt of the hammer, knuckles whitening.

"What do you want, Gabran?"

"Same thing as the king, now he must have got his hard head around it. I want traitors in a gibbet. I've lost hundreds of my boys to Tomas, and whatever yellower's responsible needs to pay. I don't like to talk and I don't like to sneak around so I'll save you some time."

"You will?"

He nodded then spat on the ground.

"Aye, it's not me for a start."

"You would hardly admit it if it were."

"Not unless I was a stupid yellower, which I'm not. But I'm from the living classes – you can probably hear that though." He pointed at his mouth. "Tomas'll see me dead before he sees me in command of so much as a latrine. There's nothing in it for me to spy for him."

"So it seems."

"And Varn and Bediri, they weren't here when Rufra lost at Goldenson Copse. Well, they made bows for Rufra, and Bediri caused trouble constantly, but they were nowhere near command."

"Maybe Tomas and Neander simply replaced one spy with another?"

He looked at me as our mounts walked slowly on.

"I thought you were meant to be clever," he said and spat again. "Varn and Bediri replaced men and women who fell at Goldenson, as did Arnst." He leaned in, speaking quickly: "And I wish I could say the spy was him. He's a right yellower and he offends the dead gods."

I did not ask him how dead gods could be offended; instead I bit on my knuckles in thought then said,

"It would be foolish for Tomas to kill his own spies in battle. And I can see no way he would know who would replace them, but that does not mean it could not be done." Gabran nodded. He was little and aggressive and acted like he truly detested having to speak to me. "Did you know Varn has a promise to avenge his people cut into his arm?" I said. "It is in an old language called Tak."

"He hardly keeps his scars secret, does he?" said Gabran. A shiver ran through the scars on my body as if they needed to remind me they were there. "Varn is from a tribe of nomads who strayed onto land held by the blessed of Maniyadoc and died for it. Tomas is everything Varn hates about Maniyadoc; Rufra is everything Tomas is not. Rufra is Varn's revenge. It ain't Varn – he's all right, for a foreign yellower."

"What about the Landsman?"

"Oh, now he is a hedge-homed yellower," he said, "but they all are, and if I'm made to tell the truth he's slightly less of a hedge-homed yellower than the other Landsmen, Fureth, his second, especially."

"But Karrick is still a hedge-homed yellower?"

"Aye."

What about the blessed, Lort ap Garron?" If Gabran was in the mood to speak, albeit angrily, I thought it best to find out how much he would say.

"One of the first to throw in with Rufra. Tomas burned most of his lands then put his entire family on a fool's throne."

"He burned them alive?"

"Women, children, the old – one by one in full view of his court to show what happened to traitors."

"Dead gods." I stared at the ground by Xus's feet.

"Lort is no spy. He knows Tomas is a sorcerer-born yellower."

"So that leaves who? Boros and Cearis?"

"They're not spies either."

"So no one is the spy?" I sat up in Xus's saddle, rolling my head to relieve some of the tension in my neck. "Well, thank you for your help, Gabran."

He narrowed his eyes, then shrugged.

"I'm glad it's your job to find the spy, not mine," he said. Then he leaned in close again. "The woman who attacked you? She was dressed as one of mine but she weren't as I know 'em all. We get bandits in camp, but it might be worth you remembering others may recognise you, eh? And Queen Adran, for all her faults, wasn't hated by everyone. Watch yourself, assassin," he said and kicked his mount on, leaving me more confused than ever.

I returned to Nywulf. We watched Gabran cantering off uncomfortably on his mount. He didn't look back.

"What was that about?"

"He wanted to assist me in catching the spy on the council by telling me it could be no one in the council."

"He is an odd one," said Nywulf.

"Why?"

"Hard to put your finger on it, in truth. He has been a soldier, I think, but he does not talk of it. He came through with a load of refugees and decided to stay. He is a skilled smith so we were glad to have him, but he gradually drifted back to the troops – he has a real skill with them."

"He could be Aydor's man then."

"I doubt it. He bears a scar on his throat where he once took a blade meant for Rufra, so his loyalty is not in question. I just wish we knew a little more about him." Nywulf stared after Gabran and then spurred on his mount to where the rest of the Riders waited. Akirin, the man who had broken his vow not to fight Rufra, knelt at the edge of the souring staring at the dead ground. Karrick stood behind him, the bent knife that was the mark of a Landsman held loosely in his hand. Everyone dismounted apart from Rufra, who remained on his mount looking down at Akirin. The man made no attempt to look up at his king.

"Akirin ap Valyan," said Rufra solemnly, "you were returned to the pretender Tomas after giving your word never to raise your blade against either my troops or my person. You did not keep that promise and as such have forfeited your life." Rufra sounded unaccountably sad, even though he was only putting a traitor to death. "Karrick has the Landsmen's book of names if you wish to sign it for whichever god you choose."

Akirin shook his head.

"The dead gods know my name." I had to strain to hear him.

Rufra gave Karrick a nod and the Landsman moved quickly, his knife coming round before being brought swiftly back, cutting Akirin's throat in one practised motion. Karrick pulled back the man's head, and as the body jerked against his knees he directed the spray of blood onto the dead yellow land of the souring. Akirin's body began to slump in his hands, and I heard his final breaths bubbling in his windpipe as his lungs continued trying to breathe, unaware his life was past saving. When he finally left for Xus's black palace he voided himself, though the stink of the sourlands covered the stink of his bowels.

New grass was already growing at the bloody edge of the sourland, worming its way through the dead yellow earth where death brought life from death. In the scars on my body I felt each blade spring from the land as if it emerged from my skin, as if the roots not only reached into the earth but reached into my flesh, reconnecting the black sea of magic to the body it flowed within. I saw a land drowned in blood, a sea of red that swept the sourings off the land like dead leaves being blown from an old tree. I saw an arrow in that final second when it hung in the air like a held breath, seemingly neither falling nor rising in the moment before it took a life. I closed my eyes. I saw a blood gibbet door swing shut, and dug my nails into my palms to rid myself of visions and the nausea they brought.

When I looked up, Rufra was riding slowly away, his head bowed as if in shame.

Chapter 12

We made camp that night at the edge of the marshes where Gabran's infantry had set up tents for us. Rufra stayed in his tent and I did not see him, nor did I stay up to talk to others around the fire; the souring seemed to have sapped the energy from me.

I was woken the next morning by a cheery soldier taking my tent down. "Good morning, Blessed," he said happily as I stared blearily up at him. "You should hurry if you want breakfast; the camp is almost ready to move."

I staggered up, made my way to the mounts and stowed my blankets in Xus's saddlebags. An early-morning mist had rolled in off the marshlands, all was silence beyond the camp except for the "'Hut" and "'Ayt" of the sentries calling out their positions and the jingling of tack as restless mounts snapped at one another. Once my blankets were safely stowed I made my way back to where a soldier was standing beside a pot of porridge. He scraped the bottom of the pot and handed me a bowl of hot stodge, flecked through with black from the pot.

"More burn than food in this," said a nasal voice by me, and I turned to see Gabran the Smith staring into his wooden bowl. "Maybe it'll give it some taste." He put a spoonful of porridge in his mouth and grimaced. "Dead gods, Balthin, what do you put in this – sandals?"

The cook grinned at him. "Only the best shoe leather for you, sir."

Gabran shook his head and forced down some more.

"Good morning, Gabran," I said.

He looked up, appraising me. Running his gaze up and down me. He had a lazy eye, and I don't think the man could have looked more suspicious if he had tried. "Aye," he said eventually.

"I've been thinking about what you told me," I said.

"Good for you," he said, and spooned in another mouthful of porridge. He was just about to turn away when his gaze alighted on my stabsword and he stopped with his spoon halfway to his mouth and let the porridge drop back into the bowl. "That a Conwy, like Rufra's longsword?"

"It is the twin to Rufra's." He could not take his eyes from the blade, so I drew it, passing it over to him.

"You the one who gave him Hope then," he said.

"Sorry?"

"It's what he calls it, Hope."

"Well, he has never been subtle."

"It's a great blade, good enough not to need a name. Its edge speaks for it." He held my stabsword, letting light play up and down the blade and there was a hunger in his eyes. "It was a very fine gift to give." He pointed the stabsword at me and I felt as if he may lunge at me rather than return it.

"He is my friend," I said. Gabran let time pass, air shifting in and out of his lungs, and then he flipped the stabsword, catching it by its blade and offering me the hilt.

"Then you are a very fine friend," he said.

"Nywulf said you fought before you joined Rufra." He nodded. "And you recognised me from Maniyadoc . . ." I let it hang.

"Men make mistakes." It was my turn to nod. "Rufra is a good master."

"Were you infantry for Aydor?"

"None of your business what I was," he said, looking away into the mist. It was a small thing, only a glance away, but

I was sure he lied. Whether it was a big lie or a small one I could not know, but he hid something.

"Do you think it is a good idea for Rufra to bring Aydor into his camp?"

He turned back to me. His thin face was expressionless, but it was like looking at a lake: the surface was calm but underneath something shifted, currents moved, but if they were the sort that may drag us down I could not tell.

"The bear is beaten," he said. "I just hope he knows it." Then he turned away, staring into the mist. He had called Aydor "the bear". Aydor had told me his men had nicknamed him "the Fat Bear". It seemed odd that he used a more courteous form. Gabran tipped his bowl upside down, letting the porridge fall on the ground. "Rufra should have sent me back with Karrick."

"The Landsman is gone?"

"Aye, went last night after giving Akirin the cut. We go to drop off the prisoners and then to meet Aydor and his men."

"We do? Rufra said nothing to me."

"Or anyone else. You would think he worries about spies." He raised an eyebrow.

"Still, it is unlikely Aydor will recognise you, one infantryman among many."

"Unlikely, aye," he said and walked away, tossing his bowl to the cook as he passed and saying, "Tasted like piss." As he walked off I thought it strange that he had not corrected me when I said he had fought for Aydor.

"Is he always like that?" I asked the cook.

"No, you caught him on a good day."

I went back and mounted Xus. It annoyed me that Rufra had not told me we were going to meet Aydor, though there had not been any real opportunity. He had been obliged to ride at the front, while I had been in the middle or rear ranks, and at night I had been so tired I had fallen asleep almost straight away. Still, it bothered me. I had come back to my friend, but my friend was a king and being king left little time for friendship. I heard the voice of Heamus, who had also been my friend, in a way, and had been slain by Neander's treachery: *"I don't think anyone is ever truly friends with a king."*

I rode that morning in silence and must have worn an expression that made it clear I was in no mood for conversation; no one approached me as the world rolled by.

The rising sun burned away the marsh mist to reveal a land slowly healing itself of the scars humanity had inflicted on it. Fields that would once have been full of grain were now speckled with the happy yellows, reds and blues of wildflowers. Tiny flying lizards buzzed around us, curious about these strange moving plants. Xus snapped at them, making a meal of more than one, and I ceased chiding him for his bad temper after one of the lizards bit me, leaving a welt that first hurt and then itched abominably. Among the fields and odd stands of trees I saw the burned remains of buildings again, and when we began to skirt the marshes at the edge of the river delta I stopped Xus to study the landscape. The river marshes were a cold and alien place. Greasy-looking water glinted from channels of unknown depth bounded by stinking, grasping mud. The view further into the marsh was obscured by walls of the tall green plants we called hauntgrass. As it died, holes appeared in it and caught the wind, letting out a low, deep "hooom" that reverberated through your bones and made the hairs on your skin stand on end. Somewhere out there were people – the marshes were an excellent place to hide. Far away a lone spire of smoke rose into the air from a lonely stilt-hut or island farm. Occasionally, as the wind blew and the hauntgrass called, I caught more signs of people: ragged hedgescares and strings of straw hobbys, a rotted boat, a wooden causeway and what I thought might be a corpse half sunk in the water – though if it was it was an old one as the black birds of Xus which wheeled above us paid it no mind.

"Damn birds," said an infantryman as he marched past.

"They are only birds," I said, turning Xus and walking him by the man. I had always derived an odd sense of comfort from the sight of Xus's birds.

"Aye, only birds, but when the birds fly, the hogs come."

"The hogs?"

The trooper spat at the ground.

"The birds have learned that soldiers bring death and they follow us hoping for food. The hogs have learned to watch the birds. They'll be here soon, mark my words." He spat again. "Bad luck," he said, looking up at me. I spurred Xus on a little, catching up with the main band of Riders.

Not long later the cry went up: "Hogs! Hogs to the south!" and Rufra brought the column to a halt.

"Gabran," he shouted. "Over that rise are the remains of Calumn's Spire. It's still got three walls standing. Set the men up there and we'll go on with the prisoners. The hogs will probably follow us, but with any luck then choose to follow Tomas's force, if it's bigger than ours."

"Are pigs really such a worry? We have a small army," I said to Cearis.

"Some of the grand boars are territorial and very aggressive. They don't generally bother cavalry, but if they have a really big herd they'll drive it against small groups, and sometimes, if they're hungry enough, they'll snap at the edges of a large column, running in and out of the stragglers hoping to bring someone down. They'll bring down a lone Rider too if they can catch them, but they can't run fast for long." She looked flushed, ready for action. "It is good to see you again, Girton Club-Foot. Rufra seems lighter of spirit already."

"He does?"

"Aye, we should talk later." She held Rufra's bonemount

higher and spurred her mount to catch up with the king, streamers of red and black material flying around the mount skull.

The infantry peeled off to our left, tramping their own road into the yearsbirth grasses, while we followed the overgrown remains of a cart track towards a copse of trees in the distance. After a quarter of an hour I saw the first of the pigs as a ripple in the grasses, then they crossed the track behind us, led by a huge boar with curling tusks. I stopped Xus, watching for over fifty counts of my-master, and still the herd kept coming.

"Canter," came the order from the front, and we speeded up. Minutes later there was another cry – "Riders!" – and I saw three mounts leave the edge of the copse and felt the tension in our group of twenty ratchet up a little. Violence was in the air, carried aloft by the squealing and grunting of the following herd of pigs. "Lances," was the next shout, and around me Riders spread out into a line and dropped their lances, keeping the four prisoners and myself behind them.

"Who approaches?" I said, joining the end of the line next to a cavalrywoman.

She squinted into the distance. "I think it is the halfmount, but you can never be sure. Tomas is a right yellower, happy with treachery and false flags."

"Who is the halfmount?"

"Boros," she said, and I remembered his flag, yellow with a draymount's head on it, one side bare skull, the other fleshed and with a draymount's huge curling horn.

"It is the halfmount," Nywulf shouted, and lances were raised once more, though we stayed in battle order to receive him.

"Hoy, King Rufra!" shouted Boros as he approached.

"Ayt, Boros ap Loflaar!" shouted Rufra. "Are we good to approach with the prisoners?"

"Aye," he shouted back, reining in his mount and letting us ride to him. "Tomas is there with Neander and Tal ap Meyrin behind the copse with ten Riders and fifty infantry. We've scouted the area and there is no one else near." Boros and his Riders fell into formation – Boros and one of his mount archers by me, his other at the far end of the line.

I heard Rufra shout, "It is time to leave those pigs behind. Ha! Bal, ha!" and he let us loose, our powerful animals growling, hooting and hissing with fierce joy as they were given their heads.

"Column!" came the shout from the front. Mounts were brought under control and fell back into two ordered lines, all except Xus. I had never had to manoeuvre him with other Riders and had to fight him. He was clearly annoyed at being forced into the centre of the herd and tried to gore any mount that came too close. Eventually I got him under control and we fell in by Boros, who had been watching me fight my mount. Because of his ruined face I could not tell whether he was amused or scornful until he spoke, his voice full of humour.

"You will have to train with us, Girton. Cearis will only forgive you such shoddy riding once."

"Why are we slowing?"

"Prisoner exchange. Rufra only galloped to leave the pigs behind. By the time we have exchanged they will have caught up, but the herds generally follow the larger group so they should be Tomas's problem then."

Around the copse waited Tomas and his men. Unlike Rufra's Riders, who had a sort of merry and colourful individuality, all of Tomas's Riders looked the same: dull armour, iron mount gildings. Even their bonemount was dull, a four-pointed skull decked out in rusty browns. Only Tomas stuck out, his mount a magnificent white and brown beast with nine-point antlers gilded in gold carved to look like ears of corn. The same motifs were chased into the hard joints at the shoulders and elbows of his armour, and the small enamel plates of his chest piece were white and gold, again made to resemble corn. The chains over his kilt and his greaves were golden; his wide helm was steel polished bright enough to look like silver, and a golden circlet of corn encircled it. He wore no visor, and when he deigned to turn his haughty, handsome face towards us, he looked every bit a king – especially compared to Rufra, who was wearing his most comfortable armour for riding and was significantly less impressive than at least half of his Riders. If you had not known who Rufra was, you would have thought him a down-at-heel Rider who had got a bit above his station.

We halted ten mounts' lengths from Tomas's forces and formed into a line facing them.

"Girton, Nywulf, Cearis, ride with me," said Rufra.

He walked Balance forward and we followed.

"Have you men for me, Tomas ap Glyndier?" said Rufra, his words as dull as the armour Tomas's men wore; they were well practised and tired.

From behind Tomas came a figure dressed in the vestments of a high priest, a nondescript grey robe pinned with rags of hundreds of different colours. From the blank white mask came a voice not even the priest's monotone could disguise. I knew it and hated the man behind the mask, Neander, who had led my first love to her death. My hand tightened around Xus's reins, and Rufra put out a hand, briefly touching me, letting me know he understood my anger and my hatred. But at the same time his touch was an order, a command that I should not move or react even though nothing would have given me greater pleasure than to put my stabsword through Neander's gut.

"As you well know, King Tomas ap Glyndier is a man of strength and does not suffer traitors to live, Rufra," he said. I found myself bristling on behalf of my friend at Neander's insolence – to not even give Rufra a courtesy title – Rufra seemed unconcerned.

"Then do you have names for me, High Priest, so that I may tell those left behind that their loved ones will not return?"

Neander recited a list of names, not many, but I could almost feel Rufra wilt with each monotone pronouncement. I would gladly have cut Neander's throat for him if he asked, and done it for myself if the opportunity presented itself. "I have men for Tomas, if you have their ransom?"

Tomas nodded, but it was Neander who spoke. "Pay him, Caren ap Galdrar." He waved a hand at a man who came forward with two small bags of coin and gave them to Cearis.

"King ap Glyndier has a gift for you, pretender," said Neander, and I found myself looking over my shoulder, expecting a trap to be sprung, but instead the same man who had paid the ransom took a package from his saddlebags. It was a weighty parcel bound in leather, and he had to use both hands to throw the package to Rufra, who caught it, held it for a moment and then almost dropped it. Now it was nearer I could see that what I had taken for leather was nothing of the sort, it was the skin of a man wrapped into a parcel. The top of the parcel was his face, stretched out into a distorted scream. Something fizzed around the scars on my skin as Tomas spoke.

"This is all that remains of the traitor Karl ap Beyler, who changed sides to ride with you," he said as if there was nothing odd about handing over the skin of a man you had once known.

"So you skinned him?" said Cearis, revulsion and disbelief warring on her face.

"King ap Glyndier would never do such a thing," said Neander, his mask scanning Rufra's Riders and the prisoners behind them. "Sadly for ap Beyler, Nonmen captured him after they came across him and some of your scouts. Your other men died quickly, but they seem to have taken against ap Beyler, for some reason. We could not spare the men to save him; it was the Nonmen who flayed him alive." The hint of a smile played over Tomas's lips as the priest spoke. "I heard it took him a long time to die. His skin was all the king's men could retrieve for you." This was a warning, and we all knew it, a warning from Tomas to his own men and to the prisoners that he would show no mercy to those he considered had betrayed him.

"Thank your men," said Rufra, biting the words out through gritted teeth as he turned his attention from the priest to Tomas. "I assure you, Tomas, that should you ever find yourself in peril I will be just as quick to assist you. Now, I have no wish to share the air with you for longer than I must. Take your men." He lifted his arm, signalling the four prisoners to be brought forward. As they advanced, Rufra cut the string around the skin, letting it fall open and unroll into a nightmare shape, a thinman straight out of the legends of the hedgings, the flapping ghost of what had once been life. "Remember your oath to me," said Rufra, holding up the skin with one hand. "You swore not to raise a weapon against me. Remember what happened in the sourlands to Akirin ap Valyan." He looked each man in the face and held the skin up so the holes where there had been eyes stared out, the hair of the scalp falling over his arm. "Remember that when Akirin betrayed his oath to me he died quick and clean. Ask yourselves if a man who would allow this –" he shook the skin, rage in his voice "– is a man you want to serve."

Rufra watched, unmoving apart from his eyes, as three of the men slid off their mounts and walked over to Tomas; the fourth watched the backs of the others and then took hold of the reins of his mount and turned it to face Rufra.

"You said I could hold a blade again if I wielded it for you."

Rufra nodded. "Yes."

"Karl was my cousin," he said quietly. "He taught me to

fight." He turned his mount, trotting it to the end of Rufra's line where he stared into the faces of men who he had once fought with – except I do not think he really saw them. I think he looked into the past, into a place where a man he had loved died screaming, and tried not to see his own face on that bloody parcel.

"So, Tomas," said Rufra. "Have you given thought to my offer, a battle of kings? Or will you have your priest answer that question too?"

Tomas stared at Rufra, his face working hard to remain impassive. I wondered why he didn't want to face Rufra; he had always been an impressive swordsman, always been sure of his own skill. Then I noticed his eyes flick to Nywulf and back again and I understood. Nywulf had once beaten Tomas with nothing but a wooden sword, and Nywulf had taught Rufra.

Tomas was scared.

"Five months, Tomas, and we either fight or you forfeit the crown."

"You'll be dead before we ever cross blades," said Tomas.

"One of us will," said Rufra. "Now come," he said to us. "We are done here." Mounts started to turn, but Boros walked his from the line. The scarred man pointed at the Rider who had held the coin and skin, a huge man with eyes so small they looked like black pits. I pitied his mount, not just because it had to carry him but because the animal's hindquarters were covered in marks from the whip, some fresh and still bleeding.

"I see you there, Caren ap Galdrar, once in service to my family. Is my brother here?" he said. "Or does he still cower behind Tomas's shield like a frightened child?" I thought the man would reply but Neander silenced him with a glance.

"I am sure Barin has heard your challenge," he said, "and would love nothing more than to finish the job he started at Goldenson Copse, but you are a lucky man today, Boros ap Loflaar. Tomas is a merciful king and has forbidden Barin from meeting you. He thinks it is wrong for such a renowned Rider to victimise the mage-bent."

Laughter came from Tomas's party, and if Rufra had not ridden up and taken hold of Boros's reins I am sure he would have charged into the opposing line. Tomas's laughter stopped as he appeared to notice me for the first time. His eyes ran down my body to my club foot.

"Girton ap Gwynr," he said. "I had heard you were back in the Tired Lands and I have a message for you." He was full of himself now, enjoying the laughter Neander had caused at Boros's expense – but he forgot he dealt with someone who had been jester, someone who knew how easy it was to puncture the skin of a man puffed up with his own importance.

"A message for me, King Tomas," I said in my brightest voice and pulled an exaggeratedly thoughtful face, tapping my lip with a finger. "Yes, hmm, well. Maybe, oh well why not?" I grinned at him. "I am sure King Rufra will allow you to deliver it," I used a voice loud enough for all to hear and a manner more suited to a king than a cripple. Now our lines rippled with laughter and Tomas gave me a look that said he would not soon forget the insult.

"I have not forgotten the part you played at Maniyadoc, mage-bent," he spat, "and you will be dealt with."

"I am honoured you remember a man as lowly as I," I said and performed an elaborate bow from the saddle of Xus. I could hear Rufra chuckling beside me.

"Come," said Rufra. "We should leave. I cannot watch Girton bait you any more, Tomas. As you know, I cannot bear cruelty." More laughter as we turned our mounts and walked away. From the corner of my eye I could see Tomas, so angry he looked like he'd been boiled, and for a moment I thought he may charge us with his Riders, but Neander held on to the reins of his mount.

"Laugh all you want," Tomas shouted after us, standing in his stirrups to make his voice carry. "Enjoy telling your jokes to Aydor when you meet him!"

We formed back into a column and rode slowly away. Up ahead I saw Rufra speaking with Cearis, Nywulf and Crast and pointing back at us. Cearis and Crast split from the front, Cearis walking her mount more slowly so she could speak quietly to Boros and I.

"That was well done, to goad him so," she said as she fell into step by us. "Tomas is a fool when he is angry and he said too much; no wonder he uses Neander as his mouthpiece. It seems Tomas knows we go to meet Aydor next and he should not. There is no way he can allow Aydor to come to us; it is an insult to him and in the eyes of many it legitimises Rufra's claim to the throne. We are no longer going to meet up with the infantry – Rufra does not think we have time. When we clear the copse we ride for the meeting with Aydor. Rufra suspects we will find him under attack."

"We are only twenty," I said and inwardly I cursed. I had been nursing ideas of going after Tomas at night and then finding Neander to settle my own score.

"Aye," replied Cearis with a wink, "only twenty, but we are twenty of Rufra's."

"And that will be enough?"

"It will have to be," said Boros, and though I could not read his expression I could hear in his voice that he would be happy for a chance to lash out.

"Boros," said Cearis, "you are to take Crast and another Rider back to Gabran and have him march for Arrot's Lee, that is where Rufra has arranged to meet Aydor. Tell Gabran to go as fast as he can go without tiring the troops."

"But you will need all the Riders you—" he began.

"This is an order from Rufra," said Cearis, and her tone left no room for argument. Boros looked at her a moment too long for it to seem anything but insolent, and then turned his mount, shouting out a name and putting spurs to the animal as Crast and the second Rider joined him.

"Rufra asks you to ride with him, Girton," Cearis said, and we trotted to the front of the column. Rufra was riding head down, looking tense, and it struck me how far away this man was from the boy I had known five years ago.

"Rufra?" I said.

"Girton –" my name little more than a growl "– I cannot believe I have been so easily duped. Aydor is in danger from the Nonmen, I should have known they were riding in numbers when I saw so many hogs."

"Pigs and Nonmen. Maniyadoc is a place I no longer know."

"The big herds often follow the Nonmen. They know there will be food where the Nonmen go."

"Why did you send Boros away?"

Rufra glanced over his shoulder in the direction Boros had gone.

"Because I cannot trust him, not in this."

"I don't understand. You said you trusted all of your council."

"In most ways, Girton." He stretched, rolling his neck and glancing over his shoulder to see if we were out of sight of Tomas's men yet. "You have seen the Boarlord, Chirol?" I nodded. "Chirol is a recent name the man has taken as his family want nothing to do with him any longer." I felt I knew where this was going.

"He is Barin? Boros's brother?"

"Yes, though it does not do to mention that in front of any of the ap Loflaar. The pretence Barin is still with Tomas is kept up by them."

"And by Tomas, from what he said."

"Aye, it suits Tomas not to be tied too closely to the Nonmen."

"But Boros hates his brother – surely that should make him fight harder?"

"Harder but blindly," Rufra said sadly. "Boros will pursue his vengeance against Chirol with a singular purpose if he sees him. If Chirol attacks Aydor our best plan is to drive him away and escape. But Boros will chase him, alone if he has to. In battle he will ignore orders if it means he will get his vengeance. At best I will have to discipline him, at worst I will lose him, and I cannot have that. He is loyal; his Riders love him, and I need his family as they hold the port town of Hart."

"So you sent him away. And Crast to make sure he does as you say."

Rufra nodded, and I wondered at how he made these decisions. Losing three Riders could mean defeat against the Nonmen, but Rufra had thought past that point and to what it would mean to lose Boros in the long run.

"It is hard to be a king, is it not?" said Nywulf quietly from beside me. I nodded. "But he does well, and he has a task for you, if you will take it."

I glanced back at Rufra, who looked almost embarrassed. "You must think me a fool, attacking with only eighteen Riders."

"That depends how many Nonmen there are." I grinned and he nodded.

"It does. If you were right and Aydor has two hundred troops then I imagine the Nonmen will have gathered a larger force than is usual for them, maybe three or four hundred."

"How do you know Aydor is even in danger?" Rufra glanced across at me, then at Nywulf, and there was a struggle on his ugly face, making him seem to age decades in seconds. "I need Aydor. For him to come to me is for the previous king's son to acknowledge my right to rule. I have arranged to meet him and bring him to my camp under cover of the prisoner exchange. As I was leaving the camp anyway, I thought I could keep the meeting secret and get back with a minimum of fuss."

"But Tomas knew."

"Maybe." He glanced at Nywulf, who was doing his best not to look smug. "Or he has guessed. He is not stupid."

"Rufra," I said, "you cannot think Aydor is worth risking your men for. You should—" He reached out, putting a gloved hand on my arm, and I had to pull on Xus's reins to stop him biting my friend.

"Peace, Girton. The Nonmen have no real cavalry, and you have not seen my mount archers in action."

"How do you even know it is Nonmen? Tomas could have an army waiting."

Rufra shook his head. "If an army moved through Maniyadoc I would know, and Tomas would not risk his own men this far from his lines. It will be Nonmen, and my mount archers will cut them to pieces."

"They may be fine cavalry, Rufra, but at close quarters cavalry can easily be overwhelmed."

"Maybe." He smiled at me and I wondered what I was missing. "But this brings me to my favour. I do not mean to downplay your skills in any way, but you have not trained with my mount archers and could not keep up with them. So, if you would, when we go against the Nonmen they will create a distraction so you can ride for the back of Aydor's troops and get to Aydor with me."

"You want him dead?" The thought of finishing Aydor was like the thought of fine food: my mouth became wet with saliva.

"No." He looked puzzled. "Did you not listen to a word I said? I need him. I want you to keep him alive."

"Again? We should all regret I was so successful last time."

"This is different to when his mother ruled, Girton." Rufra's voice was low, his temper bubbling somewhere underneath.

"But Rufra, this could be a trap. It could be Aydor who let Tomas know where he was. An army could be waiting for you."

"Aydor has given me his promise," he said, word by careful word.

"Aydor's promise is worth nothing. You should let me kill him. Nothing panics an army like losing its leader. If I finish Aydor the Nonmen will wipe out what's left of his army."

"Girton," said Rufra quietly, looking ahead with his jaw set, "I am asking you to do this as a friend. Keep him alive as long as you can and if we cannot win then get Aydor away."

"But—"

"Don't make me ask you as your king." Hard words, spat out in haste.

I stared at him, unable to find a reply.

"Then I will do as you ask, King Rufra," I said and pulled on Xus's reins, slowing him so the column had to split around me. Some of the Riders grumbled and swore at me for ruining their formation.

I fitted in nowhere. Not with my master, who kept secrets and now sweated, close to death in bed. Not with Rufra, who I barely recognised, and not with his men, who were a tightly knit group where I would only ever be an outsider, a spy.

From the front came an order to drop into the long run, a mile-eating stride that mounts could maintain for hours without becoming tired.

I let the rhythm of the animals' feet on the ground and the swaying of Xus' back lull me into a hypnotic trance.

And I dreamed of being another Girton in another life.

Coil the Yellower

And in my dream I am death and I wear his face.

I am a corn hobby doll wrapped in layers of material; the rags and scarves that cover my body and face hold my breath as a warmth against my mouth and nose.

Wind has taken the sourlands, and we lean into it, we push hard against it, we are two obtuse figures struggling doggedly onward. Strict, fast gusts pulls up the loose yellow earth and throw it into our faces. Our eyes ache with squinting to see through opaque air. Despite our wrappings the dust always works its way in. Even when we close our eyes it is felt, it is a reminder of the world outside: grit between our teeth, abrasive dust in every crack and crevice of our bodies. It mingles with sweat to rub away skin, making every step its own small torture.

Above it all, that extra smidgen of misery – the rotten-eggs stink of the dead land only grows stronger.

There is a third presence. It follows us through the sourland. We know it is there. It is a rasp in our throats. It feels no discomfort from the dust and has no bile in its mouth from the stink. When I glance over my shoulder I am frightened I will see it because it brings only misery and I have had enough of that – too much for my fifteen years. Out there is the hedging lord, Coil the Yellower, spirit of the sourlands, herald of ill fortune and pain.

He hunts me.

The air stills, but the wind continues to howl. The miasma of yellow dust slowly settles and I am alone. My master is gone and there is only one set of footsteps stretching behind me in the dust. A dead forest towers above me, a hundred thousand denuded trees are a black lacework against a bulging and swirling yellow sky.

The gibbet door swings shut.

Panic holds me close. Behind me is Maniyadoc.

The knife leaves tracks.

Why have I left?

And he is here, tall, bent and twisted, a figure made from swirling dust. A tarantella dance of shaking immateria, he is a dryness of mouth, he is a forewarning of misfortune and he is beckoning me on with fingers of sharp flint. On the horizon is a new land; a group of men wait and Coil laughs and dances and spins.

Animal.

No!

I lunge, blades twist through it, and Coil bends and whirls around them, his body twirling and dissolving, his voice a rasping laugh. Attack. More laughter. Sharp blades are useless against a creature made of dust and when I need her my master is gone. Where is she?

"Master!"

The leash marks my skin.

A thrust, meeting only air, and Coil is in my ear, in my airways, choking me. We twirl on, a stumbling, ungainly dance, coughing and slashing blindly at the laughing hedging lord. Then I am falling, spitting, puking up bile and grit onto good green grass, and smelling, even above the high stink of the sourlands, the thick sweet smell of death.

"This is what the high king sends us? A puking mage-bent cripple and a woman?" Around me are men, ten in pieced-together armour with pinched faces and mean weapons. The speaker is on a mount, and seeing him makes my blood run cold. A Landsman, he is smiling, he is Gosaile, and his smile is as cold and mocking as Coil's. A gentle hand closes around my arm as he speaks. "Still, if you can fight I'll take you. The more swords I can throw at the marchlanders, the fewer men I'll lose."

My master helps me up. It is her hand that is tight and warm on my arm.

The leash holds me.

"My name is Merela Karn, and this is Girton Club-Foot," she says. "And we are here to fight your battles in the far borders for you." The Landsman laughs at her and she speaks to me in the Whisper-that-Flies-to-the-Ear. "This is the last place any will look for us, Girton. Stand fast."

I am numb.

I hear Coil the Yellower laughing.

Chapter 13

We had ridden for about an hour, judging by the height of the sun as it dipped behind towering black clouds. Nywulf fell into formation beside me. I ignored him and he made no attempt to talk to me, at first, but as we hurtled onward, the land a colourless blur, he shouted over, "Drop back a little, Girton."

I let Xus continue long enough to feel like I wasn't jumping to Nywulf's orders before reining the mount in.

"What?"

"Will you do it?"

"Do what?"

"You know what. Will you protect Aydor?"

"Well, my king has commanded me—"

"Do not act like a child." He did not shout, and that made it more of a slap in the face. "He is not your king, not unless you have accepted him as that. And he would not force you to do anything that conflicted with whatever you call morals, assassin." He let the last word hang.

"I thought I would find a friend here, Nywulf, and instead I find . . ."

"A king?"

"No, it is more than that. Rufra is different in a way I do not understand. One moment he laughs and then he is cold to me. Maybe it is being a king, maybe it is just a burden I can never know." I let Xus walk a little further and wrapped myself in my cloak, a cold wind had sprung up. "I will do as he asks, and as soon as my master is well enough we will move on. I should not have come here."

"He needs you and you him, even if neither of you see it yet."

"No," I snapped, "he does not. He needs Heartblades and warriors and people who can keep up with his precious mount archers; he does not need—"

"Areth and Rufra had a child. He died."

Such small and simple words, but they contained so much heartbreak and he said them in such a way that I knew Nywulf shared in the pain. Nywulf had been like a father to Rufra: he had guided him, trained him, been there for him when he was needed and protected him when the world was against him. Nywulf was unassailable, even my master had said she would think twice before taking him on, but in his voice was a shard of pain that he could not hide. The shock of it made me pull Xus to a stop.

"Died?" I said.

"Aye. A boy, they named him Arnlath."

"For Rufra's grandfather," I said. It was barely a breath.

"Yes, he was born about a year and a half after you left."

"When did he die?" I had the sudden, unreasonable belief that I had brought death with me, Girton Club-Foot, servant of Xus the unseen.

A cold rain started to fall.

"About a year and a half ago. He was a beautiful boy, full of life and smiles. He was Rufra's joy, and then one day he sickened and no one could do anything about it. The healers failed. Rufra even asked about wise-women until the Landsmen put one in a blood gibbet. Everything that could be done was done, but Arnlath still died."

"He never said anything."

Nywulf stared at the ground and it was as if he was sucked dry of life.

"No. I had hoped he would confide in you, but he talks to no one about it. He will not even speak to Areth."

"He blames his wife?"

"No, Girton." Nywulf glanced at me as if confused by how stupid I could be sometimes. "Of course he doesn't. Rufra blames who he always blames when things turn bad, he blames himself."

"But no one can fight a sickness."

"No, and no one could have won at Goldenson Copse, which happened at about the same time, but Rufra does not see that. When he sees Areth he thinks she must blame him the way he blames himself, she does not. He is in a place where I cannot help him." I saw beyond Nywulf then, past the iron-hard warrior into a man desperate for help. "I hoped you could."

We walked on for fifty counts of my-master.

"I will protect Aydor, Nywulf, if that is what Rufra needs me to do," I said quietly. "And I will find this traitor, if there is one. I swear it on Xus the unseen."

"You will do whatever needs to be done?"

"Aye."

"Swear that too."

"I swear it."

"Good. Now Rufra will be wondering where I am. Be ready. We are not far from the meeting place."

The battle was heard before it was seen. To the casual eye Maniyadoc is a flat place, but that is an illusion; it is an undulating land, like a cloth carelessly thrown across a table. It rises and falls, creating valleys deep enough to hide a small army, creating false horizons and sudden, steep gulleys that will trick a careless rider and send them tumbling to their death. So death was hidden from us at first, but we heard the beating of spear on shield, we heard the high shouts of mettle-chanters, men or women who let out an ululating wail calling down hedgings on their enemies. When the wails finished we heard the massed troops shout. "Huh!" as they stepped forward.

Rufra pulled his Riders to a halt on the crest of a hill so they could look down on the forces below.

"Wait here," he shouted. "I want the Nonmen to see us. Aydor too."

The mass of Nonmen looked fierce, though many did not wear armour, only skirts, and they had their long hair spiked up with white lime, dark mud, dung or blood – all will do the job. Many had scalps hanging from their belts and their massed shields were painted with skulls and the faces of the worst of the hedgings, Dark Ungar, Coil the Yellower, Fitchgrass and Blue Watta. They shouted promises that souls would be taken in battle and tied to the land for the shatter-spirits. In the centre of their line, surrounded by a hundred or so well armoured men, I could see Chirol, or Barin as I had known him, and behind him were his standards. He flew no loyalty flags and carried no bonemount, his bearers carried sticks hung with the bones and skulls of humans and boars. Everything about the Nonmen spoke of ferocity and terror, and Rufra had been right about them coming in numbers: their force was well over three times as big as Aydor's. But they were a rabble, a collection of the Tired Lands' worst, who relied on fear and superior numbers to win their battles. I had seen their like before. I had killed their like before and I would do so again. The only worry was the better-equipped warriors surrounding the Boarlord.

Aydor stood in the centre of his wall of shields, shouting something as he held his stabsword above his head. For a moment I thought his cavalry had deserted him, but then I saw Captain Thian at Aydor's side and in the distance a small group of mounts standing idle, and I knew what had happened. Aydor and his men had seen the Nonmen coming and thought this was their end. Maybe they thought Rufra had betrayed them. They must have decided there was no escape and either wanted to show the enemy they had no intention of running or simply wished their animals to live so had driven them away. My eyes strayed back to Aydor, who was shouting to his men again. Now he was pointing his sword up the hill at us.

I found I could hear Aydor, the trick of the assassin's ear. "Rufra is here! We will survive today, Rufra is here! Let us show him we are worth tiring his mounts for!" With that his shieldwall moved forward. Usually the battle of shield on shield is a slow thing, halting, but this was a rush, a wave of men that crashed against the spears of the Nonmen. As battle was joined a freezing rain began to lash us: below someone screamed, someone cursed, someone died.

Rufra walked his mount forward and turned it so he could look each warrior in the eye. He did not seem to feel the cold or notice the rain.

"Cearis will hit their right; Nywulf will give their left something to think about. Girton and I will ride round the main force of Nonmen and join Aydor in his wall."

"There's a lot of them, Blessed," said a Rider in front of me.

Rufra looked over his shoulder, glancing through the curtain of rain at the Nonmen as if he'd not given their numbers a thought.

"There is." He grinned. "Nywulf once told me about these men who carry fear before them – they get used to easy victories against soft targets. What is it you say, Nywulf? A real warrior is like a good sword." He drew Hope, his shining Conwy blade, letting the light dance along it, and stood in his stirrups.

In my head I had continued to see him as the boy I knew, but he was a man now, not tall but broad and thick with muscle. His armour was dull apart from the circle of brass worked into his helmet and the black flying lizard made of small enamel plates on his chest piece. He was nondescript:

thick brows, broken nose, small mouth – you would not have looked twice at him in a crowd – but here there was no doubt he was a king. He radiated power and confidence. "A real warrior," he shouted, "needs a good beating to harden them, otherwise they become brittle and break easily." His voice seemed to swell, becoming louder. "So come! Let us raise the bonemount and break some swords!" He snapped down his visor, a grimacing face, shouted, "The bonemount rides!" and put spurs to Balance.

I had never seen mount archers before, never even heard of them, but as I watched Nywulf and Cearis lead them I realised that Rufra had not been insulting my skills when he said I was not one of them. He was right. I also saw why he was not worried about them being swamped by infantry – they never approached near enough for the Nonmen to catch them.

Cearis struck first. Although she was heavy cavalry she carried a short bow as she charged the rear of the Nonmen right, loosing arrows that tore through unarmoured backs. When the mount archers reached the range a spear could be thrown they doubled back on themselves. Cearis rode normally, but the mount archers in their lighter armour turned in their saddles to face backwards and continued shooting. On the other flank Nywulf and his mount archers were doing the same, diving in towards the enemy lines and then pulling away. Without cavalry of their own the Nonmen had no answer to this, and their shields were paltry things of hide that could not stop the arrows.

"Come Girton," shouted Rufra. He sounded ecstatic. "I think the they are distracted." We rode hard around the right flank of the Nonmen. Some had straggled out our way and pity to anyone who came within range of Rufra's sword or the warhammer I carried. A Nonman in rags ran at Rufra from the left and Balance lowered her head, tossing the man aside with a vicious sweep of her antlers. Rufra's sword cut out, slicing through the head of another man. I drew level, swinging the warhammer and smashing the arm of a woman, running at me with a club, into a useless pulp. Ahead a small group tried to arrange themselves into a shieldwall. Xus and Balance, screeching with excitement, lowered their heads to bring cruel antlers down for attack, and the Nonmen panicked. Those who stood their ground were too slow to lower their spears. Xus hit them first, scattering men like a child's ball does hedge pins. For a moment there was a Nonman skewered on his antlers, then he threw him aside with a scream of triumph and we galloped on, our animals furious and unstoppable.

We brought our mounts in fast, skidding round to the rear of Aydor's lines and dismounting. Rufra took his red and black shield from his mount, I grabbed a purple shield from a dead man, and we forced our way to the front of Aydor's line. Rufra took a place by Thian, and I found myself next to Aydor. He stank of apple wine, but though he was drunk he was also strong. As I pushed my way in, two Nonmen rushed Aydor, he thrust his stabsword into the guts of the first attacker. The man screamed and grabbed Aydor's sword arm, locking them together and making a gap for his companion to thrust a blade in.

I could let Aydor die and no one would be any the wiser. Soldiers died in battle all the time no matter how hard their comrades tried to protect them. No one would blame me.

My stabsword flashed out and parried the Nonman's blade. With a reverse slash I opened his belly and Aydor managed to reclaim his blade. He glanced at me, giving me a nod of thanks. His eyes widened in surprise when he realised who I was. Then he put his back into his shield and shouted, "Push! We nearly have them now! One more push!"

Then we fought. It was grim work. The Nonmen bayed like dogs which set me on edge – all my life I had feared dogs. I controlled it now but it was there, in the back of my mind. Blades flashed. From my place by Aydor I could see the Boarlord; his pig-skull headdress marked him out though his face was covered. The men who surrounded him were not like the rest of the rabble, who screamed and flailed, making them easy to cut down. Chirol's troops had discipline. They formed his second line, while he threw the rest of his men at us first, tiring us. I slashed my short blade underneath my shield, feeling the hit in my wrist when my sword cut into bone, seeing a face turn from one screaming in fury to one screaming in agony.

Aydor used his stabsword like a scythe, putting his strength behind his shield and pushing to create a gap, the blade coming out and drumming across Nonmen shields. By his side Thian cut out, exploiting any opening. Rufra fought like he was born to it, holding his shield seemingly without effort, sometimes using the short spike on the front, picking his moments, other times sliding his blade between shields and nearly always finding targets.

Chirol urged the Nonmen on, screaming abuse but remaining out of reach. Over the noise of the shieldwall I heard the beat of mount claws, the hissing of arrows and the shouts when they hit home. Occasionally I would see the mount archers harrying the back and sides of the Nonmen formation, killing without ever coming within reach of their weapons.

And then the Nonmen broke. Some simply ran and quickly fell prey to the mount archers, who wheeled and spun on the battlefield like hunting flying lizards, but the majority showed an unexpected discipline, locking shields around the fierce figure of the Boarlord and withdrawing in a surprisingly orderly fashion for a bunch of outlaws. Nywulf, Cearis and their archers harried them until Rufra let out a high whistle, calling them back.

"Let them go," he shouted. "We have not the numbers to finish Chirol here and Boros would never forgive us if we did." As his mount archers returned I watched the Nonmen retreat into the shelter of a wood and vanish, as if they had never been.

There was a strange atmosphere after the battle. Aydor's troops had already decided they were about to die, and to be reprieved had left them in a sort of daze. They walked around smiling aimlessly and collecting trophies from dead Nonmen. Thian came over to personally thank me for saving his king, and I shrugged his thanks off quite rudely, though he did not seem to mind. I could not concentrate on what Thian was saying anyway as I was watching Rufra and Aydor, seeing something I thought I would never see and wishing I did not have to. They spoke only a few words and then they clasped arms like brothers. They smiled at each other, and it looked almost genuine. I could not believe it. This was Aydor, who had made our young lives miserable and come close to having Rufra burned to death to cover his own and his mother's ambitions and mistakes.

I had put a stop to that.

I would put a stop to this.

Chapter 14

The journey back was miserable. A light rain fell, the type that is only seen as a succession of puddles seeping out of the earth and only felt as a gradual dampening of the rough wool beneath your armour, making it chafe against your flesh, leaving it raw and red. We met Boros half an hour after we left the site of the battle. He stared at Aydor and Rufra as they passed, then chose to ride with me. It seemed, for the day and a half it took us to journey back, we did nothing but stare resentfully at the head of the column. Boros was angry because he had been denied the chance to face his brother and I dropped further into a dark place each time Rufra and Aydor laughed together, like they were old friends.

And I had used magic before the battle. It had not even occurred to me I was doing it, listening to Aydor's voice from a distance on the battleground, but that was the way of magic – it was insidious. It had been weeks since my master had cut me with the Landsman's Leash, and the scars on my skin felt as if they had come alive – incandescent trackways of binding symbols oh so gradually migrating across my flesh to create new patterns, new ways, subtly altering themselves to channel the power of the land rather than deny it. The thought terrified me and it thrilled me. As long as there was life in the land the power of a sorcerer was limitless, so if Rufra chose to ally himself with Aydor I could wipe them both from Maniyadoc with a thought, and all that would be left of them was a souring, a yellow mark upon the land that I would call Rufra's Folly, and . . .

"Girton?" I turned. Rufra rode beside me and I was staring at my hands as if they belonged to another. A shiver ran through me. Was this how the Black Sorcerer had thought before he almost destroyed Maniyadoc? "Are you cold, Girton?" said Rufra. I nodded, putting both my shaking hands on the saddle horn. "It is the rain, but at least I am free of Aydor now. He has gone to join his troops so he can enter the camp at their head. It is a relief, if I am honest. He would not stop talking about how well we had fought together. I thought I would never get away."

"You looked to be enjoying yourself." I tried my best not to sound like a sulking child but from his expression I did not do very well.

"Well, it is fun to be around a drunk for a while, but it quickly becomes wearing and, dead gods protect me, a king must meet a lot of drunks."

"He's not just a drunk, he's dangerous, Rufra. Don't be taken in."

He shrugged. Rufra had been a remarkably plain boy and had grown into a plain-looking adult, his face only coming alive at the thought of battle, but when he was puzzled or sad he became downright ugly.

"I am a king now, Girton." He gave me a crooked smile. "It seems everyone I meet is dangerous and few can be trusted, really trusted." He locked eyes with me. "Nywulf told you about Arnlath." For a moment I thought he was about to be overwhelmed by the weight of his grief, then he added, "My son."

"Yes," I said simply. There was nothing I could add. I had no balm for his grief.

"I am sorry. It should have been me that told you, but it is—"

"It is all right, Rufra." I reached across and put my hand on his shoulder, and for once Xus decided against trying to bite Balance. "You do not need to say any more, if it is difficult." He reached up, giving my hand a brief touch of thanks. What could have become uncomfortable was ended by Xus snapping at Balance, having tolerated enough closeness between them, and I had to pull hard on his reins while Rufra laughed at me.

"I am afraid Xus will never make a true cavalry mount, he will always be one to ride alone."

"Yes," I said and patted Xus on his neck. "It is the way he is."

"We will be entering the camp with ceremony, Girton," said Rufra, "and it will take us at least an hour to get ready, if not longer." He sounded and looked tired, but something passed between us, a resetting of the past two days, and I knew that, though our friendship could not be as it had been when we were young, it survived. Rufra would let the mask of kingship fall in front of very few people but I had been allowed to see the pain behind it, if only for a moment. "You do not need to ride in with us, though you are welcome to," he added quickly, "but I thought you may wish to ride ahead and see how your master fares."

"I would like that."

"Good. Go then. I must return and let Crast polish my best armour until it will give any onlooker a headache to look at."

"It is hard to be a king," I said solemnly. "I know how much I would miss having to polish my own armour with old kitchen fat."

"It is my burden, Girton –" he smiled "– and I must bear it."

I left Rufra behind me, angling Xus towards the twisting columns of smoke that marked the fires of the camp. The dampening rain of the past days had subsided and now the sun burned and the fields and hedges were alive with the small movements of animals. The black birds of Xus wheeled high in the sky, dipping, falling and playing like scraps of ash caught in the wind. Flying lizards zipped through the air, some with wings beating so fast they were a blur, others gliding on wide wings of translucent skin. I could hear the grunting of pigs, which had always been a homely sound – most in the Tired Lands kept a pig if they could – but the thought of those vast predatory herds lent a darker edge to the brightness of the day. When I glanced behind me the clouds of the Birthstorm towered on the horizon as if about to fall over Maniyadoc. Sometimes figures danced on the edges of my vision, some of bone, some of grass or wood or water, but most often they were clad in black and simply standing and watching. I had seen shades of Xus before and they always preceded death, so the nearer I got to the camp the more worried about my master I became. She had been awake when I left, but only just. What if she had died while I was away? What if she had died and I had not been there for her?

In my worry I barely noticed the camp when I got there. As soon as it had started to take form on the horizon I had pushed Xus from an easy lope into a gallop. I had to slow him when I entered the camp, and eventually the press of people forced me to drop from his back and lead him through the crowds, all the time talking to him in a calming voice to stop him lashing out. When I reached our tent I tethered him and gave a child half a bit to go to the stables and get the mountmaster. There was no sign of Neliu, who was meant to be guarding my master, and I feared the worst. Taking a deep breath, I entered.

To be met with laughter.

The laughter of a man and the laughter of a woman.

In the gloom I could not make out who they were, and I was ready to be angry. Was Neliu in here when she should be guarding the door? Or – *a fear unreal* – was my master dead and the tent given to someone else?

My eyes slowly became more accustomed to the low light, and I saw Mastal, the healer, sat on a chair by my master's bed. She was propped up on cushions and a small candle burned on a little table beside her.

"Girton," she said. She still looked tired and ill but she was talking. There was a light in her eye I had not seen since I was very young and had learned some new trick that pleased her. And though I had heard her laugh before, of course I had, it had always been a quick there-and-gone-again laugh, not the throaty chuckle heard when I entered.

"Master, you are well?"

"She is not truly well," said Mastal, a smile on his face, "but she is better, much better."

"I . . ." I did not know what to say. There was something wrong here, something too close in the way Mastal sat with her, something too light in the way he spoke.

"Girton, did you know that Mastal is from the Sighing Mountains, just like I was, once," she said.

"No. I have never heard of the Sighing Mountains."

"That is because it is our people's name for them," said Mastal, "not yours."

"You would call them the Slight Hills," my master said gently.

"That wounds me every time I hear it said." Mastal laughed. He mimed a dagger being thrust into his heart. I did not laugh, and Mastal's laughter slowly died away. He looked from my master to me. "You two must have much you wish to speak about," he said and rose. "I will leave you to talk." He brushed past me, stopping to give me a short bow and quick smile.

"That was rude of you, Girton," said my master. "Without him I would be dead."

"It was I who fought off the rest of the Glynti and dragged you here, not him," I said, sitting.

"Of course," she said, putting her hand on my forearm. "You got us to Rufra's camp, and for that I am thankful." She took a sip of water. Her hand shook slightly, and I noticed she made no attempt to move the arm that had been poisoned from where it lay on the bed.

"You do not need to thank me," I said. "Besides, I had Aydor's help."

"Aydor?" She raised an eyebrow.

I leaned in close. "You must not trust Mastal. He is one of Aydor's men and has secrets."

"We all have secrets, Girton."

"We are not all sent by Aydor though, Master."

"And yet we are here and not dead. Maybe life is not as simple as you wish it to be?"

Rather than be angry with her for being unwilling to listen, I put her replies down to her illness and told her what had happened while she had been asleep. Told her how Aydor had ingratiated himself with Rufra after sowing dissent in his camp by saying there was a spy, and how I had been attacked.

"And do his council seem suspicious?"

"Some, for different reasons, though I have not talked to them all yet. But Rufra trusts them."

We talked some more. She quizzed me about our ride and my attacker, but all the time I felt she was filling the air with words rather than saying what really mattered. Eventually, after a lengthy silence, she said quietly,

"Girton, how long was I asleep for?"

"Surely Mastal has told you that."

"But you do not seem to trust him, so I ask you. How long?"

It felt as if a frost was working its way through the tent, seeping out of the heavy felt sides and from under the groundsheet to coil around and up my legs. She had no real interest in how long she had been away from the world. What interested her was magic and sharp blades that scored symbols which squirmed and bit into my skin. This was about cutting something into me that would sever me from the world, deaden taste, turn music into noise, emotion into numbness and the colours of spring into mud.

"Too long," I said. She nodded, and another long silence between us followed. "There has to be another way."

"I know you don't like the knives, I know it hurts, but—"

"No!" The word shot from my mouth, my body shuddering. "It is not the pain. It is not that." And I was standing over her, my hands bunched into fists. I had to force myself to unclench them and sit back down. My master watched impassively. "Master, I have to learn to control it, not simply stamp it down."

"That is the magic talking, Girton," she whispered.

"No, it is not, what if you had died?" I leaned in close and whispered, "What if you had died? I would be alone and what then?"

She stared at me. For too long. She was tired – I could see it in her eyes – tired and disappointed in me. She was always disappointed in me.

"Very well, Girton. See how it is. Clamp down hard if you feel it move and promise me at the first sign of you losing control you will let me cut the leash into you again."

I nodded. "Thank you, Master."

"But you must return to the path, Girton. Without discipline there is no control. You must put that aside –" she pointed at the warhammer but would not look at it "– and take up your blades again. Practise the iterations, and if Rufra needs it you must be ready to put on my motley."

I was about to reply like an angry child, telling her that I had survived alone and she could no longer tell me what to do, when we were interrupted.

"Girton? Girton Club-Foot?"

I turned. It was Areth, Rufra's wife, and she was as utterly captivating as the first time I had seen her. It was like looking over the side of a boat through clear water to the floor of the ocean deep below: fascinating and for ever beyond my reach.

"Yes," I said eventually. I was dizzied by her, though she did not seem to notice. Maybe she had this effect on all men and was simply used to it. "This is Areth, Master, Rufra's queen."

"Welcome to my tent, Queen Areth," said my master.

"You are awake, Merela Karn. I am glad of it. Rufra has told me much of you, but you have been gravely ill and must rest. I do not want to bother you but I would speak to your charge if I may?" She nodded. "Outside, please."

"Go," said my master. "I need to sleep." I followed Areth out of the tent.

"I had hoped we would meet in better circumstances," she said, "but I am afraid time does not allow for niceties. You left with Rufra?" As she spoke I noticed Xus was still there. It annoyed me that the child had taken my money and not done his job.

"Yes, I did."

"But you have come back alone . . ." She left it hanging, and it was only then that I saw how worried she was.

"Rufra is well. We met Aydor, and Rufra is getting ready to enter the camp in triumph; he sent me on ahead."

"Good," she said. "Good, but he must not enter in triumph; he must come back now. He is needed."

"Why?"

"Arnst is dead."

"The priest?"

"Murdered, and the camp is ready to tear itself apart over it. I have held the peace as well as I am able, but Rufra needs to return now or he will come back to a riot."

Now I was glad Xus remained.

"I will go and get him."

"Thank you," she said. I crossed to Xus and pulled myself up into the saddle. As I prepared to leave I leaned over to speak quietly to her:

"I heard about your child and I am sorry."

For a second I thought she would cry, but then her face hardened – not in an unpleasant or cruel fashion, she was touched by my concern, though she also knew she did not have time for it.

"Children die here, Girton," she said. "Princes, living and thankful alike. The Tired Lands are a hard place to be a mother, but we must move on from death. And more will die if Rufra does not end the war. We cannot afford to sit and brood or blame."

"Have you told Rufra this?"

"I have tried, he is not ready to talk, not yet. Has he spoken of Arnlath to you?"

"A little, not much. He seemed sore hurt by it."

"It is good that he has spoken to you, Girton." She reached up and placed a hand on my sleeve. "Be a friend to him, for me. It is harder for a man to take, I think, the death of a child."

It cut me to see her shouldering such pain.

"But you bore the child . . ."

"And I am heartsick at the thought of him still. But blessed men? They teach you to win and to fight where they tell women to expect pain and grief – we are prepared for it all our lives. Rufra feels he failed Arnlath, like he lost the fight and he blames himself."

"He is wrong."

"I know," she said quietly, and then as the silence grew between us she added, "Look after him, Girton, because he will not let me, not yet." She removed her hand from my arm and I trotted Xus out of the camp. Soon his great legs were stretching out in a gallop that ate up the land, but it was not the speed that made me dizzy, it was the thought of Areth ap Vthyr.

Chapter 15

As I approached the column, Nywulf rode out to meet me. He listened as I explained that Arnst had been killed and then he swore, running off a list of the worst of the hedge spirits and the unlikely things they did to each other in the bedchamber, before telling me to wait while he gave Rufra the news. Five minutes later Rufra rode past me on Balance, his head down as he pushed his animal as fast as it would go. Behind him came Crast, Boros, Cearis and finally Nywulf, who signalled me to join them.

We did not speak.

The crowd that had slowed me when I arrived at the camp parted for Rufra to pass. He pulled Balance to a halt in front of the tent that served as a meeting place for his council and slid off the animal, storming through the flaps of the tent and ignoring the salutes of his guards.

Nywulf grabbed my arm as I tried to follow. "He will want to speak to you later. Now he needs to speak to his council. Do not go too far away."

I nodded and found a bench where I could wait and let the sun warm my leg where my club foot ached. I wondered how I had missed the difference in the camp when I entered it earlier. There was a quietness about the people that had been lacking before. The camp had the air of a castle under siege, and people stood about in small groups whispering to each other. Children who had previously run around getting underfoot were now being herded by groups of adults, and when I tried to talk to a little girl all I received from her guardian was a suspicious look.

Mastal joined me. The healer smelled of herbs and dust and when he sat, his thick brown robes rubbed against my armour. I shuffled along so he was not touching me.

"Girton, I must speak to you about your master."

"You have done well, Mastal. Thank you," I said, but the words were ashes in my mouth. I could not bring myself to like him.

"It is not I, it is these." He opened his robe so I could see the hand he was shielding from those around us. In it were some dried leaves about the size of my palm.

"Doxy leaves?"

"They are not doxy leaves." He smiled. "I wish that they were, Girton. Doxy leaves are common as pigs and these are far from that."

"They look like doxy leaves." I moved even further away from him.

"Yes, they are a related plant I imagine, and where doxy is good if you have a headache, this is a leaf we call yandil and it is a far more powerful healer. The poison in your master has its roots deep in Glynti ways and, though they would never admit it, what they do is a kind of sorcery." He reached into his pouch and took out another leaf, seemingly identical. "Here, this is a doxy leaf. Smell it." I did. It smelled of earth and had a bitter green background note, like unripe fruit. "Now smell the yandil." He passed me a leaf from inside his robe and I lifted it to my nose. At first I thought it smelled the same, but then came another scent, very faint at first – honey, pepper and warm sunlight. The threadwork of scars on my body pulled against my skin as if attracted to the herb, and for a moment I was in a barn full of amber light while a woman I had loved put her hand on mine. I pulled my hand back from the yandil as if stung.

"Do not be scared, Girton," whispered Mastal, "and do not make a scene, but what you smell is magic." He took back the yandil leaf. "Not the type that sours the land in the hands of sorcerers; what you smell is the scent of life, and the yandil hoards it. I have used the leaf to stave off the poison and to help your master build up her strength so she can fight off the Glynti sickness."

"And it is working."

"Yes, it is, but I do not have enough yandil to keep her well for long."

I stared at the doxy leaf in my left hand, it felt somehow less substantial after holding the yandil, it was simply a dead thing. I folded it and put it in my pouch.

"You have looked in the markets?"

"Yes, both the night and day markets, but it is not the sort of thing anyone would choose to display with the Landsmen in camp, and I am too obviously a stranger here. They are suspicious of me. You, on the other hand . . ."

Could end up in a blood gibbet and he would not care. Or did he do this to remind me of the difference between myself and my master? Or to remind me of the similarity between him and her? That they shared some perfect mountain land and I was from sad and broken Maniyadoc, more torn and sundered by sorcerers than any other place in the Tired Lands.

"You want me to look for it?" I could not look at him.

"Yes."

"How much of it do you need?"

"At the moment I give her a quarter of a leaf, ground into a paste, each day. As her body becomes accustomed to it, I will need to give her more to see the same effect. I have maybe a month's supply, but she needs three months at least, maybe even six."

"And if you can't find it?"

"Yandil grows thick in the Sighing Mountains."

"So you would have to go and get it then?" I tried not to sound too happy about him leaving.

"No, I must be with her to administer the herb."

"So you want me to go?" I did not like the idea of leaving my master with him.

"No. My people are as suspicious of strangers as yours can be, more so in many ways."

And then it struck me, what he was saying.

"You want to take her there?"

"Only to treat her, Girton, because—"

"No!" I stood, trying not to shout as it would attract attention. "I saw how you were with her, how you looked at her."

"Girton –" he looked shocked, as if his veneer of calm should somehow have fooled me "– it is not what you think. Only the talk of two people sharing memories of a land they have loved, nothing more."

"I am not a child, Mastal," I hissed.

"I am not so sure of that," he said quietly, standing and brushing imaginary dust from his robe. "Think on what I said, Girton. I have no interest in your master the way you imagine. Is it more important to have your master here with you? Or more important that she lives? You are young, Girton. The world is not all about you."

"It has never been about me," I said. "If it was about me, do you think I'd be standing here with a warhammer at my hip and a soldier's armour on?" From somewhere tears were threatening, tears of frustration, and there was something else, a voice I recognised, one that I had not heard for a long time. It whispered to me from very far away.

"I can make this all better."

Mastal walked away, stiff with irritation, as if he had been utterly reasonable and I was the problem. "I will find your leaf," I shouted after him. "I will find you more than you need!" He ignored me and, when I turned, a woman and the children she shepherded were staring at me with wide frightened eyes. "He does not understand," I said to her. "He is a foreigner."

The woman looked me up and down and said, "So are you," then hurried her children away. Before I could say anything Neliu approached.

"Shouldn't you be guarding my master?" I said.

"Crast is with her. Shouldn't you be finding traitors?"

"It is not quite as easy as guard duty," I snapped back before concentrating on my breathing and speaking more slowly. "I am sorry if I was sharp – my day has been long – but as you are here I should ask you if there is anyone on the council you do not trust."

"I would have said Arnst, but if the traitor was him someone has done your job for you." She pointed at the warhammer hanging from my belt. "Are you as good Nywulf says?" I shrugged. "I don't think you are," she said, "or you wouldn't have that ugly thing or get jumped in a wood. You'd use a real weapon." She tapped the blade on her hip.

"It does its job."

"It is not a dancer's weapon. Nywulf said you were a dancer." Her eyes shone. "I had hoped to dance with you, see if you are worthy of the blade you carry." She pointed at the Conwy stabsword on my belt. I had moved it there from my back when we joined Rufra, so he could see it. While I was distracted her hand shot out, making a grab for the hilt. Before she got anywhere near I had hold of her wrist. We locked gazes, and then, for the first time since I had met her, she smiled. "Gusteffa identified your attacker," she said.

I did not let go of her wrist. "And?"

"A woman called Callin, a mercenary and, it turns out, a murderous thief. In her tent we found a sword from an officer we thought had fallen over and smashed his head, as well as a few other things."

"So you are saying it was a robbery?" She was very near to me, her eyes gleaming.

"Looks that way."

"She knew who I was."

"She probably asked about you – ambassador's assistant, likely a rich target."

"Likely," I said.

"Rufra wants you," she said, then added, "I have a bet with Crast that you would let the king down." She glanced down at where I held her, and I let go. She rubbed her wrist. "You're quicker than I expected."

"Maybe you have lost your money, eh?"

"Only if you're quick enough when it counts," she said. "Are you quick enough when it counts, Girton Club-Foot?"

Now it was my turn to shrug.

"I am still alive, Neliu, that is what matters. Lead me to the king."

Rufra waited for me with Nywulf and Areth in a back room of his two-storey caravan. Neliu went to stand by Nywulf, the floor creaked as she crossed it and in the windowless wooden room the heat was stifling.

"Girton," said Rufra, "we have a problem. Arnst has a following, a loyal following of at least a hundred, probably far more. They are already blaming the priesthood for his death. The followers of the dead gods are in their turn glad Arnst is dead, though they are not being too open and singing out their joy, not yet anyway."

"Trouble will surely follow that song," I said.

"Yes." He moved nearer to me and spoke quietly: "I want you to forget about Nywulf's talk of traitors. The Triangle Council are all loyal so do not waste your time on them." Neliu was absent-mindedly nodding her head as he said this, as if she also thought I wasted my time. "I want you to find out who killed Arnst."

"Me?"

"You are the one who uncovered Kyril's killer at Maniyadoc."

"But my master—"

"Is awake now, so you can consult with her if you need to. I will give you a letter of authority to go anywhere and talk to anyone."

"We would be obliged if you did this for us, Girton," said Areth. I nodded, although I did not intend to stop hunting for the traitor. Events are often interlinked. If there was a traitor it was possible he was also mixed up in the death of Arnst: in fact it would be stranger if he wasn't.

"Very well. I will need to see the corpse."

Rufra took my arm by the wrist and squeezed. "Thank you. Come, he is in the butcher's hole."

We left the caravan to find the clearing outside had filled with people. There was a palpable sense of tension in the air. The crowd was clearly divided between Arnst's followers in their black rags and the rest of the camp in bright colours. Two of the camp's priests, Darvin and Tarris, stood at the head of a small group of acolytes, and the air fairly crackled with the ill will between them and Arnst's followers. I was in no doubt the crowd could turn ugly at any moment.

Nywulf pushed past me and I heard him whisper to Rufra, "I will bring more soldiers." Rufra nodded and then stood on the lower bars of the stair to the caravan so the crowd could see him.

"Listen!" he shouted. "Listen to me!" The crowd quietened. "Arnst was part of my council but I know there are those here who bore him no love."

"Aye. Good riddance to him!" shouted a woman from somewhere to the left of Rufra, he ignored her and continued talking.

"And there are also those here who loved him greatly! But no matter which opinion you hold, you are united in one thing. As Arnst and I were also united!" The crowd was now silent. "We all want to see Tomas beaten, aye?"

"Aye," came the reply, but it was a weak shout.

Rufra raised his voice further:

"You want Tomas beaten? Aye?" This time the reply from the crowd was much louder. "Good, because there is nothing that would please Tomas more than for us to turn on each other. Do you understand? We must stand together."

"And so you would have us forget Arnst?" This came from the right.

"No!" shouted Rufra. "I would not have you forget any life taken before its time, but this is a matter for the king's justice, do you understand?" There was murmuring in the crowd, a ripple of disquiet passing through them and I felt Rufra's hand on my shoulder. "Do you see this man?" I knew what he was about to do and I wanted to tell him not to. Do not do this, Rufra. My place is not by your side in view of all. My place is the shadows, on the edges of your life, doing the things you do not wish to be seen to do. But it was too late. "This is Girton Club-Foot, and when we were young he solved a murder in Castle Maniyadoc, an impossible murder, a murder where there was no mark on the body, a murder no one believed could be solved. No one!" There was silence again though I was surprised no one could hear the sound of my cheeks burning with embarrassment. "Girton Club-Foot solved that murder! And Girton Club-Foot will find out who killed Arnst. He has the king's trust in this and, I hope, he will have yours." He paused to let the crowd think about what he had said before continuing: "I ask you to trust in me, as you have done before, and to trust in Girton, as I do, for he is a good man. Now go back to your tents and keep the peace."

During Rufra's speech soldiers had slipped into the clearing, and now they moved forward into the crowd, politely assisting those who may not have been quite as willing to leave to change their minds.

"That was well said, Rufra," said Areth.

"It will not hold them for long." He did not look at her

as he spoke. "There will be more deaths over this." He turned to me. "Work quickly, Girton, for all our sakes, or Tomas wins the fight without ever drawing sword."

Rufra then took me to the butcher's hole, a cave in a small hill used to keep meat cool so it did not spoil. It was not a hard place to find for anyone with a nose as the smell of offal and meat fat tarred the air around it. Arnst's corpse was on a wooden table, covered by a dark cloth making the contours of his body a twilit landscape in the gloom.

"You are sure it was murder?" I asked, remembering the body of a boy named Kyril, which had lain on a similar stone slab, unmarred and perfect because he had been killed by magic wielded by my first love, Drusl.

"Quite sure," said Rufra as he pulled away the cloth.

Underneath lay Arnst, though at first glance it was hard to tell. He had been stabbed multiple times, and his stomach had been slashed so fiercely that his entrails had escaped. An attempt had been made to push his guts back in and secure them with a filthy cloth. His killer had also put out Arnst's eyes and, on closer inspection, I found his tongue had been cut out.

"When did this happen?" I asked.

"Yesterday. He was found in the evening in his tent. His man has guarded it ever since so it is not disturbed."

I had not liked Arnst much from our brief meeting but I had not wished death on him. I inspected his hands and found marks where ropes had dug deep into the flesh, rubbing and burning the skin of his wrists as he had fought against them.

"He lived through at least part of this," I said, gesturing at the carnage of his body. "Someone hated him."

"That is the problem, Girton," said Rufra sadly. "Arnst was not an easy man to like. A lot of people had cause to hate him, finding his killer will not be an easy task."

I looked once more at the ruined body.

"Nothing is ever easy."

Chapter 16

The huge Meredari, Danfoth, stood before Arnst's tent as a steady stream of people pinned small scraps of rag to it, as the living often did when mourning those they loved. Danfoth did not pay attention to any of those who approached, and if they talked to him he ignored them, only staring forward with his hand on the hilt of his blade.

"Danfoth," I said, the black face paint around his eyes was scored by the tracks of tears. The Meredari believed a man or woman would be judged by the weight of tears cried for them. "I need to enter Arnst's tent."

He turned his head to me, blond curls shifting in the wind.

"None may enter," he said.

"I have been sent by—"

"None may enter," he said again more forcefully. "The last place of Arnst must not be disturbed. One day many will wish to see where he had his revelations. He was a great man."

"A great murdered man." He stared at me as if I spoke a foreign language.

"He foretold his death, but his words will live on." Danfoth turned his gaze away from me and I decided to try a different tack.

"Danfoth, I understand your respect for Arnst, but Rufra has sent me to investigate his death." I produced the letter but it held no interest for Danfoth.

"It does not matter who did this. Arnst's words will live on and so will he." The Meredari still did not look at me, and I put the letter away.

"Will they live on under Tomas and Neander?" Now Danfoth turned his head back to me. "Because Rufra will allow Arnst's words to live on, but I think we both know Neander will not." His brow creased, and I wondered if he was drugged. There was something in his movements that spoke of the fugue of those whose minds sailed other seas.

"Rufra will triumph over Tomas. Arnst saw this. He said Xus had a plan and Rufra was part of it."

"But if the people do not know who killed Arnst, the camp will tear itself apart, Danfoth, and if that happens Tomas has won." I realised I was talking slowly, as if to someone whose mind was mage-bent.

"Tomas will not win," he said and turned his head from me again.

"What if unmasking his murderer was part of Arnst's plan?" Danfoth turned back to me again. Behind us a quiet stream of people hesitantly pinned more rags to the tent. Some of the Meredari's curls had stuck to the make-up caked onto his face and created greasy whorls between the black and white.

"Touch nothing," he said and stood aside so I could enter, then followed me in.

Danfoth had kept the lamps burning, and once my eyes became accustomed to the gloom I scanned the contents of the tent. It was clear nothing had been disturbed since Arnst's body was removed. Under the chaos and dried blood of a violent death I recognised an ordered mind. Piles of books had been knocked to the floor, falling so they exposed their labelled spines, while on one table stood glasses and bottles – ordered by size and miraculously untouched. Arnst's bed was neatly made, and in the centre of the tent a table and two chairs had stood – now overturned. The carpet sheet was thick with blood, now black, and I knew it would be tacky to the touch. The tent smelled like the butcher's hole.

"Did you hear anything?" I asked Danfoth. It seemed unlikely such violence could have been done without him hearing.

"No." His voice was thick with sorrow. "Arnst had sent me to tour the drinking tents and get the feel of the camp, see how his words were sitting on those who must fight." Odd, I thought, that it was those who must fight that Arnst had been interested in, or maybe it wasn't. Maybe it had only been an excuse to get rid of his guard.

"Did he send you away a lot, Danfoth?"

"I was his right hand. He had many tasks for me." I reached out for a book that lay on the undisturbed table atop another. "No!" Danfoth was in front of me, his hand on his sword. "Those are the words of Arnst and they are not for you." I took my hand away.

"Who are they for, Danfoth?" I asked.

His eyes were very far away, and he was almost lost again. "For those who follow. They are for those who follow him to Xus's dark palace."

"And of those who follow, would any of them hold a grudge against him?"

"Never. He was loved by his followers." His words spoke of surety, but there was something else there, some oblique untruth which I would not pick at now. Danfoth wasn't the most talkative man, I did not think calling him a liar would make him any more forthcoming. I could always return when I had more information to press him with.

"Was he expecting anyone on the night of his death?"

"No. He tells me when he must meet people. Some hate him and he needs protection."

"I think he was meeting someone."

"Why?"

"Two chairs." I pointed at the chairs on the floor, the type that folded up to be put out of the way or easily transported. Then I noticed a sword lying beneath one of the chairs and went to pick it up. Again Danfoth stopped me touching it. "It may belong to who killed him, Danfoth."

He shook his head. "Arnst's possessions are not for you."

I glanced back at the blade. It was a fine piece of work, a solid-looking blade that shone with quality. The hilt was inlaid and carved with scenes from the deaths of Adallada and Dallad, the queen of the gods and her consort. One edge was red with blood.

"You are sure? It is a strange thing for a man who preached the death of gods to own such a blade," I said.

Danfoth nodded.

"Before he was Arnst, he held another name and was one of the high king's guards. That is one of their swords."

"What was his other name?"

"That name is no longer spoken; it is dead."

"So is Arnst. It may be important." I had been too flippant.

Danfoth turned from me.

"You should go," he said. "There is nothing more here for you."

I left but I had plenty to think about. The high king, Darsese, ruled from Ceadoc, though he was a paper king with little real power outside his own castle. Still, Ceadoc itself was rich, being the seat of the the Landsmen's power and where their leader, the Trunk of the Landsmen, sat. It also it held the sepulchres of the dead gods, which attracted pilgrims from all over the Tired Lands. If Arnst had been one of the high king's guard then he would know how to use a blade, so whoever had killed him must surely have been trained to use a blade also. And two chairs. Had Arnst sat peacably with his killer until there was some falling-out? If so it must have been someone he knew. He had sent away his bodyguard to meet whoever this person was, so maybe it was not someone he wished his loyal man to see him meeting. Who could that be?

I decided to look around outside, pushing my way gently

through those still bringing remembrance rags. By Arnst's tent were two others: to the left was a small round tent covered in old, worn leather, its entrance opening on to the clearing in front of Arnst's tent from which an aisle of military tents stretched away. To the right was a drinking tent, though they were usually rowdy places it was quiet now, no noise coming from the closed flaps that acted as doors. I approached the drinking tent first, surprised to find the flaps tied so I had to brush the chimes to get attention.

"We are closed," came the shout of a woman from inside.

"I am not here to drink, I am from the king," I replied. A moment later a hand reached through the flaps and pulled on the ties, undoing them. I slipped through and into the tent, which was spacious, rows of benches set up around long tables, each just wide enough to hold a couple of pots and nothing else, the better to fit more people in.

"I am here about Arnst's murder," I said to the woman, who was compact and chubby-faced with small eyes. One of those lucky people with good skin that makes ageing them hard.

"Well I did not kill him, if that is what you think. His followers supply most of my business."

"But not today?" I waved behind me.

"No. Berit – he is my man – said we should close out of respect for Arnst." She looked like she had found something dead on the table she was cleaning.

"You do not think he deserved respect?"

"He was trouble," she said, "as are plenty of his followers. More than once I've had to get my pig-sticker out." She pointed at a huge boar spear leaning by the barrels at the back of the tent.

"You use that?" I said.

"Aye. Would Berit could wield a weapon as large." She laughed to herself.

"Did you open the night he was killed?"

"I never shut, apart from today –" she stopped cleaning and mopped her brow "– and even then I get no rest as my useless man is off, leaving me with all the work."

"Just you and he run the place?"

"Aye, us and our daughter did." She shrugged. "But a battle camp is no place for a young girl and we found her a better place to be."

"So you are left all the work?" I stepped over to her, took a cloth from her bucket and started to clean a table down. "If I am to ask questions then at least I can pay for them with a little help, eh?"

"Ha!" She grinned. "A useful man? Maybe King Rufra really is changing the world for the better. Ask away. What is your name, useful man?"

"Girton," I said, scrubbing at a particularly stubborn stain. "On the night Arnst died, did you notice anything unusual?"

"We was busy that night," she said. "Always a little busier when the king is away. Plenty of Arnst's followers were in, as is usual, and we had some trouble."

"Oh?"

"Priests," she said. "I was out with the cart getting more perry. Berit could tell you more if he was here but, aye, we had a priest in."

"Is that usual?"

"They do come by, try and get those in here to see the error of their ways, but they don't generally stay long."

"It gets heated?"

"You could say. People been saying Fitchgrass has been stealing women, and the Priests said he was here to calm them. Wrong crowd for a priest to talk about hedgings to. They were practically accusing him of causing it when I left, and Berit had chucked him out by the time I returned."

"Which priest was it?"

"He wore his mask, and I wasn't paying much attention." She stopped scrubbing. "No, wait. Grey robe he was, so one from the healer's. We weren't happy having him here, bringing bad luck. Berit is the one to speak to though."

"When will Berit be back?"

"Who knows? When this work is finished, I imagine, lazy yellower that he is."

I stayed another half-hour helping the woman, Ahild, and left after declining the quarter-bit she offered to pay me for my work. Then I went to the smaller tent, and though the tent flap was untied I brushed my hand against the chimes. A man's face appeared.

"Yes?" He was small, and the hand holding the tent flap back was covered in tiny cuts. I wondered if they had been given by a sword.

"My name is Girton. I am here to look into the death of Arnst for King Rufra." The man seemed to shrink a little.

"You should come in then." He moved back, holding the tent flap open. "My name is Hossit, Blessed," he said with a small bow before catching himself. "Sorry, the new ways are still very new to me." He gave me a nervous smile. I glanced around his tent and smiled back. The reason for the cuts on his hands was obvious now: he was a woodworker, though I noticed a spear stood by his door.

"Are you expecting trouble?" I said, pointing at the weapon.

"Oh no," he said. "Tis a hunting spear and just where I left it. Arnst's followers are no trouble." I nodded, but sometimes a denial may reveal more than is intended, and this man appeared oddly sad or maybe frightened. I picked up a model of a mount, intricately carved, though one of its legs had broken off.

"Your work?"

He nodded. "Yes, made for my son." He pointed to the back of his tent where a young boy, five, six maybe, was playing quietly with some wooden figures in front of a small shrine to the dead god Lessiah.

"It is good workmanship," I said, turning the mount in my hands. "There are just the two of you here?"

"My wife has . . . gone to spend some time with her sister at the castle," he said. "The boy stays with me as he is learning my trade." The boy turned and smiled shyly at me and I wondered if his wife had left him, and that was why he appeared sad. I would intrude upon the man as little as possible. He did not strike me as a killer.

"Did you hear anything on the night Arnst died?"

"Not really," he said, looking at the wooden floor. "The sound of the drinking tent drowns out everything else, and Arnst and his people are generally quiet."

"You are not aware of any visitors he had that night?"

"We keep to ourselves," he said, gesturing at the shrine. "We are not of them."

"So you saw nothing and heard nothing?"

"No." He was turning away when his son spoke:

"There was the hedging, Father. It comes at night."

"Quiet, Dwilan. Girton is the king's man and has no time for your fancies."

"A hedging?"

"A fancy of the child's," said Hossit quickly. "It is a current fascination, nothing else."

"When did you see it, Dwilan?" I said.

"At night. Sometimes I look out of the tent and see him. He steals women – he took mother."

"The boy hears women's rumours and then sees them in dreams," said Hossit, moving in front of his son. "Please do not chastise the boy. His mother has gone and he misses her is all."

"I will not chastise him." I crossed to the boy and knelt, taking a quarter bit from my pouch and putting it in his hand. "Tell me of this hedging." I smiled at him. "I have heard of hedgings but have never seen one, so tell me, was it Dark Ungar you saw?" The boy smiled and shook his head.

"Who then? Coil the Yellower? Or maybe Blue Watta dripping down the path?" I pulled a face and Dwilan laughed.

"No, none of those. Just a field hedging, but not tall and thin like everyone says they are. It was big and strong."

"And how did you know it was a hedging? Was he made of prickles, or road dust and spit?"

More laughter.

"No, it looked just like a man wearing a cloak."

"Then how did you know he was a hedging?"

"Because I saw him on the night Gildera vanished. She used to live in the tent opposite. The wind lifted his cloak, and underneath his skin was green just like a field hedging's is in a story."

"Green skin?" He nodded. "Thank you, Dwilan. I must leave now, but if you remember anything else then please find me." I turned to the boy's father. "Thank you for your time, Hossit." He showed me out, and there was little doubt he was glad to see me go.

Danfoth watched as I walked away up the aisle of military tents, inspecting the back of each in case it had been slit to allow someone through. I found nothing more than the usual small patches and fixes any tent has. From the length of the grasses around the tents they had all been there for weeks, and in truth I did not expect to find anything. This was not a killer who sneaked in and out; this murderer was brazen.

The boy had spoken of a hedging with green skin, and his father did not believe him, but I did, in a way. A murderous hedge spirit made no sense, but in the night and to a small boy a man wearing a cloak over green armour might easily be mistaken for a monster. The Landsmen wore green and had cause to hate a man like Arnst, who preached the death of the gods they served. And they were formidable warriors, trained as well, if not better, than the men who guarded the high king at Ceadoc.

And if I was honest, nothing would give me more pleasure

than to see a Landsman join the desolate to bleed out for murder.

Dusk was falling as I made my way back to our tent. I noticed in the distance a fuzzy glow in the sky. At first I thought it was fire and a chill passed through me – fire in a camp like this would be deadly – but there were no shouts on the wind so I made my way towards the light. I heard laughter and the buzz of conversation; nearer I heard the shrieks of children, and a huge plume of flame shot into the darkening purple of the sky. It was a night market. Night markets were a common feature of the Tired Lands. During the day many were too busy trying to scratch a living to look at stalls, so markets always set up at night at least once before moving on. In a military camp a night market made even more sense, as during the day most of the troops would be training or on duty; at night they liked to carouse and spend their wages.

I entered the night market and recognised that, just as the Landsmen had a small enclave in the camp, so did Festival. Figures wrapped in triangular cloaks stood behind stalls laden with wares, though I noticed the food stalls were sadly depleted. Traders shouted out what they offered in sing-song, overlapping voices.

"Pots, pots, buy my fine pots."

"Plays and stories, ancient voices."

"Rags, rags, many-coloured rags."

"Toys and treats, good to meet."

"Plays and stories, ancient voices."

"Toys and treats, good to meet."

"Pots, pots, buy my fine pots."

I reached into my pouch and took out the doxy leaf, rubbing it between my fingers. If the yandil my master needed was to be found anywhere it would be found here. I still felt angry with Mastal but I was not sure why. My master was not celibate and took lovers, but they were casual, and she rarely seemed to take much joy in their company. Something about the way she had laughed with Mastal though, it felt different. Was that the root of my anger? Was I really just a jealous child?

Maybe.

But it felt wrong. Something about him felt wrong, though I could not put my finger on it. Had Aydor sent him to distract me? Was that Mastal's purpose? To give me something else to think about while he cause turmoil in Rufra's camp? On to land me in a Landsman's gibbet, buying his hedge-cursed leaves?

I approached a pot seller, the stall decked out with straw hobby dolls, and glanced over the teetering piles of bowls made from pale clay. At the back of the stall were signing bowls, made so thin you could almost see through them.

"A bowl, boy, or a pot to piss in?"

"I can afford neither." Behind his mask of corn stalks I could not tell if the trader was disappointed or amused by me. Those of Festival often saw the world differently to the rest of us. "Is there a herb dealer in this night market?"

"Aye." He may have nodded but his stiff robes made it impossible to tell. "Up past the weapons seller and right at the courtesans." I thanked him and moved further into the market. A troupe was performing *Elit, Who Scorned the Gods and became Dark Ungar*, and a crowd had gathered around them, jeering and whooping at the dancer playing Elit. He was no great talent and a part of me itched to push him aside and show the crowd how such a dance should be done.

"Bread, bread, soft as your head."

I paused at the weapons seller, inspecting her wares, stabswords and longswords, knives and axes. I picked up a hand axe, hefting it and getting a feel for the way it swung.

"That is a good blade," said the stallholder, a woman bigger and more muscular than I was. "Good size for you, boy – better than that thing at your side." She pointed at the warhammer.

"I'm not so sure." I tipped the axe so I could see where the head was attached to the wooden handle and spotted a telltale pattern of tiny pits. "I suspect this may break the first time I try and cut butter with it."

"Ha!" She laughed, an explosive, certain sound. "This boy knows his blades then. Ha!" She leaned forward to whisper, "Ignore what is on show in front, boy, look at what is behind." I glanced up, enjoying conversation with one who recognised my worth. Along the back of her stall she had a few blades that were much better, as well as a selection of knives, including the strangely curved knives the Landsmen used to cut their symbols into those who practised magic. They sent a shudder through me and my desire for conversation suddenly died.

"Thank you, madame stallholder," I said, "but I cannot afford such wares." She waved me off with a friendly gesture.

"Juices, juices, sweet and good."

I passed the courtesans. A man and woman stood, stock still, oiled and almost naked on either side of a large tent. A tall thin man who wore antlers made of twig and spiralled bands of hard bread around his arms served as howler, shouting out his delights.

"You boy –" he pointed at me "– carrier of a mighty weapon, I see, come do battle in the tent. Enjoy the cut –" he leered at me "– or thrust of our beautiful courtesans . . ." I walked past, ignoring him, as I had learned that to talk to howlers only invited embarrassment. Around the corner I ran into Rufra's healer.

"Tarris," I said, "have you been to the herb seller?"

"I would not touch her wares," the priest said, and I sensed venom, even through his mask and modulated voice. "Festival is rife with ills, a bed for hedgings and hungers." The courtesan's howler approached but went in search of easier prey when he saw Tarris. "Is your master dead yet?"

"No," I said, "in fact she is awake now. I go to see her

when I am finished here. Would you like to come and wish her well?" I said guilelessly, unable to resist the jibe.

"Why would I do that?" He seemed genuinely puzzled, though it was always hard to tell with a priest.

"Did you hear about Arnst?"

"Aye, murder is a terrible thing." He did not sound like he thought it was that terrible. "But I must wonder if Xus the god of death acted to protect himself from desecration. Arnst was nothing but a danger to all."

"Did you know anything of him?"

"As little as I could manage," he hissed. "Now I must go." He pushed past me, and I watched him go before carrying on to the herb seller. A priest in a grey robe had been in the drinking tent. Tarris or one of his acolytes?

"Flesh, offal, bone and caul, all that lives to Xus must fall."

The herb seller was situated next to a butcher whose wares were so rank that the stink would scare away a yellower. Nonetheless, a steady stream of ragged and starved-looking people took away cloth wrapped parcels of dripping meat. I turned my back on his stall and tried my best not to breathe in through my nose.

The herb woman was old, old in a way not often seen in the Tired Lands. Her long white hair looked like untreated sheep's wool and her face was deeply lined, washed-out cataract-pale eyes stared out from parchment paper-thin skin. I held out the doxy leaf to her, and the hand she used to take it was more like a bundle of twigs, its joints huge and swollen with age's kiss.

"Doxy," she said quietly. "I have plenty of doxy if you wish, boy, but much cheaper for you to go pick your own – it is common enough around the paddocks."

"I do not seek doxy leaf," I said, "but a leaf that looks like it and is called yandil."

She looked at me, and I wondered if she were deaf, but

before I could repeat my words she spoke again, drawing out the word so it sounded like a yawn: "Yandil."

"Aye. It is rare, I know, but—"

"You will not find yandil here, boy," she said, her voice much stronger. "If you are here on the say of the white tree and its green Riders then begone. I have work to do." She turned away and resumed grinding something up in a small mortar and pestle.

"I am here on no one's say so but my own," I said, "and I seek the yandil for—"

She turned back to me, leaning over her stall and her voice was harsh, discordant with fear.

"Get away, boy, and do not mention the name of that herb again. The Landsmen are ever eager to fill their gibbets and even talk of yandil will find you a home in one. Now go, before you bring a hunger down on us both." She brought the tips of her thumb and fingers together and touched her nose and mouth as I had often seen people do to ward off hedgings, and then gestured with her head, making it clear she wanted me gone. Dejected, I turned, only then noticing that the butcher was staring at me, his muscles tensed and a cleaver that dripped rancid meat juices held loosely in his hand. There was no help here. I left, feeling like the darkness was closing in on me. At the edge of the night market I heard my name called.

"Girton!"

I recognised the voice immediately, a sound like a flaming torch.

"Areth, what do you do here?" It seemed strange that a queen should walk unescorted among her people. "Is it safe for you to walk alone?"

"I believe in Rufra's accord, and these are my people, Girton." She swept a hand around, gesturing at the market.

"Just because the assassins are not killing does not mean others may not. Arnst is dead and any fool can wield a knife.

Rufra is lax with his Heartblades too," I said, more to myself than to Areth.

"Yes," she said, and linked her arm through mine, making my heart leap in a way as joyous as it was uncomfortable. "Because it would never occur to him to send a common man to kill Tomas he thinks that Tomas will act in a similar fashion." Her voice became cold: "He is a fool in many ways."

"No," I said, and unlinked my arm from hers. "Rufra is no fool; it is only that he wishes to see the best in us all. It is to be admired."

"What use is admiration to a dead man?" she said, and then she softened. "You will watch for him, won't you, Girton?"

I nodded.

"Is it safe for you here, Areth? You are the queen. I would have expected people to mob you with their grievances."

"They would have, once," she said, "but now they are used to seeing me here, and besides –" she looked away into the dark and I thought I saw the sparkle of held-back tears in the torchlight "– everyone here has lost someone. They respect grief."

I did not know what to say, settling for a question instead of a consolation."Why are you here?"

"It is easier to be among people," she said. "Sometimes, at night, I close my eyes and see the face of Arnlath as he died, so thin, his skin grey, his breath . . . his breath . . ." I saw her gather herself, push the grief down so she could carry on. "I do not think his death was natural, Girton. He was such a strong child, so full of life. So I walk the camp. I put everything I have into hearing what is said of him in case some word is said that may lead me to how he truly died."

"And what do you hear?"

"He was loved. He is missed. It seems every woman in the camp looked upon him as they would their own child. I walk the markets and hear them talk. I sit and I listen for the barest mention of his name."

"I wish I had been here, Areth," I said. "If it was poison, maybe I could have . . ."

"Or maybe it was only a sickness." She shook her head, forcing a smile onto her face. "And why are you here, Girton Club-Foot? I mean in the market, not the camp."

"Seeking a herb," I said and took the leaf from my pouch.

"Doxy?" She laughed. "Someone has been tricking you. It's little better than useless. You should pick it from the fields and do the farmers a favour – doxy will take over the fields given half a chance."

"No, I do not seek doxy but a herb which looks much like it called—"

She put a finger on my lips, and her touch kindled a fire within.

"Do not say its name," she said. "I know what you seek."

"How?"

"I left no stone unturned when Arnlath was sick, no medicine untried. Come with me."

She led me back to the herb woman and her guard, the rancid meat seller.

"Irille," she said, "this is Girton."

"We met." She did not sound overly enthused about renewing my acquaintance.

"Girton is a friend of mine, Irille," she said. "It would be good if you could help him."

The old woman turned back to me and looked me up and down.

"You are sure, Areth?"

"Absolutely."

"Very well." She vanished into the tent behind her stall and after a minute or so of banging about within returned holding a sheaf of leaves wrapped in rags. "Here." She thrust them at me.

"How much?" I said, reaching for my pouch.

"It is not the sort of thing we take money for," she said. "Just leave before you draw attention to me."

"Thank you," I said.

"I hope it helps," said Areth as we walked away. "Rufra tells wonderful stories of your master."

"She is wonderful, mostly. But strict."

"Maybe she should marry Nywulf – they sound like a matched pair." She smiled at me, and talk of my master led me to thoughts of Mastal.

"Areth, you know the people of the market well?" She nodded. "Is there anyone who knows languages?"

Her brow furrowed, and she rubbed at the crease between her eyes. There was something breathtaking in it, a simplicity of movement that made me skip a breath. "Bowan the Toymaker. He has been all around the Tired Lands and beyond and delights in books. If anyone knows languages it is him. Why?"

"Nothing. Just something I was curious about. It has nothing to do with Rufra."

She shrugged and pointed towards the far corner of the night market.

"He has a tent over there. You should find him at work if you hurry."

"Thank you, Areth."

I hurried to the toymaker's tent, my club foot had started to ache and my limp became more pronounced with every step. Outside the tent hung hobby dolls, many of straw and some of bulljuice, the kind used by children to play with rather than to keep hedgings away. More bulljuice toys hung from the top of the tent like so many corpses, sickly white limbs bent into a strange shapes, painted faces seeming to mock me. Inside, Bowan was busy and the sweet and sickly smell of bulljuice, like over-fermented perry, filled the tent as he crouched over his moulds. He used an animal bladder, its end tied around a stick of hauntgrass. He pushed the hauntgrass into a mould, glanced over his shoulder at me and nodded.

"The trick," he said, "for bulljuice dolls is to get the juice right to the bottom of the mould and fill them quickly, or the juice will set." He imparted this with the air of a man sharing a great secret, irritating me almost immediately. Before I could reply, he turned away, squeezing the bladder between his arm and his body, slowly drawing it out of the mould. "Smoothly, see. Fill the entire thing."

"Don't let me disturb you – I can wait," I said, and he took me at my word, carrying on with his work. He was much younger than I expected, late twenties maybe, and he had shaved his head bald, exposing ears that were too large for his head. Which was a strange shape. When he had finished he put down the bladder extremely carefully, as if it were fine white bread. Two more bladders hung from the cross-poles of his tent, tightly tied with twine from which lengths of haunt-grass dangled.

"I must, of course, work quickly," he said, taking down another bladder. "The bulljuice does not keep long." He set about his next set of moulds, again, as if I were not there.

"How quickly does it dry?" I said as he put down the second bladder.

"Almost instantly when it's out the bladder." He pulled a doll from his first set of moulds, a ghostly white, faceless figure ready to be painted. It looked like something from a nightmare, a man made of maggots, but it gave me an idea.

"How much is one of your bladders of bulljuice worth?" He screwed up his eyes, blinked twice. "An odd question," he said. "Let me think." He thought. For too long. "A bladder makes four dolls, and each doll is a quarter of a bit." He thought again and I was about to do the maths for him when he held up a finger. "Two bits."

"Are you afraid of the dead?" I said.

"Who can live in the Tired Lands and be afraid of the dead?" He smiled, managing to look pleased with himself and slightly tired of me, then he wiped bulljuice from his hands. "Why?"

"Come with me," I said, "and bring your last bulljuice bladder." He frowned and opened his mouth to argue, but I headed him off. "I will pay you three bits, up front." I held out the money and the toymaker grinned at me.

"Well, only a fool turns down a certain coin." He took the remaining bladder from its hook. "Lead me to these dead then."

As we walked to the butcher's hole Bowan chatted about himself. He was not interested in me, and when I asked about his travels he talked at length about them. At no point did he ask my name. I tried to hurry him a little, but he said the bulljuice did not spoil that quickly in the bladder, as if this were something everyone knew.

"I have heard you know languages. Maybe you could translate something for me, if we have time?" I asked.

"Of course," he said. "It is always a joy to school someone."

I took the papers I had copied from Mastal's packs from my jerkin and passed them to him. He paused under a torch, studying them in the light and I almost found myself hoping he would not understand them.

"This is the language of the Slight Hills, though they hate it when we call them that."

"Do you understand it though?"

He squinted at the paper. "This is a copy," he said.

"Yes, it is." He glanced at me then nodded and went back to the paper.

"It is not a very good one."

"It is quite exact." He looked at me again.

"Maybe the original was written by someone with poor handwriting then," he said. "I am not overly familiar with the language of the Sighing Hills, but I think this is a list."

"Of what?"

"People." My insides twitched.

"People?"

"I think so. There are quite a few." He brought the paper

closer to his face. "Here it says, 'Comhyn, who went to . . .'" he paused, peered "'war' I think it says, and then it may refer to a place but I am not sure. And after that is an offer of three sheep. The next one says—"

"How many names are there?"

"Hokhyn, Histal, Jaada, Medula—"

"Wait!" He looked up, blinked twice.

"Where it says Medula, are you sure of what it says?"

"As I said, the letterwork is not the best—"

"Could it say Merela?"

He furrowed his brow and looked again. "I suppose, in fact, yes, I think it does." He shrugged. "But as I said, the penmanship is—"

"What does it say afterwards?"

He rubbed his left eye. "'Daughter, went to far lands with her family to trade many years ago.'"

"Daughter?"

"They use it the same way we use 'woman'," he said. "She is worth knowing, this Medula."

"She is?"

"Her family offer fifty times her weight in flour for her return."

Now Mastal made sense. He hunted people for reward. And a reward that large would tempt any in the Tired Lands.

My immediate instinct was to kill him, but I needed him to treat my master, at least until I could work out how to do it myself. But now I had the advantage. I knew why he was here, what he wanted and that his friendly demeanour was a sham. How many others had he fooled in the same way?

"If you have a purpose for this bulljuice," said the toymaker, "we should hurry or it will harden." We walked the rest of the way to the butcher's hole and I explained that I wanted him to inject his bulljuice into a wound on Arnst's thigh so I would have an impression of the knife that had made the wound. The thigh was a good place, all muscle, and it would hold the shape of the blade. When Bowan saw the body he turned a strange shade of green, and when I held the wound open so he could insert the hauntgrass straw he had to go outside to vomit. Thankfully, after that he no longer spoke and simply got on with the job.

An hour and several more false starts later, I returned to the tent I shared with my master, flushed with triumph. I paused as I approached. Light shone through the felt and I could hear laughter inside again. I stood outside, strangely unwilling to enter. The laughter sounded so real, my master so happy. Crast materialised, seemingly out of thin air, by my side. Making me jump.

"Evening, Girton," he said. "Come to join the party?" He gestured with his thumb at the tent.

"I'm not sure I'm invited," I said.

"Wish I was." He shrugged. "Sounds like they've been having a right old time, laughing all afternoon. They even had a boy bring them food and perry." He rubbed at his running nose with a sleeve. "I keep expecting them to start humping." His words slowed to a trickle and dried up at the look on my face. "Sorry," he said. "Didn't mean to make you uncomfortable."

"I'm not," I said, but I don't think either of us believed it. Crast raised an eyebrow and suddenly I found myself laughing. Something about Crast reminded me of me before I went off to fight in other lands. He had an irreverence, though underlying it was something else, something darker, but this was a land at war and everyone was scarred by it.

We were interrupted by Mastal.

"Crast," he said, "I must speak to Girton alone."

"Welcoming as always, Mastal," said Crast, and stepped back into the darkness.

"What?" I said. It came out as a harsh bark.

"I know it is difficult for you," said Mastal softly, "and I spoke in anger when last we discussed this, but if I am to make your master well we must leave for the Sighing Mountains soon. If you could talk to the king about transport, then—"

"I need to speak to my master first."

"Very well." He dipped his head. "I am glad you are ready to discuss this like an adult." I nodded, not wishing to speak to him in case I said something cutting. In my pouch the package of yandil weighed heavy, but I did not mention it – he could not have expected me to find so much so quickly. Instead I watched while Mastal walked away into the night.

Inside the tent I found my master bright-eyed and healthy-looking, almost herself again. She was dressed and sitting on the edge of her bed.

"An eventful day, Girton?"

"Yes, Master."

"But you still wear that at your hip?"

I looked down at the warhammer.

"I had an idea about Arnst's murder." I went into my pouch, pushing aside the package of yandil leaves and bringing out a white and red shape. "In fact I think I have solved it."

"What is that?"

"Bulljuice, Master. I poured it into one of the knife wounds on Arnst's body and look." I held up the shape the bulljuice had become. It was not obvious what it was at first. Still smeared with blood in places, it looked a bloody fried egg missing the yolk and ragged edged. My master reached out and touched it, her eyes following the lumps and bumps, and then she touched the raised parts, looked a little closer. Smiled.

"The knife that made this wound," she said, "was not straight. It had a kink about halfway down, which is why the bulljuice mould is this strange shape, A normal knife would leave straighter edges."

"Yes."

"Arnst was killed with a Landsman's knife," she said. "That was a clever thing to do, Girton."

"Aye." I smiled at her. "And it puts the noose around the Landsman Karrick Thessan's neck, doesn't it?"

"You are very quick to assign blame, Girton," she said, and I felt a withering inside that in turn fed an ember of anger.

"Not at all. I spoke to a boy who saw a man in green. And Karrick left Rufra's patrol early, coming back the night Arnst was killed, so he would have been here. And now I know his knife was used to kill—"

"His knife? He is not the only Landsman in the camp, Girton, and those knives, though uncommon, are not impossible to get hold of. Have you considered who else may have wanted Arnst dead?"

I felt deflated, and angry, that she would pull down what I had achieved rather than help. I almost blurted out what Mastal was up to, just to see her face when she found out what her new man really wanted.

Be careful

That voice, the magic – I had not heard it for so long but it was right. She had family in the Sighing Mountains. What if, when she found out, she wanted to go to them?

To leave you.

I bit down on the harsh words and put them to the back of my mind.

"You always say it is a fool that climbs a wall when there are stairs, Master."

"And it is a fool that uses stairs without checking whether or not they are guarded, Girton. I do not say it is not the Landsman; I only say that you do not appear to have considered any other, and that you may want it to be a Landsman because you do not like them."

"They are killers. All of them. You hate them too."

"I would wipe them from the Tired Lands, Girton, but consider that if you misstep you let a real killer walk free, and that may leave your friend in danger. Be thorough." I wanted to say something that would show her how wrong she was but could think of nothing. "I am very tired, Girton," she said. "I should sleep."

"Do that then." I stood, and as I left she blew out the light.

Annoyed with my master, and myself, I found the largest drinking tent in the camp, a place I could lose myself among Rufra's troops and a place where I could sit alone and know no one would bother me – soldiers understand the need to be alone. The tent was loud, but I found a dark corner at the end of one of the long tables that ran the length of it and there I nursed a cup of watered perry and a bellyful of resentment. Unconsciously, I ran my hand under the edge of the table and found an old inscription in assassins' scratch, some of the words missing through age.

Captain Sarand steals from -- who can ill affo-d it. 5 bits is all -- can muster. -- is a worthy task/ CS steals no m--
Gostis

Someone sat down beside me.

"I wish for my own company tonight," I said.

"A pity," said the man as he placed a pot of perry in front of me. "I wished to thank you for speaking up when Boros found us." I glanced up. It was Thian, Aydor's captain.

"Aydor has entered camp then?"

"Aye. Rufra thought it best we enter camp quietly after what has happened. He wanted no more upset."

"If you have come here to plead your king's cause then you may as well talk to the stones of Maniyadoc."

"No," said Thian. "Aydor told me some of what went on

between you though . . ." He let the words die and, despite knowing he was playing me, I kept my gaze on him and waited for him to continue. "Well, in truth I do not recognise the man I serve in the stories he tells of himself as a child."

"He was not a child," I said. Thian had no reply to that.

"I also thought you may want to know that . . ." He did not finish. A silence fell in the tent as Aydor walked in. There was no mistaking him, his bulk filled the entrance to the tent. I was surprised to see he was alone and wondered whether Thian had been sent into the tent with a few of his men to make sure he would be safe. I noticed, as Aydor stood in the doorway surveying the room, that he wore twinned stabswords rather than a longsword and stabsword.

"Why does he wear two stabswords?" I said to Thian, who looked at me as if I were a fool.

"You really do not know?" Before I could answer, a soldier stood up at a table near the door. "You are not welcome here."

"But I am here," said Aydor, full of the belligerence I remembered. "And I am here at the invite of your king."

Now we see the yellower's real colours, I thought.

"Well, Fat Bear," said the soldier, "you can leave by the invite of his army, with my boot up your arse if needs be."

Aydor stared at the man, his tongue exploring the gaps between his teeth. The tension in the tent rose, people shifted, breath was held.

"You have small boots," he said, "and I have a large arse. You might get lost up there if you're not careful."

A spattering of laughter across the room – which the soldier silenced with a glare.

"You are not welcome here, Aydor ap Mennix," he said quietly and slid his stabsword from his belt. "Do you understand me?"

"Are you offering to duel me?" said Aydor.

"I would, happily." I believed the man, he had the air of

one who had fought his whole life and had no fear of another's blade. "But a living man cannot duel a king, eh?"

"True, said Aydor. "But now we have Rufra's new ways, eh? All are equal. So –" he pulled himself to his full height, which even I had to admit was impressive "– I accept your challenge." The soldier looked surprised.

I made to stand, but Thian pulled me back down. "Wait."

"Rufra's camp is already on a knife edge over the murder of Arnst, Thian. If Aydor kills one of Rufra's troops there will be carnage."

"Just give him a moment, Girton. As I said, he is not the man you knew."

"Then let us go outside, Aydor," said the soldier.

"Yes." Aydor nodded slowly then held a finger to his forehead as if remembering something. "Forgive me, but what is your name?" He sounded as if he had not a care in the world. "If I am to duel a man I should at least know his name."

"I am Bonal," said the soldier.

"Well, I have not actually duelled before, Bonal, but as I understand duelling, it is the one who suffered the insult who gets to choose the weapon?"

The silence in the tent was utter.

"Aye," said Bonal. Someone moved and the creak of their leather armour filled the room.

"Well," said Aydor, "it was you called me a fat bear."

"I did. What of it, Fat Bear?"

"So I get to choose the weapon?" Bonal crumpled his brow, searching for some sort of trick, and then nodded. Aydor scanned the room, meeting the hostile gazes of the men and women around him. "You are not the only one who hates me here, Bonal," he said and looked straight at me, finding my shadow in the edges of the tent. "There are many deaths between myself and Rufra's men, and I would have all hostility end here –" he raised his voice "– so I will duel you all. Every single man and woman in here. One at a time or all at once, I do not care." There was a massed intake of breath, and I thought again, here it is, the arrogance I expect of Aydor ap Mennix. He reached out to the table in front of him, closed his meaty fist around a drinking pot and held it up. "This is my weapon," he shouted, holding it in the air, "and we will fight to the last one standing!"

"We fight with pots?" said Bonal, who was clearly puzzled and possibly not the greatest intellect in Rufra's army.

"No, we shall fight with drink," said Aydor. "Potwoman," he shouted, "I will pay for every drink poured tonight, and mind you keep the pots filled. The last one standing wins the duel." He stood on a table, which creaked under his weight, and raised his voice further – he was already half drunk. "We have all lost friends in this war. I have taken yours and you have taken mine. We will remember those lost, we will put aside old hatreds and come together for King Rufra!" He thrust his stolen pot into the air, spilling perry all over himself, and to my shock his speech was met with a massed shout of "Aye!"

Aydor carried on: "We will drink! Drink to the fallen! And we will make new friendships, forge new bonds! And maybe when tonight ends you will no longer hate me, but . . ." He left the word hanging, and the friendly atmosphere he had been building started to peter out as Aydor squinted around the room. "In the morning," he said quietly, a grin spreading across his face, "you will call me Aydor Headsourer –" he raised his voice again "– and all will hate me anew!" With that he fell backwards off the table and onto the floor in a crash of armour and the place exploded into laughter. Some of Aydor's men started to enter the tent and Rufra's soldiers greeted them as if they were old friends.

"See," said Thian. "He is not the man you remember."

No, I thought as I got up to leave, he is far more dangerous than the Aydor I knew ever was.

I slipped out of the tent. Outside, more of Aydor's men were milling about, still unsure of the welcome they would receive within. Something caught my eye, or rather someone. A man was hurrying away and trying to do so without me seeing him – he would have done better to stay still and I may have simply walked past. But he did not, so I wandered back through the camp, wondering what Gabran the Smith, who had tried to avoid any mention of Aydor in the patrol camp, had been doing with his troops outside the drinking tent.

Back in our tent I lay in my cot thinking the day through. Mastal had moved his cot nearer to my master, and from where I lay it looked like the two were abed together. I took the doxy leaf from my pouch, then took out a yandil leaf and compared them, then glanced over at my master and Mastal, then back at the leaves. Both looked similar, but one was special, unique, while the other, what had Areth said about doxy? "It's little better than useless . . . and will take over given half a chance."

I can make everything better.

I hatched a plan.

Chapter 17

What my master had said about me not being thorough enough haunted me in the darkness, chasing all sleep away. That or thoughts of Mastal, leading her away under false pretences to claim a reward. I was sure Karrick was my murderer, but now I had seen Gabran acting suspiciously it would be wrong not to check on him, just in case. So if I could not sleep then I would put the night to good use. I would break into Gabran's tent, and he and I would have words about betrayal.

The camp in the deep of night was a different place. I could still hear the echoes of the night market, though from the height of the moon it should be near to closing. That aside the only noises were the "Huts" and "Ayts" of the perimeter guards and the unnerving cooing and trilling of night lizards. It was cold too. Until the Birthstorm broke, the weather would not settle and nights were often freezing. Cold air danced along the scars on my skin, lifting the hairs on my arms and sending uncontrollable shivers down my body. I had to wait, crouching still and letting myself become accustomed to the temperature of the night to regain control. That done, I set out

Gabran's tent was far over on the other side of the camp in the smiths' enclosure. Even in the middle of the night the smiths still worked and the sound of hammers on anvils rang out. Gabran's tent was easy to find: his flags hung outside and he did not bother with a guard. I slid into his tent, which was basic, the tent of a man who was always ready to move on. It contained nothing expensive or personal and the furniture was the same general camp stock as would be found in any trooper's tent. All in all it fitted Gabran's personality. This was what he had known all his life, and this was what he was comfortable with. He slept curled up on his side under a thin blanket on a camp bed. I approached quietly, sliding my Conwy blade from its sheath. When I was close to him I leaned over and placed the blade against his throat.

He woke immediately.

"Gabran," I whispered, "let's talk about lying yellowers." He opened his mouth and I shook my head. "No shouting, no calling for help or I leave a corpse in your bed, you understand?" He nodded. "Good. Now, Gabran, you were quick to tell me your thoughts on traitors and how you were not one, so you can imagine my surprise when I saw you sneaking away from Aydor's troops."

"I was simply passing," he said and swallowed. His neck pressed against the blade of my knife and a thin red line of blood welled up.

I leaned in close.

"Lie to me again, Gabran, and I will prove to you what a yellower I can be. Understand?"

He smiled then, which was unexpected.

"You're a clever one. Rufra is right to trust you."

"But is he right to trust you? What are you up to? What is Aydor up to?"

"I don't know what—" I pushed the blade a little harder against his neck and he raised an arm, not in threat, simply to tell me he was not finished. "Truth! Absolute truth!" I slackened the pressure on the blade. "I have no idea why Aydor has come here, and I counselled Rufra against allowing it."

"So you know he cannot be trusted," I said. I saw the start of a lie in him then. I saw the idea he could feed me what I wanted to hear move over his face. Then I saw it leave, saw him decide to tell me the truth.

"No, I don't know that, not at all. My reasons for not wanting Aydor here were selfish, that is all. That is why I was there. I went to see him."

"Explain."

"One night," he said, "Aydor was allowed to take out a patrol and—"

"He got lost, ran into Rufra."

"You know about this?" I nodded. "Right. Well I was with him, acting as his second in command. I'd never met Aydor before that night. I was only a lowly troop leader, only ever seen him pass on his mount, but even though the yellower couldn't read a map to save his life he was all right – a drunk, but all right. I thought I could serve him until I saw Rufra. Then I knew I was wrong. Knew who I wanted to fight for after that. So after we made it back, I ran. I didn't care about rank, I just wanted to serve Rufra in some way."

"But you knew Aydor would recognise you."

"Aye. And me having been close to Aydor, one of his troop leaders, well, it would make me look bad, wouldn't it? Especially with talk of a spy about. So I went to beg for his silence."

I waited, staring into his face, looking for any hint of deception, finding nothing.

"And what did he want for his silence?" I removed the blade from his neck. What he had said made sense and he wasn't a good liar, or a comfortable one. Telling the truth seemed like it had taken a weight from his shoulders.

"That's the weird thing – he didn't want anything. Made like he didn't know who I was."

"Aydor did? Could he have forgotten you?"

"He was drunk but not that drunk. I thought we were going to die when Rufra appeared on that ridge and I can remember the face of everyone with us, like they were my own brothers and sisters."

"Aydor set you free."

He nodded. "He's still a yellower though."

"You should tell Rufra," I said. "And if you don't, I will. So when Aydor eventually does want some favour from you, and he will, he will have nothing to use against you."

"I'll tell him," said Gabran. "You know, you're a right yellower, you are. You might be the worst of 'em all –" he spat "– but I'm glad you're our yellower."

I left Gabran's tent more confused than ever. What was Aydor playing at?

Chapter 18

In the morning I woke early, washed and left the tent before either my master or Mastal could speak to me.

"Crast? Neliu?" I called. Somewhere a lizard trilled a fluting plea for the sun to rise.

"Girton." Neliu appeared by my side, and I shivered in the cold of the yearsbirth morning.

"Where is Nywulf? I want to get some practice in with my blades."

"And Nywulf chooses this day to put me on as guard for the invalid." She smiled, twisting a lock of fire-red hair around her finger. I was glad she was thawing towards me a little. "Crast will be training with Nywulf now. If you hurry you may catch them. I train in the evening, if you fancy a real challenge."

"I may," I said. "And my master improves, so maybe soon you will not be stuck outside a tent all day."

Neliu nodded. "They plan to take a walk today, when the sun is at its zenith. The foreigner says the sun's heat will give her strength." She shrugged. "He seems to know what he's talking about."

"Maybe he does." I did not want to talk about Mastal. "I will talk to Nywulf about letting you away when I am here. We do not need a guard then."

"I'm sure you don't," she said, but it didn't sound like she believed me.

I jogged over to the training ground, my feet guided by the thud of wooden training swords coming together and the voices of officers drilling troops. A number of fields had been set aside, and the soldiers' feet had turned the ground to mud through hours and days and weeks of training. I found Nywulf and Crast easily enough. Rufra's flying lizard flag fluttered above them, and the king watched as the two sparred gently, warming up. By the king stood the Landsman, Karrick.

". . . he is barely a man," said the Landsman as I approached. I felt my temper rising until I realised he spoke of Crast, not me.

"But you have seen how he fights."

"Aye," said Karrick. "What Nywulf has done with those two astounds me."

"They are almost as terrifying as Girton was," said Rufra.

"Is," I said. Rufra turned, momentarily abashed at being overheard before grinning at me.

"Rufra has said you are a great bladesman," said Karrick, and as he spoke his gaze strayed to my clubbed foot. I felt his disdain even if it did not show on his face.

"Do not be deceived by Girton's small stature," said Rufra. "I have never seen the like of him with a blade, though I've not seen him fight recently and would never have thought a warhammer his weapon."

"It is now," I said.

"I imagine a warhammer slows you some," said Karrick.

"I'm fast enough to stay alive." My words were sharp and Karrick looked wounded by them.

"I see age has not made you any happier in the mornings, Girton," Rufra clapped me on the back. "Don't let him rile you, Karrick. Girton has always been a little spiky."

"If he is a little spiky, maybe a mace would be a better weapon."

Karrick and Rufra laughed. I did not join in, and their laughter soon died away.

"Are you here to spar, Girton?" asked Karrick, and I nodded, letting my hand fall to the hilt of the warhammer.

"I have neglected my work with blades, and my master would have me practise. But if you wish to test my skill with the hammer, feel free, Karrick. You would not be the first Landsman to question my skill." I smiled at him but it was not a friendly smile.

"Sadly," said Karrick, "I have injured myself." He touched his arm.

I remembered the bloodied sword on Arnst's floor.

"Someone caught you with a blade, Landsman? But you did not see action with Rufra." I held his gaze.

"A sparring injury, nothing more." I was sure he lied. "But if you really feel you must—"

"How is your master?" interrupted Rufra.

"Better." I kept my eyes locked on Karrick's. He was a Landsman, a killer, and he had a wound he could not account for. He had looked oddly hurt by my tone, and I realised how strange my hostility must appear to Rufra when he did not know I believed the man a murderer. I wanted to tell Rufra what I knew but could not, not yet. I had the cast of a Landsman's blade, but I wanted more and did not want to say anything in front of Karrick.

"I think I should leave," said the Landsman.

"You do that," I said.

"There is no need," said Rufra, moving between me and Karrick.

"It is no problem," he said. "I told Gabran I would help him drill the infantry, and they are strangely sluggish this morning."

Rufra watched him walk away.

"That was not well done, Girton," he said.

"I cannot believe you have let a Landsman onto your council. You say you want a fairer land, but they murder with impunity and—"

"What they do is necessary, Girton." Something in me tightened. "It is not murder to end a sorcerer – they are a greater danger than even Tomas. You have seen the sourings, more of them than most, I reckon. What the Landsmen do is unpleasant but necessary, and besides –" his voice dropped a little "– if I offend them they may ally with Tomas, and I cannot afford that."

"So you make a deal with the smaller hedging?"

"In a way, but Karrick is a good man."

"I'm sure that is what men say of Dark Ungar until they find themselves shatter-spirits."

"Girton, you must try and learn some diplomacy."

"He killed Arnst." The words escaped my lips.

"No . . ."

"He did. The wounds on Arnst's body were made by a Landsman's knife, and a boy saw a green man that night."

Rufra held my gaze, searching my face in case I played some trick.

"Those knives can be bought in the night market, and did the boy say he saw Karrick?"

"I have not yet confir—"

He leaned in close so he could whisper. "I cannot accuse a Landsman of Arnst's murder, Girton, not on so little. And I do not believe Karrick a murderer. He had little love for Arnst, but Karrick is a man who enjoys living by rules, not breaking them."

"You do not want it to be him," I said, incredulous.

"No," he said simply and looked lost. "I do not. It would cause me endless problems. It would be best for me if it turned out Arnst was killed over money –" he left a gap just a little too long to seem innocent "– or a woman."

"Would you make that the truth even if the killer was Karrick? You would do that, Rufra?"

"No," he said quietly, "I would not. But I must be absolutely sure before I make a move. Absolutely."

We stood in silence, watching Nywulf and Crast warming up. "I am thinking of asking your master's healer to stay on," said Rufra. "All that stops me is I worry old Tarris may poison me if I do." He tried a furtive smile.

One, my master.

Two, my master.

"Given Tarris's attitude to medicine, he may poison you whether he means to or not."

I was rewarded with a laugh. "Indeed. I may ask him to study Mastal's ways simply to see the look on his face."

"Make sure I am there when you do that." I gave Rufra a smile.

"I was hoping you'd tell him for me." Before I could reply Rufra pointed at the sparring ground. "Look, they start for real now."

Nywulf held a wooden longsword and stabsword and Crast held the same until Nywulf glanced over at me and told him, "Stabswords only." After Crast had changed weapons he and Nywulf set to sparring, the older man circling the younger like a hunting animal. Nywulf darted in, flicking his long blade, and instead of dodging out of the way Crast spun inwards along the edge of the blade – *twenty-first iteration: the Whirligig* – and darted out his blade at Nywulf's throat, forcing the older man to block with his stabsword, he did it with a lazy ease. Nywulf came back at Crast – short, efficient thrusts of his longsword to keep the younger man at bay – and Crast danced around him. I watched, and it was all I could do not to stand there like an idiot with my mouth open. Crast was an assassin. He fought just like an assassin. How could Nywulf have brought an assassin so near to Rufra?

It was only after they'd sparred for five minutes that I started to notice the differences between my style and Crast's. Of course he could fight like an assassin, just like I could fight like a soldier. Nywulf had trained him to be a Heartblade, so he would naturally have a fighting style designed to counter an assassin's. As I watched, the differences became more apparent. Where the assassins' style had its roots in the dancers and acrobats of travelling troupes, Crast's style was more military, uglier. His movements did not flow and I found little art in them. He fought well, very well, but he would never make a dancer, and he made no attempt to tumble or leap; instead he kept his feet firmly placed. It was a utilitarian style based around defence, where the assassin's style I followed, Xus's black bird, was all about swift attack, but Crast was no less dangerous for all his artlessness.

Eventually Nywulf signalled a halt and, puffing slightly, took out a rag, wiped his face and came over to Rufra, who picked up a bucket of water with a ladle in for him to drink from.

"Well, the lad's coming along, eh?" Nywulf said to Rufra.

"Indeed he is. I feel safer already." The king passed the ladle to Crast. "Well done."

"And you, Girton, what did you think?" said Nywulf.

"He fights well," I said.

"But?" said Rufra. "Anyone with ears can hear a 'but' in your voice."

"Nothing. It is just, it is not . . ."

"Not what?" said Nywulf, an unpleasant grin on his face.

"It is not beautiful," I said and immediately felt like an idiot.

"You can keep your beauty," said Nywulf. "I'll settle for keeping a blade out of the king's ribs."

"Would you test me, Girton?" said Crast shyly. "I have heard how well you fight from the king."

"Well, I had hoped to spar with Nywulf," I said.

"I am too old and too tired for you," said Nywulf. "Spar with Crast. Do him good to fight the real thing."

We walked to the centre of the sparring ground and I picked up a pair of wooden stabswords. Even the weighted practice blades felt light in hands so used to the warhammer.

"Ready?" said Crast. I moved into the position of readiness and nodded.

First we circled each other. Crast was short, even compared to me, so I had the advantage of reach, but he had two good feet which made us even. He tested me, coming forward – *the Precise Steps* – and his blade snaked out. I beat it away with a flick of my wrist.

It felt good.

He came in again, harder this time, using something like the Quicksteps. I let him push me backwards. As he lunged I countered – *the Boatgirl's dip* – but a blade blocked my move, and I had to dance out of the way as he attacked with his left hand. He pushed forward, and I countered, but every time I attacked he was there, a blade high, a blade low, a blade waiting for me to impale myself on. I was slow – I felt it – slow and out of practice. Whenever I tried to string together the dance I was either stopped by Crast or, worse, by my own lack of practice.

Irritation hampered me further, annoyance an extra weight on my hand and my mind. I wasn't thinking clearly. Instead of backing away and studying Crast, I was pushing in, attacking and getting angrier and angrier with each block. Everything I had, he answered. Then he slipped just a little, and it let me in – a perfect string of moves: *first iteration: the Precise Steps*, pushing him back; *fifth iteration: the Boatgirl's Dip*, up and around Crast as he tried to regain his balance, and straight into the *thirteenth iteration: the Fool's Embrace*, grasping Crast from behind with my blade coming round to open his throat. I could have held him there, but I let him wriggle out and come back at me with three short thrusts. He was wary now – he knew I was better than him. Who I am was coming back, slowly, but it was coming. At that moment, as I congratulated myself, Crast cracked me on the knuckles; I dropped my blade and found his at my throat.

Gentle applause from Rufra and Nywulf. I glanced over

at them. Rufra was smiling, like he was proud of his me but I did not know why. Nywulf did not smile at all, but then he rarely did.

"You let me win," whispered Crast in my ear.

I had not, not really. Rufra must think the same.

"Well, it does not do to disappoint Nywulf, right?"

"You should not have let me win," he said, "if it had been real. I would not have let you win." He lowered his training blade. "But thank you. Nywulf will have no excuse to make me clean latrines now. I owe you and I do not forget my debts."

It was hard not to laugh at such an earnest oath from someone so young, but I kept my face straight.

"Good," I said, and wondered whether he really did think I had let him win or if he knew I had been distracted. If nothing else, sparring with Crast had woken in me a hunger to practise with stabswords and shake off some of my rustiness.

"Well done, Girton," said Rufra. Nywulf was silent. "My court is in session today," he said. "I wanted you to see—" Before we could talk further a Rider arrived on a sweating mount. "A messenger has arrived for the king," he said. "He waits in your pavilion."

Rufra looked crestfallen. "It will have to wait," he said as the Rider slid from his mount and offered the reins to him. Rufra climbed up and rode away. Nywulf and Crast jogged after him, the trainee Heartblade giving me a happy wave as he left.

They vanished into the camp and I made my way to the rear of the sparring field. I had spotted a thick patch of doxy leaves and stopped by them. An idea had been growing in my mind, a thought that had seemed ludicrous at first, but with time had gathered weight. I picked enough doxy to fill my pouch, telling myself that it was in case I had a headache and at the same time knowing it was a lie. Then, with the sun approaching its zenith when my master and Mastal would go for their walk, I headed back to our tent, feeling a tightness inside at what I was thinking of doing.

I detoured, going to the day market, where I bought food, though I could have found it in many other places nearer our tent. As I ate the filling and tasteless porridge I wandered until I found the stall selling pots, from which I bought a mortar and pestle. Then a jug of perry from the stall next door before I returned to our tent. Still I told myself this was all just a passing idea, but with every step an insistent voice in my head became louder and louder.

Why should you trust Mastal?

Why should I? He was Aydor's man and a foreigner who intended to take my master away. Aydor knew how good she was, how quick and clever. If he had some plan he would want her out of the way, and what better way to do that than to dangle family and home in front of her? I wondered how long Mastal had searched for her and how he had found her.

In the tent I began angrily grinding my doxy leaves into a green paste that resembled the one in the small glass bottles Mastal had lined up by my master's bed.

A voice inside told me that what I planned was dangerous and foolish, but it was a quiet voice almost entirely drowned out by another which told me Mastal must not be allowed to take my master away. If he did I was sure I would never see her again, and who knew how far Aydor's plan went? Or even if there was really any family waiting for my master in the Slight Hills. Besides, what I intended was not madness, not really. Touching the yandil leaf had woken something within me. Just the thought of it sent a fizzing along the lines of scars on my body, it fountained an incandescence in my mind. The dark sea within me was shifting again, but it was not so dark now; it was cut with lines of oh-so-bright surf that washed gently against my consciousness, and when they withdrew they left tidemarks of understanding. I knew this leaf. I could feel the bundle of yandil leaves in my pouch throbbing metronomically against my thigh, they were connected to me in a way Mastal could never understand. Magic ran through both me and the leaf, he was only a healer.

I can make this better.

This would work, and I was as sure of it as I was of Karrick's guilt. I would solve two problems in one fell swoop. If Mastal saw his cure was not working he would have no reason to stay. My master dead was no use to him, and then, when he was gone, I could use the yandil I had to cure her myself.

Once I had the mixture of doxy leaves and perry at the same consistency as Mastal's paste, I took my eating knife and removed a small amount of it from each bottle. The yandil glowed gold in my mind and seemed light in my hand, as if it would float away if I let it go. I did not need to measure the doxy paste. I felt it as a dark weight and judged my doctored doses by the tarnish in the golden gleam of the yandil. Once I had diluted all of the bottles, I moved the remaining yandil leaves to my pack, then thought better of it. It would not do for Mastal to find them and I could not trust him: it would not surprise me if he searched through my possessions when I was not here. I pulled up the flooring in the corner of the tent and buried my pouch of yandil leaves in the earth. That done I took the mortar and pestle outside, rinsed them in the filthy stream that ran through that part of the camp, then went into the centre of the small copse of trees behind our tent and hid them in a thorny bush.

When I returned to the tent Mastal was dosing my master with yandil. Although I was not ashamed of what I had done, I found I could not watch him and turned to cleaning my armour and weapons. Mastal and my master chatted happily while she spooned down the mixture, which tasted foul – I knew as I had tried some myself.

"I must be getting used to this, Mastal," she said. "It has started tasting sweeter."

"It is your regained strength and the knowledge you walk the road to wellness that gives it a sweeter taste," said Mastal as he rinsed the empty bottle in a dish of perry. I wondered why he did not use water. "Girton, Merela has decided to make the journey to the Sighing Mountains as soon as she can. I know this is not what you want, but—"

"Rufra cannot spare a cart just yet," I said, the lie coming easily to my mouth, "but he says in a day he will have something for you to use."

Mastal nodded slowly then turned to me, looking me carefully up and down.

"I am glad you have accepted what must be, Girton," he said, his deep voice filled with a pretence of understanding. "I know it is hard for you, but it is what must be for Merela to get well."

"Yes," I said, and I did not know what other words I could use to fill the sudden silence, not without becoming angry that he used my master's name so casually.

Mastal's expression changed, his eyebrows rising in an unspoken question.

Without warning I was filled with fear. What had I done? I was no healer. The gentle surf inside my body had gone, and instead I was nauseous with the upswell of darkness within. I was drowning. I felt sure Mastal could see something was wrong, and if he did not my master would. And she did: her brown eyes were bright as my breathing became shallower, faster, out and in and out and in and out and in.

"Breathe slowly, Girton," she said softly. "Remember, this is the same fight as the one carried on with blades. Only the battleground is different."

Mastal looked between us, his head turning slowly from me to her, aware of some current of understanding in the tent that flowed around him but did not touch him. His eyes narrowed, then he nodded and I wondered whether she had told him about the magic within me.

"It is a curse, a temper," he said, "and it takes strength to control it." He turned back to me and put his hand on my shoulder. I wanted to brush him away but stopped myself. "I believe you have that strength, Girton. You will not let your anger control you as I once was controlled. Now I am a grey man without a home." He stared into my eyes. "Be stronger than me, be stronger than I am for her." He gestured towards my master with his head, and the sea within me rose and smashed against my ribs, robbing me of breath. Nausea – almost overwhelming – I could banish it by admitting what I had done. It was not too late. I could tell Mastal, give him the yandil and get him the cart for my master. What if I had killed her? What if doxy leaf and yandil combined was a poison? What if—

"Girton."

I turned, brushed off Mastal's touch. Nywulf stood in the entrance of our tent.

"Yes?"

"We have received notice that Tomas intends to raid the village of Gwyre using the Nonmen."

"Why?" said Mastal.

"They have supplied us food in the past. They have sold food to Tomas too, but now he wishes to make an example of them so the other outlying villages will stop supplying us."

"It makes sense," said my master, "though it is just as likely to be a trap." Nywulf stared at Mastal and the healer stood, leaving the tent. Nywulf waited until he was sure the man was out of earshot before speaking again.

"Our source in Tomas's camp is well placed," he said, "and Tomas does not know we hear his military plans."

"It is foolish to think that—" began my master.

"He has never led us wrong before, and Rufra is no fool," said Nywulf. "The attack is due in a week. We will send a small advance party of Riders to Gwyre to evacuate the village if it is still peopled, or to return and warn Rufra if it is full of Nonmen waiting for us. Behind them will come carts for the villagers with enough troops to escort them back here safely and garrison the village. When Tomas attacks we'll be waiting. If we're lucky, Tomas will be leading the force himself and the war will be over. Attacking a defenceless village is about his level."

"And if you're not lucky?"

"We'll give Tomas a bloody nose and weaken his army further."

"You want me to come," I said.

"Rufra has asked for you to ride with the advance party." I wondered if he wanted me out of the camp, away from Karrick and the difficulties I would cause when I proved he had murdered Arnst. "He thought you may find purpose in protecting the innocent."

"It is a worthy thing to do," said my master. "You should go, Girton."

She did not want me here. My master and Mastal would be happier with me gone. Aydor's healer was like a hammer falling on a wedge, forcing us apart. I wondered if he acted for Aydor or simply out of selfishness because he wanted the reward for my master.

"Go, Girton," said my master. "Your friend needs you."

Hedgings take them. I left.

Rufra greeted me in the stables, empty apart from him and I. He was leading Xus, who was letting out a constant low, rumbling, warning growl.

"I readied your mount for you," he said.

"Do you still have all your fingers?"

"What is a finger or two between friends." He smiled and tied the reins to the hitching post in the centre of the stables then led me back into Xus's stall. "I wanted to talk to you before you rode out." The smile stayed but it became a faded and ghostly thing.

"I suspected you were not only here to play groom, and also that you are about to tell me something I do not want to hear."

"Yes –" he put his hand on my arm "– but don't smash your hobby doll before I dress it."

"Why does everyone keep acting as though I am unable to control my temper?"

"Well," said Rufra with a shrug, and the smile returned for real, "you are a little more caustic than the Girton who left for foreign lands."

"Only a little?"

"No," he said. "Actually a lot." The silence between us felt uncomfortable. "Girton," he said, "will you tell me about that?" He pointed at the warhammer but I do not think that was what he really wanted to speak about.

I shrugged. "I took it from a man."

"What did you do out there in the world? You are not the boy who left here."

"I killed, Rufra. My master put us in among a Landsman patrol going to pacify the far borders. Ten Landsmen led by a man called Gosaile, about twenty mercenaries and a blood gibbet on a cart. I think Gosaile hated me from the moment he set eyes on me." I tapped the hilt of the warhammer. "I begged my master to let us travel as entertainers but she would not. She said it was better to be among those who were armed, better for us to become comrades with them. Safer." I kicked at a clod of dirt. "Comrades? They were barely human. Gosaile had led many raids into the borders, said they were a hotbed of magic. The villagers seemed aggressive, always meeting us with violence, and we fought for three years. Small armies at first, warbands – you know, twenty or thirty at most."

"It is a necessary job, Girton," said Rufra gently. "You saw Grandon's Souring, and you have seen the Great Western Souring."

"I never saw Gosaile do any form of test for magic, Rufra, not once."

"The Landsmen guard their secrets.'"

"No, he made no attempt to. He laughed about it. And every village we found, defended or not, he killed them all. Men, women, the old, the children . . ."

"He will have had a reason." Rufra put his hand on my arm and I shrugged it off.

"Of course, he always had a reason. A magic user was born here . . . We do not have the numbers to guard prisoners . . . We cannot leave those who hate us at our backs. He and his men would take the most attractive boys and girls and use them, then kill them too."

"But you did not?"

"No, I did not take part in what they did," I said quietly, "but I could not stop it either."

"He used the blood gibbet?"

"He only used that the once." I stared at the floor, and before Rufra could speak carried on; I did not want him probing me about that once. "After three years there were very few of us left. He used the mercenaries hard and most were dead. He said we should turn back. He agreed to pay my master and I and let us move on, but he had no wish to waste his money on a boy and a woman. He sent me to scout a village and sprang his trap there – ten Landsmen against me."

"It was not enough." Rufra tried to smile.

"No. It was not. And I took this from Gosaile." I lifted the warhammer. "It is a weapon for an animal, and I carry it to remind me that I was an animal, no better than him."

"But you did the right thing, Girton," he said. "You killed him."

"I should have done it a lot sooner."

"But you could not. His mercenaries and Landsmen would have ripped you apart."

"That is what my master says."

"You should listen to her."

"Listening to her had me end up with the Landsmen."

"She could not foresee that Gosaile would be a monster, Girton."

"It is hard, Rufra. I had hoped to find my place and some peace here, but . . ."

"You have a place here, Girton." He drew his longsword from the scabbard enough to show me the shining blade, twin to my stabsword. "Brothers, remember?"

I nodded but all I wanted to do was change the conversation.

"I spoke with Areth last night, Rufra."

"Oh," he said, and let the sword fall back.

"She walks the night market listening for mention of your son."

"I know."

"Perhaps if you were with her more she would not."

He glared at me, and I felt like a stranger trespassing on ground sacred to others.

"She wants to talk," he said quietly, turning away from me and leaning against the side of the stall. "She always wants to talk."

"She needs to. Maybe you need to also?"

He let out a snort of false laughter. "You swing from lost and angry to mother hen in a heartbeat, Girton. Can we talk of something else, please?"

"She thinks Arnlath was poisoned."

"I know. That is one of the things she wants to talk about." There was an ugly undercurrent in his voice.

"Do you think your son may have been poisoned?"

"No." There was no movement in that word, no room for

doubt or any invitation to further conversation. Nonetheless, I have never been one to take a hint, no matter how unsubtle.

"I have heard his symptoms and how he died, Rufra. Speaking as an assassin—"

"I do not ask you speak as an assassin, Girton." Cold words.

"He was your heir. It would suit Tomas, or Aydor, to—"

"No assassins work in the Tired Lands while there is war."

"You cannot be sure."

"I am." There was a hardness in his voice I had never heard before. "I am sure, Girton."

"Even if the true assassins will not work, there are always people who will kill for money, Rufra."

"Tomas would not have my son poisoned. He believes himself a king if nothing else. An agreement was made."

"Rufra, you cannot think that all kings are like you. Do you forget the sewer that was Maniyadoc before you took it? Tomas would happily—"

"No!" he roared, taking two stiff-legged steps towards me with his fists bunched at his sides. Xus growled and pulled on his reins but could not free himself. "Tomas is a king! We will not have this conversation."

I met his anger with anger.

"Being a king does not stop a man being a murderer."

Rufra's hands flashed out and he grabbed me by the loose collar of my armour and pulled me across the stable. Surprised, I stepped badly on my club foot and a lance of pain ran up through my leg. I grabbed Rufra's collar, the sharp enamel edges digging into my hands. A black fire flared in my mind and I bit on my tongue, using the pain to extinguish it. I expected more shouting, even violence, but it did not come; instead he whispered to me, his face no more than a hand's breadth from my own, and I saw his anger was not true anger, not true fury, it was desperation. Tears ran down his face.

"If I believe Tomas or Neander had my son killed, Girton, then I will have them both taken alive, whatever the price in blood and bodies. I will chain Tomas and cripple him and make him my pet. Do you understand? He will live a long life, and every day of it will be spent discovering new ways to endure the pain I will visit on him. I will take Neander's fingers, toes, eyes, tongue and cock and keep him alive and broken in a cell, Girton. I will never forgive and will visit such atrocities on those responsible that in turn their families and the priesthood will never forgive me. And the war will never stop. There will be nothing left in Maniyadoc and the Long Tides but pain and vengeance, and that cannot be who I am. It cannot be my legacy." His eyes searched my face as if I were a mirror and he looked to see in me what burned in him. He would not find it. My path was already a dark one and I could see no light for me. "Do you understand? That cannot be who I am. Not if I am to create anything lasting in the Tired Lands." His grip loosened and he looked almost surprised that he had been holding on to me so violently. When he spoke again it was in a broken whisper. He shook. "Help me, Girton. Be my friend and help me be the best man I can be. That is what I need from you, that is what I need you here for. I need your friendship more than I need your blade."

My own anger and shame was still there, writhing black along the scars on my chest, but Rufra's naked pain and his control of it made me feel like a spoiled child.

"I will be your friend." I let go of his armour, it had cut lines into my palms. "But as your friend I ask one thing of you."

"One?" An edge in his voice, something dangerous.

"Talk to Areth, Rufra. She does not blame you. Tell her what you have told me." He bowed his head but I was sure there was a nod there. "And no matter what, do not keep Tomas as a pet; that would be worse than you having a dog." He looked up, almost a smile on his face. "You know how much I hate dogs."

And he laughed, not true laughter, a sad bruised laughter that made me wonder if we would ever be friends the way we had been once before. But at least he laughed, and I swore if I could not be a good man for myself I would be one for Rufra. I would hold in my anger and my hatreds and try my best to obey his wishes.

My new oath was to be tested almost straight away.

When I joined Nywulf and his Riders I found out what Rufra had been meaning to tell me and had forgotten in his anger:

Aydor would lead us to Gwyre.

Chapter 19

Sparse trees dotted the landscape and the setting sun was a red ball gilding their tops with a blush as we approached Gwyre. Imploring shadows stretched stick hands towards us and we rode on regardless, ignoring the stinking herds of hogs that shadowed us. I understood Rufra's desire to protect people but could not help thinking it was a decision based on emotion rather than strategy, and that it was not a wise move.

Gwyre was an old village, one of the few places in Maniyadoc built of stone rather than mud and thatch, and from a distance it looked like the jutting teeth of a blackened and discarded jawbone against the skyline. Boros told me it wasn't much more than one street. It had once been a small fort and the houses had been built against the curtain wall, in many places the houses had grown higher than the wall which formed their backs. It held a strategic position, topping a low hill and commanding a swathe of land sown with crops. It made Rufra's desire to garrison the place a little more sensible, if only a little. Hedgescare statues stood in twisted poses, rags blowing in the breeze where they were not plastered down by the insistent drizzle. Huge triangular barns thrust into the skyline – there had been more of them once but many had been burned and only blackened timbers remained, leaning as if caught mid-fall by an invisible hand. Far to the right of the village was a wood of pines that made it look like the land had been pierced from beneath by barbed spears.

"The gates are shut," shouted Boros from the front of the

column. I rode a few mounts back from Aydor and Nywulf. Aydor I did not want to speak to, and Nywulf I felt betrayed by for dragging me along in the first place. I did not care that Rufra needed Aydor sweet, or that having the man who had once been king-in-waiting take his orders made him look good. Aydor could not be trusted and should not be here at all, never mind leading us.

All in all it had been an uncomfortable ride, partly because I was unused to riding as cavalry – Xus disliked the large shield slung over his rump and refused to find a steady rhythm to his trot so the saddle had rubbed my thighs raw – but mostly because I had been forced to listen to Aydor chat with the men and women around me like they were old friends. I had ridden with Cearis for a little while, but she had tired of my sullen silence and gone back to join the priest Darvin, who also accompanied us.

"Aydor, stay here and command the column if you will," said Nywulf. If riding with Aydor stuck in his throat the way it should have he did a good job of hiding it. "Boros, Girton, ride forward with me." He glanced towards the wood on the horizon and clicked his mount forward. "Quickly now."

I let Xus follow Nywulf's mount and then had to rein him back as he tried to lead. He let out a low growl when I pulled on the reins and then lowered his antlers in response to the smell of blood. Now I was nearer to the gates of Gwyre I could see why Nywulf had stopped the column.

"We have ridden into a trap," I said.

"Aye," said Nywulf, "but it remains to be seen how much of one."

The wall around Gwyre was as high as a man and half again between the tall, narrow houses that overtopped it. The outside had been plastered with a sandy-coloured render which was flaking away in places to expose hefty rocks beneath. The village's wooden gates were firmly shut and nailed to them was a man, his arms and legs splayed out in a star shape and his stomach slit so his entrails could be looped around a spear stuck in the ground in front of the gates. Blood had run down the gates from where his hands and feet had been nailed to the wood, and black streaks marked the pale pine.

"He died hard," I said.

"It looks like my brother's work," said Boros. He sounded pleased as he slid off his mount, drawing his sword and cutting the rope of the dead man's entrails. He plucked the spear and its gruesome decoration from the ground and threw it to one side.

"Is this Rufra's spy, Nywulf?" I said, gesturing at the corpse. "The one Tomas would never suspect?"

He nodded.

"Hallan ap Bessit," he said quietly as he watched Boros pull the nails from the gate, letting the body fall. "Gwyre!" he shouted. "I am Nywulf, come from King Rufra." He glanced towards the distant pinewood and I followed his gaze, sure I saw movement there. "Open your gates, Gwyre!" No answer. "Open your gates!" he shouted again. I heard a mount behind us and turned. Darvin had brought his animal up.

"I can talk to them . . ." the priest began.

Nywulf shook his head, too angry for diplomacy.

"Open your gates," he shouted, "or I will send a man over the wall to open them for you!"

"Go away." The voice that replied was barely audible.

"Talk to me properly," said Nywulf, no longer shouting though he spoke loudly enough for his voice to carry. "Let me see you."

A man in his forties or fifties appeared on the thin bridge above the gate.

"If you send a man over the wall our archers will shoot him."

"We have been sent by King Rufra to help you."

"If we let you in," said the man, "they will do to us what

they did to him." He pointed at the tortured corpse on the ground. "It took him a day to die."

"And you did not help him?" said Boros.

"They would not let us," the man said. He looked on the edge of panic. "The Nonmen would not let us."

"Did Chirol lead them?" said Boros, stepping forward.

"Yes."

"You watched this man die." He pointed at the corpse. "And you did nothing?" shouted Boros. "You could at least have cut him down."

"We were scared, there are women and children in here. We are farmers and . . ."

"You could have been heroes!" shouted Boros. Darvin walked his mount forward.

"Peace, Boros," he said, raising an arm, the purple rags of his robe swinging to and fro. Nywulf glanced at the distant wood again. Dust was rising, and I estimated whoever was causing it would be here within the hour, sooner if they rode. "What is your name?" Darvin asked the man. When he spoke I realised how quiet it was. No lizards trilled, no grasses hissed in the breeze. The only sound was the faint cawing of the black birds of Xus drifting across in the still air from where they spiralled above the wood.

"I am Ossowin. I lead the people of Gwyre."

"Talk to Nywulf, Ossowin," said Darvin. "The Nonmen are a symptom of our sickness. They are in the grip of a hedge-hunger that will never be sated. You must know that."

Ossowin looked lost and frightened. His eyes moved from Darvin to Nywulf but he found no comfort in the eyes of either man.

"Has my king ever done you wrong, Ossowin?" said Nywulf gently. "Has he ever short-changed you on the price of your crops, ever stolen from you or hurt your people?"

"No, and I respect Blessed Rufra truly, Nywulf."

"Then let us in, you old coward," said Boros conversationally.

"Quiet!" Nywulf roared in the voice I knew well from the squireyard at Maniyadoc, and Boros seemed to shrink in on himself. "I am sorry, Ossowin. Boros has only ever been a soldier, and he has a score to settle with the Boarlord. He does not understand what it is to have a family to protect. Look to the wood. What do you see?" He pointed to the growing dust cloud.

"Men," Ossowin said. I could hear the fear, strong in his voice. "Men are approaching."

"Not just men, Ossowin; it is the Nonmen," said Nywulf, "and they come for us, but we are on mounts and they are on foot. What do you think they will do, Ossowin, when they get here only to find we have ridden away?"

Ossowin stared down at us.

"They . . ." he began. "They will follow you," he said, but I knew he didn't believe it.

"No, Ossowin," said Nywulf, who sounded tired. "They will take out their anger on you and your village. Your archers and your walls will not hold them. Your children and your men and your women will become the playthings of the Boarlord, and those few that escape will be prey for the herds." He stared at the ruined corpse of Hallan. "We are a hundred armed and trained men and women, Ossowin, and Rufra marches behind us, half a day away at most."

Ossowin glanced over his shoulder at the late sun as it set the clouds alight.

"This night Rufra will not be here; he will be in a camp far away, and you cannot hold the Boarlord all night. He has many hundreds with him."

Annoyingly, he may have spoken the truth, but Nywulf did not care. "We can hold him longer with you than you can without us."

Ossowin stared down at us, as frozen in place as any

hedgescare. I heard a scrabbling sound on the other side of the gates and Ossowin was joined by a woman. She said something to him and then put a hand on his shoulder, a small gesture that spoke of a lifetime's partnership.

He nodded, a picture of misery. "Open the gates," he said in barely more than a whisper. "Let them in."

We had to dismount to pass under the bridge over the gates as it was not high enough for a mount and Rider. On the road behind the gates stood the villagers of Gwyre. The road was muddy, and the same grey mud coated the villagers' legs from foot to knee. Some carried bows, but I only spotted three or four of the weapons. In all they were a bedraggled lot who watched us with wide and frightened eyes. Most had rags over the bottom of their faces, as if they could hide from the fate that awaited them by hiding their faces. Nywulf saw in our column then told them to unsaddle their mounts and drive them away. "We will not be riding away from here until Rufra comes to relieve us, and there is nowhere to stable them anyway," he said, and he made sure the villagers heard him. "We'll keep Xus and Dorlay for now, and round the rest up after Rufra arrives. Boros, check the wall – look for weak points." I glanced around. Most of the houses had been built against the wall so their steep roofs made parts of the wall far higher. "Ossowin, how many archers do you really have?"

"Seven," said the woman standing by Ossowin.

"You are?"

"Aisleth, his wife." She linked arms with Ossowin. "Everyone in the village can use a bow, but there are only seven I would trust not to panic and waste arrows."

"Thank you for your honesty," said Nywulf. He turned to a woman unsaddling her mount. "Farriya, pick twelve to go with you and Aisleth's seven. I want you to take down anyone trying to climb over the walls between the houses or coming down the roofs."

"Yes, Nywulf." She pulled a hornbow from the case on her mount and started calling out names.

"Blessed Nywulf," said Aisleth, "can you get the children out before the Nonmen come?" Nywulf strode over to the gate and looked at the oncoming force. It was large, three hundred at least.

"No," he said. "If I try they will catch them and use them against us."

Aisleth nodded and moved closer to Nywulf.

"I have been a soldier," she whispered. "Your man will tell you the big house at the back of the village has weak walls, and I know you cannot hold this place all night." There were tears in her eyes.

Nywulf put a hand on her shoulder. "We are Rufra's troops and we will hold for our king." He glanced at her before adding, "Do you have children here?"

She nodded."One. My girl, Dinay."

"Does she ride?" She nodded again. "As well as anyone."

"Dinay," shouted Nywulf, and a girl came forward, no more than twelve and thin, as all are in the Tired Lands. "You ride, girl?" She bobbed her head, shaking in her sandals as Nywulf grabbed me by the arm. "This is Girton, Dinay. He will introduce you to his mount, and you will ride to the king for me."

"You would give her my mount?" I said. "Why not Aydor's? He—" I was silenced by Nywulf's stare.

"I would have this girl get safely to Rufra, Girton. Show me a faster and fiercer mount than Xus and I will put her on that." I glared at Nywulf but I did not have an answer to his truth.

"Very well," I said. "Come, Dinay." The girl was plainly scared of me, and though I was annoyed at Nywulf for making me send Xus with this child, I knew it made sense. I pushed her up onto a mounting block and brought Xus over, then put my hand over Dinay's and got her to stroke the mount's muzzle. After a few moments of growling and annoyed whistling, Xus allowed me to lift the child onto his back. I led them to the gates and took a moment to stare at the approaching force of Nonmen I could hear their screamed curses on the wind.

"I am sorry for taking your mount, Blessed," said the girl. She could hardly speak but did not look away from me or hide her face as some children would. Her brown eyes were wide with fear and her hands trembled on the reins. She was more scared of me than she was of the Nonmen, and I felt small and cruel. I used Xus's bridle and stirrup to pull myself up. Xus growled at the unfamiliar weight on his side."

"Listen to me, Dinay." I forced a smile. "You strike me as a brave girl." She nodded. "Then I am glad it is you I must give Xus over to. Now, you must ride like you have never ridden before. Xus is the fastest and the fiercest mount that has ever lived, do you understand?" She nodded again. "Give him his head, steer him south and he will look after you until you meet King Rufra. No one will catch you, and if someone tries then I pity them as Xus will let no one hurt his rider." The girl returned a fluttering smile, only for it to be driven away as what I had said sunk in.

"I will meet the king?" she stuttered the words.

"Aye. Rufra is a good man, Dinay. He is my friend and he will be yours too."

"A king will not want to speak to me," she said. "I am only a farm girl."

"And I was once a thankful with nothing. Do not worry. Rufra does not judge a person by their origins, and he will see that you ride Xus and know you must be special. He knows I would not let just anyone ride my mount, and he knows how few can master Xus." She still looked worried. "Some of his best Riders have been thrown from Xus's back." I leaned in and whispered, "Even Master Nywulf," and got another smile. "But look at you. Xus sits quite still for you." Spots of drizzle were collecting in her black hair, like jewels.

"Your task is important, Dinay, Tell Rufra we are here and we are under siege. Tell him Girton Club-Foot says he is not to dawdle."

She mouthed the words I had spoken and then said very quietly, "Blessed, will you look after my mother and father?"

I did not know what to say. I knew the chaos of battle, the fear, the confusion, how difficult it was to keep track of those by you who you had known for months, never mind a couple of strangers you had only just met. Why should I lie to the girl? Why give her false hope?

"I will do the best that I can," I said, because I knew it was what Rufra would have said. The girl smiled at me and I smacked Xus on the rump, sending the mount careening out through the gates. I watched him run and felt another body come to stand by me.

"That was well said, Girton."

"It was a lie, Nywulf," I replied.

"Sometimes we must lie."

"Aye." I drew my warhammer. "How long do we have until the Nonmen are on us?"

Nywulf peered through the drizzle into the increasing gloom.

"A quarter-hour until they are here. The gates are flimsy and will not hold them long. Maybe an hour until the real fighting starts."

"How long until Rufra gets here?"

"Too long," said Nywulf, "but it always is. We will hold."

"We will?"

"We must," he said, and turned as Boros came up.

"The walls are stout in most places, but one house at the rear of the village has been used to store grain, and its rear wall has a big hole in it to allow easy access to the fields. Hedgings curse farmers." He spat. "They have ruined a good defence the better to bring in grain. I've got troops packing it with what they can and putting spears in among the packing. It'll hold for a bit, but it's going to end up being a way in no matter what."

"I'll hold the house." I turned. Aydor stood behind me, a stabsword in one hand and a huge shield in the other. He looked ridiculous.

"How many will be needed to hold it?" Nywulf asked Boros.

"You won't fit more than three in there without them tripping over each other." He glanced at Aydor. "Maybe only two."

"I'll find a place in the shieldwall defending the gate," I said and took a step away from Aydor.

"Dead gods," said Nywulf, "you two are still the same idiots I tried to train in the squireyard." He turned to me. "Girton, give me that warhammer."

"My warhammer?"

"Unless you have another." He strode forward and wrenched it from my hand. "Aydor, that stabsword, give it to me."

"This is my weap—"

"I don't care." He pulled it from his hand and replaced it with the warhammer. Then he strode back to me and forced the stabsword into my hand. "This will be a hard enough fight even with you both playing to your strengths; we will not make it any harder. Girton, I need your speed in that house back there." He pointed to the rear of the village. "Aydor, I need your strength to anchor my shieldwall around, and now you have the weapon you need to do some real damage."

Before I could complain, Nywulf turned away, shouting orders, assigning troops to the shieldwall, telling the villagers to hide their children and ordering every able-bodied man and woman to find a weapon. I mounted the wall as Nywulf put together his defences and watched the girl on Xus as he galloped as hard as he could. A small contingent had split from the main group of Nonmen, but they were on foot and would not catch Xus. I was more worried about Chirol as he rode at the head of his men, his boar-skulled head turning, watching the girl on Xus. Then he leaned in close to say something to a man running beside him and wheeled his animal round to ride in pursuit.

"Fly, Xus, fly," I said into the air, and it seemed the mount heard me. The girl leaned into him, and Xus ran as hard as he could. I hoped it would be enough.

The main Nonmen force was near enough to Gwyre that I could make out their shouted threats as the gates to the village started to grind shut. It was time to prepare for battle. Below, Nywulf was standing on the mounting block and shouting to the troops and villagers assembled before him as the din from outside grew louder.

"This man is Aydor!" yelled Nywulf, pointing at him. "Once he was a king who fought against Rufra for the crown, and now he chooses to follow King Rufra, because he has seen that it is right. Two days ago, the Nonmen, these same Nonmen that are outside your walls, attacked Aydor. He had only a small force and no village to shield him. He was outnumbered by far more than we shall be and yet he fought them off. He made them run as if Dark Ungar himself had come for them." Nywulf's gaze passed across the crowd before him, troops and frightened villagers. "And we will do the same this night!" he shouted. "The Nonmen only win because they use fear as a weapon. Without fear they are nothing more than mage-bent thinmen, stumbling into battle. Now, are you afraid?"

I joined in with Nywulf's troops as they shouted, "No!" The villagers' response was less assured, so Nywulf made them shout it again and again until we were all as loud as one another: No! No! No! "The Nonmen will never take Gwyre!" he roared. "We will not let them! We do not fear them!"

It was a good speech that Nywulf made that day.

But, as he had said, sometimes we must lie.

Chapter 20

With Chirol gone to chase Dinay on Xus, his second in command stood outside the village of Gwyre, just out of bowshot. His shadow stretched out behind him as if he were a giant, and the villagers watched from cracks in the gate and the ramparts of their wall. Those who could not see listened carefully as the Nonman, Chadat, listed what he would do to them if they did not give us up to the Boarlord. It was not a pleasant list or one I have any wish to recount.

Nywulf stood between Boros and I above the gate. I was surprised that Aydor had not demanded to be up there as Rufra had put him in charge, but he had happily let Nywulf lead, preferring to be among the men and women below. I did not complain, though I worried what poison he may be whispering in their ears. I remained the only one not taken in by his false humility. Nywulf had told Boros and I that he would not reply immediately to the Nonmen – he did not want to give them the honour of our leader speaking to them – and had told Boros he could say what he wanted until he interrupted.

"Where is my brother?" called Boros. "It seems whenever we are likely to meet he finds an excuse to be elsewhere."

"The Boarlord will be back," Chadat shouted, "and when he returns he will be wearing the skin of your messenger." I heard a gasp from below.

"A young girl sounds like his sort of opponent. Fighting children is all he's good for – all any of you are good for. You should run now, Chadat, before you and your men are humiliated by a bunch of farmers."

"We shall cut you all to pieces!" screamed Chadat.

"But to do that, you will have to get past the farmers, and I do not think you are up to it."

Before Chadat could reply Nywulf stepped forward, raising his voice to make sure all of the Nonmen could hear him.

"Go," he said calmly. "Rufra is on his way, and if he catches you here you will be trapped between us and him. He will smear the walls of Gwyre with your blood."

"You lie," shouted Chadat. "If that were true you would not have sent a messenger. It is you who will adorn the walls of Gwyre, Nywulf, and you shall have a long time to regret your folly here just as Hallan had time to regret spying on Tomas."

"I do not lie," said Nywulf. "If I do, may Xus strike me down now." He waited, and those crowded around the gate held their breath in expectation.

Nothing happened of course, as Xus the unseen is rarely so punctual. The rain continued to fall, torches still guttered in their sconces, throwing strange shadows, and if I fancied I saw Xus's shadow cast then it was no shock that the god of death would be in this place in this hour.

"It seems Xus does not want me yet," said Nywulf. "Maybe it is your hand he will take and lead along the path to his dark palace." He stood back and said quietly, "Girton."

I picked up the bow by my feet and strung an arrow, pulling on the cord once or twice to get a feel for the tension in the string and wood, glancing at a tree to gauge the wind, watching Chadat as he saw me test the bow. Alarm crossed his features but it quickly turned to amusement. He was sure he was out of range, and for most archers that would be true.

But I am not most archers.

I drew, asked Xus to guide my arrow, and let fly. Chadat gazed up into the sky, a big grin on his face, and he opened his arms as if to mock death, but Xus the unseen should never be mocked. A roar went up from Gwyre as the arrow took Chadat in the chest, punching him to the floor and pinning his body to the ground. As we climbed down the ladder Nywulf was already speaking.

"Boros, sometimes you are an idiot and sometimes you are a genius." He raised his voice. "Farmers' clothes! I need farmers' clothes. Bring them quickly, big as you can, whatever you can find." Nywulf ran over to some villagers and Boros stared after him as though he had gone mad.

"I suspect, Boros," I said, "he means to dress the front rank of the shieldwall as farmers."

"Why? That won't scare the Nonmen."

"No, farmers won't scare them, but how often have you seen a shieldwall of real soldiers fall in the first fight?"

"'Hardly ever . . ." A grin spread across his face as he realised what Nywulf was doing. "The Nonmen will think a bunch of farmers beat them."

"Exactly." I heard Rufra's voice echoing back from my past when we trained as squires together, and then, as if in reply, my master's voice saying the same words: *"Half the fight is always in your head."*

My master, how was she?

I was flooded with guilt. Was she suffering already from what I had done to her medicine? What if I died here and never got to correct the mixture? Why had I done it? I was such a fool. I would tell Mastal what I had done and make it right, whatever it took.

We will make her well.

A scream came from outside the village, followed by the sound of hundreds of swords and spears beating against shields. Above the clatter I heard the high shouts of mettle-chanters and the wail of spinners as the chanters whirled them around in their frenzied dance, working themselves and the Nonmen up for the attack.

"Open the gates," shouted Nywulf.

"But that is our only protection," said Ossowin. From somewhere he had found leather armour and a spear; he at least looked like a warrior.

"We will meet their first charge head on, and it will focus the attack in one place, at least for now." There was a huge grin on Nywulf's face as he went to stand by Aydor, who wore armour covered with sacking and farmers' rags. "Let's show these yellowers what farmers are made of," he said and slammed down his visor.

I joined the archers on the bridge above the gate. Nywulf was sure the Nonmen were not great tactical thinkers, and he was right. They slammed into our shieldwall in a great screaming wave but they were not disciplined or well equipped, they had a ragtag assortment of weapons and little in the way of armour. The small opening of the gates neutralised the advantage of their superior numbers, and our curving wall of brightly coloured shields held. We did not loose our arrows, not yet; our supplies were limited and they would be needed later. For now we crouched behind our shields, and when spears were thrown at us we threw them back. Occasionally a Nonman would scramble over the shieldwall, avoiding thrusting spears and blades and landing on the other side, only to be cut down by those waiting for just such a manoeuvre.

Mostly I watched Aydor, I suspected he may use the chaos to kill Nywulf. Depriving Rufra of his most experienced man would be a shrewd move, but he was too busy with the Nonmen, and the more I watched Aydor the more he seemed made for the place he held in the centre of the wall. He was strong enough to wield my warhammer in a way I had never been able to, battering aside those that came at him, using the clawed haft to thrust between his shield and that of the woman on his right the way others would use a stabsword. When space opened in front of him he used his height to whirl the hammer around his head and bring it smashing down on those coming in to fill the gap. He was ferocious, lost in the battle, and it was partly his ferocity that won the first fight for us.

And almost lost it.

The Nonmen withdrew, and rather than fall back and let Nywulf shut the gates so the troops around him could rest, Aydor followed the retreating Nonmen, berating them as he did.

"Beaten by farmers! By farmers!" he shouted as he strode after them. "Remember that and run while you can . . ." I cursed him from above, but he could not hear. Nywulf frantically called for him to return to our lines.

There was always one, always some unruly fool who pursued a retreating force and they all suffered the same fate for their lack of discipline. When Aydor was too far from the gate to easily return eight of the better-armed warriors split from the retreating Nonmen and circled back to kill him. Part of me rejoiced – he was nothing but trouble for Rufra and this would be a good way for him to die. But my master's voice was in my head, telling me to study the whole battle and not just my own part in it. Dead gods' graves, if Aydor fell now it would take the heart out of the men and women who had seen him fight so hard with them, to the farmers he must seem unbeatable, like a giant of war.

"Black Ungar take you, Aydor," I whispered under my breath. I was moving before Nywulf shouted my name.

I leapt from the wall, rolling in the mud and coming up with my stabswords drawn and a sharp ache in my club foot. I ran hard, foot in front of foot, my gait lopsided and my mind full of anger. Four of the Nonmen readied themselves to meet Aydor, who charged them like a bull mount in full rut. The other four circled round to come at him from behind. It was them I aimed for.

Foot in front of foot.

Breathe out, breathe in.

No pain, no fear.

I am the weapon.

My thighs ached and my club foot burned. I'd not run hard like this for too long.

Aydor met the first Nonman, catching an overhand blow on his scratched shield and shattering the man's skull with a return blow of my warhammer. Then Nonmen were in front of me, unaware of my attack as yet. Aydor would have to fend for himself while I dealt with them.

Twenty-third iteration: the Kissing Skip.

Building up momentum with a hop, skip and a jump. Landing with both feet on the first Nonman's knee, forcing it sideways. A crack of shattered bone and ripped ligaments. Using his body as steps, propelling me up into the air – *twentieth iteration: Swordmouth's Leap* – coming down with my stabswords held like the fangs in the beak of the flying lizard that hunts fish, blades straight through the face of the second Nonman as she turns at the sound of her friend's scream. The remaining two spinning to face me, caught off guard and shocked to see two of their number already lying in the mud behind me.

Quicksteps.

Pushing the Nonman forward, forward, forward, panic in eyes half hidden behind bars of dirty hair. He makes a poor lunge at me. I bat it away and – *eighth iteration: The Placing of the Rose* – blade into his throat. The last remaining Nonman drops his weapon and runs. I ignore him.

Aydor.

Foot in front of foot.

Too slow.

Foot in front of foot in front of foot.

Run, Girton.

He has his second attacker down, but the other two are moving around behind him. A blade comes in towards his back

The Speed-that-Defies-the-Eye.

I am there.

The Meeting of Hands saving the life of a man who would have had me killed. The Nonman is dead. I came from nowhere and he had no time to prepare. My blade is in his heart. The second backs away and the warhammer comes around, breaking his neck.

For minutes it seems we stand there listening to the whimpering of the man with the broken knee and staring at one another.

"Thank you, Girton."

I don't want his thanks.

"No filthy Nonman is taking my warhammer as a trophy because of your stupidity. Get back to our lines."

Aydor stared at me for a moment longer, then raised an eyebrow and shrugged.

"Well, thank you anyway." He laughed then. And I found myself laughing with him at my own prickliness, though it was laughter which came from the tension of battle fleeing and not any form of camaraderie. I still thought him dangerous.

Before we headed back to Gwyre, Aydor turned to the fleeing Nonmen and screamed at them, "Beaten by farmers! Beaten by farmers and a mage-bent cripple!"

We rejoined the men and women waiting for us, a jeering, screaming mass. Nywulf watched with a look of amusement on his face and then he shouted in his best parade-ground voice, "Quiet! We've given them a bloody nose, that is all." The troops nodded and the villagers, who a moment ago had looked elated, became rather less full of celebration. "They'll come back, and they'll come back harder and cleverer." He looked up at the bridge across the gate where he'd stationed his sharpest-eyed trooper. "You see anything, Geest?"

"Aye." The woman sounded bored. "Ladders and what looks like a ram, but they've got no roof for it so we can rain merry hell on them before they get through."

"You hear what she said?" He let his gaze play along the faces around him. "They're bringing up siege weapons – not big ones, but enough to cause us a little trouble. "I want a child in every house – if the Nonmen start cutting holes in the roofs I want to know. And I want someone boiling water, and if we can get some torches up on the roofs of the houses we should do that too." People were nodding, listening attentively to what Nywulf said. "Troops, if you are not in the shieldwall I want you protecting the archers and whoever else you can from arrows. Any villager or trooper who has nothing to do should collect fallen arrows and keep our archers supplied. Do you all understand?"

He was met with a chorus of "Ayes."

"Right, everyone get a drink. Those who want to see Darvin or your own priest to sign your god's book do it now."

"I could do with some perry," said Aydor with a grin.

Nywulf grabbed his arm. "Over here," he said and took Aydor aside as the others queued up at water and perry barrels. I melted into the shadows so I could hear what they said.

"You fought well, Aydor." And the huge man gave a smug grin that made me wish I'd let him die. "But do not congratulate yourself too much. You were lucky out there at the end. Don't be a fool again. If not for Girton you'd be a corpse."

"Sorry, Nywulf." Aydor bowed his head. "Something happened, I do not know what."

"Battle madness, Aydor. Sometimes Xus the unseen whispers in the ear of those who do his bidding, and his words are powerful." I felt a sudden stab of jealousy. In Maniyadoc five years ago I was sure I had been led to safety by the god of death, and for Nywulf to say he spoke to Aydor felt like I had been betrayed, though it was foolish of me – death comes to all. "Now you have heard his words, you will recognise them next time the madness tries to take hold. I do not want to have to send Girton after you again."

Aydor smiled at him.

"For years I dreamed of fighting Girton one on one," he said. "Now I am glad that never happened or I would not be here. Dead gods, but he can fight."

"Yes, and he fights clever, Aydor. You should too. First rule, don't fight unless you have to, you understand?" The Aydor I once knew would have cursed Nywulf for telling him what to do; this one bowed his head and I wondered how long he had been working on this contrite act. "And the second rule, Aydor, is that you don't drink before a fight."

"But everyone drinks before—"

"Not officers, not Rufra's officers, and that's why he wins. Drunk officers do foolish things, you understand?" Aydor nodded, and I watched him walk away and join the queue for water.

"Girton," said Nywulf, "you can stop skulking now."

"We shouldn't trust him."

"Maybe not, but right now we need him to fight the Nonmen. I want you and your bow in the middle of the village watching the roofs until I need you in the house at the back. My troops will call you when it's time."

"Very well."

"And did you learn your lesson out there?' he said, putting heavy emphasis on "your".

"That Aydor is a fool?"

"No, that you should play to your talents and stop running from who you are. Your strength is not in the warhammer; leave it with Aydor." He grabbed my wrist, lifting up the arm that held my Conwy stabsword. "You are fast, Girton Club-Foot, so be fast."

"I'm out of practice," I said, looking at the ground as he let go of me.

"They come!" A shout from above.

"You're about to get plenty of practice," grinned Nywulf, then shouted, "Places! Cearis, get on the wall and cause trouble for that ram. Aydor, the shieldwall. Village archers, I want you ready in the middle of the village. Boros, form a second line behind the shieldwall." As Nywulf barked orders men and women ran to obey, he was in his element. This was a man doing what he was born for. "Telkir, Halda." He stopped two soldiers. "Get in that house with the hole in the wall and take some spears to keep away any Nonmen trying to clear the hole and get in. They won't get through yet, but when they are near send a runner for Girton to join you. When he does, you are to watch his back, you understand?" They nodded and jogged to the rear of the village.

Everything was illuminated in orange by the light of the fires lit in the gaps between the houses, and a column of thick smoke rose above Gwyre like Birthstorm clouds. Outside the walls the Nonmen had started up an eerie chant backed with hauntgrass flutes, and it sounded like Dark Ungar himself was coming for us. As I went to join the archers in the middle of the village I passed Cearis. She gave me a wave, and I saw the ink on her fingers from where she had signed the priest's book. Darvin and Gwyre's priest, Coilynn of Lasurd of the fields, had taken over a house and as I passed it Coilynn appeared. She was tying a rag of grey material above the door so we knew where to take the wounded. The priest already had blood down the front of her gown of green rags, and I wondered if it was hers or from the wounded.

As I passed she stopped me, touching me gently on the arm.

"King Rufra, will he really come?" she asked, and even though priests are trained to modulate their voices I could hear fear there.

"Yes," I said simply, remembering a moment clear as a summer pool – Rufra clad in silver, appearing out of the dark when I needed him most. "He will come."

"Good. I would like to see him. I have heard much that is good about him."

"Even about his new ways?"

"I am not against them as some priests are. If the grasses grow and change, then why shouldn't people? Lasurd told us the seasons changed for a reason, so change must be for a reason." She finished tying the flag. "I must get water now. Darvin is still taking signatures, so if you would sign for Lasurd or Lessiah now is the time."

"I must prepare for the next attack," I said. She nodded and went back into the house.

I walked on though I felt guilty about my small lie; Coilynn's simple faith in her god and her king had touched me in a way I did not understand. It had been long on long since I had felt faith in anything. Irritated, I joined the group of archers in the middle of the long central street where it widened. They looked frightened, holding their bows and quivers tighter than lovers. I had no quiver, only a handful of arrows I was gripping too tightly. I loosened my fist, watching the white retreat from my knuckles and be replaced by a more human pink. Down the street I saw Aydor laughing as he took a ladleful of water from a trooper and I thrust my arrows into the muddy ground with such vehemence the men and women around me took a step back. I must have looked like something from a nightmare to these people, my expression grim, body mage-bent and harlequin armour splattered with the same Nonman blood I could feel drying on my face.

"Empty your quivers," I said. We were surrounded by the men and women Nywulf had sent to shield us. "Stick your arrows in the ground."

"Why?" said a woman. It was Aisleth, Ossowin's wife. She at least looked like she had some spirit.

"It makes them easier to get hold of, allows those gathering arrows to see who is running low and, more importantly, the dirt on the heads will poison a wound. If your target doesn't die now, they will die later."

"That would be a bad death," said a small man, "like Vorle who died seeing Fitchgrass after he cut himself on the plough."

"Good," said Aisleth. "these Nonmen do not deserve to die clean. Hedgings take them all."

"What about the Nonmen arrows?" said a man at the back. I pointed at the troops with shields around us.

"That is what they're for, and—"

"Arrows!" The shout came from the walls, and I instinctively ducked; the villagers followed my lead and we were quickly encased in a shell of shields as a hard and deadly rain fell. Somewhere outside our refuge arrows found flesh, and screaming heralded the second Nonmen attack, followed by the shouting and whistling of the mettle-chanters and another rain of arrows.

"Magic curse them and sorcerers take their spirits," muttered someone behind me.

"I think they already have," said a soldier. There was a low chuckle from the men and women holding the shields. That they seemed so calm about the falling arrows helped to calm the villagers around me a little.

"My hand shakes," said Aisleth.

"Mine too," said another villager.

"Hold fast," I said, turning to meet the eyes of the village archers. "Waiting is always the worst part. We'll get our turn at them soon. Action will steady your aim."

I could feel fear around me, the stench of sweat and piss and the gradual ratcheting up of tension as the Nonmen's ram beat upon the gate and arrows rained down on us again. The trooper holding a shield above me flexed his fingers.

"Arm ache?" I said. He nodded. "I can hold the shield for a while if you wish."

He shook his head. "Save your arm for your bow, Blessed," he said, and I wondered at how, even though Rufra had brought his new ways, people still clung to what they knew.

"Archers!" Nywulf's call was loud and clear. In a bigger battle a warleader would use a whistle, flags or a horn, but here Nywulf's voice was enough.

The shields were removed from above us and a shudder went through me as the cool night air replaced the warmth of bodies huddled under our protective roof. Torches flickered and flared all over the village and for a moment I saw nothing. I let my eye run along the top of the wall, up to where it met a house, along the roof, down the other side to where the wall continued until it met the next house. A silhouette on a roof caught my eye – arrow-to-string, draw, aim and loose. A scream of pain and a body rattled down the slates.

"Shoot at anything on a roof or coming over the wall," I said. "Take your time and aim well." – *aim, shoot* – I sent another arrow into the night and was rewarded with a scream. "You don't have to kill them. The fall will do that, and if it doesn't there are plenty of our troops waiting at the bottom to finish the job." Soon silhouettes were swarming over two of the houses, one to the left and one on the right. – *aim, shoot* – The archers over the gate were no longer firing exclusively down at the men with the ram – *aim, shoot* – now they had split their attention between the ram and the walls and I knew the momentum of the fight had changed – *aim, shoot* – *aim, shoot* – we were reacting to the attackers this time rather than having them do what we wanted – *aim, shoot* – I heard the splintering of wood – the gate was starting to give.

"Where is our water?" roared Nywulf into the night. Two women struggled past carrying a huge steaming metal cauldron. Aydor left the shieldwall, which stood idle in front of the splintering gate – *aim, shoot* – and joined Nywulf, taking the cauldron and carrying it up two parallel ladders. As they got it to the top of the wall, an arrow hit Nywulf, bouncing off the metal of his shoulder piece. Nywulf shouted, "Signless filth, you need a wash!" And they tipped the cauldron of boiling water over those below. – *aim, shoot*. The steady boom of the ram was replaced by anguished cries.

"Arrows!"

The shields came over us. A hard ratatatatat as arrows fell. The Nonmen archers' attack seemed to go on for a long time. Though there were probably no more than ten flights launched they staggered them, so just as I thought it was over another rain of arrows would fall. No doubt they caught out more than one of us.

Beneath the shelter of the shields Aisleth gave me a smile. "You were right." She held out an unshaking arm. "The waiting was the worst part, my hand no longer shakes."

"Girton!" I scuttled out of the haven of the shield roof to find Cearis waiting, her shield held above her head as she strolled along as calmly as if she walked through a rainstorm. "Nywulf wants you to kill some of their archers, see if you can drive them back a bit." We jogged over the ground to where Nywulf was inspecting the gates.

"Pull them down," he ordered.

Ossowin started to protest. He headed a small group of angry villagers that had gathered in the lee of the wall.

"Eight of ours have died already, Nywulf, and four more will succumb to their wounds soon enough," he shouted. "And for what? They still come."

"Thirteen of my troops have died, and they have died for you," said Nywulf. I winced – that was more than we could afford. "If we let the Nonmen choose our tactics, they'll rain down arrows on us or put their numbers into coming over the roofs of the houses and the wall. And we will lose. If we take down the gate, they will focus on this place." He was right, but I knew it was a desperate tactic. Our troops were no longer as fresh as they had been at the start.

Another volley of arrows fell. I peered through a hole in the gate to see where the Nonmen archers were. Like fools they had bunched up their archers with the torches and fires of the army behind them, making them an easy target. "We need to kill some of them," said Cearis into my ear. "If they fight sensibly they will just wear our numbers down. We have to make them angry, then give them a target and let them grind themselves to dust against it."

"Will this work?" I called as she climbed the ladder beside me. I crouched behind the parapet and put an arrow to the string of my bow.

"I hope so. Nywulf worries that the villagers, Ossowin especially, will crack and decide it is better to give in to the Nonmen than to fight. He wants to keep them busy and focused, fighting will do that." I nodded, stood – *aim, shoot* – a shriek in the dark – *aim, shoot* – another cry. The group of archers broke up and retreated.

"How long before they come again?" I said.

"Not long," said Cearis.

This phase of the battle went on for another hour and I stayed with the archers. Each time the Nonmen met our shieldwall they were repulsed, Aydor screaming at them, "Beaten by farmers! You're being beaten by farmers." I don't know if that demoralised the Nonmen or made them more furious. Whichever, it annoyed me intensely.

Screaming had been the background noise ever since the battle started, but it was late into the night, in the hours when the knowledge of our mortality haunts us and the dead are usually taken away, that a different type of screaming started. The screaming of the tortured. Out in the darkness among the myriad flickering fires of the Nonmen someone was being hurt. I stared out, while our numbers had steadily dwindled the Nonmen's had swelled. Aisleth came to stand by me. She was covered in blood but I was glad to see it was not hers. She held a spear in one hand and I quashed the feeling of hopelessness that had been growing within me.

"What is that noise, Girton?"

"Sometimes Nonmen brutalise their own, I do not know why."

"Nywulf!" The shout came from outside the walls. "Nywulf, I would talk peace. Do you give me safe passage?"

"Chirol!" Boros strode past me.

Nywulf followed, grabbing him by the arm.

"Not now, not here."

"I am sworn vengeance," said Boros. "He is here and I am—"

"Not now," said Nywulf. His voice was very calm, a dangerous sign to those that knew him. "When there is another attack, he will lead it. Then is your chance."

"Let me speak to him," said Boros.

"No."

"Nywulf, I—"

"You will go to the house at the rear of the village and help build that wall back up. It will not stand another attack, but whatever you do will help buy a little time." Before Boros could say anything Nywulf raised his voice: "Cearis, take Boros and help him shore up the rear wall." She came forward, walking Boros away. As the young warrior glanced back over his shoulder I could see the hate on his face, even through his scars. Nywulf watched Boros go and then ascended the ladder and stood on the wall.

"Talk then, Chirol. I will hear the terms for your surrender but do not promise I will accept them." A laugh came from the darkness, followed by another terrible scream.

"Later, Nywulf, I will have you at the point of my knife, and what a talk we shall have then."

"I look forward to it," said Nywulf. "Now, speak if you would speak. I do not have time to natter like a laundry man."

"Very well. Your beloved Rufra is not coming, Nywulf, I caught your messenger. That is who you hear screaming."

"No!"

Aisleth made to run for the hole where the gate had been but I grabbed her.

"Wait, Aisleth, wait. He lies."

"How do you know?" she said, stricken.

"Your daughter rode Xus and she wore no armour. No one could ever catch my mount with only an unarmoured child on him."

"But what if she fell? What if—" She was interrupted by Nywulf chuckling. "You have our messenger, do you? Then what is her name, Chirol?"

"Ah. Sadly my men were too keen with their knives and cut out her tongue before we could find out her name."

"Cut out her tongue, did they?" Nywulf laughed. "Then bring her forward, Chirol. I am sure her mother will know her."

"I doubt that, Nywulf. If what we have done to her was done to me, well, even my own mother would struggle to recognise me."

"I hear she does not anyway," said Nywulf.

"He does not have her, see?" I whispered to Aisleth. I let go of her arm. "If he did he would bring her forward."

"Know this, Nywulf," shouted Chirol. "What we do to this girl is as nothing to what we shall do to those villagers in there with you, but if they give you up now we will let them live."

Aisleth's husband had appeared beside us with a gaggle of villagers.

"Aisleth, we should take him up on this. They have our girl and we cannot survive the night. We—"

She turned and slapped him hard across the face.

"See him?" She pointed at me. "A mage-bent boy with more mettle in him than you have ever had. This Nonman no more has Dinay than you have balls. You shame me and your village."

Then she turned and before I could stop her she was up the ladder and standing by Nywulf. Ossowin put his hand to his slapped cheek and gave me a glare of such vehemence it felt like a blow.

"I hear you, Chirol, Boarlord of the Nonmen," she shouted. "It is my daughter who rode out for the king and I do not believe you have her, or that you will let us go free. But know this: if you have laid a finger on my girl, your death will be one so slow and painful it will be told as a tale by mothers to frighten their children for generations! Come near us, and—"

The arrow came out of the night, a single, well aimed streak that took Aisleth in the heart. The wicked point emerging from her back. For a moment she still stood, and then the life went from her and she fell, ragged clothes billowing around her and she crashed lifeless among the troops of the shieldwall.

"No!" cried Ossowin.

The Nonmen charged. I grabbed Ossowin, anger welling up in a dark tide. "You did that, fool." The roar of the charging Nonmen rose. "Your cowardice put her on that wall. It should have been you up there!"

"No," he said quietly, "not I. You did that – you gave her spirit in a hedging's deal."

"Be quiet," I hissed, "and fight for your village. Fight for your wife and her memory. Give your daughter someone worthy to look up to." I picked up a shield and a spear and shoved them into his hands, pushing him towards the shieldwall "All of you," I screamed at the villagers standing around me. "Fight! Fight for Aisleth! Fight for Gwyre!" I pushed a woman forward. "For Aisleth!" I shouted, and they took up the shout, running to put their weight into the shieldwall.

And then the Nonmen were on us, the presence of their leader spurring them on. I ran for the house at the back of the village where our defence's weakest point was and hoped we could hold.

Arrows fell around me. This would be the Nonmen's biggest attack. Chirol had not stopped the girl or frightened the villagers into surrender, so he had to throw everything at us now and hope to break us before Rufra arrived with more troops. I did not know if we would live to see Rufra come or not, but I would make the Nonmen pay dearly for my life.

In the house with the broken wall it was worse than I had hoped. The flickering light of the torches showed me two soldiers, Telkir and Halda, with tired faces and spears wet with blood, some of it their own. Broken spears lay on the floor and by them a small pile of broken furniture was all that remained to barricade the hole with. The wood jammed across the gap was scored and scratched and the only good thing about the building, from a defensive point, was that the upper floor had been removed and I could look straight up into the rafters high above, which would make it hard for anyone to come through the roof and surprise us. Behind me arrows and bolts had peppered the door I had come through.

"They will bring ropes next time," said Halda. "They have been using grappling hooks on the wood over the hole and distracting us with arrows when we try and get them off. Then while we deal with the hole they come in through the roof." She pointed at a pile of bodies in one corner. "None have survived the fall yet, but they will bring ropes." She sounded resigned to her fate.

"If we could bring down the entire back wall," said Telkir, "that would stop them."

"Have you tried that?" I said.

He nodded and kicked the wall. "Solid as Halda's thighs." He grinned at the woman across from him. Halda smiled back then wiped hair from her face and grabbed her helmet from the floor. "Listen." The high whirring of mettle-chanter's spinners filled the air. "They come again."

First came the shadows, figures like bad dreams, flitting past the hole and momentarily eclipsing the light. Telkir and Halda crouched, spears in their hands, and I unsheathed my knives.

"Don't waste your time trying to get those running past," said Halda. "They are only trying to tire us. Save your energy for when the real attack comes. You may be better using that –" she pointed at a bow leaning against the wall behind me "– to keep them from the roof." I nodded, sheathing my blades and picking up the bow. With a crash something hit the boards across the hole making them shudder against the nails holding them. Halda's spear darted out and there was a cry from outside. Another crash. Telkir's spear shot out and there was a scream. A bloodied hand grabbed the spear and a hook was pushed through the gap between two boards. There was a shout of triumph from outside and the hook bit into the boards as the tension was taken up. With a loud creak a board bent and then snapped in half.

I watched all this open-mouthed, like a child in their first battle.

"Move!" shouted Halda. She threw herself into me, pushing me to one side and knocking the air from me as crossbow bolts shot in from the darkness. I heard her take the hit for me, heard her pain in the out-take of her breath. It was not a scream and not a shout, more a sound of disappointment – like she had been given a long-hoped-for gift that did not match up to her expectations. I wanted to check her wound, see if I could help her, but there was no time. Slates started to fall from above where Nonmen hammered on the roof. Halda placed her hand on my shoulder and pushed herself up, her bloody touch like a fire against me. My mind lit up with life and a dark tide moved within. She pulled the crossbow bolt from her side with a grunt and picked up her spear, stabbing at Nonmen who screamed curses as they grabbed at the remaining boards. Slashing swords hacked at what remained of the barricade. The rhythm merged with the frantic beating of my heart, it slowed, and changed, *everything changed*. I saw shades at the holes in the roof and a snake fell, twisting and turning in the air as it struggled to find and bite. I raised an arm, stepping back to avoid poisonous fangs then *a rope, it is only a rope*. My hand closed around the bow. I existed in a strange and slow, silent world.

– aim, shoot –

The world rushing back.

Fight.

Move.

Live.

My arrow took a Nonman in the throat, and I rolled aside as he hit the floor where I had been a moment ago. Another arrow – *aim, shoot* – into the rafters. Another Nonman fell. An arrow aimed at a Nonman on the rope – *aim, shoot* – As my arrow found him another was already climbing down. A second rope fell in a welter of slates and wood. Further along a third hole was hammered in the roof. Too many of them: a million grasping hands at the hole, a thousand hedging-faced monsters staring down. The stink of blood and damp hay. A gasp from behind me. I turned. Telkir fell to his knees, his mouth gasping for air like a landed fish as a Nonman, filthy skin, matted hair, wearing the spine of a man as a belt, scrabbled through the barricade and stabbed him again and again and again. – *aim, shoot* – The arrow punched the Nonman backwards, but it was too late for Telkir. Halda was barely holding her own against a Nonman as he squeezed through a tight gap. A Nonman dropped from a rope, landing behind me and I span, smashing the bow into his face, dropping the weapon and going for my blade as a Nonman sword found Halda's throat.

Three Nonmen against me.

Four coming down ropes.

One reaching for the closed door into the village. My left stabsword snaked out, hamstringing him before he could open it. I didn't have time to finish him. *Never leave a live enemy behind you.*

An attack came from my right – *a Meeting of Hands* – forcing me on to the defensive. A hand grabbed my club foot, filthy nails digging hard into twisted flesh. Even through the leather of my boot it was agonising. My concentration fled. Pain flooded in.

Breathe, Girton. A whisper from very far away. My master's voice.

Nonmen coming down the ropes. Nonmen hammering at the remaining boards.

Breathe out.

Too many.

Breathe!

All is lost.

Breathe in.

Too many.

Breathe.

No time for fear.

Too many.

No time for pain.

All is lost.

Breathe out.

Sell yourself dearly.

You. Are. The. Weapon.

Stamping down hard on the hand holding my foot. *The Archer's Crouch.* A filthy blade whistling over my head. I counter with a thrust to the gut rewarded with blood and the stink of open bowels. *The Twitcher's Flip,* a handspring sending me backwards, and I stand against the back wall. Two down of seven; more coming down the ropes. More coming through the hole.

If you die. I die.

My master's voice. How does she know?

How does she know?

Forward. Into the Precise Steps. Shock on filthy faces at my attack. Right blade deflects a spear point, left blade slides in opening a chest.

Breathe in.

Place the rose in his mouth. Kick the body into the man behind him, sending them both sprawling backwards over Halda's bloody corpse. Longsword coming for me.

No retreat.

Into *the Maiden's Pass,* spinning down the length of the blade. Marry it to *Jubal's Spin,* both blades coming up and out as I twist, razor edges finding throats. Axe from the left too heavy to parry. *The Boatgirl's Dip,* going under his swing and elbow swinging back to knock him off balance, letting the momentum of the movement bring round my blade to cut a furrow across his back.

I can do this.

Yes! I can do this.

Stabsword from the right. Easy parry, blade into throat. Nonmen flowing like water through the holes. Nonmen dropping like rain down the ropes. I am at the far end of the room. I have cut through them like a scythe.

I am the weapon.

Turn.

I am the weapon.

The Nonmen are wary now.

Breathe.

They are scared of coming within reach of my blades.

Push.

"Yes, Master." Whispered under my breath. And attack.

Dogs!

"Dogs?" There are no dogs, but the sudden word, heard clear as day in my mind, brings with it the cold sharpness of an old terror.

I am six. I am a slave trapped in a cage while dogs tear my friends apart.

I falter, and in battle that split second is all an enemy needs. Nonmen, coming all at once, blades and spears held out. The spaces that I need to fight in denied me. Death inevitable.

Let me help you.

Master?

No.

Not her voice. It was never her voice. Her voice is a light across the scars of my skin. This voice is old and dark and insidious.

I recognise it.

I hate it.

I fear it.

Spear points reach for my flesh.

There is a pause.

All is quiet. All is still. The cold night air is golden. Dying men bleed life into the land. They make a well that is sweeter and deeper than my needs require. I see every danger. I count the glittering spear points; I count the shining sword blades; I count the rusty axeheads. I see faces twisted in hate, blackened teeth, roaring mouths. I see weak points in the walls that will bring the building down around me. I see my master sweating on a bed as poison blackens her flesh.

"Help me."

I say it.

I welcome it.

Because I do not want her to die. Because I am frightened of death.

The scars on my body twist and pull. They rip me apart and they put me back together. They burn my flesh and they freeze my spirit. I am a single point of light in a dark land that stretches out for ever around me.

I am single point of fury.

A black spear point springs from my open mouth. I vomit black birds of hate and death. They twist through the air around me echoing the patterns of the scars on my body. They shoot into the rafters of the house. They are a sparkling darkness shot through with motes of white hate; they are a cold mirror of the night sky. Birds twist and slice, spin and cut, pierce men and sever ropes before forming into a thick, inky snake. It hammers into the house, hitting the wall, passing through the thick stonework in a hail of razoring shards then turns on itself, smashing in the other side through the medium of four men. It fountains from me, neither solid nor liquid, and my mouth is stretched so wide it feels like my jaw will crack and my teeth will shatter. I would scream but I cannot move: every muscle is tensed, every thought excised. More Nonmen enter through the gaps in the barricade and the blackness pierces heads. Ruined bodies block the holes. The black fountain anchors itself into the walls, seeping into the stonework and making huge black plugs. My body is shaking. The black snake pulls and I feel the wall giving, feel the stress running through the building in a web of fine lines like the glowing scars on my skin. The building starts to give, creaks – shifts – relaxes – groans, and it is falling, the walls and the roof coming down in a smoking heap on top of the massed Nonmen outside.

And then it is quiet.

It is quiet.

Outside there is screaming and fighting. I know it but I cannot hear it. My ears sing a high-pitched song and my skin is white with dust. I rub my eyes, making dark pits on my white face.

And then I hear a noise.

In a corner, unseen, has been a watcher. A girl, no more than five or ten, it is difficult to tell her age amid the dust. Her hair is braided with cornstalks and her eyes are the blue of hailflowers. She stares at me, terrified.

No one can ever know what you are.

And this time it is the voice of my master, or a memory of it. No one can know of the magic. My Conwy blade is in my hand. The hilt is warm and blood drips from the tip.

Tap. Tap. Tap.

One more body. No one will notice one more body.

"Go." The word escapes my parched mouth. "Go quickly and tell no one what you saw here. I saved your life. Remember that. I saved your life."

She squeezes out of her hidey hole, skips over ruined bodies and around fallen stones to push the door open and run out into the night. The door opening shatters the strange quiet that has infused the room.

It feels like every muscle in me has been tightened to breaking point, and as the adrenalin drains away I start to shake. The grass that covered the floor of the house is dead, like ash – soured. Nothing will ever live here again A glance around the room: bodies, broken and twisted beneath fallen woodwork and masonry. Miraculously, an oil lamp still burns, hanging from a hook by the door. When I pick it up it is warm in my hand and it brings with it a flush of sensation: a cold breeze on my skin, the stink of ruptured guts in my nose and the noise of voices full of fear and pain. Screaming. People are screaming, and the screams are twisting, moving, coming together in the night and forming words.

"They're in! They're in!"

I don't know what the magic I used here was. It is not something I have heard of from the old stories, not something I recognise. I glance at the dead grass, wonder what other telltale marks I may have left on the bodies for those who know what to look for. I toss the oil lamp onto a pile of shattered wood hoping there will be enough material to start a fire and hide what has happened. Hide the terrible thing I am.

Then I head into the night.

The Nonmen are in the village.

My work is not yet done.

The Boarlord, framed in the open gate by fires behind him, watching as his men flood the small village in a screaming, shrieking mass. Nywulf is pulling back what remains of his troops and the villagers, about fifty in all, to create a rough semicircle in front of the building being used by the priests for our wounded. In front of them is Aydor, standing with his legs apart and my warhammer in his hands. He is covered in blood. It sticks his chained skirts to his bare legs and his once-grand purple armour is hidden beneath a viscous covering of gore. His helmet is gone, and his face is a mirror of the grimacing rictus that was on the visor. He is screaming like a madman. At some point he has lost his shield and as Nonmen attack he lays about himself, creating space while Nywulf's pitifully thin shieldwall forms up behind him. A Nonman runs past me, screaming with joy as he pursues a woman and I cut him down with a single, hard, downward slash of my Conwy stabsword. I walk forward, foot in front of foot. Another Nonmen rushes at me with a spear. *The Maiden's Pass* – slipping around him and forcing my blade up into his gut, once, twice, three times, letting him fall as I walk, foot in front of foot, on into chaos.

"Aydor, now!" shouts Nywulf, and the shieldwall breaks, allowing Aydor to slip back in.

"Form up! Form up!" Chirol is screaming at his men. "We'll gut them like sheep and leave them hanging from the walls for the false king!"

I stagger forward. The after-effects of magic hang around me in trails of gold and silver and I cannot understand why no one is pointing and screaming at me. I am the real horror here. As Aydor squeezes into the shieldwall another body squeezes out.

Boros.

He runs shouting obscenities at his brother. "Mage-bent,

sorcerer's get!" He sees nothing else. The first Nonmen he passes are too surprised to do anything but the third is ready with a spiked mace. As Boros passes he swings it, knocking him to the ground. He raises his weapon to finish the job, and I sheath my blade, stoop, pick up a fallen bow and an arrow – *aim, shoot* – The arrow takes the Nonman in the throat. I hear laughter, the strange otherworldly laughter that I have only ever heard once before, when I walked the dark halls of Xus's palace. This is a dream and I am already dead. We are all already dead.

I drop the bow, cut down another Nonman. I do it carelessly, without thinking, the movement of my blade and body automatic. Finally the Nonmen notice me. I am a dust-white apparition with black-pit eyes.

Gwyre is a blur heavy with exhaustion and death.

The Nonmen are hedgings, screaming and whooping as they come to claim the fallen spirits promised to them.

Nywulf is shouting and his words are spikes of ice in the air.

A group of Nonmen pull together before me. Shields lock into hide, spears grow into bristles and they become a creature of hard scale and sharp teeth. It is not a strong creature but it will be enough to finish me. I know it and so do they.

Nywulf rallies his survivors: "Sell your lives dearly. Make the yellowers pay. And for the dead gods' sake, don't let them take you alive!"

I have lost one of my blades, I don't know where, but the ground is littered with weapons and I pick up another. The Nonmen before me are no longer human. I see them as Dark Ungar, a creature warped by loss and hate and hungry only for more of what pains it. *The Swordmouth's Leap*, straight onto the teeth of the bristling spearbeast before me, that is how I shall go. Laughter bubbling up within, a final grand gesture that no one will ever see or talk of.

I can help you.

That voice, so reasonable, so beguiling.

A village wiped from the map, the Nonmen gone with it, and in its place a yellow pit, dust rises like smoke. Girton's Souring, they will call it. You will live for ever.

But they will not call it that because no one will live to remember my name. Power moves within me. I am a ship on a sea of darkness. I sail an ocean of life. I am the shifting tide.

A horn sounds.

It is a single golden clarion call, it is a note of such exquisite and utter sweetness that it stops every man and woman in the village where they stand. Swords do not cut, arrows do not fly. Even the Nonmen hold and look to their leader.

"Rufra!" shouts Nywulf. "It is the king! Rufra sounds his horn. He comes!"

Do I imagine it or can I hear cavalry? Is that really the drumming of mounts' feet on the ground? The growls of mounts smelling blood? The horn sounds again and the beast before me devolves back into men and they turn, running for the gate. The Boarlord stands at the gateway to the village and, as his men stream past him and out into the night, he points his sword at Nywulf as if to say, "later, you and I" and then he joins his troops, running out into the night. In the light of the burning house behind me I watch the faces of the troops and villagers as they turn to each other, each seemingly more surprised than the last to find that they are still alive.

Chapter 21

Rufra smashed the Nonmen at Gwyre. People would tell you, later, that it was a golden battle where a good king struck down a great evil. So loved was he by the dead gods that Xus the unseen did not take any of his troops to the dark palace, and when they spoke of glorious cavalry charges it was Gwyre they imagined; the king leading his Riders to glory like Duvell who slew the twin sorcerers – a shining silver figure wielding an unbreakable sword that protected him from all harm. It was true, to a point. His cavalry lost no one and he slew the Nonmen almost to a man. Only a few escaped, though Chirol was among them. He would vanish from the Tired Lands for many years – though sadly, not for ever.

But of those who defended Gwyre few survived. Nywulf led one hundred in and only thirty walked out. Boros survived – just. He was carried out unconscious with the other wounded. Among the villagers the death toll was even higher, a hundred and fifty had lived in Gwyre but only forty-two left it, and most of them were children. The mood in the cavalry that returned to Rufra's camp was jubilant – they had sliced an arm from Tomas's army and made victory that bit more likely – but among the defenders of Gwyre there was no celebration. We had fought hard and it had taken all we had from us. Many Riders lent their mounts to the villagers, who walked like the dead, still coming to terms with what they had seen and lost. For a long time they would look back over their shoulders at the column of smoke rising over the wide, flat land, showing where Rufra had torched their village and crops to deny them to Tomas. The girl, Dinay, had lost her mother but was being treated as a hero; her ride would become a song and a dance of its own one day. I had told her to ride Xus back, and Rufra had asked her to ride at the front of the column and made her his swordbearer, trying to dull the girl's pain with his generosity of spirit.

I walked at the back of the column and my spirit was not so generous, it was sick. My teeth felt rotten with the memory of magic and every part of me ached: my club foot burned and my limp was more pronounced than it had been in years. I walked with Darvin, the priest of Lessiah, and though his face was covered his every move was that of a man weighed down by what he had been through.

"The hedgings are loose in the land, Girton." He trudged on a few steps over ground churned up by mount feet and claws. "Darkness is abroad and I hear talk of yellowers being seen. A sorcerer will arise from this chaos, mark my words." I was taken by a coughing fit and fell to my knees, bile spewing from my mouth onto the ground. "It is a poison, magic," he said, and I felt cold. Did he sense what was in me? "The taint of the hedgings does men no good, and we have been too close to it. We must fight against it with whatever we have." He helped me stand and stared straight into my eyes, behind his dirt-stained mask his eyes were a vivid blue. "Even when we think we have done enough we will always find there is more to be done –" he seemed inexpressibly sad "– and we must reach deep inside ourselves to find the strength to push on further than we believed possible."

I nodded, uncomfortable in his unwavering gaze.

"Where is Coilynn?" I asked. I had liked the young priest.

"Dead," said Darvin. "Nonmen got into the cellar. She tried to protect the wounded and had her throat cut for it."

"A pity," I said, and looked inside for grief but found only a numb place, a grey lake of nothing. I did not know what words may comfort Darvin at the loss of his fellow. "I spoke to her," I said. "Rufra would have liked her."

"Yes," said Darvin, "I am sure he would." He let go of me, folding his hands into his robe and staring at the ground as we staggered on.

Behind us, Gwyre continued to burn.

Carts arrived eventually, and with them came food and drink. We clambered into them, and I found myself sitting with Ossowin, Dinay's father.

"I am sorry about your wife," I said.

He turned to me. There was a shallow cut across the bridge of his nose, but the real damage was in his eyes which were wild, like a pig that knew it was being taken to slaughter. "You," he said, there was no forgiveness there. "I will not forget you. I will make you pay for what you brought upon me. Now my wife is dead and my daughter thinks I am a coward and does not want to know me." He spat on the floor of the cart by my feet.

"Much is said and done in the heat of battle that is later regretted," I said. "You are not a coward. I will speak to Dinay."

"You will? Nywulf's pet will speak to my child? Nywulf I understand; he is a man who knows nothing but war, but you are simply a follower and barely a man at all. Because of callous child-men like you I have lost everything."

"Not everything. You have your life. If not for men like me you would have lost that too. You and your family would be playthings for the Nonmen." The words were harshly spoken and leaped from my mouth.

"Would we?" He pushed my shoulder. "Or would the Nonmen have passed us by? If your usurper king had never—"

My hand was at my blade hilt before I even thought; only the firm grip of Darvin stopped me drawing my weapon.

"Girton, peace, peace," he whispered in my ear. "Perhaps you are not the person to be dealing with this, eh?" The wheels of the cart creaked out circles of time. Darvin let go of my sword hand.

"I'll find another cart," I said, and jumped off.

We camped as the sun hit midday and I was called to to sit with Nywulf, Rufra, Cearis, Crast, Aydor and the girl Dinay.

"Welcome, Girton," said Rufra. "We sit and drink to the hero of the hour." He nodded at Dinay. "Hers is a ride that will be talked of for generations." The girl blushed deep red as I sat by her.

"You should be proud, Dinay," I said. "Few can tame Xus – even King Rufra almost lost a finger to him."

"Not almost," said Rufra, holding up a hand with one finger bent back so it looked like it was missing. Gentle laughter rippled around the fire. "We had a great victory at Gwyre, Girton," said Rufra, "and I am aware that a high price was paid by you and those who defended it, but—"

"—it will not be spoken of," I filled in.

"It will be spoken of," said Rufra, "just not as loudly as people will speak of our victory." He stared into the fire.

"It is how it must be," said Nywulf.

"I hear Aydor fought like a maned lizard," said Crast. Aydor smiled so widely I thought his stupid face would split.

"A mad lizard," said Nywulf. Aydor's face dropped until Nwyulf gave him the smallest of grins across the fire. "But we would not have held without him."

"That could be said of anyone who was there." Aydor tore off a piece of pork, stuffing it into his mouth and carrying on speaking with it full. "And you, Girton, you saved my life. I saw the bodies around the house you defended. You must have fought as if a sorcerer sat on your shoulders." I shuddered. Did he suspect? Was this a threat? His mother must have known what I was; had she told him?

"I would have died many times over if not for Telkir and Halda," I said. "They were not as lucky as I, that is all."

Aydor nodded and lifted his cup. "Telkir and Halda," he said. Rufra lifted his cup and, keeping his gaze locked on the young girl who shared our fire, said, "And to Aisleth, spear woman of Gwyre who spat in the face of the Boarlord."

"The fallen," added Dinay and began to raise her cup, but she was shaking with tears she could barely suppress – and tears she should not. We all understood loss.

Cearis put her hand on her arm. "Come, Dinay the Rider," she said softly. "Let us find Darvin and write a plea for your mother in his signing book, then you should sleep. You have not slept for too long."

We watched her lead the girl away.

"A brave girl," said Rufra. "She will make a good Rider."

"You will make her a squire?" I said.

"Already done," said Rufra. "She has fallen out with her father, and—"

"The man is a coward," I said.

"The man was faced with a hard decision," said Rufra, steel in his voice. "He sought only to protect his people."

"And so he let a man die horribly on his village gates."

"Better that than letting his whole village die." I remained silent. "I will speak to Dinay about her father and see that there is a reconciliation. It does not do to split up families and the girl needs someone, otherwise Nywulf will have another stray on his hands."

"Stop, Blessed," said Crast. "You will make me jealous if there is someone else for Nywulf to force latrine duty on." Laughter. Then Nywulf spoke and the laughter stopped.

"This proves there is a spy, Rufra."

Rufra stared into the sky, watching the clouds scud by. "How so, Nwyulf?"

"Who knew about Hallan? Who outside of your close council?"

"No one," said Rufra. "Only you, Cearis and Karrick."

"You trusted the Landsman?" I said. I felt a coldness like I had sunk my hands into icy water.

"Karrick is trustworthy in this. He carried messages."

"Girton may have a point," said Nywulf. "The Landsmen do not like you or what you bring."

"Karrick is different, and besides, Hallan may have given himself away."

"He was a careful man," said Nywulf.

"Even careful men make mistakes," replied Rufra. He stood and emptied his cup into the fire. "We should move on or we will still be in hog territory come nightfall. Girton, you should ride. Speak to the mountmaster. She will find you a mount, or Xus if you want him, but . . ."

"He is a comfort to the girl?"

"Yes. But you need to ride. You look half dead."

I felt it too, though not for the reasons Rufra believed.

There was an ache in my teeth and the web of scars over my skin felt like a net of burning light.

When the mountmaster brought me a mount, the animal shied, growling and bucking as I neared.

"I do not understand this," said the stablemaster. "Stuy is usually the most placid of my mounts." I tried to calm him and he bit at me, slashing with his tusks. "Stuy!" she said, shocked.

"It must be the blood," I said. Dried blood was caked onto me, it had worked itself into the enamelling of my armour and between the plates at my shoulder and elbow, it stifled the clinking of the chains in my skirts and it stiffened the material, making it scratch wherever it touched my skin.

"Maybe it is the blood," she said, though she did not believe it. A war-trained mount has no fear of blood. It was me that scared the animal, me and what ran through me like a pulse. I may have been tired to the bone but since Gwyre the world had become more vibrant and alive than it had been in years. I walked through a rainbow, a place of iridescent colour and sensation. I felt the land around me, felt the men and woman and the blood running through them, felt the animals as they moved around us and further out I felt the herds of feral pigs as they tore into the cold corpses of Nonmen left around Gwyre. I felt the sourings like an ache in my bones, like a sore, a throbbing centre and the aching itch around the edge as the body fought a losing battle to save itself. I felt the rivers and the streams in cold currents along my skin. I felt the armies of Tomas as a dull glow of life far to the north of us. And I felt a million other things I did not and could not understand; I only knew they were there; alive. And this feeling had been growing and growing. As I stood there watching the mount I was overwhelmed. My tiredness was a crack, a weakness, a fracture of glowing lines around my body.

The world rushed at me.

A sudden focus.

I hear a tree branch cracking in a silent forest. See the land as a circle in my vision, a flat spinning plate of sky and earth that curls around itself. It refuses to make sense, it is a reeling vertiginous spin. A sound like the whine of a biting lizard twisting around my head, getting closer and closer, high-pitched and irritating. It is all I can hear. It fills my ears, my mind. My vision telescopes, the colours blurring and twisting into a single dark point surrounded by colour. The world expands and draws in, taking on a weight that would pull me to the ground if the tracks on my skin were not threatening to pull me apart. Then the single point of darkness expands, and it contains everything: me, Rufra, the Tired Lands, the world. It is so big I can barely believe something as insignificant as me can exist within it. Pain follows. The lizard bites me in the centre of my forehead, the world slaps into focus and I am me again. Girton. Not glowing, not lost in a world beyond understanding.

"Girton?" Rufra's voice.

I shook myself out of my reverie. I had been lost in sensation, lost and confused. I had somehow expected Tomas's forces to feel different, malignant, but in the low pulse of the magic all life was the same, from the heavy powerful throb of the mount by me to the thready life of the grass it crushed underfoot. All the same.

"Yes." My voice wouldn't come, and I had to cough to clear my throat. "Yes, Rufra." He looked on the point of panic.

"Saris, the mountmaster, brought me. She thought you were ill. She could get no reply, said you were frozen like a hedgescare."

"Tired, that is all." The mount growled again and I put my hand on its flank. "Be calm," I said, and the mount stood still. To those around it would look like it relaxed, but I could feel it was not so. The animal was taut, hard and on the edge of panic as I forced my will onto it. The mountmaster knew something was wrong but not what. How could she? "I am tired, that is all," I said it again in the hope I would believe it.

"Of course," said Rufra. He rubbed his forehead with the heel of his hand. "I am used to thinking of you as more than most men. I did not think about the toll Gwyre must have taken on you when I asked you to ride. You should take a cart and get some sleep, Girton. That is what you need, sleep."

"Thank you," I said. I realised that Rufra's soldiers were watching. Rufra had put his trust in me publicly and I knew he had told stories of me, of my skill as a warrior. The men and women around me had expectations. I glanced around at those watching and in their eyes I saw a terrible need I had previously been unaware of and I understood the constant pressure Rufra was under. It was not enough that he was a good man; he was a king, and that meant he must be more than just a man, and as his chosen I must also be more. I coughed. "I think it is only clear air that I need, Rufra. To ride will do me good." I pulled myself up into Stuy's saddle. "In fact," I said, raising my voice, "the harder I ride, the better I will feel. I shall scout ahead, if that is all right, King Rufra."

Relief. He tried not to show it but he was ever a poor actor. I had not let him down, not shown weakness, and by doing that, in the eyes of his troops I had proven him right in choosing me. I wondered how precarious he believed his throne was.

"Thank you," he said quietly and pulled himself up on Stuy so he could whisper in my ear. "For the dead gods' sake, Girton, find yourself some comfortable moss in a copse and get some sleep." Then he dropped down and stepped back, shouting, "Now ride, Girton Club-Foot, champion of Rufra! Ride hard!" I put the spur to Stuy and, wishing it was Xus, galloped from the makeshift day camp to the sound of thunderous cheers I did not deserve.

Night had fallen by the time I approached the main camp, and I smelled the place before I saw it. The cold air of the plains had driven away the familiarity that had allowed me to stop noticing the stink of the camp while I was in it. Riders had arrived ahead of me, even though I had not stopped as Rufra had suggested, and I found a camp in a jubilant mood. Stiltwalkers loomed out of the darkness and huge torches had been lit. Music played and fire-eaters spat great plumes of flame into the air. But all I wanted was my bed, my body ached and I smelled even worse than the camp. I handed Stuy over to a mountmaster and stumbled through the crowds. I had never enjoyed crowds and the people felt like a pressure on the top of my head, flames on my cheek. Men and women recognised me as a warrior and tried to push drinks into my hand. A garland of wildflowers and hobby dolls was placed round my neck as I staggered through a night that was red and black and black and red. Eventually

I found our tent and stumbled in. It was quiet. My master did not lie abed; no doubt she was out with Mastal, dancing and feasting, enjoying herself. I was glad. It meant the doxy I had put in her medicine had not killed her. The bottles of medicine were lined up by her bed. I meant to put it right, immediately, but a voice in my head was telling me to lie down, if only for a moment. When I did, my exhaustion was such that I fell straight into the deepest, blackest sleep.

Blue Watta

In the dream of the past. I am death and I wear his face. In the darkness she is against me. Her warmth seeps into me. Our desperate land is fully explored, our bodies are sated. I breathe slowly and list into sleep: I topple, I fall.

Down
And down
And down.

In the darkness the currents have me, they are as strong as the weeds that tangle around my feet – *cannot fight them cannot cut them dead gods let me breathe*. A hand pulls me free but as I am about to break the surface I let go. Blue Watta laughs, Blue Watta pulls me on. The water is an insistent lover, it explores me, holds me, smothers me and will brook no escape. It pulls me on.

I surface.

Our first meeting is a hesitant one. She drops the bread, we both go to pick it up. She laughs. I laugh. I pick up the bread. Her name is Hattisha, she was the daughter of a man who made weapons for the Landsmen before he died. Now she makes bread for them. Her name is Hattisha, she makes me laugh and warms my bed and when I have a spare moment I always seek her out. She mixes secret herbs and leaves into unguents and rubs them on tired muscles. She cleans blood from my skin. She is not Drusl, my first love, and I do not love her.

Down
And down
And down.

The current is a storm that binds, pulls me hither and thither, steals the air from my mouth and gently closes my eyes. Blue Watta is a dancer that will not be denied, everything in the water is his, including my life. I am a toy, a plaything to be tossed from side to side without care. I am hollow and bound in weeds. I rot into nothing and Blue Watta enjoys the spoiling of his prize.

I surface.

Her name is Hattisha and her skin is warm and sweet like biscuit. The work with the Landsmen is grinding – "Do this, mage-bent, do that, mage-bent." I am latrine digger, gibbet raiser and executioner. I fight in the front line, cutting down the desperate who fight with makeshift weapons. I do it in the name of gods long dead. I kill without thought or belief. I fear being discovered. I fear being myself. I am a wheel that turns without volition. At night I squeeze my eyes shut and try not to see the faces of the dead. I am a canvas of scars.

"Shhh, shhh. It will be all right, it will be all right."

She is not Drusl, my first love, and I do not love her.

It will not be all right.

Down
And down
And down.

The water is full of bodies, sexless and amorphous and they are drawn past me in the current. Some are slack as backwater, some as watchful as the moon shuddering and shimmering far above the drowning water. Hands without fingers, faces without noses, mouths and eyes. Cold flesh is crushed against me, desperate to share my warmth. I struggle.

I push. I drown. I beg for air as the bodies around me become more real: faces form, hands reach. I struggle. I push. I drown.

I surface.

Her name is Hattisha and a Landsman tried to drag her into his tent. She cries in my arms, she shakes with anger and shame. She tells me how much she hates them. Speaks animatedly of the time I will have earned enough to leave their employ and we can run away, set up a life in a village somewhere and she will bake bread. Then she cries herself to sleep in my arms. I entertain ideas of being the night, drifting out into the darkness, mixing herbs and leaves into a water bottle, watching a Landsman slowly wither and die knowing that I did that – I avenged the woman in my bed.

But I do nothing, the scars on my body numb my anger. She is not my first love, Drusl; I do not love her and it will not be all right.

Down

And down

And down.

In the water we are dislocated, we exist in another world. Blue Watta says and I do – my actions are not my own. I cut through the water with blade hands and water hedgings fall apart at my touch and reform behind me. The fight is endless and unchanging, my actions desperate and futile. I cut and slash, cut and slash, and all that wears down is my blade arms until I stand in front of Blue Watta. He is a million tendrils of weed bound in water ice and fish skin, he is a construction of weathered bones and broken ships and he laughs.

"You dive too deep."

Her name is Hattisha and she mixes unguents and herbs like a village wise woman. Her name is Hattisha and she is too trusting around cruel men who hold grudges. My master's hand is on my arm, my master's knife has cut my flesh. The Landsmen wait for me to act as the cage door swings shut.

"Girton, don't leave me here, Girton!"

Beneath the weight of the scars I am screaming.

I am too deep.

The weed tightens around my feet.

The sound of the river running is a gentle gurgle. It is a mocking laugh. Her cry fades on the wind and a blood gibbet crowns a hill behind us. A pattern throbs on my chest. I feel nothing and I do not betray what we are. My life goes on. The next village to be pacified awaits.

Her name was Hattisha. She was not Drusl, my first love. The scars on my chest burned all the colour out of the world and I did not love her.

Down.

And down.

And down.

And down.

And down.

Chapter 22

I awoke, tiredness gone but my limbs strangely leaden. My master and Mastal were still absent. For a moment I was struck with fear – had they gone? Had he already stolen her away to the Sighing Mountains? If so maybe it was for the best. But as I emerged from the warm cocoon of sleep I saw their packs were still there and my master's knives were stowed under the bed where I had put them. She would never leave without her knives. No doubt they had bedded down together somewhere, drunk and giddy like children.

While I had slept in the filth of death, as she had trained me to do.

I stood, stripped off my armour and washed in a bowl of cold water, the icy sting making me feel far cleaner than the meagre amount of dirt it removed. That done I headed out into the camp, thoughts of my master's medicine forgotten behind a wall of old resentments woken by my dreams.

I intended to steal into the Landsmen's compound and find Karrick's tent. He would think himself safe there with his people, and I was sure I would find the proof I needed to place before Rufra to show that Karrick had murdered Arnst. Then Rufra would have to act, and if there was definite proof one of their own had betrayed the king the Landsmen would not be able to move against him.

I glided through the camp, skills I thought I had forsaken the day I picked up the warhammer coming back to me. I moved between people like a silver fish through water, my passage barely disturbing the busy current of their lives.

Not that anyone was paying attention; it was clear that Rufra's victory at Gwyre had been celebrated well the night before. Shattered pots and cups lay at the sides of the paths, and men and women moved carefully, nursing sore heads. I ran into Neliu who, unlike most others, looked fresh and happy.

"Practising your assassin's tricks, Girton, Champion of Rufra?" In her mouth the title became a mockery.

"If you said that a little louder everyone would hear you." She grinned at me. "You seem happier than you have been before, Neliu."

"I am no longer bound to guard your master."

"Why?"

"She made an impassioned plea to the king last night, saying that she was back to strength, and she proved it by beating two warriors in hand-to-hand combat."

"She is better then." I could not hide my relief. Maybe what I had done to the medicine had not had any effect at all. Maybe Mastal didn't even need the yandil leaf. Had it all been a lie to get her away from me?

"No," said Neliu. "She beat them but she tired quickly. She must have been a sight to see in her prime. Anyway, she proved she has enough energy to protect herself from an assassin." I remembered my master duelling Sayda Halfhand in a badly lit Maniyadoc courtyard and knew that, though Neliu affected an air of worldliness, she knew very little of assassins. "Where do you go today, Champion of Rufra?" she said.

"Why do you keep calling me that?"

"Aydor was singing your praises to Karrick."

"Aydor was talking to Karrick?"

"Oh they get along famously. Then Nywulf told everyone about you shooting down the Nonman general, and Rufra informed us all of the title he'd bestowed upon you. You're quite the favourite." There was an edge to her voice, something hard underneath the words and I wondered if she was jealous. "You've been practising with Crast as well, haven't you?"

I nodded. "Helping him train, when I get the time."

"You should practise with me next time. I'm better, not as soft."

"I'll try and find time to train you too then," I said.

Her grin, all bared teeth. "Will you be at the court tonight?"

"Court?"

"Aye. Just because you're off fighting, the business of being a king doesn't stop. People have grievances, anger, reasons to be at one another's throat. These people –" she gestured around her as though we were not part of the crowd "–they are like a storm-tossed lake and Rufra must pour oil upon it to calm them." There was no mistaking the sarcasm. "Gusteffa will perform – she at least will be interesting."

"I may come then." I glanced over her shoulder. A phalanx of men in green armour was pushing through the crowd followed by a chorus of swearing, though people were careful not to do so when the Landsmen were looking at them.

"Enjoy your day, Champion. I have important things to do for my king." She jogged off.

"I have important things to do for the king also," I said under my breath, and made off after the Landsmen.

Their compound was walled, which annoyed me. The palisade of sharpened stakes around it was a naked statement of distrust in Rufra. It made me want to spit that they called themselves his allies but acted as if they could not trust him. The irony – that I was thinking this while looking for a way to break in was not lost on me, but it only served to make me more annoyed. The palisade made it difficult to get in, but not impossible. I would wait and watch. My master always said that patience was an assassin's greatest ally. All I needed to do was melt into the background and—

"Champion?" I turned. A child in sacking and rags stood in the mud, whether a boy or girl it was hard to tell. "You are Girton, the champion of Gwyre, aren't you?" I nodded, unsure what to say, and the child – it was a girl – took from her rags a small package wrapped in the same filthy cloth she wore. "Bread," she said, "for you, for saving us." I considered saying no, but she clearly had very little and this act meant very much to her. I did not want to insult her.

"Thank you," I said, taking the bread. She very solemnly bared her throat to me and I nodded back, then she walked away.

When I turned, a Landsman was watching me from the top of the palisade. "You want something?" he said. At least he did not recognise me as Rufra's champion.

"Maybe you could help, Blessed," I said, my mind racing as I made myself appear as small and meek as possible, contorting my body to seem far more crippled than I was. "The night before Aydor came to camp, my uncle said he made a bet with a Landsman called Karrick over some hog meat and he has sent me to collect it."

"Go away, mage-bent," said the Landsmen, "and take your ill luck with you."

"If I do not get his meat my uncle will beat me."

"Your uncle is lying to you. Karrick was away with Rufra that night. He did not return until the next day; he came with Aydor."

"Oh," I said. "Maybe my uncle was mistaken."

"He was. Now piss off before I put an arrow in you."

I let myself blend back into the crowd. So Karrick was not where he should have been on the night Arnst died. More than anything now I wanted to see his quarters, and so I looked for a new place to watch from. I found one quickly enough, but it was spoilt by a woman bringing me a piece of rancid mutton. My next place was ruined by a half-blind man who wished to touch my hair. And so it was for the rest of the day: any chance I had of sneaking into the Landsmen's compound was ruined by a constant stream of good cheer and well-wishing. With each approach I became increasingly uncomfortable and started to understand my master's desire to keep away from people. At one point I had to chase after a woman after she heard me mutter, "Xus save me from generosity of spirit," under my breath and ran away in tears. Only profuse apologies calmed her. By then it was clear I had no chance of sneaking into the Landsmen's compound. If anything untoward happened, it would be my name on everyone's lips. Every Landsman in their camp must have seen me.

I walked away and my name was called again. By this time I was truly tired of the attention and turned, spite bitter as magic on my lips, but the harsh words died in my mouth.

"Areth."

"I am glad I have found you, Girton. I wanted to thank you."

"You did?"

"For talking to Rufra, for whatever you said. He came to me last night—"

"I don't think I need to know the details."

"—to talk." She batted at me, gently slapping me on my arm. "At first anyway." She gave me a sly look and then burst out laughing. "Girton, you have gone as red as a berry! I thought you a man of the world, well travelled and having had many lovers!" She linked her arm through mine.

"I had a lover . . ."

"Oh." She stopped and the smile fell from her face. "Drusl, I am a fool, I did not think before I spoke." I felt bad for making her uncomfortable. "But there must have been others since?"

"A couple." My insides tightened and I dug my nails into my palms.

"I do not just mean someone to warm your bed for a night, Girton." She giggled and then was suddenly serious. "If you are to stay here you cannot be lonely, and there will be dances and feasts when the bonemounts are finally stabled.

You will need a partner then." She turned me towards her, holding me lightly by my forearms. "Listen. Come to court tonight. Gusteffa will dance and after the court there will be a feast. I have many friends, all of whom would be glad to meet the king's champion, if you understand my meaning."

I heard her words but did not reply. A cold truth was stealing over me, a mixture of sadness and guilt that was entirely new to me and so uncomfortable it made me want to run away from this place, run and never return. Where Areth touched me a glow ran along my scars. Her face was warm like the sun and I could not turn away from her. No matter who Areth may introduce me to they would pale into insignificance beside her.

My friend's wife.

I can give her to you.

A jolt, the stink of pondweed thick in my nostrils.

"Girton, are you all right? You have gone ghostwhite."

"Yes. Sorry." My jaw ached. "Just tired is all, Areth." I needed somewhere quiet. The magic within was shifting again. An hour to myself was what I needed, somewhere to think and breathe and pin the magic down.

"Very well. Get some rest, but promise me you will come to court. Promise."

"I promise."

"Good. Rufra will be pleased to have you there."

I nodded and watched her walk away.

I can give her to you.

"No," a word said through gritted teeth. And like a dog beaten by its master, the king's champion went to find somewhere to hide from the world. Much to my annoyance it seemed every place in the camp was full of happy people, and so I sought shelter in our tent. Even there I found laughter, a small world of warmth and light, though the laughter stopped when I came into the tent.

Mastal stood. "I must leave," he said, giving my master a

small bow. He ignored me, and I him. No doubt he went to report to Aydor.

"Girton," said my master, "I see you do not have the warhammer at your side today."

"Nywulf gave it to Aydor." I sounded petulant, like a child.

"And you still fought."

"I have returned to my stabswords. As you wished." My words were cold, and she stood, placing her hands lightly on my arms – like Areth had done. "You look tired, Master," I said.

"It comes and goes." She searched my face, her hand coming up, and she almost-but-not-quite touched my cheek. Her bent fingers traced a line above a new cut on my face. "We should have toured as players," she said quietly. "We should have tumbled and storied and sang."

"I said as much."

"You did –" her hand came down to her side "– but we cannot change what was." Silence, a counting of moments.

One, my master.

Two, my master.

Three, my master.

"There was no cart, Girton," she whispered. "Rufra knew nothing of it. There was never any cart to take us to the Sighing Mountains, was there?" I shook my head. "Why, Girton?" Abruptly I was six again and I had picked up one of her knives despite knowing they were not for me. I echoed the words of that six-year-old boy.

"I do not know."

"You do not know," she said slowly, "and that is the best you have?"

"I was scared," I said, finding my voice and pushing past the discomfort in my throat, the sudden threat of tears. "I was scared you would leave and never come back, and I would be left alone. He wants to take you away." I could not tell from the look in her eyes whether she was angry, disappointed or touched; maybe it was a little of all those things.

"Oh, Girton," she said, and suddenly she was holding me, wrapping me in a fierce embrace. "I would never leave you for long. I would always come back, always."

"I am sorry, Master." A flood inside me, now tears blurred the world. "I thought you were dead! I thought you were going to die. I did not—"

"Shh, shh, my boy." She rocked me from side to side like she had when I was small. "Quiet, quiet. It does not matter." She cooed the words to me, like a mother calming a babe. "It does not matter. I understand."

"I will put this right," I said. Behind her, the bottles of medicine were lined up on Mastal's trunk

"I know, I know."

"I will do it now." I removed myself from her embrace, and she stepped back so that only her hands rested on my shoulders. She looked into my face.

"What we are is hard on you, Girton, and sometimes I am sorry for what I have made you into. But I am never sorry for you. I am never sorry I have you."

I nodded, wiped mucus from my nose and tears from my eyes. "Rufra has his court tonight." I sniffed back tears. "I am to be there. I will talk to him and arrange the cart for tomorrow. I think I should talk to Mastal as well."

"Thank you, Girton, and I will return as soon as I can. Are you still angry with with him?"

I shook my head. I was but could not find the words to tell her why. Maybe when I confronted him with what he had hidden in has papers we could put the medicine right and he would not take her away. Both of us had something to hide. We would fix my master, and the matter would be done. I would protect his lies if he left her here – and he would protect mine, and we would never speak of it again.

"No, I am not."

"Then go. Do what you need to do to make this right."

"I will."

And I took my leave, thinking nothing of the small tremble of my master's hand, thinking it a symptom of strong emotion, not something deeper.

Something darker.

Outside, Mastal waited for me a few paces from the entrance to the tent and as I approached he backed away. Words of contrition waited in my mouth.

"I thought you an adult," said Mastal, "and I treated you as one, but it seems you are only a child." There was fury in the lines of his face. "Your king knew nothing of a cart."

The contrition vanished to be replaced with anger.

"Because I knew of your plans, Mastal." He stared at me. Shocked or simply angry, it was hard to tell.

"Plans?"

"I read your papers. You are no travelling healer; you seek rewards for finding people."

"You went through my things?"

"It is a good job I did."

He took a step closer as I spoke, his taller frame filling the space in front of me. "Among our people such a thing would be a huge insult. I should walk away from here for this."

"Maybe you should."

"If I leave, your master will sicken and die."

"You only want her well so you can take her away and make your coin."

He shook his head. "No, those are not my reasons. The yandil is in the Sighing Mountains, as are people who have loved her and missed her and wondered where she is for many years. She has family there. You would deny her that?"

"She has family here."

"She has an apprentice here –" he snapped the word back at me "– one who long ago should have found his own way in the world. Does a shopkeeper count his delivery boy as family? Does a smith count the child he teaches to hammer metal as family?" I was taken aback by his anger – it was me who had been wronged, not him.

"It is not the same."

"Is it not?"

"You should leave us, Mastal. Go."

"No, I will stay. I must, to make her well."

"And if she does not get well? What then? If you cannot take her away and get your coin? If her health fails?"

"It will not. I will make her well."

The anger within me was so strong I was shaking. My hands itched for the hilt of the blade at my hip.

"If she sickens," I said, "you will leave us alone."

"Leave?"

"Yes."

"You are such an angry child you would rather she die than met those who love her?"

"No, but if you do not make her well you must leave."

He looked me up and down as if I had just landed from the sky. "Very well. I do not doubt myself so I will agree to that," he said quietly. "But when she gets well, you will let her go without complaint."

"Promise you will leave."

"My word is—"

"Promise it!" I shouted the words in his face and he took a step back. He was not a man used to physical anger, I could tell it from the way he moved.

"Very well, Girton Club-Foot. Should your master sicken again, though she will not, I will pack up my trunks and leave."

"Good, and do not think you can wheedle your way

further into my master's affections. When I return later I shall tell her why you are really here." I was about to turn and leave, pleased at having struck the final blow, but instead of looking shocked or worried he only shook his head.

"Girton," he said, "she already knows. I told her long ago about her family." And then he turned and left me with nothing but fury and nowhere to aim it.

Dead gods, I wanted him gone.

I will give you what you want.

I will give you what you want.

Chapter 23

When I arrived at the king's court the session was already under way, it had the rowdy atmosphere of a theatre. Rufra's throne was on a raised dais, and next to him sat a radiant-looking Areth. At his shoulder stood Nywulf, severe and forbidding as ever. Behind them were some of his Triangle Council: Gabran the Smith, looking uncomfortable in a formal kilt – I knew how he felt – and my heart leaped with a small joy when I saw that next to him sat Boros, his scarred head swathed in bandages. I had thought he would die from his wounds and was glad he had not. Bowmaster Varn and Bediri Outlander sat on the other side, and my heart fell when I saw Rufra had allowed Aydor to sit with them. Bediri leaned over and said something that made Aydor laugh and my guts clenched. How well did she know him?

Areth saw me in the crowd and whispered something to a retainer, who vanished and returned with a chair, putting it next to Boros and nodding towards me. As I worked my way through the crowd I let their mood lift mine. They were a happy lot, full of joy at Rufra's victory, and it probably helped that Rufra had killed a lot of pigs on his way back from Gwyre – the air was full of the smell of roasting pork; nearly everyone either had meat and bread in their hand or a face greasy with meat juices. I spotted the copper hair of Neliu weaving through the crowd and her mirror image on the other side, Crast, both no doubt looking out for threats. Crast gave me a cheery wave when he spotted me and I waved back as I sat next to Boros.

"I am glad you live," I said.

"I am not. My head aches like a mount is running around in it and Tarris is making me drink a concoction that tastes like vomit. Twice a day!" His voice was filled with mock outrage. "I see you're wearing armour, Girton? No kilt?" He pulled at the material of his own and grimaced – a truly frightening sight on his scarred face. It seemed no one liked kilts.

"As I am now Rufra's champion I thought it more fitting to wear armour and blade."

"Any excuse to get out of a kilt."

"Well, in the next fight I will try and get hit on the head and let you win the glory."

He laughed. "Maybe getting to sleep through a battle is worth wearing a kilt for." The smile fell from his face and I knew he thought of his brother, Chirol, who had managed to escape.

"He cannot run for ever, Boros. Chirol will turn up again."

"Dead gods, I hope so," he said. "My blade thirsts for his blood."

"How does this court work, anyway?" I asked, keen to get off the subject of his brother and the peculiar madness it instilled in Boros.

"See those sad-looking fellows over there." He pointed at a circle of men and women to the left of us with a rib bone he had been gnawing. I nodded. "Well, they come in front of Rufra, put forward their case, and Rufra consults with us and we give them a decision. Mostly it's disputes between traders, petty stuff that's not worth the king's time."

"Is that all?"

"Sometimes it gets exciting. See the bound man on his knees? He murdered another guard. Violence between guards is always popular with the common folk."

I glanced at the group Boros had been talking about, the only people in the clearing who did not look happy.

"How do you bring a case?"

"Why, got a grievance?"

I wondered where Karrick Thessan was.

"Not as such," I said.

"You do it through one of the Triangle Council, usually. Approach us, and we judge whether it's worthwhile and give Rufra a quick rundown of the case before the court."

"So it's decided beforehand; this is just theatre?"

"Justice must be seen to be done, and the crowd has its part to play also. Rufra can be swayed by their reaction, to a point."

"Is he a good judge?"

"You will see," said Boros, then he sighed. "But first we have to watch the bloody dwarf prance about."

"Gusteffa? But she is a master jester."

"I forgot you liked that sort of thing," he said.

"It will not hurt you to appreciate a great artist, Boros." He shook his head at me and took a swig of perry. Then Gusteffa appeared, and the dance truly began.

The Story of Aseela, the First Queen, and How She Brought Us Mounts

Long before the balance was upset and even before men and women knew the names of their gods, mounts ran wild in the hills and no man or woman could ride them. One morning, in these long forgotten times, Aseela woke to find her husband standing outside with their children, holding his bow.

"Aseela," he said, "today I shall hunt and bring us back a fine haunch of mount to feed our family."

"Mind you do, husband," she said, "for your children are hungry. But be careful, and if there is danger run like the wind."

"I shall be careful," he said.

But as night clothed the sky he did not return, and Aseela worried because she had also hunted mounts and knew mounts were fierce. And in the morning, when the sun woke the flowers, he did not return, and Aseela worried because mounts were fierce. And when he did not return by the middle of the day Aseela decided she must find him. She took up her bow, left her children and headed into the hills where the mounts ran to find her husband. Aseela trekked across streams and through mud, following the hunter's path until she found blood. And Aseela, heavy-hearted Aseela, followed the blood until she found her husband. He had not been careful as she had instructed, and when danger came he had not run like the wind.

A mount had gored him, and he had as little breath left in his body as he had blood in his veins.

"Oh Aseela, I was not careful as you instructed. I did not run like the wind. I saw a black mount, a king among his tribe," he said, "and took aim. But just when I was about to shoot, a giant golden mount appeared and gored me. I am sorry, Aseela, but you must raise our children alone now." And with that he died and Aseela rent her clothes in grief and swore to the sky she would hunt down the great golden mount that had taken the man she loved away from her. So Aseela, huntress, headed up into the hills, following the mounttrails until she heard the sound of mounts in fury. And above the whistles and growls of mounts she heard the roaring of the maned lizards which hunted in packs and knew no fear. Down went Aseela, down into the ferns. She felt the wind on her face. She smelled the lizards and the mounts they preyed upon. Forward went Aseela, huntress of her people, through the long ferns and past high trees. Coming to a clearing where she found a mount at bay – huge and golden, queen of her herd.

Aseela strung her bow with her best arrow, cut straight as a kill, cut to pierce the heart of a mount. And Aseela waited for her moment.

The golden mount stood over another, black as death and wounded. Around and around the mounts the lizards prowled, five in number and fierce as any of their kind. As one darted in, the mount lunged and another tore at her rump. Bite by bite they began to wear the queen of mounts down.

Aseela aimed her arrow for the heart, thinking only of vengeance.

Then stopped.

She saw a queen guarding her wounded mate from danger, even to the definite cost of her own life.

Another lizard darted in, jaws slavering, teeth snapping. Blood was drawn.

I know this, she thought. Despite we have always hunted mounts, I see myself in you. I see you fight for what you love and I see us more alike than not. Those great antlers tore the life from my lover, but he would have torn your lover from you. I come in vengeance for what was mine, on you who acted only to protect what was yours.

And then.

Almost against her will.

The bow shifted aim.

The mount lowered her antlers to fend off an attack.

A lizard lunged.

An arrow flew.

It took the lizard in the heart. Another beast is swept away on the crown of the golden mount. The three remaining lizards turn to face Aseela and the golden mount attacks. A furious rage. Arrows fly! One, two, three. Together the woman and the mount slay the lizards.

And all is quiet.

The mount steps forward, huge and threatening, blood on her antlers. Behind the queen of the herd her mate stands.

From out of the brush came more mounts, the queen's herd, a forest of sharp antlers and razor tusks.

Aseela calls to the sky, "What a fool I have been! We have hunted mounts, and mounts have killed us in return! This is how it always was, this is how it always will be! My time on this earth is done. My children will be raised alone. What do animals know of mercy?"

But the queen of the herd spoke:

"Human, I killed one of your scent, and yet you saved me."

Aseela fell to her knees and rent her clothes to bear her breast for the sharp antler.

"Mount, I saw you protecting what you loved, and saw myself in you."

"But you must know our people are enemies. You shoot sharp arrows and we gore and trample. That is the way of life, unchanging."

"Then gore and trample, Queen of Mounts."

"I cannot return love with blood," said the great beast. "As you saw yourself in me, so I see myself in you. And as we act, so are changes wrought. Let us be change. Now take my gift." Two young mounts, one black, one white stepped forward. "Take my children, ride upon them and let them help you in your labours, and as long as you do not hunt my herds they will serve you."

And Aleesa, who had once run like the wind, now rode like the wind and knew a joy like no other. And since that day no man or woman has hunted a mount. And that is right and that is just.

When Gusteffa finished, the applause was rapturous, and I marvelled at her. She was a fine acrobat but more a great judge of people. She had danced well and presented a story that mirrored the performance the people were about to see now – justice in action. Gusteffa raised a hand in triumph, gave me a wink and a quick, happy, flash of her teeth before cartwheeling out to the side of the arena and vanishing into the crowd.

"She was wonderful, wasn't she, Boros?"

"If you say so," he said, leaning forward. "Mostly she just gets under my feet, being everywhere. But it seems everyone else likes her, even that yellowing priest, Darvin, likes her." He shook his head. "But now it is the real business. First case is our murderer."

A guard captain walked forward, her metal shoulder pieces polished to within an inch of someone's life so they gleamed like silver in the yearsbirth sun. Behind her two guards dragged forward the bound man and the chatter of the crowd died away.

"King Rufra, I am Captain Vellit of your fourth cohort; behind me is Guard Elithon. Two nights ago he got drunk and killed a guardsman called Untire because he would not spend the night with him."

"You have witnesses?" said the king.

"Both Polik and Calkini behind me saw the act. Elithon himself does not deny it."

"Does Elithon have anything to say?" Vellit moved to one side and the two guardsmen helped the bound man stand. Now I could see him clearly I saw eyes red from crying and bagged black by lack of sleep.

"Is what they say true, Elithon?" said Rufra, his voice sounding deeper, sterner than I was used to hearing.

"Aye, Blessed," he said. "We was drunk." His voice broke and he fought for a moment to bring his tears under control – though strangely, he did not appear at all frightened. "I only wanted him to come back to me, that were all. Then he were dead at me feet and my blade was wet. It were like Dark Ungar took me."

"You do not deny it then?" The guard shook his head. "You know at this time I need every blade I can get?"

"Aye. I have let you down, Blessed."

"You have. Do you have anything to say before I pass judgment?"

"Quick," he said, though it was barely audible. "Just make my end quick." The man stared at the floor. Rufra nodded to himself. "Elithon of the fourth cohort, a death is met with a death, and you will be taken to the nearest souring by your captain, your blood will bring life to the land." Elithon nodded at the judgment, and out of the corner of my eye I caught Gabran the Smith doing the same. He must have brought this before Rufra.

"Was that a good judgment, Boros?" I said.

He nodded.

"Aye, though a pity. I always thought Elithon rather handsome."

More cases followed, and, as Boros had said, they were mostly dull – arguments over goods, tents being pegged too close together and neighbours who could not get on. Little of it interested me. We were in the middle of a case about a lost draymount – the man who had found it would not give it back unless the man who owned it paid for the fodder it had eaten – and the crowd were jeering and booing at the two men involved, when the steady tramp of soldiers' feet brought quiet to the small arena.

Boros, who had been using the cover of his bandages to disguise that he was on the point of sleep, sat up in his chair.

"Well, this looks like it may get more interesting than arguments about half a rick of hay," he said as the crowd split to allow a phalanx of Landsmen through. At their head was Karrick and – a shock ran through me – behind him stumbled the old woman who had given me yandil leaf. "Or I could be wrong," he said. "It might just be awful. Blue Watta curse the Landsmen, they bring nothing but misery."

Karrick stepped forward, and another Landsman pulled the old woman after him by her stick-thin arm. I glanced over at Rufra. He looked annoyed. Areth looked stricken.

"King Rufra," said Karrick. His voice carried over a crowd now silent and cowed – only a fool didn't fear the Landsmen. "I am sorry to interrupt this court—"

"Then do not do it," said Rufra. "There are ways to bring

a grievance, Karrick, and you know them. You helped me draft the rules we follow."

"Aye, but this is more important than squabbles over money." With a heave his second threw the old woman into the dirt. Karrick did not even look at her. "This woman is a sorcerer, and as you have decreed the Landsmen cannot act in your camp without your say-so I must have your judgment on her."

"There is only one," said his second. "A sorcerer is questioned and then goes in a blood gibbet."

"Quiet, Fureth," said Karrick sharply. "I speak for the Landsmen here."

"Rufra, this is wrong," said Areth and she stood. "She is only an old woman, a herb seller. I bought herbs from her when our son was ill, and . . ." Her voice died away. Rufra's face paled, then visibly hardened.

"No wonder your son died if you trusted this sour-wombed creature." There was a shocked intake of breath at the way Fureth spoke to the queen. Then the Landsman brandished a bunch of leaves above his head.

A ripple of laughter passed through the crowd. "Doxy!" shouted a woman. "He's gone soft in the head if he thinks doxy is for sorcerers – he'll have to gibbet every women in the camp!" More laughter.

Karrick gave his deputy a filthy look and spun on his heel. "Fureth may speak out of turn," he shouted, "but what he holds is not doxy. It is yandil leaf or, as you common folk call it, sorcerer's balm." There was another gasp at that and I became still from the inside outwards. The old woman had given me yandil. What had she told them? She looked exhausted, her hair lank and her ragged clothes bloodied.

"What has been done to her?" said Rufra quietly.

"Nothing. She ran is all, tired herself out," said Fureth from behind Karrick. "Then we had to subdue her."

"Silence, Fureth!" barked Karrick. "My apologies, King Rufra. I did not command this woman to be put to the question nor punished. We abide by the rule that the only law in your lands is yours. Landsman Fureth will be punished if he has overstepped the mark." I did not believe Karrick, and behind him Fureth sneered underneath his wide green helm.

"So I must decide if she is a sorcerer," said Rufra sadly.

"There is no question of that, King Rufra," said Karrick quietly. "Under the high king's law possession of sorcerer's balm is proof of sorcery." Rufra nodded but did not look happy. "And even you must bow to the high king's law, King Rufra." Karrick did a good job of sounding regretful. He probably practised in front of a mirror.

"He is right," said Aydor. "We cannot allow a sorcerer in camp." I felt like opening his guts, especially knowing what he had been involved in with his mother.

Rufra looked at Aydor and for a moment I hoped he would dismiss him, or shame him publicly for speaking when he was not part of the council. Then he turned back to Karrick.

"Very well. This woman shall be taken by Captain Vellit to die alongside Elithon." Rufra put his hand on Areth's hand. "Her death will be quick at least."

"No," said Karrick, his voice full of mock regret, but there was iron within it. "She must be questioned. I am sorry, but if she has sorcerer's balm she may have been supplying it to others. And then she must go into a blood gibbet. A sorcerer must be seen to die." The crowd had become silent; nothing stirred a crowd's hate quite like Landsmen and sorcerers.

"No!" Areth stood, and when she spoke she did not speak to Rufra or to Karrick, she spoke to the crowd. "That is barbarism. She is an old woman who may have done nothing more than mistake something forbidden for doxy. She could be any of us." There were murmurs among the crowd – hadn't one of them just mistaken it for doxy?

"If that is true it will come out when we question her," said Fureth, and Karrick shot him a foul look, his fury at being undermined plain for all to see.

"It is the high king's law, and even though High King Darsese is far away, it is him the Landsmen ultimately answer to, Queen Areth," said Karrick.

"From what I hear," whispered Boros, "the high king is far more interested in feasting and his catamites than what the Landsmen get up to."

"I do understand, Queen Areth, that your background leaves you unfamiliar with the laws of the blessed," Karrick said, and he may have believed this, but to the crowd it sounded like an insult and Areth was loved.

A cynical voice within me said that the queen was simply worried the woman would mention her name. A louder voice told me she genuinely felt for the woman and would have interfered even if she not been involved with her.

"The blood gibbet is wrong," said Areth.

"You question the high king's law?" said Fureth. Karrick shot him another dark look. "Quiet, Fureth," said Karrick, "I will not tell you again. Areth simply cares for her people, as a queen should."

"Do not fear for me, girl," said the old woman, and the crowd went silent, the better to hear her words. "I do not fear the burning tongs or ripping blades." I believed she would protect Areth, but what if she protected her queen by offering another to the Landsmen – me?

"Were I a man," said Areth, "I would use your high king's law to fight for her innocence."

Did her gaze stray away from the Landsmen, just for a moment?

"But you are not a man, my queen," said Karrick, "and you cannot."

Did it stray to me?

I stood.

"She is simply an old woman, and you are cruel men in search of a victim." I put my hand on my blade so there could be no mistaking my meaning. "I say this. And I am a man."

As one, an intake of breath from the crowd.

"Girton . . ." said Rufra. I could hear how much more he wanted to say, it was caught up within the two syllables of my name: warning, reproach, fear. I glanced over at Areth. She looked, not pleased, relieved at what I had done, while both Nywulf and Rufra were warning me off with their eyes. But it was too late. I had chosen a path. What was it Gusteffa had said? *"My path is set. You still have a choice."*

"This is not your fight, Girton Club-Foot," said Karrick. He sounded reasonable and I knew he was right. To challenge a Landsman to a fight over an old woman accused of sorcery would probably arouse suspicion. I could already feel it, the crowd starting to wonder, to turn.

But I had other reasons to challenge Karrick.

"I say she is innocent, and I also say you are not. You are a murderer, Karrick Thessan." A storm of excited noise from the crowd. "Rufra charged me with finding Arnst's killer – you all heard him do so," I shouted. "The day Arnst died, Karrick left Rufra's Riders to come back here. He should have been here by nightfall with little trouble, but he was not back in the Landsmen's compound until the next morning, and he told his men he rode in with Aydor."

"That proves nothing," said Nywulf from behind me. I ignored him, though it bothered me he was defending the man.

"But there is more," I said. "Arnst was killed with a Landsman's knife," a ripple of shock ran through the crowd. "And Arnst did not simply give in; he fought, and his sword was bloodied." I stepped forward, raising my voice and spreading my arms in the manner of a Festival storyteller. "I saw the bloodied sword myself, a fine blade." I spoke to the crowd as if we conspired together against a common enemy and then turned back to the Landsman, speaking casually, but loudly enough for all to hear. "You are wounded, are you not, Karrick Thessan?"

"It is from training . . ." he began, but I could feel the

crowd turning against him. "This is not a play, boy," he said, I spoke over him using all the skills my master had taught me as a jester.

"Most damning of all, a young and innocent boy saw a Landsman going into Arnst's tent that night." The crowd let out a hiss. What I said was a lie, a small one, but I needed to push Karrick. I knew he was guilty but I could not prove it. Instead I had to make him fight me and prove his guilt that way.

"Girton," said Rufra, "this is not enough. There are many Landsmen here, and even if it was one of them this boy saw—"

"You protect Arnst's killer?" From the crowd stepped Danfoth the Meredari. "You say you have new ways that are fair for all, but you protect this man." He pointed his huge hand at the Landsman.

A strange look crossed Karrick's face. He seemed resigned, almost as if he were glad to be caught. He stepped forward. "Girton is your champion, King Rufra," he said softly, "and he defends this woman –" he pointed at the stallholder "– and accuses me of murder. This cannot stand." He drew his sword. "Let our blades decide it, Girton Club-Foot. Let blood bring life and truth."

I stepped down from the dais and Nywulf grabbed me by my arm. "Why are you doing this?" he hissed.

"He is a murderer," I said, "and probably the spy you set me to search for."

"Girton," he said quietly, his grip tightening painfully around my arm, "I forbid this and will knock you on your arse to stop it if I have to."

I met his intent gaze and took a deep breath.

"You owe me," I said "Remember a night long ago in Maniyadoc? You said you owed me for Rufra's life. Well I call in that debt here and now."

He pulled me in close.

"You had better be right about this, Club-Foot, because you are perilously close to ruining everything Rufra has built."

"I am right," I said, "I am sure of it." Nywulf let go of my arm but a shudder ran through me. Ruining everything? What did Nywulf know that I did not?

"If you're that sure you're right, make sure you win," he said.

I nodded and stepped forward. Before me Karrick was strapping a long oblong shield, marked with the tree of the Landsmen, to his arm, and Fureth was tightening the straps on Karrick's helmet. Karrick pulled down the visor, blank and polished to a mirrored sheen, the mark of the Landsmen elite. I had heard of these warriors but never seen one. They were feared.

But so was I.

I made sure my own helmet was secure on my head. I did not use a visor – they were useful in a melee, but in one-on-one combat I preferred to be able to see clearly over protecting my face from scars.

Behind Karrick the Landsmen, about fifteen of them, had lined up in two rows, and the parched branch had been raised, their green standard hanging limp in the cold air from the twisted wood. I had no standard to raise but Danfoth walked forward with a pole in his hand and stood in front of the raised dais where Rufra sat. He unfurled a flag: a black background with a white circle and within that a cross of mount antlers. I had never seen such a sigil.

"The chosen of Arnst stand with you, Girton Club-Foot," said the huge Meredari. "Avenge the fallen."

There were two loud crashes as Karrick banged his spear on the inside of his shield.

"Shall we do this, Girton Club-Foot? Or do you wish to stop your foolish crusade against me before it topples you?"

He crouched behind the large shield, his body almost totally hidden by it, only the eyes and the crest of his helmet showing. His long spear twinkled in the light. He looked unassailable, a man without fear or doubt.

I drew my weapons.

"I am not frightened of you. I have chosen this path," I said, "and have no choice but to travel it."

He shrugged. "Very well, but the King must start this." I glanced over my shoulder and Rufra stood, he looked furious. "I ask you both, once more, not to do this," he said. Danfoth's hand tightened around the haft of his spear.

"Girton must renounce his accusations and allow us to take the woman," shouted Karrick.

I looked at Rufra and behind him saw Areth, her head in her hands.

"I cannot."

"Then make ready," said Rufra, "and Xus guide the right blade." I took his mention of Xus as tacit support until I remembered that the Landsmen also paid homage to the god of death. Then all was forgotten and we began to circle.

Of all the foes to face, a man with shield and spear is the hardest in many ways and the easiest in many others. If you can get past the spear they are usually finished, but the shield Karrick carried also had a frontspike, a great barbed point that he could use to impale an attacker. It made the shield into a weapon or, at the very least, gave him time to draw his sword if his spear was beaten or broken. And the shield was big, giving him excellent cover and my stabswords had little chance of puncturing it. His left side was vulnerable because the shield interfered with his spear and it should have been easy to dash around the side of him and attack, but I knew only a fool would try that; a gap so obvious could only ever be a trap.

But if I did not test him I would have no idea of his skill.

The hush of the crowd, a lead weight on my back

We continued to circle, Karrick always keeping me to his

right side. When I felt it was becoming a little dull for those watching I made my first feint, a few skittering steps that took me round to his left. He did nothing, leaving a huge gap I could run into, but as soon as I moved closer he pivoted, almost inhumanly fast, and if I had made the move seriously I would have run myself onto his spear. What the crowd did at that moment, whether they shouted, sighed, called my name or his, I have no idea; all my concentration was on the spear tip thrusting forward to impale me. His reach was far longer than I had expected. I fell back, and we continued our slow revolve. I could feel the crowd becoming impatient but made no further move. Karrick had too many advantages in defence for me to be hasty, but he was also carrying a heavy shield and, no matter how strong he may be, he would eventually tire against a quick man with light weapons. Karrick would have to move on me soon or I would wear him down, like the sea does a rock.

When he came he came fast – like a riptide, crouching behind his spear, jabbing the point at me as he advanced, trying to herd me backwards into a place I could not escape from. I made to roll away, but he had been waiting for it and his spear was there. I turned the roll into a spring and that into *the Carter's Surprise*. Had I been more practised, more ready and more sure of myself, I would have reversed, vaulted his shield and gone for the killing blow, but I did not. Instead I threw myself feet first at his shield. As I hit it Karrick hunkered down, digging the rim into the ground and taking my hit. I hacked down with a stabsword at his head, but the armour of his helm was thick. I did not care – that was not the aim of my attack. My weight fell onto the shield's frontspike, and I used it as a springboard into a high somersault. Landing hard in the mud I saw my aim achieved: the frontspike now hung from the shield half broken, not only useless as a weapon but a dead weight dragging on the shield to tire Karrick further.

He dropped his spear, drew his longsword and smashed the spike off his shield. Then he was back down behind it, longsword out, a lethal spine of silvered steel.

The crowd cheered but I could barely hear them over the thundering of blood in my ears. My club foot ached from the hard landing, but more worrying was the sharp pain in my good foot and the blood I could feel pooling in my boot. The razor hooks of the spike had cut through the sole and into my foot as I had pushed myself off. Now I was the one who would tire quickly.

He will beat you.

A moment of distraction.

Karrick attacked, slashing his sword in front of him, creating an arc of pain I could not get past. Back and back I went, waiting for my moment and . . .

Now.

Stabsword out, deflecting the tip of his blade and disrupting his rhythm. Forward. Running the edge of my stabsword along his steel. Pushing in close. Forcing his blade to the right and getting ready for for the moment I was near enough to either go under his guard or round his back.

He threw his shield at me. Totally unexpected.

While he had been slashing at me, somehow he had loosened the straps holding the shield on to his arm. The heavy wood knocked me backwards and I went careening into the crowd, who pushed me forward. I tripped over my club foot, the sharp pain of the cut on my good foot stopped me righting myself and I fell, scrambling onto my back as Karrick came in.

He will beat you.

I almost used the-Speed-that-Defies-the-Eye, but caught myself at the last moment – to use magic in front of fifteen sorcerer hunters would be suicide. Instead I rolled left and right as Karrick, screaming like Coil the Yellower, brought his blade down again and again. My rolling brought me up against his fallen shield, and I pushed the roll further, dropping one stabsword and grabbing the handle of the shield. Rolling again so it covered me and the thunder of Karrick's blade filled my ears as it started to cut through the wood, only moments until it was through. The Landsmen chanted, "Ka-rrick! Ka-rrick!" banging their spears on the ground. They thought he had already won.

I can end this.

A momentary image of a black sword skewering Karrick through the gut, leaving him writhing in agony as I stood to claim victory.

Madness. The crowd would rip me apart.

The black antler, jagged, branching lines of magic holding up a hundred bodies on a thousand spines.

My teeth hurt, my jaw ached.

Black arrows pouring from my mouth.

No magic, no more.

As the shield splintered, my position became untenable. Karrick must have been sure he had won. If I threw away the shield he had me, if I kept the shield it would only be moments before he could thrust his sword straight down through it. All must think me beaten.

But, magic or not, five years of battle had made me hard to kill.

Looking down past my feet, I saw Karrick's legs. He stood with his feet slightly apart and his knees locked to give him strength as he rained blows on me. His metal greaves shone, the chains of his skirt swung. I slithered down and kicked out hard with my club foot. The boot I wore was built up with wood to make walking easier but it also made a weighty club. Karrick's knee had nowhere to go and I heard it dislocate, the joint tearing itself apart, the sort of sound that makes you want to vomit. He fell with a scream of agony and, sure I had won, I threw myself on to him.

But just as I was not someone easily beaten, neither was the Landsman. He grabbed my wrist as I brought my stabsword down on him and with his other hand he brought his own short blade out. I grabbed his wrist. The fight became about strength. He tried to roll me; I stopped him by spreading my legs, digging my feet into the earth.

My stabsword moved down two fingers' breadth towards his face. I angled the blade at the eye slit in his visor. To threaten an eye brings on soul-sucking fear. The crowd chanted my name but it was a faraway noise, almost drowned out by my harsh breathing and the grunts of Karrick as he tried to hold me off.

No. It was not grunts, it was words, thickened almost beyond understanding by his desperate efforts to live.

"Why . . . do . . . you . . . lie?" Because of his mirrored visor it was as if I heard the words from my own distorted face.

"You lie," I hissed back and my blade moved closer. He was tiring, the agony of his ruined leg sucking his strength away like the wind takes leaves from a yearsdeath tree.

"Forven Aguirri," he gasped out. He dropped his blade, and his hand came up, gauntlet clawing at my face, but I simply raised myself out of his reach. His hand joined the other on my wrist.

"What?" I pushed the blade down a little further.

"Chase that name," he said. "I am innocent." He let go of my wrist with one hand and pushed up his visor so I could see his face. "Innocent," he said again, grabbing my wrist once more, but he could not stop the slow descent of my blade towards his eye.

I doubted. I saw nothing in his face that spoke of guilt. Oh I hated him. I hated him for being a Landsman, I hated everything I had experienced at their hands, but as he gasped out, "I did . . . not kill . . . Arnst," and the blade descended until it almost touched his eye, I doubted.

What if I was wrong?

"Forven . . . Aguirri."

I could let him live. None would doubt I had won. And I saw in him hope. Saw him think he may survive. Then, with our faces almost touching, with sweat from my brow dripping onto his face, he took in a great lungful of the air we shared and sealed his fate. Shock on his face. Eyes widening. He drew another lungful through his bleeding nose, the air bubbling and snorting through the blood.

He could smell the magic.

Dead gods curse all magic. He knew what I was.

None can know.

"Sorcer—" he began but never finished. I put all my weight and strength into the blade and it passed through his eye and pinned his skull to the ground. Beneath me his corpse shook, and his muscles twisted and shifted as they gave up his spirit to Xus.

I pushed myself up, wincing as I stood on my bleeding foot and wincing again as I transferred my weight to my club foot. There was only pain.

I pointed my blade at the old woman in front of the Landsmen. "She is innocent," I said. "Now release her."

Fureth held a blade in his hand and I wondered whether he had been about to come to his master's aid. Then he gave a small bow of his head and his blade came down on the old woman's neck where it met her shoulder, hacking into her flesh the way a butcher would hack into meat. She groaned as she fell to the ground, and was dead before she landed face first in the mud. A silence fell over the crowd.

"She is released," said Fureth.

I walked forward, every step like walking on fire, blade held tightly, legs stiff with anger.

"Girton!" The shout came from the dais behind me but I walked on. The Landsmen drew their weapons. A dark voice whispered promises in my ear:

We can end this.

The sky was puce, purple and dull – bruise painful. The Landsmen were paper-thin men, skin greasy with loathing, and I could pick them up on the wind and dash them against the rocks to burst like overripe fruit. My ears felt gravid, heavy. All sounds were hollow, weighty and echoing as the crowd cheered each step I took towards the Landsmen. Lines, silver and flowing, surrounded the crowd and their faces contorted into wood and souring, hate and hunger, hedgings excited by pain and violence. Is this what I fought for? Were any of them worthy of Rufra? I could clear this ground, remove this rabble from Rufra's—

"Girton!" This time the voice reached something inside me, and I halted. Stumbling to a stop. The pain in my feet crippling. Fureth in front of me, blade in hand, an almost-smile on his face. I turned back to my king to see him balancing on the edge of fury. "Return to your place, Girton. You have proved your point." I stared at him, and he screamed at me, squireyard loud. "Do it now!" And I did as he asked. I would not defy him in front of the crowd.

As I neared the dais Danfoth the Meredari moved to stand in front of me with his strange flag. "You have defended Arnst, and for that the followers of his ways will follow you. We will call you Blessed of Arnst and Chosen of Xus."

I didn't know what to say, the words in my mouth were misshapen. I knew I did not deserve any honour, and over Danfoth's shoulder I could see Nywulf, fury on his face and his hand on the hilt of his weapon. If I accepted Danfoth's loyalty it would undermine Rufra.

"You can serve me by serving Rufra," I said eventually. "It was his authority that allowed me to fight Karrick, and only his." Danfoth's face furrowed in confusion, behind him I saw Nywulf relax a little.

"Very well." Danfoth turned. "Many heed the words of

Arnst," he said, "and they will follow you, King Rufra. For now," he added.

Rufra lifted his head, baring his throat to Danfoth in the old way of showing respect. "I am honoured to have you at my side," he said. Then he looked around the clearing at the crowd. Fureth had been watching us, bright eyes following every movement, his bloody sword still in his hand.

"You had no right to kill that woman, Fureth," said Rufra, and a silence fell on the clearing. The crowd may as well have been absent for all the noise they made, though their expectation of some further violence was an almost palpable force.

"I had every right," said Fureth, "and you know it. In fact she got off easily. Karrick paid you a courtesy and nothing else, and now you ally with those who speak against the dead gods." He pointed at Danfoth. "We would take our dead," he said, "or will you deny us that too, and pay us further insult?"

"No insult was meant," said Rufra, and for a split second only I saw the lonely boy I had known in Maniyadoc. "Take Karrick and honour him, as I will." Fureth did not reply; he simply pointed with his blade at Karrick's corpse. Four Landsmen came forward, lifted it onto their shoulders and marched in lockstep out of the clearing, followed by Fureth. He did not sheathe his bloody sword.

Rufra watched until they turned down a row of tents. As excited chatter broke out among the crowd, he shouted, "The court is over, and we will have peace among ourselves again as Arnst's killer has been brought to justice."

He retreated back into his tent with his council, leaving me standing on the field of battle aching and pained and, worst of all, no longer sure I had brought any sort of justice to Rufra's court at all.

Far to the east, great black pillars of cloud grew into the sky. The Birthstorm gathered strength.

Chapter 24

I limped back to our tent, every step agonising. Twice I saw Landsmen standing and watching as I passed. They made no move to stop me or attack, only turning their heads to follow my passage and I could not fail to understand the unspoken threat of their presence. I had taken one of theirs and they had marked me for it. But even if they had wanted to move on me they would have found it difficult as I was followed by a small crowd of ragged people in black clothes. They did not speak, though occasionally one would dart forward and touch of the edge of my armour.

Eventually I tired of this and caught one by the wrist. "What are you doing?"

"I . . ." she stammered. She was young, no more than twelve or thirteen.

I let go of her. "I will not hurt you, girl."

"I only wanted to touch the chosen of Xus. Get meself the unseen's blessing."

"I am only the champion of Rufra, and please," I said as gently as my pain allowed, "I wish to be left alone."

She nodded and returned to the ragged group, talking in a low voice with them. As they turned to leave she said, "We will return tomorrow, Chosen," and I cursed under my breath. The last thing I wanted was a following of fanatics.

My master and Mastal were talking quietly but fell silent when I entered the tent.

"Girton," said Mastal, "have you arranged for the cart? We . . ."

My master took one look at me, bloodied and battered, and silenced him with a hand on his arm, a familiar gesture that caused a surge of dark anger inside me.

"Leave us, Mastal." He looked at her as if confused by her words. "Please," she said, and he shrugged, walking out of the tent without giving me a second glance. I listened to his footsteps. It did not sound like he went far away, not as far away as I would have liked. "What has happened to you, Girton?" She stood.

"I fought the Landsman, Karrick. I killed him."

"But he hurt you?"

"I cut my foot."

She crouched down, undoing my boot. "I told you not to confront the man until you were sure."

"I was sure," I said, but she could hear the waver in my voice and glanced up.

"And now?" She went back to pulling on the knots in my laces.

"Less so."

She pulled frustratedly at the lace of my boot and then made me sit. I watched her hands move, noting how she struggled with her right hand and how the bandage covering where she had cut her arm to remove the Glynti poison was marked by fresh blood. Behind her were the rows of medicine bottles.

"But you still killed him, even though you were unsure?"

"He knew what I was."

"Then you had no choice," she said. There was no trace of doubt or remorse in her, and I shuddered as she pulled bandages and unguent from under her bed. When she started to treat the long cut running across the sole of my foot I let out a hiss. "It is a painful place to be cut, but the wound is not deep. Keep it clean and you will be fine."

"He said he was innocent and gave me a name, Forven Aguirri, but it means nothing to me."

"There is no 'ap' in that name, so he is likely not from

Maniyadoc – probably from outside the Tired Lands," she said. "But that is all I can tell you. Karrick must have thought the name would mean something to someone, or why say it? If you think he may have been innocent and you wish to protect your friend you must chase it." She started wrapping a bandage around my foot and I found the repetitions – such small and perfect movements – mesmerising. "I will help you," she said.

"But you are going away with Mastal."

She made a face, wrinkling her nose and smiling.

"He is a good man, but I am starting to think he fusses too much. I am far better now than I was. I have even returned to training – only gently, mind – and what would I want with the Sighing Hills? They are a long way from all that matters to me." She tied off the bandage and stared into my eyes. "There, Girton. Everything is better now, yes?"

I swallowed. The next words were hard to force past my lips – it was as if some force sat between my mind and my mouth. "You have to cut me again, Master."

"Cut you?"

"Aye, the magic – I can feel it growing. It wells up, and I am not sure sometimes where what I want ends and what it wants begins."

"You said you wanted to learn to control it."

"I almost killed everyone at Rufra's court, Master," I whispered. "It was overwhelming, like when Drusl died. I saw how easily I could end ev—"

"But you did not." She put her hand on my knee and smiled. "You controlled it, you won."

"Only because Rufra called my name. If he had not . . ."

"But he did. And next time you feel that way you will remember Rufra's voice and you will know you can control it. You were right, Girton: I cannot cut you for ever, and you are not weak or foolish. Just remember, do not give it what it wants." Behind her the rows of bottles gleamed, catching a shaft of stray sunlight.

"Master, there is something else . . ."

An odd expression crossed her face, one so strange it stopped my words dead. Her brow furrowed and she glanced down at the hand on my knee.

It shook.

Around the bloody bandage on her arm was a thin line of black flesh which extended as I watched it, as though drawn on her arm by an invisible scribe.

"Girton, I . . ." She froze. From the black line around her bandage more thin lines were drawn out, and these hairs of black flowed along the veins of her arms, tracing out delicate antlers on her skin. Her expression became slack, then tightened and locked into an agonised grimace. She made a sound, like none I had ever heard before – part grunt, part scream. Her eyes opened so wide I thought they would start from her head, her whole body bowed, shaking the bed and rattling the bottles on the trunk to the floor. She collapsed into my arms.

"Mastal! Mastal!" I screamed, and the healer came running, scooping my master out of my arms and placing her on the bed. He stared at the black lines and I backed away, dread mounting.

"No," he said: upset, puzzled, angry. "This cannot be happening. The dose was right; the poison was beaten. We beat it!"

"What is happening to her, Mastal?"

"Hold her hand, Girton," he said. "Let her know you are here. It may be some comfort at the end." He made no move for his medicines and his words were without hope – final.

"End? No! You cannot simply give up without a fight! Help her."

"I cannot." And my knife was at his throat. "Help her," I said.

"I cannot. This should not be happening. The power of the leaf is broken and the poison floods back in."

"Do you need more yandil?" I dropped the knife and ran to the back of the tent, scrabbling at the floor like a hunted animal desperately burrowing for safety. "I have more yandil, lots more of it." Understanding slowly grew on his bearded face.

"Why didn't you tell me you had that?"

"I was going to." Panic filled me, burning and fizzing through my body, and I gave no thought to my words. "I was going to give it to her when you had gone."

"Gone?" He looked puzzled. And then he didn't. "You changed the dose? That is what you have done? That is why you had me make that promise to leave? You changed the dose?"

I did not reply but he didn't need me to – he knew.

"Give her more," I said, pulling the package from the hole in the ground and returning to my master. I lifted her limp hand and spoke in a voice low and full of threat while dark lines swirled over her flesh. "Give her more, Mastal."

"You stupid boy," he hissed. "There is no going back once it has failed. It is useless now. By being too cowardly and suspicious to trust others you have killed her." He raised his hand, bringing it down towards my face in an open-palmed slap. I dropped the yandil and grabbed his hand, tightening my grip on it and squeezing his fingers in a way I knew must cause him pain, but there was only anger on his face. "You have killed her, Girton," he said, and there was the sparkle of tears in his eyes. "Why would you do this? Why would destroy what you love most?"

I stared into his eyes and that voice, that cold, black voice, wormed its way into my mind. *I can give you what you want.*

One hand on him and one hand on her, I felt the difference in them.

Felt her.

Felt him.

Felt the shadow as the poison eclipsed my master's life.

I can give you what you want.

She is fragile, thin as a lizard's wing bone, her spirit barely existing. She is on the edge of mortality. The poison is a ravening dog running through her – breeding, multiplying. Big dogs beget small dogs beget smaller dogs, and they grow and breed and bark and screech until soon she will be gone, devoured by the poison, taken from me by an agonising death. Somewhere on the edges of my consciousness a dark figure, somewhat sad, somewhat terrifying: Xus the god of death. Here to take his due.

I can give you what you want.

Mastal is strong. Burning with life and anger. All he is becomes open to me and I can peel his mind away, see his life moment by moment, but I do not. There is a split second without end – it gives me as long as I need. Shows me what I want and how to do it. A decision is made, a sad, scared, lonely, grieving boy hears the voice of a thing that wants to be used.

I can give you what you want.

And says yes.

All that was Mastal – his life, his hopes his fears, his loves and lusts – it is extinguished. It is instant and it is eternal. I felt the moment he realised what was happening. His question, how? Not why. I felt him accept what was happening. I understood the man in a way I had never let myself before and I knew how utterly I had wronged him. He had only ever had one desire, and that was to heal. And so he did. In death he was as true to his calling as he had been in life. I sucked the strength from him in a rushing wave, a riptide of life barrelling up a river. It flowed from him, through me and into my master, drowning the poison dogs in a foam of hot, powerful life. The transfer seemed to go on for ever but cannot have taken more than moments, and when it was finished my master breathed easily, and Mastal, or what had been him, lay on the floor, a husk of flesh, dried out and curled up as if he had spent a year in a blood gibbet.

"No," I said. What had I done? I said it again, "no," as if denial could somehow alter this terrible thing. This hadn't been meant to happen. I had only meant him to go away. Seconds after the act all that was left was regret, regret and fear. How would I hide Mastal's corpse? How would I explain this to my master? Would she ever understand?

We can make her understand.

An image of a terrified mount bending to my will.

"No!" The world was wavering, the air around me moving as if made up of strangely coloured weeds, my movements languid, like I danced a sleeper in a story. The scent of spices and honey filled the air.

"Girton?"

The word.

The world.

Solid again, hard and unyielding. The stink of death filling my nostrils, and now everything was worse. Now there was a witness who could not be allowed to live.

I spun, scooping my knife from the floor and only just managing to stop before I opened the throat of Areth.

"Are you going to kill me –" she showed no fear "– or do you want help hiding the body?"

"What?" I stumbled over the words, confused beyond all bearing. How could she be so calm? Why was she here?

"I felt what you did from the other side of the camp," she said, "but it took me half an hour to get out of the council meeting I was in."

"Half an hour?" I had only been here minutes, I was sure.

"Yes," she said and, very gently, took the knife from my hand and laid it down. "I suspected you were one of us from the start but could not be entirely sure."

"One of you?"

"One of Neander's children."

And suddenly it was explained. The feelings I had for Areth were not real; it was the same force that had first drawn me to Drusl – a shared magic. It was not love even if it could become it. It felt like drowning, being overwhelmed by something so vast that to fight it is to only to waste what precious moments of life were left.

"Control yourself, Girton, or we're both dead."

I could barely speak.

"You know magic?"

"How else would I be here, or know about yandil?"

"But how?"

"I told you. I was one of Neander's girls, like your Drusl." And my knife was in my hand and at her throat again.

"You are the spy!"

She laughed and pushed the knife away as if I were no threat at all. "The only thing I owe Neander is a blade in his black heart. He sent me here as a spy, and Rufra knows that –" she lowered her voice "– but he does not know about the magic. He would not countenance that, not even in me."

"How do you explain your scars to him?"

"I have no scars. I was not beaten. Neander did not treat us all so physically, Girton. Some of us he found other ways to hurt." She put her hands on her hips. "Now, do you wish to interrogate me or to save yourself from a blood gibbet?" She pushed me aside and stared at Mastal's body.

For a moment I thought she would vomit. His corpse looked like he had been burned alive, his body shrivelled and bent into a foetal position, but instead of being charred and black it was desiccated and yellow. The same dry, dead yellow as the sourlands.

"I have never seen anything like this; what awoke within me is for healing."

"But you did not try and save my master," I said.

"And I could not save my son either." The words came quickly, angrily, and I felt only two fingers tall. "Besides, you had Mastal, he seemed to know what he was doing." She pulled up a corner of the carpet. "Are you going to stand there like a lost child or help?" I helped her pull up the carpet and roll it around Mastal's corpse. "Magic was how I knew my child was poisoned," she said, her voice quiet, "but, of course, I cannot tell Rufra that. But I can tell you."

"You do not think Karrick was the spy, or the killer?"

"No," she replied. We finished wrapping the corpse and she searched Mastal's packs for string. "I am thankful you stopped him interrogating the old woman. She would have told all eventually – they always do – and that would have been bad for me and you, but Karrick would never murder, he was too obsessed with rules."

I thought about what she had left unsaid: that Karrick may not stoop to murder but I would.

"What do we do with Mastal's body?" I asked.

"It is dark," she said, "and there is a copse not far away." She pointed through the back of the tent. "You can bury him. I'll make sure the way is clear. We need to do this now."

"Why are you helping me? All I do is kill people who do not deserve it."

"I did not say Karrick did not deserve death, Girton – he was a Landsman after all – but I help you because they're wrong about us, about what we do." As she spoke I stared at the carpet which contained the husk of Mastal. "That was not your fault." She touched my arm, and her touch was a fire running through me. For a second our eyes met and I saw clothes falling, felt warm skin and heard quick breaths in the dark heat under the eaves of a castle. Areth stepped back, her chest rising and falling, a flush across her neck and face. "They make us hide, and this –" she motioned at the body, avoiding my eyes "– is the end result. It is meant to heal, Girton, that is what the magic is for, and if we bury it, hide it, then it lashes out. Even what you did here, really, was to heal."

I nodded even though I knew she was wrong; nothing about the power inside me had anything to do with healing.

What I had done may have healed my master, but I had needed a death to do it.

"Being here puts you in danger, Areth."

She put the finger that had brushed my arm against her lips, as if to taste it, then, realising what she was doing, clasped her hands behind her back.

"You stood up for me," she said. "You fought Karrick to protect me, and I owe you thanks for that no matter what trouble it causes Rufra."

"Trouble?"

"Karrick was a calming hand on the Landsmen. He did not agree with Rufra about many things but he was no Fureth. That man is a fanatic."

"You mean I killed the wrong Landsman?"

"In a way, but through Irille and her yandil leaf he would have discovered us eventually, Girton. He was a methodical man. So no, you did not kill the wrong Landsman, and maybe events turned out for the best. Let us just say your timing was off and it is unfortunate it could not have been handled another way."

"How?"

"An accident would have been better." She smiled and I wanted to cut my hand in annoyance. What a fool I was, so cocksure and angry that I challenged a highly trained warrior when that was not my way. My way was the quiet way, the poison, the blade in the back or the tumble down a stair. "Now come," said Areth, and pushed past me out of the tent.

Hefting the carpet over my shoulder, I followed her. It weighed surprisingly little. Areth walked ahead but the camp was quiet. When she vanished into the dark I waited between two tents, listening to the hissing of the night lizards. Then she reappeared and we made our way to the small wood.

"Girton, I must leave you here. If I return to Rufra covered in dirt and twigs questions will be asked." I felt a brief touch on my arm, and white shock through my body. "Bury him well, Girton, or the black birds of Xus will give us away."

"What will I tell my master?" My words were barely louder than the wind brushing through the trees.

"Tell her he left – that he could not stomach his failure."

"She will know I am lying, she always knows when I am lying."

"Then send her to me, Girton, and I will tell her it is true," said Areth, and it felt like all the pain in the world was in her voice. "I can lie. I have become very good at it."

Then she was gone, and there was only the sound of her swiftly retreating footsteps. When they had faded I wondered how I had come to find myself in this place, alone with the corpse of a good man at my feet.

It would not be the last one of course.

I would always walk with death.

Chapter 25

I did not sleep that night. I spent the dark hours lying next to my master, willing her to wake up but at the same time frightened that she would. I could not look at her face as I stripped the wound on her arm. The deep gouge was still raw and frightening to look at. I had seen deep cuts before on the bodies I left behind but it was rare I saw the weave of another's life while they still lived. In the flickering candle-light I searched for signs of the black lines that had risen to overtake her flesh but found nothing, only layers of white bone, creamy fat and red muscle. There was something about her now that I could not place – she felt different, the way the Tired Lands felt washed clean after the Birthstorm has come and gone. I was sure that she would wake even if I did not know when, and I was sure she would have questions even if I did not know how to answer them. As the subtle light of dawn slipped under the edges of our tent I laid her wounded arm gently down on the covers and slipped out.

I walked aimlessly until my feet were picked up by a breeze made thick and tempting by the smell of fresh bread. I followed it to one of Rufra's bakers who was giving away the king's bread. The queue parted to let me through, though I wished it hadn't. I was uncomfortable being known and unhappy with the idea people expected something of me. I took my bread and wandered away through the camp keeping my head down. As I approached the Landsmen's compound I slowed, not wanting to be recognised, and veered away. The wide paths leading from the compound had been churned into thick mud, as if by the feet of many mounts. I noticed the usual noises of a busy camp were missing.

Curious, I headed back to find the Landsmen's gates stood open, the compound empty. Tents, mounts, men, all were gone; all that was left was rubbish blowing about in the breeze. The Landsmen had left only one object for us, a bonemount in the centre of what had been their camp. It had been raised by smashing a spear through the skull and a hand axe had been buried in the top of it. One of the antlers had been broken off halfway down so it looked like the skull Rufra used. There could be no misunderstanding the message; the Landsmen had declared themselves against Rufra.

"Happy now, Girton?" I turned. Nywulf stood behind me with five troopers. "Take that down," he said to them, pointing at the bonemount.

"I did not want this," I said.

"Well it is what you got us." He was angry, his thick body tight with it. "We beat five hundred Nonmen and many died doing it, but you have cleverly managed to send Tomas a few hundred mounted and trained Riders to make up his numbers."

"The Landsmen would never have fought for Rufra anyway," I said. Nywulf stepped in close. "No, but if Karrick lived they would never have fought at all," he hissed, "and you ruined that for the life of one old woman."

"And to remove a spy," I said, but I could not put the confidence into my voice that I'd had before. Nywulf did not reply, only pushed past me and went to help his troops take the bonemount down.

"Nywulf," I called. He turned. "Have you ever heard the name Forven Aguirri?"

"Aguirri?" he said and his brow furrowed. "No. Now leave, Girton. I am too angry to look at you and I have real work to do."

I walked away from the empty Landsmen camp to find a

quiet place where I could think. At one point I saw Ossowin, the headman of Gwyre, who glared at me, his eyes full of hate, and then gave a curious smile before turning away. I considered following him, to apologise for his village and his wife and his daughter, but for what? He would not accept it. I had got everything wrong: Gwyre, the Landsmen, Mastal, even my feelings for Areth. Only when I finally stopped and sat down did I realise that my aimless walk had taken me back to the small wood in which I had buried Mastal. When I tried to eat my bread it tasted like dust.

Why had Karrick given me that name? Was it simply to curse me with indecision? Maybe he had been angry that he had been caught out as a spy and angry I had beaten him with a blade, and this was his revenge – this lingering, ghostlike doubt.

That was it. I had not been wrong. He was a killer and the spy.

I tried to make myself believe it but could not.

One of Xus's birds landed on the ground between two trees and I threw it some bread. It screamed a harsh bark of thanks at me and was joined by more of its kind, so I threw more bread. Maybe I should ask Danfoth the Meredari about the name. He had been closest to Arnst. I ripped up the rest of the loaf and threw it to Xus's birds, then headed back into the camp.

Around Arnst's tent flocked a different kind of black bird – the followers of Arnst. They sat together quietly, causing no trouble, only wanting to be where their master had been. In front of them stood Danfoth, reading from a scroll. As I approached he stopped speaking and rolled up the scroll.

"Chosen of Xus," he said, and a hundred heads turned to me: shy smiles, hopeful eyes. "See, Xus's chosen has come to us as Arnst said he would." He spoke like he was in a dream. Dead gods know, I felt like I was.

"I am no one's chosen, Danfoth, but I wish to speak to you." He nodded and led me into Arnst's tent. It was tidy now, the mess of Arnst's death cleared, though I noticed that the bloodstained part of the carpet and a section of the tent itself had been cut away and carefully rolled up and tied with black material. Danfoth did not speak, only gazed at me silently from blue eyes sunk within black make-up.

"Arnst is gone, his murderer found," I said. "Will you stay here?"

"Arnst said he would die, Xus's chosen would come, and we would begin again at the place of his death."

"And did he say he would return to life then?" I could hear myself sneering as I parroted the words of a thousand market hucksters. "That you should collect coin and wait for him to return? He will not but you may become rich."

"No," said Danfoth, "we are not about such foolish tricks. Arnst waits in Xus's dark palace for us; our bliss will be found with him. When Xus reaches out his hand we will take it gladly."

"You are a death cult?"

He leaned in close, his voice a low, angry rumble. "Ask yourself this: when only one of your gods lives why do none give him allegiance? Arnst told us to live well, but to welcome death when it comes."

I saw something frightening in Danfoth's eyes. This was not what Arnst had said, to my recollection, but I knew a little of the Meredari people's beliefs. They were warriors, honouring those who had died in battle, exalting them for it.

"Arnst told you this?"

"It is in his writings." I reached out for one of the scrolls but Danfoth held up a hand, stopping me. "I have not finished translating those yet." I had thought him stupid and now realised how wrong I had been. Quiet was not the same as foolish. "Our priests will not wear masks," he said. "We will only speak truth so will have no reason to hide our faces."

I wondered whose truth they would speak, Arnst's or Danfoth's?

"Does the name Forven Aguirri mean anything to you, Danfoth?"

"No." Danfoth turned away from me. "Why do you ask that?"

"It is just a name I heard."

"It is of no interest to me," he said. "Arnst's killer has been found and ended. He either answers to Arnst now in Xus's keep or starves where his hedging has chained him to the land."

"What if he wasn't Arnst's killer?"

"Then you are not the chosen of Xus," said Danfoth, and he turned to me with the face of a warrior not a man, "and you should leave."

I nodded and slipped out of the tent. From there I headed next door to the carpenter's tent but was stopped by a young woman.

"That is the prayer tent. Would you like to pray with me?"

"No," I said, confused "Where is the carpenter?"

"Who?"

"The man and the child who lived here."

"Gone," she said. "They gave their tent to the people of Arnst."

"Where did they go?" She shrugged and I turned, looking across to the drinking tent, which I had not thought about until now. It seemed strangely quiet. "What about Ahild and Berrit in the drinking tent."

"Berrit died – fell, broke his neck. Ahild sold us her tent as a meeting place."

"And where did she go."

"You should pray with us," said the girl. "Xus will hear you."

She was wrong, they were all wrong. I had felt the presence of Xus and it was a soft, shy thing that desired no glory. He would not be found here, and this place and these people made me uncomfortable. I walked away feeling uneasy and made my way to the day market, but instead of the usual bustle found it oddly subdued. The loss of the Landsmen was rippling through the camp. Everyone knew what an efficient fighting force they were – for as long as anyone could remember they had been one of the strongest armies in the Tired Lands – and for them to join Tomas was a huge blow to Rufra's ambitions. Where there should have been theatres, performers and jesters there were only empty stages and people scurrying around to buy what they needed before returning to their tents. Guards were everywhere, watching, and the atmosphere in the camp was far more martial than it had been before. I wandered through the market until I saw a man selling small wooden figures.

I picked up a figure of a Rider on a mount. "How much?"

"Half a bit."

"Very well." I reached into my pouch. He was clearly surprised that I had not tried to haggle down his exorbitant price. As he reached out for the money I held it back. "Is this the work of Hossit, the woodcarver who lives over by Arnst's tent?"

"Aye, good carver is Hossit. Sad he's gone."

"Where did he go?"

"To join his wife at the castle, driven out by those black and ragged yellowers."

"I thought his wife left him."

"Left? No, dead gods never seen a couple tighter than Hossit and Milder. No, he sent her up there."

"Why?"

"Half a bit," he said, opening his hand.

I gave him the coin. "Why did he send her to the castle?"

"She didn't feel safe here." I felt let down. No one here felt safe. But then again most stayed.

"Why didn't she feel safe?"

"Well –" He looked around him. "– this is a war camp. Maybe she was afraid of there being a war, eh? Hossit didn't talk much about it." A dead end, then I had another thought.

"Which of the traders here are Festival?" I leaned across. "I know they are not meant to be here to support Rufra, but I am sure there are some."

The trader looked around at the guards but they were paying no attention. "We are all Festival, but Irille, the herb seller, was a little more Festival, if you get my drift. You could try the butcher who was by her, though last I heard he was packing up."

I ran, slipping and sliding in the mud, to where the herb seller had been. The butcher was indeed packing up, folding away his bloodstained tables. As I approached he put a table down and picked up his cleaver.

"I need to speak to you," I said.

"Irille is dead because of you," he said. "Leave."

"I tried to protect her."

He shrugged. "I once tried to get water from a stone but I was still left thirsty."

"Please, I was told you may help me, that you are more Festival than any other here. What I ask may be the difference between Rufra's success and his death."

He blinked at me and wiped his bald head, leaving a smear of animal blood across it.

"One question, then, that is all."

"You travel, you meet people. Does the name Forven Aguirri mean anything to you?" As I said it I realised how foolish and desperate I sounded. Even if the butcher was Festival, there were thousands of people in the Tired Lands, to expect one name to jump out was bordering on madness. But why would Karrick have given me a name if he did not think it was a trail that could be followed?

The butcher stared at me, then he spoke.

"There was a man in the high king's guard called that, once."

"Really?"

"Aye. I only remember because there was a fuss about him when Festival stopped at Ceadoc that year. He was kicked out, had his armour and blade taken. I dare say anyone who was there that year would remember it. Rare someone is forced to leave the high king's guard."

"What did he do?"

"Women," said the butcher and picked up his table, "which would not bother the high king usually, even though this Forven was using his position to force himself on them, but he went too far – chose some married relative of the high king and got caught."

"They didn't simply kill him?"

"No. From what I hear they were going to, but he talked himself out of it." He placed the table on his cart. "Remarkable really. Court is brutal. Reputations are ruined on a word, and he had ruined many women, to their foolish way of thinking. A glance can ruin someone at Ceadoc, and Forven had done much more than glance. When he could not convince, he took, brutally, is what was said. The high king delights in cruelty and any excuse for it, which is probably how Forven survived until he picked someone too powerful. He should have ended there, become one of High King Darsese's entertainments, gone to the menageries –" a shudder ran through him "– but it is said his words enchanted the court, held them in some sort of spell." He picked up a case, the muscles in his arms tensing like ships' ropes holding against a tide.

"So what happened?"

"They exiled him. That help you?"

"I'm not sure," I said. "Did you see this happen?"

"Some of us have a living to earn," he said and turned away, placing the case on his cart.

"Do you know what he looked like?" The butcher shook his head. "Or where he went?"

"What do exiles usually do?" He gave the case a shove, pushing it along the bed of the cart. "He took up religion, up at the old place in the bonefields."

"The one that was destroyed?"

"Aye." He picked up another case, and the smell of spoiling meat wafted across from him.

"Do you know anything more?"

"The temple was destroyed at the beginning of the war by the Nonmen, though they weren't called that then. All the priests were killed, but a man like that, with his appetites and ability to sway people? I half expected him to end up leading them." He slammed the case onto the cart and then spat. "Rapists. They should make them eat their own cocks."

"But you never saw his face?"

"That's what I said." He turned away.

I thanked him but he did not acknowledge me. As I walked away bits of puzzle started to slide into each other. The people around Arnst – not his followers, those on the edges of his movement – had something in common, but until now I had not noticed it because I had not been looking for it. The first woman I met had clearly despised Arnst, and I had put it down to her dislike of incomers, but what if it was more than that? I had thought the woodcarver's wife had left him, but that was not the case; she had gone away to be safe. And Ahild, who had depended on Arnst and his followers' custom for her drinking tent, she had also sent her daughter away. Women had not been safe around Arnst and I had not seen it. Had Karrick known this and recognised Arnst as Forven Aguirri? But why hadn't he said anything? If he knew Arnst had been ejected from the high king's guard as a rapist why keep quiet? If. Such a small word and yet it contained so much possibility.

I should have listened to my master. She had told me to delve deeper and I had ignored her because I had wanted Karrick to be guilty. My hate for Landsmen had overridden everything. What a fool I was. If I had only scratched at the surface of the problem I would have seen I was following no scent but my own.

I needed to speak to Rufra. If Karrick had known, surely he had told Rufra?

But Rufra, my only friend in the whole world, had not told me.

I stormed my way through the camp at a fast limp. I was so angry with myself for being a fool that no one barred my way until I met Crast, guarding Rufra's door, he blithely ignored my anger.

"Girton," he said, "if you want to see the king you'll have to wait. And given what's happened you might want to steer clear of him for a while."

"Let me in, Crast."

"Can't, can I?" he said, mock serious. "I'm a trainee Heartblade, and you're an assassin in an obvious temper who's trying to get at my king." Suddenly he brightened. "Am I going to have to fight you? After your training I might even win. Neliu will be so annoyed."

"Shut up, Crast." I pushed past him and he let me, walking along by my side. It was difficult to remain quite as angry in the face of his unrelenting good cheer. "I won't enjoy killing you of course. I feel like we're becoming friends despite the bruises you've given me."

"You wouldn't be able to kill me."

"Are you sure?" He was suddenly serious. I glanced down. His stabsword was at my belly. I met his eyes and was glad to see a mischievous sparkle there. "See? I've been paying attention."

"I have no wish to kill Rufra."

"You might have once he's seen you." The blade was gone again. "I'm not sure you're his favourite person after killing Karrick. Nice fight, by the way. Messy, but you got the job done."

"Messy?" I stopped. "What do you mean?"

"Well, you're Girton Club-Foot, the great artist with a blade, and you ended up beating him by rolling about in the mud."

I stared at him for a moment, unsure whether he was joking or not.

"You've never killed anyone, have you?" I said.

"Of course I have," he replied but he looked ashamed, like someone caught in a lie.

"Let me give you a little advice, Crast," I said. "In the end it is not about being an artist, it is about being the one who walks away."

"You sound like Nywulf."

"I heard it from him, that's why. And he is usually right."

"He said you shouldn't have fought Karrick."

"And now we're back to me needing to speak to Rufra," I said.

Crast shrugged, though we were already at the inner door in Rufra's tent. "I'll have to ask if he'll see you," he said.

"I'll wait." Crast ducked inside and returned a moment later.

"He'll see you, Girton. I'm just glad it's you and not me going in there."

Before I could reply Aydor walked out, looking distraught, disappointed and angry all at the same time. He glanced at me.

"Girton," he said sharply. There was none of his false bonhomie now. I wondered whether Rufra was starting to see through him.

"Your turn," said Crast. He held aside the tent flap and I readied myself for the rage of kings.

Rufra sat in a corner of his tent, the light from outside almost totally blocked by the closed curtains. He was hunched over the table with the mock-up of the battle at Goldenson Copse set up on it. He did not pay me any attention when I entered; he was lost in the pieces before him, or pretending to be, and I watched him move cavalry and infantry about, shake his head, put them back and start again. Each time he only made a few moves. Maybe he had tried them all before and realised their futility as soon as he started.

"It cannot be changed, the past," I said softly. He put down the figure of a man he was holding, placing it in the centre of the board. It was a jester, mid bow, taking the acclaim of the crowd.

"Aydor wanted to join my Triangle Council," he said. "I told him no."

"It was the right thing to do."

"He offered to publicly renounce any claim to the throne." That stunned me, but I had trained to perform all my life and did not let it show.

"He will say anything for power." Rufra sighed at my words, shook his head and went back to moving his little figures. It seemed an age passed before he spoke again, and when he did there was rage in his voice, tightly suppressed.

"I told you that if Karrick were to be dealt with, I would do it."

"The way you dealt with Arnst, or was he really called Forven?" His mouth opened and closed, and in that instant I knew I was right.

He closed his eyes and sighed. "I should have known you would discover the truth of Arnst eventually." He put down the piece he was holding, a mounted Rider. "By the time I knew about him it was too late."

"You could not remove him?"

"He had many followers – brought some with him and added a lot later. Many of them are my soldiers."

"So you set a rapist free in the camp and covered for him to keep yourself in power. I thought you said you were going to be different?"

He stood, knocking the table and the pieces to the floor, and everything about him – the hands balled into fists, ugly expression, muscles on his neck like hard shadows – said anger.

"What do you know?" he said, struggling to keep his voice low. "What do you know? You left!" He walked over to me, small quick steps, raising a hand and pushing it against his forehead, chewed fingernails catching in his long hair. "You left! You left for five years, and for so long I expected you to return and you did not. You left me with a handful of men and a castle. And now you come back with your black-and-white morality and see nothing past what is in front of your face. Do you have any idea, Girton? Any idea at all what it has been like?"

"You were not alone." I stood, my own muscles tensing. "You had Nywulf, Cearis and Boros and your council . . ."

"They are not my friends!" It was almost a shriek, almost a shout, and yet he did not raise his voice. He took a deep breath and spoke softly: "They are not my friends. They are my teachers, and the council often seem as much my enemy as my helpers." He looked at the floor. "I have been alone, Girton, and so many have died because of my mistakes, and now –" another breath "– just when I seem to be getting some semblance of control, you come back and it is like Dark Ungar has cursed my camp."

"We beat the Nonmen," I said, but there was no force in my voice.

"And you have replaced them with the Landsmen. I'd rather fight the Nonmen a hundred times than the Landsmen once!" He was shouting now. "The Landsmen give Tomas a legitimacy he has lacked until now, do you understand? And all because you could not obey a simple command!"

"I thought you said you wanted a friend, not a servant." Now I was shouting.

"I want a friend I can talk to, that I can trust!" He threw the goblet he was holding into the corner of the tent. "Someone who will think before they act!" I had cutting words ready in my mouth but I did not unsheathe them. I had moaned and whined about my own pain but Rufra had been thrust into kingship, forced to cope, and then he had lost a child – where had I been then?

Rufra turned from me to sit on his throne and filled a new goblet from the barrel of perry by it. When he spoke now it was softly, as if he was seeing a place far away. "I should have told you about Arnst the minute you said a Landsman was sneaking about."

"Why didn't you?" I said, looking around the tent. Only now did I notice how bare it was. He had nothing of himself here, nothing except the broken table and scattered pieces, all else was simply the trappings of a king, not my friend. I had pitied myself and my loneliness while failing to see the same in others. What a fool I was. What a fool I had been.

"I felt stupid," he said. "Here was Girton, having gone off to all these far exotic places and become so worldly. Taken a stand against an evil man, taken his weapon even. And then you come back to find your friend so committed to a good cause he has lifted a rapist to a place of power on his council, and here I am, forced into colluding with a Landsman. Every time Arnst became fixated on a woman I had Karrick spirit her away before Arnst could hurt her." He poured the perry back into the barrel. "I did not know what he was until too late. I warned Arnst I would not stand for it, had him watched."

"Why Karrick?"

"Because Arnst was persuasive, but I knew he could not convert a Landsman to his ways. Especially one like Karrick." He made a small movement of his hand, a fluttering, a momentary affirmation of the mistake he'd made.

I saw how he must have struggled. He had trapped himself in an impossible place, needing those who were loyal to Arnst but worried by the influence he had in the camp – while at the same time desperate to protect his people from him. I had blundered in, come to all the wrong conclusions and made everything immeasurably worse.

"I have been a fool, Rufra," I said. "I should not have acted without your permission. You were right.'"

"Small consolation, Girton," he said, a sad smile on his face. "Have a drink" He waved a hand at the perry barrel.

"It does not agree with me," I said, because I feared what the magic would do if I let myself become drunk.

He shrugged.

"Me neither," he said, staring at his empty goblet. "Do you still believe Karrick guilty?"

"No," I said quietly. "With what I know of Arnst now, the number of suspects has increased beyond thinking."

"I should have told you," said Rufra again.

"And I should have looked harder," I said, more forcefully. "In truth I wanted Karrick to be guilty. I barely looked past him at all."

"Not all the Landsmen are like the one you took that warhammer from, Girton," he said, and the ground beneath my feet seemed to shift.

"They are still cruel – it is their reason for being."

"The Tired Lands are cruel, and if another sorcerer rises they will become crueller still."

I had no answer to that, not without telling Rufra truths about me I knew he could never accept.

"You are not cruel, Rufra."

"I hope not to be, but being a king –" he wrapped his arms around himself "–it is a cruel business, Girton."

"Surely you have some distractions? It cannot all be miserable."

"Gusteffa does her best to amuse me. Sometimes it has only been Gusteffa's clowning that has kept me sane."

"A jester is a good companion," I said.

He grinned.

"Aye. Maybe I have kept her because the jester I wanted was not here, but I have come to appreciate her talent and her council." He stood. "Listen. Do you hear?"

I did. People shouting. The voices of men and women raised and demanding order. "What is happening?"

"Tomas presses me hard, and when the Landsmen left they took half our flour with them, Fureth is a man full of spite." A cloud passed over his face. "Now I must replace what they took and food is more scarce than ever, so I am forced to choose between providing free bread and paying my soldiers. The proclamation has just gone out that bread must be paid for. I will be lucky if there are not riots."

"Your people will understand."

"Will they? Maybe they will today, Girton, but what about in a week, when they are hungry? Or in two weeks, when their children are hungry?" He went down on one knee, picking up the figure of the jester. "I need Tomas to attack," he said under his breath.

"But what about Karrick, Rufra? What do we do?"

He stared at the figure.

"I will let Karrick's death stand," he said quietly and picked up the map table, starting to set the figures back on it. "It pains me. He was a good man, but if we say Arnst's killer is still out there it will only lead to more turmoil, and if the people believe the Landsmen harboured a murderer they will trust them less and their defection will not seem such a blow."

"But if there is still a spy you are still in danger."

"I am always in danger, Girton." His eyes flicked to the door flap, and from outside I could hear more voices raised in anger. "But I am used to it, and Nywulf, Crast and Neliu will keep me safe."

"They are not here now."

Rufra smiled. "Do not be so easily deceived. Neliu hides somewhere in the back of the tent."

"You did not trust me?"

"I did –" he grinned "– but Neliu is not the trusting type, and if I had sent her away, she and I would have had to answer to Nywulf."

"No one wants that," I said, and we laughed – a small laugh, a slow repair to the material of our friendship which had become torn and ragged with distrust.

"I will continue to look for anyone who threatens you. I will not rest."

"You do not need to do that, Girton. Simply be my friend."

I nodded.

"I will." But it was not enough. Never enough. I had done so much damage to what he was trying to build and yet he forgave me so easily and asked for so little in return. It was more than I could have done in his position, and I felt a need, a deep need, to wash away my foolishness. To wash away the blood and bitterness of my years in the wild here in his tent and recreate myself. I fell to my knees before him, raising my throat in the old way of respect and finding old words, words from the stories of great Riders I had told as jester, springing into my mouth.

"I pledge myself to you, Rufra ap Vthyr. I will be your servant and friend –"

"Girton," there is no need for this." But I carried on.

"– and my blade will be as your hand. It shall not be unsheathed without your command. It will make no cut without your permission."

He looked at me so strangely I wondered if he thought I was making a joke. Then he nodded, clearly unsure of what to say, the moment seemed so solemn, so serious, but a small smile crept onto his face.

"You don't need my permission every time though," he said. "If someone tries to kill you, don't die simply because I am emptying my bowels in a bush."

And suddenly we were laughing again, like children.

Chapter 26

I spent hours talking with Rufra. We avoided the years I had spent with the Landsmen, instead talking of where else I had been and what I had seen, and I realised the time away with my master had not all been bad – I had seen wonders few others ever would. We talked of victories gained and losses we had suffered and, in low tones with many pauses, he told me of the day Gusteffa brought news of the death of his child. I had no answer to the pain – so obvious and raw on his face – all I could do was listen and hope the release of words helped ease him somewhat. Each time we heard shouts from outside his face was like a skyscape: clouds of worry, doubt and fear passing across it, all to be burned away by his determined scowl. Occasionally, reports would be brought to him, words were whispered into his ear and he would nod then issue instructions. Sometimes he told me what was said – scouts reporting on troop movements, men reporting on the mood of the camp – and sometimes he did not, and I did not ask. If it mattered he would tell me. Eventually, the camp became quiet.

As I stood to leave he lifted his Conwy sword slightly from its scabbard so I could see the shining blade.

"Brothers," he said quietly.

"Brothers," I said, lifting the stabsword slightly from the scabbard at my thigh, he nodded and grinned as I dropped it and it slotted back into place. I left feeling stronger than I had in months, years maybe – stronger through my friendship and stronger because at some point during our talk I had decided to stop running from myself. Maybe I would never be a good man like Rufra, my path was set, my black deeds were done. My blade would only ever wreak havoc – it was my fate – but I would give my life for Rufra and his new ways. For the first time in days it seemed my club foot did not ache.

The day had fled. It was that moment before twilight when the promise of day and warmth is fading, but – and it may have been my imagination or the pleasant buzz my renewed friendship with Rufra had given me – despite the darkness gathering her skirts it seemed like the heavy air that threatened the Birthstorm had retreated a little. Maybe this would be one of those rare years when the Birthstorm existed only as threat on the horizon but never came into being, simply dissipating – giving way to the long, dry, heat of yearslife when the grasses ripened and hissed with the promise of bread to come, but also when the wells dried out and people balanced on the knife's edge of life.

Twilight was when people thronged to the priests to hear their sermons and sign the books. I wondered if it put folk on edge to sign the books above ground in a tent rather than trailing down steps to the traditional buried chapels. I passed the congregants outside Darvin's open tent. He sounded hoarse and the crowd overflowed from his tent, so eager were they to hear what he said. It was a comforting to see so many drawn to the words of a good man, and I stopped, joining the back of the crowd and listening.

". . . and remember, people you love may fail you or seem to let you down, but you must forgive! You must try to understand that what they do, even when it hurts, even when it seems terrible to us, is for us all!" His masked face regarded his congregation as if he were beseeching each and every one. "Sometimes we must cause a small pain to avert a larger one. We must sacrifice what we think is important so that good may persevere and the true gods be reborn . . ."

I nodded and walked away. Darvin was trying to make

them understand Rufra's changes and ready those who followed him for a world that may become even harder as Rufra tried to remake it into something fairer.

I was thirsty, and there was a well on one of the small wooded rises that overlooked the camp. I could slake my thirst there and have a moment alone. I headed up the slope deep in thought.

Rufra had been through much, but he had built a kingdom, whereas I had been through much and done nothing but feel sorry for myself.

And kill.

I had always said I hated the path I had been taken along, that I would rather have been a performer, bringing joy and laughter instead of death and sorrow, but what had I done to avoid it? Nothing. I picked up the bucket by the well, its wood worn smooth by long use, while idly thinking about putting on my motley and make-up and entertaining the crowd in the night market for nothing but the joy of it.

The arrow punched the bucket from my hand and it bounced along the ground, violently unspooling the rope from the winch in a screech of complaining metal. I froze, for the barest moment, trying to understand what had just happened and then dived to the side. As the bucket rolled to a stop a second arrow cut through the air, smashing its tip against the stone lip of the well where I had been standing a moment before. Panic. In the gathering dark the archer could be anywhere. No. He must be in front of me. I vaulted backwards, my hands gripping the cold edge of the well – a third arrow cut through the air with the sound of material tearing – I pushed off the stone, going over the wooden roof of the well and feeling-rather-than-seeing the arrow pass below me. Landing on the muddy ground, I slipped down behind the well.

I can help you.

No. The voice did not help.

Silence.

Was the archer moving? I listened for the crack of a twig or the subtle brush of cloth against branch. I couldn't stay here; I needed to be among the trees. Even though their cover was thin it would be enough for me to work round and get behind whoever attacked me.

Breathe out.

Breathe in.

I can help you.

No.

Breathe out.

Breathe in.

I ran for the treeline, stepping awkwardly and erratically to make myself a harder target. Another arrow, this one from slightly to the left of where I thought the first arrows had come from. The brush of fletching against my cheek. The archer was good but not good enough. I made the trees, hiding behind the slim cover of a young pine. Two arrows in quick succession bit into the tree, showering me with splinters and astringent sap. Fall and roll, coming up behind another tree. Repeat, this time in the opposite direction. Stop, listen.

I can help you.

No.

I listened.

Nothing.

Run. Tree to tree, breath loud in my ear, waiting for the arrow to hit. The punch of it. The pain. The shock and the gasping for life as it runs out through the wound. Don't think like that! Another tree, more cover.

No arrows.

Was the archer waiting, hoping for me to become complacent? Or were they gone, knowing they had missed their chance and taking the opportunity to melt away until they could try again.

Let me help you.

I felt it call to me – the well of life beneath, the darkness within. I could reach out into the wood and pluck the archer from his perch, dash him against the ground. Smash him into pulp and . . . *"The Tired Lands are cruel, and if another sorcerer rises they will become crueller still."*

What would I ever bring Rufra but trouble and sorrow?

I stepped out from my tree, arms open, all senses working, waiting for the arrow. Ready for it. Ready.

One, my master.

Two, my master.

Three, my master.

Nothing.

Four, my master

Five, my master.

Six, my master.

They were gone.

No.

A sound. The rattle of wood on wood – a dropped bow. I ran, sliding behind another tree. This part of the wood was on a steep slope and the trees barely clung on, the ground little more than loose scree. A bow on the ground, one of the hornbows used by Rufra's mount archers. I picked it up as I ran past, skidded to a stop at the edge of the wood where the tents of the camp started. No one there. Whoever had attacked me was already gone. I inspected the bow, nothing special about it, no markings or personalisation. I wandered around the wood, finding a place where the leaf litter had recently been disturbed, following tracks and admiring the skill of who had attacked me. I wondered how long they had lain in wait then shook my head. No, they must have followed me. My visit to the wood had been an impulse. Had my attacker picked me up at Darvin's tent, or had they been waiting for me outside Rufra's tent? Either way it was unlikely I would find someone who remembered them; a man or woman with a bow was too common a sight in the camp.

Still, I walked up and down the lines of tents, looking for

a sign, keeping alert for someone following me. Every face that passed looked suspicious. Did that man's eyes follow me? Did that woman signal to someone behind a tent? Were those children, gathered around an old woman with their hands out, taking coin or marking my movements?

This was madness – I could not suspect everyone who passed me. I returned to our tent, resolutely looking only ahead. When I slipped inside I was surprised to find no lamps lit. My eyes accustomed themselves to the low light. My master's bed was empty.

The impact came from behind, high in the centre of my back, throwing me forward.

An arrow.

I knew the way they killed. Felt its ghost as it ruptured my lungs, split my breastbone and burst from my chest. I hit the floor, dust billowing from the carpet. The weight on my back forced me down into the choking cloud.

Not an arrow.

A person. I tried to roll. A hand grabbed my hair, pulling my head back and baring my neck for the blade at my throat.

"What did you do, Girton?" My master's voice, raw and full of pain. "What did you do?"

"Nothing." The word spat out, eyes closed to hide the lie from her even though she was behind me.

"Where is he?" Her weight altering, knees becoming painful shards in my back as she moved, her lips by my ear. "Where is Mastal? What have you done with him?"

"Gone." I spat out dust, coughed. "He left."

"Don't lie!" My head pulled further back. "What did you do?" I had never heard her so angry. "I can feel it, Girton. Feel the magic in my bones, feel the poison is gone. Before it was always there, like a weight, but now I am free of it. What did you do?" She bit out each word like she was forcing down filthy medicine.

"I did not mean it," I whispered. My mind raced and I

felt like a child again. I could not tell her the truth. That I had killed Mastal was bad enough, but that I had used his life to save hers? I did not know what she would do, to me or herself. When she had taught me to lie she had taught me to always hide a lie within a truth.

We can stop her.

A terrified mount bending to my will.

"I doctored your medicine." I choked the words out, eager to be rid of their filthy taint.

"What?"

"With doxy leaf. I found a supplier of yandil and—"

"You could have killed me." Disbelief in her voice.

"I did not know!"

"Mastal thought he had failed and that you would die. I used that to drive him away. Then I treated you myself with the yandil I had gathered."

One, my master.

Two, my master.

The weight left my back but I did not try to move.

Three, my master.

Four, my master.

I sat up.

Five, my master.

Six, my master.

In the corner of the tent I could see a vague shape. She sat with her arms around her knees and her head down, long hair falling in curtains. When she raised her head all I saw were two eyes sparkling in the dark.

"Get out," she said quietly.

"Master, I—"

"Get out!" And this time she screamed it, grabbing a bottle and throwing it at me. Glass showered me, and I scrambled away. Another bottle followed and hit me on the back, though the impact did not hurt as much as my master's third scream. "Get out, Girton!"

I ran out into darkness. Rain had started, the sort of non-committal rain which was enough to be uncomfortable but not hard enough to really curse at. I staggered through the camp. Far away I could hear the night market: whoops of joy and laughter that were as alien to me in that moment as flight. I fell over a tent rope, sprawling in the mud, and the sob that escaped me was not one of physical pain, it was from the sort of vicious inner pain that I had not felt since Drusl had died all those years ago – but worse. Drusl's death had been beyond my control – it had been engineered by others – this time only I was to blame. Any who saw me must have thought me drunk, stumbling from tent to tent, using their small support to push myself onwards. In the dark, with damp hair covering my face, no one recognised me as I blundered through the camp. In the end I found myself in a small copse and curled up on the ground in the damp leaf mould like an animal.

As I lay there I found a small bright point of relief within myself. I was free of the worry I had felt like a crushing weight on my shoulders since I had killed Mastal. She knew. I did not know how, but she did. Now the storm had broken and the worst had happened, my ship had been wrecked and I was cast adrift. The nagging fear of discovery had been replaced by a much cleaner, more focused fear: fear of travelling the new and unknown sea before me. I could not change my place in life and I could not shrug off the hurt that ran through me every time I thought about my master and her voice as she had ordered me away.

But I knew pain.

I was familiar with pain. And if pain was the ocean I was lost in, then I would take some comfort from the knowledge that I had swum these seas before.

And I had survived.

I would survive.

My eyes closed and I wished fervently for warmth.

Fitchgrass

And in my dream I was death and I wore death's face. On the plain of grasses a hobby hangs from every seedhead; they have the faces of those you have killed. Fitchgrass the green hisses through the leaves. Fitchgrass the yellow not seen but heard. Fitchgrass the black who tangles the unwary. Fitchgrass the white who knows your secrets.

Fitchgrass, Fitchgrass,
Tied up in stitchgrass.

Heard in the night in the field, heard in the day in the haystack, heard as he steals away the bad children to blight the harvest. Clanging shut the gibbet door. Chasing you, chasing you, a tangle of corn and thistle, flower and fear. Run, mage-bent, run! Run through the fields pell-mell, ground churning underfoot, straw in the air and the scent of sun and mounts in your nose. You know what happens here. Leave her behind. Leave her dead on the stable floor. Leave her dying in the blood gibbet. Leave her black and lined and wracked with pain. You never loved her.

Sour boy, sour boy,
Lost-all-the-flour boy.

Fitchgrass crawls through the fields. Fitchgrass ties knots in grasses. Fitchgrass trips the unwary. Leads you down the path. Only fears the scythe which reaps and opens a vein – blood flows. *"Don't forget me, Girton."* Blood slows, bends and twists, becomes elastic and wraps itself around the dying body of a woman whose face you cannot see. Blood becomes grass, a net of dry yellow stalks as brittle as ice and as unyielding as the cold. You never loved her.

Fitchgrass, Fitchgrass,
Tied up in stitchgrass.

You run from Fitchgrass, king of mischief. Fitchgrass, fast as wind and light as a sigh. A web of dry grass has you and you cannot lose yourself on the endless plains of hissing hobby seedheads. Blood gibbets filled with dolls watch you, point the way for Fitchgrass the green. You are tied and, when you look behind, you drag a net of dry grass. The door slams shut on the woman. *Master!* It holds you back and you cannot cut the stems and stalks. *She is slowing you down.* She is slowing you down. You never loved her.

Sour boy, sour boy,
Lost-all-the-flour boy.

Fitchgrass closes, striding, ratter-tatter. Fitchgrass is stilt-stagger above you, poised to strike with his warhammer. The ground beneath you ruptures as you suck the magic from it. The fields around you die. *Tear it all apart.* It is so easy. Easier than breathing, easier than running, easier than dragging a weight. Black fierce you rip the hedging lord stem from stem to scatter on the wind like chaff after harvest, and as you rend him he does nothing but laugh.

Fitchgrass, Fitchgrass,
Tied up in stitchgrass.

And when the air clears, when the hedging lord is gone you are all that remains. The wind blows, the land turns yellow as Fitchgrass' body. The bodies in the gibbets die and rot to bone. There is blood on the grass, but hedgings do not bleed and the blood is not yours. You look for the woman in the net but she is gone.

Only you remain.

Only we remain.

Chapter 27

I woke to lizard song, the gentle trilling of a small flying lizard as it called to its mate. For a moment I suffered the strange dislocation of waking in an unexpected place: this was not my tent, not my bed.

I had no tent. Had no bed.

But I was warm. In years of campaigning I had slept outside many times and was familiar with the feeling of waking outside, and it was never one of warmth. In the early morning, frost still cracking the blades of grass and the only stable relationship I had ever had in my life in tatters, I should have woken cold and shivering – with self-pity if nothing else. But I was calm, calm and warm, and the world, though still dark, was full of the promise of morning. I could smell flowers, a subtle, honey scent full of exotic spices, sharp and sweet as it teased my nose.

I will give you what you want.

I stood, spun, looked at where I had lain. Scorched into the ground was the shape of my body in yellow, my own souring in the earth and leaf litter of the wood. Here was a small place where nothing would ever grow or live again, where I had stolen the life from the land to keep warm throughout the night. Magic had been succour to me, and it had felt good. How many of the giant sourings that scored the Tired Lands had started with small patches like this? An almost insignificant patch of dead earth. Had the Black Sorcerer's journey towards murdering thousands and ripping a crevasse in the earth started with an act that appeared harmless, a desiccated yellow patch of ground that he thought no one would notice?

I fell to my knees and brought up what little food was in my stomach, retching, burning, spitting. This wasn't me. This was not what I wanted to be. I'd let it creep up on me despite all the warnings, despite knowing that the magic wanted to be used, that it had its own low and animal cunning, I had simply let it through. No, it was worse. There had been no volition on my part; it had acted of its own accord. I kicked leaf litter over the shape in the grass, hiding the souring and my vomit. Then, making sure no one saw me, I slipped out of the wood and back into the life of the camp sure that, somehow, people would be able to tell there was something terrible in me, that I carried some guilty mark.

The morning sky glowered and the air was heavy with the promise of the Birthstorm. A sudden burst of stinging hail swept across the camp.

But I pulled my tunic tightly about myself and the morning sky glowered, the air heavy with the promise of the Birthstorm. A sudden burst of stinging hail swept across the camp but the cold was not as chilling as the thought I may have become the puppet of magic.

I needed purpose or my thoughts would chase me into hiding and darkness.

Arnst's killer was still out there, and it seemed unthinkable that his death was not somehow related to the spy who was betraying Rufra. If I could not control myself, I could at least control what I did and would put right Karrick's death. And the place to start with that was Arnst's camp.

No. It was not.

It was at the beginning. Start at the beginning.

When I had first come here I had met a woman who clearly disliked Arnst. She had not given me her name but she had told me the name of her child, Collis. I should start with her. I felt no grief at Arnst's death – I would happily have engineered it myself – but I owed a debt to Karrick, however much it annoyed me, and it was like a nagging pain in the back of my head. There was also still a traitor loose in the camp, and it was entirely possible that the death of Arnst had nothing to do with who he was; his death could well have been an attempt to destabilise the camp.

I had to know the truth.

The camp woke as I passed through it, like I was the foam on a wave pushing sleep away before me. Though Rufra's camp was big, it was not large enough to grant anonymity, and I tracked down Collis's mother quickly enough. She was at a signing sermon, and so I sat down outside to wait and think.

"Girton?" I turned to find Areth, wandering the camp as she often did.

"Areth, I was just sitting."

"I sit, often," she said, and nestled down beside me. "I am worried, Girton," she said after a while.

"Worried? About what?"

"About Rufra." She lowered her voice. "Last night a messenger rode in – not one of ours – Rufra has been in council ever since. And Nywulf is missing."

"Missing?"

"He left yesterday after speaking to the priest Darvin. He said nothing to Rufra either, just rode away."

"You think these events are linked?"

She nodded. "The Rider was from Tomas," she whispered. She had the posture, the flying-lizard quickness of one overrun with worry. "It was the call to battle."

"So Rufra will be moving out his army."

"Yes, but without Nywulf? Despite what he may think, Rufra needs him, needs his experience. And Tomas, curse him, has chosen to fight at Goldenson Copse as he knows the place preys on Rufra's mind."

I sensed Neander's hand at work.

"Do you want me to find Nywulf?"

She shook her head, her eyes wet with tears.

"What if Nywulf is the spy." The words escaped her mouth as if they were a guilty secret, something she dreaded letting loose. A tear ran down her face. "What if that is why he has gone? If Nywulf betrayed Rufra it would kill him." Her voice fluttered around the edges of panic and I touched her face, fighting down the shiver of pleasure that ran through me. I applied gentle pressure, moving her head so she looked at me.

A terrified mount bending to my will.

I pulled my hand away.

"Nywulf would never betray Rufra," I said, though my heart fluttered inside at the thought.

"But he knows everything about Rufra – his contacts, his battle plans . . ."

"And he loves him like a son, Areth. No. I cannot believe that. Nywulf will be back. Rufra without Nywulf is like . . ." I could not think of what it was like.

"Like you without your master?" she said. I nodded, and inside me something hurt. "What happened last night, Girton?" she said gently. "I felt you out in the camp somewhere, like a glow."

"How do you control it, Areth?" I said.

"Control what?"

"The magic. How do you stop it overwhelming you?"

"Overwhelming me?" She let out a quiet laugh. "I can barely draw enough to heal a cut. If it was powerful enough to overwhelm me do you think I would not have let it when my son was dying?" She glanced up at me, her eyes blue as sea, but in them was a mote of fear. "Is it different for you?"

"A little," I said, suddenly wary. "Maybe it is because I am not as used to it."

"Maybe," she said, and another shiver, this one like a warning, ran through me, spinning and twisting over the network of scars on my body. She knew too much, and if she was scared she may tell someone. What would happen to me then? Who would believe me if I tried to tell them the queen was also a sorcerer? No one. She was safe, but I was far from it. I could almost feel the danger, like a pressure.

I can help you.

I stood.

"Areth, I have to go."

"Is it something I said?"

"Yes." She looked hurt and I shook my head. "Not like that. It is something you made me realise."

"You will be ready though, if Rufra marches? You will be there? You have to be there."

"Of course. I will be waiting for his call. I think I always have been." Then I vanished into the crowds leaving the signing sermons, but I was no longer looking for Collis's mother; I had something else to do first. If I was to serve Rufra I must have control of what lived within me, and there was only one person who could give me that: my master. And more, I owed her the truth of what had happened to Mastal no matter what it cost me, no matter how much it hurt.

I stopped outside our tent, taking deep breaths. If I was to be hated by her, so be it, but it would not be for a lie. I stepped over the threshold and into the darkness. She was still exactly where I had left her so many hours ago, sat with her elbows on her knees, her head down.

"Master?"

"I told you to leave." She said it very quietly.

"I did." I remained in the doorway of the tent. "And now I have come back."

"And you can leave again."

"I cannot," I said.

"Why?"

"I lied to you, Master. If you wish to hate me then I would have you hate me for the right reasons."

She looked up, eyes sparkling in the gloom.

"Talk then," she said, short words full of impatience.

"Mastal is dead." I waited in the dark for some sort of reaction – anger, tears, anything – all I heard was the slow susurrus of her breathing. "I killed him," I added in case she needed some clarification.

"Why?" a sharp word.

"Well . . ." I could feel my brow furrowing, the words becoming a stutter. Why? I did not know. I knew it had seemed right then, I knew it had seemed like the only way, but now I felt lost, like I was flailing at a reality that slowly drifted away – like I walked a dream. "You were ill, and—"

"Did you doctor the medicine? Was that true?"

"Yes. Mastal showed me the yandil, and it seemed to speak to me. I could feel the hurt in you, feel the poison, feel what should be done with the leaf. I thought I could make him go away, save you myself." I sounded desperate and took a breath, slowing my words. "But it did not work." Tears were fighting to escape my eyes. "It did not work, and Mastal said that once the yandil had ceased to work, that was it – death was the only escape you would have from the pain."

"And you killed him for it." She sounded disgusted, pulling herself to her feet and starting to turn away from me.

"No, not for that, though I am entirely to blame, I accept that." She looked over her shoulder.

"And yet, Girton," she said quietly, "I live."

"He said I should be with you. At the end." *Breathe out.* "I held your hand while Xus approached." *Breathe in.* "I felt the brush of the unseen's cloak, and Mastal, in his anger—"

"His righteous anger."

"I know that." The words were angry, and I saw her blink at me, slowly, like a predator measuring distance. "I know he was right to be angry. I was wrong about him. As I have been wrong about so much. Mastal raised a hand to strike me."

"And you struck back. So much training and yet you had so little control."

"I did not strike back," I said softly and relived the moment of Mastal's death, the horror of it; the exhilaration of it. "He struck at me and I stopped him. I grabbed him by the wrist and in my other hand I held you." My voice as dry as a souring in yearslife. "I felt everything, Master. I felt your pain, I felt the poison as it hated its way to your heart and I felt the love that Mastal had for you." I stared, but where I looked into was a bleak place dominated by a mountain whose scars and peaks and crags were the desiccated face of a good man. "I took his life and I used it to drive the poison from you. But it should have been my life, not Mastal's. I should have given my life for yours. I should . . ." I could barely speak any more, and my last words had to struggle to escape my mouth. "Cut me," I said. "I cannot cope with it. Cannot control it. The magic, it is too much for me. Cut me. Send me away if you must but you have to cut me first." And then she was there, like she always was, giving more than I expected or deserved. Holding me in her arms as I sobbed like a child, repeating over and over again between the tears, "I did not mean it, I did not mean it."

She stroked my hair, talking in nonsense words that brought no meaning, only comfort.

"Oh my boy, my boy, I should have seen this, should have known."

"No, Master, no excuses. There are no excuses."

She pulled away, putting her hands over my ears, holding my head so I had to look into her eyes.

"You are growing up, and it is harder for you to do than any other." Through the blur of tears I saw her concern, her love, but there was a hardness there, and I knew that I could not ask for her forgiveness, not yet. The way she looked at me had changed. I had never realised how constant was the sense of pride she felt in me, not until today. But now when

I looked into her eyes it was no longer there, and I felt that absence as a pain more crippling than any wound.

"Master, I have got so much wrong. Done so much wrong."

"Then you must put it right. No, we must put it right." I nodded. "You shall tell me everything, all of it, and then we will work out our next move."

"But first the knife," I said quietly.

"Aye," she said, "but first the knife."

I left the tent two hours later, my chest throbbing and bleeding from the wounds, the world a greyer place. Maybe it was the gathering of the thick blanket of Birthstorm clouds above that caused this, but most likely it was not. There was a chattering in the camp, an excited noise, but I could not bring myself to be curious about it. Each time my master had cut in the wounds my reaction had been slightly different. Sometimes I had wept and begged her to stop, often I had fought, and for a time she had needed to bind me before starting her work, but not this time. This time I had removed my top and sat in a chair while her knife made its, deep, intricate lines in my flesh. Afterwards we had spoken of Karrick and Arnst and murder and spies. She had told me to find Collis's mother and speak to her, bade me keep my eyes open and follow only what could be shown to be true, not what I wanted to be true. The leash made this easier. It dulled my emotions as much as it dulled the world, and that voice, that seductive voice full of promises was quietened. Though it was still there.

I could have helped.

But it was now more like a sudden memory of a bad deed long past, the type that makes you clench your fist but is then forgotten again. It would not affect me as it had, and my master told me that, some time in the future when I felt ready, I would undoubtedly master it.

"There is no greater teacher than hard lessons, Girton. And your lessons have been harder than most."

I hoped she was right.

Collis's mother was not hard to track down. It seemed everyone knew her, and she was popular as she often looked after the children of those busy with other tasks around the camp. I found her shepherding a school of squealing children as they played on and around a long-suffering draymount.

"Ascilla?" I said, having picked up her name as I questioned those who knew her.

"Yes, can I help?" I was glad she did not recognise me.

"I spoke to you when I first entered the camp and asked you about Arnst." Her face screwed up as if she smelled something bad. "I remember," she said, wary.

"You seemed to dislike Arnst," I said.

"Me and many others. Not surprised someone scratched his name on a wall."

"Did he try and force you?"

She stared at me, cold eyes.

"Bread costs now," she said, "and I have mouths to feed." I took two bits from my pouch and gave them to her. She made them vanish with practised ease. "Suppose there's no harm in telling now he's gone. Aye, he did."

"Forced himself on you?"

"Would've, but his man, the one with the painted face, stopped him. He weren't gentle about it either."

"Danfoth?"

"Aye."

"You said there were others?"

"Many, some not as lucky as me."

"Do you think they may have taken revenge – them or their lovers?"

She shook her head.

"Arnst weren't a stupid man. I used to go see him, before. His talk of Xus being the only living god, it made a sort of sense, what with all the death. He were kind too, but only to get to know you. Once he knew you then he made his move. We're well rid of him. Ain't often I cheer a Landsman, but that Karrick, he did us all a service."

"One of the other women, might they have wanted to kill him?"

"Maybe, but probably not."

"Why?"

"Danfoth. If Arnst weren't stopped you'd get a follow-up from the painted man. Gentle he were too. Sorry an' everything. All apologies, and then came the money. Might seem shallow to take money after such pain, but life is hard."

"Did anyone not take the money?"

"Some. Some threatened to take it to the king, but what would he care?"

"Do you have names? Where are the women who made these threats?"

"Names? Aye. Ginell, Fara, Belseri, Antarii. You won't find 'em though," she said. "Left the camp most of 'em, and Ginnel and Antarii both died when the wells were poisoned by Tomas's men."

"All of them gone? Didn't you find that suspicious?"

"Of course I did," she said, "but as I said, what was I supposed to do? Take the names of a few missing or dead women to the king against one of his council?"

"Yes. Rufra would not turn you away. He would listen."

"He'd protect his own – they all do, don't they?"

"What makes you say that?"

"The priest told me, and priests don't lie, do they?" She turned away at a high scream from the draymount. Two children were hanging from the stump left from one of its curling horns, causing the animal pain. "I better get back to the children," she said, and stormed off, shouting, "Collis, Lelta, let go the poor animal 'fore it tramples you both to death."

I walked away deep in thought. Those names. One of them had been familiar but I could not say which one or why. And I suppose I should not be surprised that the priest had doubted Rufra, though I was disappointed in Inla of Mayel. I had liked her and thought better of her. I made my way towards Arnst's tent to find Danfoth. I needed to speak to him.

Danfoth was talking to his followers. He was arrayed for battle and looked fearsome in armour blackened by charcoal dust and his face freshly painted, but he spoke softly. His listeners were so silent that Danfoth's voice carried across them to me.

"Arnst told us a great change was coming with his death. That Rufra would be the agent of that change, and the followers of the true god, Xus, would be swept up on the wave of that change. So now the battle is at hand." He stood. In one hand he had an axe and in the other a shield painted with the crossed mount antlers on a white circle. "So do not worry that you are not trained for battle, do not worry that you have no armour or weapons. Go into battle in happiness, knowing that Xus, the lonely god, will greet with great joy those who have rushed to meet him without fear. We will fight!" Now he raised his voice. "We will fight for Rufra, and whether we live or die we are still victorious. So, children of Arnst, say goodbye to your families, blacken your faces with charcoal and be ready for death. For today we march!"

The crowd roared, and I was surprised by how many of them there were – over two hundred easily. Only about a third were soldiers; the rest carried whatever they could find as weapons – clubs or farming tools. They would be cut to pieces in battle. Danfoth was a warrior so he must know that. I reappraised him, again. At first I had thought him a silent, unintelligent bodyguard, then a zealot, but now I wondered if he was cleverer than all of us and had some plan I could not fathom. I would tread warily as I questioned him.

"Danfoth," I called as I approached.

"Chosen of Xus," he said, "will you fight with us in the battle against the hedging's servants?"

"If Rufra commands it," I said, and sensed his annoyance. "And I hope you will follow his commands too."

"I have a higher calling," he said. I wondered if he meant it.

"To be priest of these people?"

"Arnst told us Xus has been badly served. I serve in his name and for my followers."

"Your followers?"

"It does not do for the chosen of Xus to stoop to picking at words, Girton Club-Foot," he said. It was the first time he had ever called me by my name, and it felt like he used it to add a subtle undertone of threat.

Lightly, I touched the hilt of my blade.

"I need to speak to you, Danfoth. Best we do it in private." I glanced at the blackened acolytes around him.

"Then please," he said, "enter the tent of Arnst." He stressed his dead predecessor's name as if to make up for the earlier slip.

"Thank you." I walked inside. The tent had changed again: everything that must have been Arnst's had been carefully packaged up and was now stacked in one corner. Each parcel had a small label attached with a golden ribbon.

"Are you going to start a museum?" I said.

"A temple," said Danfoth, "so a great man may be remembered."

"A great man," I said slowly. "He wasn't though, was he?"

When I turned, Danfoth stood blocking the entrance, his axe in his hand.

"What do you mean?" he said casually. I wondered how hard he would be to kill if it came to it.

"I asked you if you recognised a name, Forven Aguirri. You said you did not."

"That has not changed." His painted face was unreadable.

"Then let me tell you a little about Forven Aguirri, Danfoth."

"I have a battle to prepare for—" he began.

I held up a hand to stop him.

"This will not take long, and you will hear it. Or do you not care about the chosen of Xus's wishes?" His mouth moved a little – a smirk at being caught out or maybe a confirmation of what I suspected: Danfoth was no more a zealot than I was.

"Very well, Chosen," he said and sat in Arnst's chair before Arnst's desk.

"Forven Aguirri was a member of the high king's guard and an abuser of women," I began. "This saw him thrown out of the guard in dishonour." I waited but Danfoth said nothing. "Forven was a proud man and enjoyed the power that being high king's guard gave him, so he sought power in other ways. He changed his name, joined the priesthood and trained to be a priest. But I suspect he lacked the discipline for it. Oh, he spoke well, but the learning was too much. And, when it came to it, he could not keep his cock in his pants. Then, one day the Nonmen raided his temple and among them he found others like himself." I stared at Danfoth; he stared back. "Maybe they did not share all his appetites, but they shared something, a hunger fed by hedgings. Forven found his place among the Nonmen, and found that there were those who would follow a man with charisma and few morals. Then he fell out with the Nonmen. Maybe he met another like him, or maybe he picked a fight he could not win, but he was forced to leave. So he took his followers and used what he had learned in the temple and his words to start his own priesthood. And he ended up here, where he found himself on Rufra's council. He probably could not believe his luck –" I took a step towards Danfoth, my hand on my blade hilt "– but he still could not control himself, could he?"

"A fine story you have invented," said Danfoth.

"The story is mine, but I am sure the facts are Arnst's," I said.

"Do you think I was a Nonman?" Danfoth's face remained expressionless.

"You were Arnst's fixer, which made you someone, gave you power, which must be a good feeling for a Meredari, who most think are little more than thieves. But the higher Arnst rose in Rufra's council, the more likely it became he would be found out – shamed, and you along with him."

"Arnst's death was foretold. It was necessary for the cult of the dead god to advance," he said tonelessly.

"Did you help it advance?" I asked quietly.

He stared at me, and then he grinned. A moment later he burst out laughing.

"You are clever – so many pieces but not the right picture. I did not kill Arnst. It did not come to that," he said. "Xus is kind to those who follow him." Inwardly I cursed. As I was speaking it had occurred to me it could well have been Danfoth who had killed Arnst, though Danfoth could not know enough to be a spy so that would have seen only half my quest resolved.

"Do you believe a word of what you preach?"

He laughed again.

"Have you ever been to Ceadoc?" I shook my head. "I have. I was in the high king's guard too. The high kings are mad, Girton Club-Foot, given over to lives of utter debauchery. They care nothing for the people, only for their own pleasure and for power. But they dance to the tune of their priests, because the return of the dead gods is all they have to fear. That is what I wish for, Girton Club-Foot. I will build up the children of Arnst, and I will become the piper of kings and dance them to my tune."

"Those Arnst abused all vanished. Did you kill them to protect him?"

He looked at me as if weighing me up and then a smile spread across his face.

"I have looked through Arnst's personal papers," he said, smiling like we shared an unspoken secret, "and it is clear that on occasion he may have gone too far to protect his holy words." I was sure he lied – that any women who had threatened Arnst had died by Danfoth's hand – but I could not prove it, and I would not move against him without proof. I had learned that lesson at least. Then the Meredari added something that slotted another puzzle piece into place. He leaned forward. "If it was Darvin who put you on to this then tell him Arnst killed his daughter, if it may give him some peace, though I will deny it if asked by any other. You can also tell the priest that if he really loved her as much as he pretends he would have admitted she was his. And if he pushes me too far that fact will become common knowledge."

And I knew which of the names Collis's mother had given me I recognised and why. Fara. The woman Darvin had been searching for, saying she was his assistant. That she was his daughter changed things completely.

"I have to go," I said. I pushed past Danfoth. And I ran.

The priest's tents were not far from Arnst's, and as I ran past them events were twisting in my mind. Things that had happened to which I had barely given a thought took on a new form. Words spoken took on a new meaning. First I went to the healers' tents to find Tarris, who stooped over the corpse of a man whose stomach was bloated and gangrenous.

"Tarris," I said. He turned to me, his porcelain facemask almost hidden by his grey hood.

"Ah, now your foreigner has left I see you come back to me for healing. Well, maybe I do not—"

"I am not here for healing."

"Then why are you here? Do you chase ill luck?"

"Sometimes it feels that way," I said, "but that is not why I am here. Darvin, tell me of him."

"He is a good priest."

"Despite his child?"

"Child?"

"Fara."

"Ah," he said, "now his mania for her makes sense."

"Mania?"

"She tarried with Arnst's people, and he was desperate to bring her back. That is why he stayed when most of the other priests left, I think."

"But he did not acknowledge her?"

"Not to me." The old healer sounded sad.

"He could have though, under Rufra's new ways. And he would not have been forced to leave his calling."

"No," said Tarris, "but Darvin is a traditionalist at heart and—"

"It is a strange place for a traditionalist, Rufra's camp."

"Aye," said Tarris. "I thought that too, but Darvin seemed to be coping well enough until . . ." He turned away as if realising he had said too much.

"Until his daughter was killed?"

"She was killed, then?" he said.

"Yes, but I cannot prove it."

"Darvin said she had vanished," said Tarris. "She believed in the new ways and he hoped to teach her the error of her ways. Privately, I thought he had driven her away and knew it, so guilt drove him to find her. But if she was his daughter . . ."

"'The error of her ways'? He is not for Rufra's new ways at all then? But I heard him saying . . ."

Old eyes peered out from behind the white mask. "I have said too much." He turned away. "If you do not need healing, please leave."

I did as he asked. What had been a suspicion was growing

into a certainty as I made my way to the paddocks looking for Cearis or Boros. I found Cearis with her cavalry, saddling up their mounts and shining weapons for war.

"Cearis," I said.

"Girton, are you ready to ride?"

"Not yet. I still have work to do."

"Aye. Tomas is the only work that concerns me though. We ride out within the hour to meet him in the field. This will all be finished within a couple of days and then Rufra will be the only king in Maniyadoc." She swung herself up onto her mount. I took hold of the bridle.

"Cearis, tell me something of Gwyre."

"You were there, Girton." She looked pained at the thought of the place; we had all fought hard.

"Yes, but in a different part to you. When you fell back from the gate to protect the healers, did any of the Nonmen get past you?"

"Past us?"

"Into the buried chapel."

"I cannot see how they could," she said, "though you know what battle is like. Why do you ask?"

"No reason," I said. Although I was now almost entirely sure of what had happened, I did not want to cast aspersions until there could be no doubt, no doubt at all. I had been blind, everything had been laid out before me and I had seen none of it.

I headed to Darvin's tent.

The priest of Lessiah's makeshift chapel was gloomy and almost empty apart from one acolyte refilling the lamps. There was no sign of Darvin, though his bed and small pack were still there at the back of the tent. I had not thought it odd that a priest should live in his chapel, but now I realised it was the habit of a fanatic. I started to go through his pack.

"What are you doing?" said the acolyte. "Those are the priest's things . . ."

"Be quiet," I said, drawing my blade and pointing it at him. He scuttled back to stand by the door, watching as I went through Darvin's few belongings. I found only a change of clothes and a spare mask with a crack running across the centre of it. I sat back on my haunches staring around the tent, sure there must be something. Apart from the acolyte and the lectern holding the signing book it was almost empty.

I stared at the lectern, a wooden box as high as a man's waist. Around the bottom was a very thin line of dead grass. It had been moved, and recently. I scrabbled over the muddy floor of the tent and pushed the lectern, hard, sending the signing book flying into the mud. The acolyte let out a screech of dismay and made a dive for the book, clutching it to him and shrieking abuse at me. I ignored him. Under the lectern was another book, much smaller. I picked it up and opened it at the first page. It was a diary of sorts, the diary and fears of a penitent. I started to read.

His daughter worried him. He felt for her, loved her, but could only see in her the proof of his own weakness. Again and again he blamed the hedgings for her existence, although he seemed unsure which was to blame. Sometimes it was Fitchgrass, others Dark Ungar, Coil the Yellower or Blue Watta. He spoke of his fear of becoming a shatter-spirit, tied to the land. Then the focus changed from hedgings to Arnst and a growing sureness that Arnst had given his spirit to Dark Ungar. Strange proofs were given, odd and disjointed ideas, bizarre diagrams scrawled across the pages. Connections had been made between seemingly innocent occurrences: on one page a lost ring, a dying soldier and a bad pie had taken on peculiar weight in Darvin's consciousness. Before me I saw a mind unravelling as the world that he had known and been secure in also came apart. Then I found the page where he rejoiced in Arnst's death, called himself a true servant of the gods, a man who "carried out their will no matter the cost."

Among his ravings another name appeared, first

intermittently, then more and more regularly. In one place it had been written and then "Dark Ungar's Servant" written over it. Again and again I found this conjunction, sometimes scored through so fiercely that the pen had torn the page and the one below it.

Rufra.

Rufra the betrayer. king of the hedgings. Rufra ap Vythyr, murderer of innocents. Rufra ap Vythyr, servant of Dark Ungar.

On another page I found the word "traitor" and the name of Gwyre's priest, Coilynn, written together and pierced by lines drawn to look like thorns. No Nonman had killed Coilynn. Darvin had taken her life, judging her enthusiasm for Rufra's ways evidence she also served Dark Ungar. He called her a "needful sacrifice" and went on to write of the need for the "final sacrifice to bring about the rebirth of the gods".

I threw the book aside. Below it was a box wrapped in grey wool, the same rag Coilynn had ripped up to make a healers' flag from. When I shook it out, it revealed itself as a bloodstained grey robe, like the one worn by the priest seen in the drinking tent. The box was the sort a warrior may keep an expensive sword in. I opened it. Wool lined, and in the wool the indented shape of two blades, the first an ornate sword. I remembered how the butcher had said Forven Aguirri had had his sword taken from him, and I had thought nothing of it. But now it was clear that the ornate blade used to kill Arnst was not his own; it had been Darvin's. Below the indentation of the sword was the shape of a much smaller blade, a Landsmen's knife. A knife used for sacrifice.

And that knife was also gone.

"Where is Darvin?" I asked the acolyte. He sneered at me and then I was on him, my blade at his throat. "Tell me where Darvin is or I will kill you here and now!" He was young, no more than a child really, and his eyes were wide with terror. "Tell me!" I shook him hard.

"G-gone!" he said.

"Gone where?"

"The king leaves for battle," he said innocently, unaware of the cold shiver his words sent through me. "Darvin is gone to carry out the sacrifices for war and to pronounce the final blessing on him."

"The final blessing. Boy, you should pray to the dead gods for a small mercy."

And then, again, I found myself running.

Chapter 28

The camp was thick with people and the atmosphere high with a mixture of excitement and fear. I pushed through crowds, desperate to get to Rufra, and heard many voices, some sure and loud, talking about how Rufra could not lose, others sad and tearful as they said goodbye to loved ones hurrying to join the rapidly growing ranks of Rufra's army. I heard parents talking to children in low voices, assuring them everything would be all right when they were just as unsure and scared themselves. People crowded in from all sides to block my way, a thick stream drawn to the low hill outside the camp where Rufra would be blessed and make the speech everyone wanted to hear, the one where he would assure them they were safe and that he would win. I was familiar with the unsettled feelings of people whose warriors were about to fight and understood their need to feel like they had not chosen the wrong side – that they were not all destined to become thankful if Tomas won. They were not of course. If Tomas won he and Neander would simply wipe them out to save having to feed them.

It was probably for the best that I was not expected to make any speeches.

I gave up trying to push through. My attempt at speed was doing nothing but riling up the people around me, and in an atmosphere that was such an odd mixture of elation and tension it wouldn't take much to start a riot. So I let myself become one with the crowd approaching Rufra's cavalry and the front ranks of his army. On their mounts the Riders were awe-inspiring, their armour polished and shining, gilding glinting on the animal's antlers and coloured loyalty flags strung on moonwood wands bounced and twisted in the air, giving a strange air of jollity to the business of war.

The crowd was brought to a halt by a line of Rufra's guards standing shoulder to shoulder, their shields painted with his flying lizard and locked to create a ring around the low hill. Atop the hill sat Rufra on his mount, dressed in silver armour and a long golden cloak that fell from his shoulders. Neliu was just behind him. On his right was Cearis holding Rufra's bonemount, the skull of his childhood mount Imbalance, strewn with rags and streamers which fluttered in the air with the promise of death. On his other side, and nearer to me, was Boros, his halfmount standard raised above him. The armour of his mount archers was less bright in the sun, their bearing less impressive than Cearis' cavalry though I knew they were just as important to Rufra, if not more so. Boros was the only person wearing his visor down, his ruined face replaced by a metal replica of what it had once been – achingly beautiful. Behind Cearis and Boros's Riders was Danfoth the Meredari, armoured in black on a black mount, and with him ten men and women in the black rags of Arnst's followers. To the right sat Aydor, on his mount and looking every inch as arrogant and haughty as I remembered. He wore my warhammer, and I felt a moment of resentment that he stood at Rufra's side, and fear that he would betray us all. I saw no sign of Nywulf, which worried me. Of them all he was the only one I thought likely to recognise a threat in time to do something about it.

But would even Nywulf suspect a priest?

In front of them all was a scaffold and stage hastily erected from rough wood and old branches to create a platform high enough for Rufra to be seen by the entire crowd when he took his blessing. Across the front of the stage danced hobby dolls made of last year's straw, starting to sag and blacken where old blood stained them; above the stage some recently cut pear tree branches bent under the weight of the luck-bread tied to them.

From the bottom of the hill on the left I could see a procession of priests and acolytes, led by Darvin, making its solemn way up the hill – their solemnity somewhat spoiled by Gusteffa who danced and cavorted before them. Gabran the Smith led a contingent of troops in clearing the crowd to make a corridor for the priests, and in the resulting crush I was barely able to breathe, let alone move.

"Gabran!" I screamed, willing him to hear me, and when I got no reaction I mentally cursed his wide-brimmed helmet and the ridiculously over-the-top crest of purple lizard feathers that crowned it. "Gabran!" Did he turn for a moment, looking for a voice he half-recognised in the churning crowd? I could not be sure, but as I could barely move I had little option but to continue to shout. When Gabran did not hear me, I called to Gusteffa capering before the priest. She saw me. Even among the throng she somehow heard me and caught my eye.

"Stop Darvin! Gusteffa! Do not let Darvin near Rufra!" But she must not have been able to make out my words and all I received was a smile and wink. Fitchgrass curse the crowd. I shouted more loudly, forcing air from my lungs. "Stop the blessing!"

A man in front of me, huge and black-bearded, turned on me angrily.

"Traitor! You would curse the king by sending him to battle without a blessing?"

I opened my mouth to tell him who I was and a fist hit me in the kidneys from behind. I buckled, only the weight of the crowd kept me up. Someone stamped on my club foot and I had to fight to suppress a scream of agony. A woman in front of me hissed "Traitor!" and elbowed me in the face, opening a cut above my eye, and then blows were raining down as the cowled figure of Darvin passed at the head of the procession, a smoking burner held high, the scent of the perfumed smoke strong enough to cut through the stink of sweat from the crowd. I was knocked to the ground and more kicks were aimed at me. The press of the crowd hampered my attackers and though they kicked at me they could not swing their legs back enough to do real damage. Soon they would realise it and start stamping, and then I would be finished.

A foot came at my head and I grabbed it with both hands, giving it a vicious twist and being rewarded with a scream of pain. The owner of the foot fell beside me. I grabbed his body, twisting so it was on top of me and in the confusion I wriggled backwards from under him. Some were aware of what I was doing. Cries of "Stop the traitor" went up, and I saw legs pumping up and down, stamping on the man I had felled. A foot found my hand and I had to bite down to stifle a cry. As the foot lifted to come down again I twisted so it missed and delivered a punch to the back of my attacker's knee, making the leg buckle. The woman went down, I used her body to drag myself up.

"Traitor," I cried and delivered a kick to her stomach. Others took over where I had left off and I pushed myself away from the scuffle, trying to see where Darvin was as a group of soldiers pushed their way into the crowd to keep the peace.

The procession had stopped in front of Rufra. His cavalry and mount archers were in two loose rings around the scaffold: the cavalry Riders in the outer ring had their swords out and held loosely at the sides of their mounts ready to salute their king; the mount archers created an inner ring and held their bows ready to do the same. It was not lost on me that this was also a show of strength and an efficient way to protect the king should there be any threat from the crowd.

Only I knew the threat would not come from outside.

Rufra slid down from his mount and there were cheers: "Rufra! King Rufra! Long life to the king! Bread for the king!" My friend raised his arms and smiled at the crowd, nodding and slowly spinning on the spot. He had the uncanny talent of appearing to look right at you, but when I waved and tried to attract his attention his gaze simply passed over me. I tensed as Darvin and the procession of priests walked past Rufra, but Darvin only ascended the scaffold and watched as the king followed. I pushed my way forward, no longer caring about those I upset. Darvin not only intended to kill the king but he intended to make a spectacle of it. I forced my way through the crowd on a wave of abuse and shouts – I was all sharp elbows and knees – and wondered if Darvin was also the spy. But if so how did Darvin pass on his information to Neander and Tomas? And more, how did Darvin know of Rufra's military plans? Did he have an accomplice in Rufra's council?

It did not matter, not now, not this second. Rufra went to his knees before Darvin, arranging his golden cloak around himself. The crowd chanted the syllables of his name and they beat urgently in my ears – "Ru-fra! Ru-fra! Ru-fra!" Before me was a wall of soldiers. Getting though the crowd was one thing, getting past them another. And once I was past them I would face the cavalry and mount archers. Would they recognise me in time or would they simply react? How would they know I was not an assassin? If Nywulf had been there I could have relied on him to be quick enough to protect Rufra. But now?

I trusted no one.

Darvin raised his arms to speak, and the crowd fell silent.

"We stand here –" he did not sound like a madman, he sounded calm and sure "– in the midst of chaos and death. Let us not think death is the natural way of the Tired Lands. Life was once in balance, until the gods died, and we mourn their passing every day. But, at the same time, let us not forget that death and sacrifice are necessary – why else would Xus the unseen live on?" Behind him a pig was led forward, garlanded in straw dolls and flowers, but the sacrifice to be offered by Darvin was far more valuable than any pig. I found myself pushed up against the shield of the soldier in front of me. He held his shield well, locked into the shield next to it, in his other hand he held a spear. I looked for a weakness to exploit. "We have all made sacrifices, but Dark Ungar continues to whisper in the ears of those who should know better!" Darvin produced a knife from inside his robes.

The crowd screamed their agreement and surged forward, crushing me against the shield and forcing the soldier one step back.

"Tomas! Curse Tomas!" screamed out all around me.

Only I saw that Darvin held the bent knife of a Landsman.

"Curse all those who forsake the way of the gods!" shouted Darvin, and now I could hear the sharp edge of the fanatic in his voice, the raw cut of obsession. At the same time I saw, in the faces of those around the king, an unconscious knowledge that something was wrong; Boros's metal face tilted slightly, as if he heard an off-key sound; the bonemount that Cearis held dipped a little; Neliu's hand touched the hilt of her blade.

Inla, the priest of Mayel, passed Darvin the halter of the sacrificial pig, and he jerked the creature forward. "King Rufra," shouted Darvin; my breath stuck in my chest, my muscles froze – a ring of armed men and women stood between me and a murderer – "make the salute of the old ways." Rufra raised his head, exposing his bare throat to Darvin's blade.

Breathe out.

"And now," said Darvin quietly, though his voice carried easily across a crowd suddenly silent with anticipation, "with my blade I make the final sacrifice. I close our ears to the hungers of the hedgings. I act sure in the rising of the gods. With my blade I bring balance with blood." He raised the blade.

And let go of the pig.

Breathe in.

Everything slowed.

Grabbing the spear of the guard before me, pulling him forward and off balance. Digging my left foot in above the knee of the man on my left. He squeals in pain as I push myself higher. Right foot on the hip of the woman on my right. She screams and starts to fall.

Rufra's eyes are closed as he waits for a blessing that will never come.

The knife is coming down.

My left foot on the rim of the guard's shield, using it and his spear to propel myself up and forwards over his head. I try to keep hold of the spear, but the guardsman is well trained. Though my move has taken him by surprise he keeps a tight hold of his weapon, and it slides from my grasp. The sharp tip cuts the palm of my hand and steals some of my forward momentum, sending me sprawling.

The muscles in my bruised legs and back are on fire.

The pig is screaming as it falls from the scaffold.

The knife is coming down.

Those nearest Rufra react: Cearis pushing the bonemount into the hands of the Rider nearest to her and going for her sword; Boros spurring his mount forward; Neliu's mouth opens in shock. The two Riders in front of me pulling their mounts round to face me, antlered heads coming down, razor-sharp gilding flashing in the sun.

The knife is coming down.

I let myself fall, rolling onto the ground and my tumbling momentum carries me forward over the damp and slippery grass. I hear shouting, screaming, crying. I feel the disturbed air on the back of my neck as antlers pass over my head. In the corner of my eye I can see mounts rearing, bringing slashing claws and spurs into play, but I am already up, running towards the threat.

Boros is leaning into his mount.

Cearis has her sword half drawn.

Neliu is mounting the scaffold steps.

A mount archer is drawing his bow and aiming at me.

And the knife is coming down.

Tumbling, forward and up. A bow aimed – strung and barely taut – I grab the stirrup of the mount archer's saddle. Other archers are swinging round, bringing bows to bear.

Everything is so slow. The progress of Darvin's knife is measured in blinks of my eye, a glance of time.

Pulling myself up the stirrup as the Rider tries to lower his bow. Other hand on the quiver strung forward on his saddle. *Heave*. Upward! Using his armour like a ladder. Shoulder into his face, foot over his in the stirrup. Bow twisted from his hand and into mine, my momentum carries me, pushing him backwards off the saddle. He fights for balance. One foot on the shoulder of his mount, and the arrow *I barely even know* I plucked from his quiver flashes up into the bow. My other foot on the Rider's chest. I stand tall, high above his mount and everyone else. The falling Rider's hand locks around my leg and I feel gravity, remorseless, as he falls, bringing me down with him.

I have no time.

No time for fear.

Draw.

No room for fear.

Aim.

I am the instrument.

Loose.

I am the weapon.

DrawAimLoose.

I hear the arrow's impact. See it take Darvin in the throat, a killing shot, and he falls backwards off the stage. The blade in his hand snatched away a finger's breadth before it bites into Rufra's neck.

And I'm falling, landing heavily on top of the mount archer whose weapon I stole, the wind knocked from both of us. I am unable to move as a soldier runs at me, his spear ready to strike, and only the iron discipline instilled in him by years of training saves me from death as Cearis shouts, "Stop! Stop! He saved the king! He saved the king!"

Underneath me the mount archer is groaning, and all around is chaos. I struggle to my feet, aching all over.

Cearis takes my arm and helps me up.

"Girton, are you hurt?"

Everything hurts.

"I need a healer."

I need my master.

"I have betrayed Rufra," she said, her face stark, on the edge of breaking.

"You?"

"Darvin was my priest. I confided in him. I have betrayed my king."

"No," I said. "You will not be the only one who confided in the priest. He fooled everyone: you, me, Rufra. You cannot blame yourself for a man whose wits have fled."

She stared at me for a moment but I am not sure she believed me. I worried for her. Shame is a dangerous thing for a warrior to take into battle.

"Thank you for saving him," she said and turned away. "But we cannot let this stop us. We must still fight Tomas. We must still ride. Catch us up when you have seen the healer."

I walked away. All was chaos in the moments after the attempted killing, and none looked to me. The crowd were restless, noisy and dangerous, full of an anger that had no target. As Cearis left to return to Rufra, guards closed up behind her. Up on the stage Rufra shrugged off those trying to help him and swept down the stairs, pulling off his golden cloak and throwing it to the floor. Areth went to him, and they spoke hurried words. She touched his cheek and he put his hand against hers, nodded and smiled. Troops moved through the crowd quieting them, trying to re-assert some sense of normality. A shout of "Rufra!" went up, though it lacked the jubilation it had held earlier. I turned to see my friend pull himself up into the saddle of his mount. He waved to the crowd, smiling as if nothing had happened. I wanted to go to him, but all I would be was a reminder of what had just happened, and Rufra would not want the crowd thinking of that. As he began his speech I walked away.

I barely heard him, only some of his words seeped through as I limped back to my tent for my bruises and cuts to be treated. He spoke of danger, of how everyone there shared it and how he respected the bravery of all, from those who fought to those who made the bread or minded the children. From what I heard, it was a good speech, one that should have brought the crowd together, but as omens for battle went there could not have been many worse than Rufra's blessing ceremony.

In the sky, dark clouds gathered as the Birthstorm readied itself to break.

Chapter 29

"Will you join Rufra for the battle?" My master worked unguent into my club foot, I could already see the spreading blue of new bruises.

"Yes. If I ride now I should be able to reach them before battle is joined. Two days from now is when Tomas has said for them to meet, and it is a day and a half's ride for an army. I should be able to do it in a day."

"You need not, you know," she said, lightly touching my shoulder. "You did well with Darvin."

"I should have seen it far earlier, Master," I said. "If I had not been so foolish, Rufra would not have set out under a bad omen or lost the Landsmen to Tomas."

"But also Tomas may not have called him to the blade. Girton, you cannot know what may have been; all you can do is live with what is. And you have caught the spy, that is important."

"It does not feel right."

"People talk to priests, Girton, you know that. Cearis even told you that. What better way is there to get information than to have a priest report to you, eh?"

"I suppose so," I said, "but I cannot help feeling there is more."

"Then talk it through with me."

"Darvin had a daughter, Fara. He rejected her, out of shame, I think."

"Shame is often a whisper of Dark Ungar."

"But he still cared for her, in his own way. On the other

hand we have Arnst, who felt no shame and used his place to seduce women, and if that did not work, he would force them."

"And Arnst was involved with Fara?"

"Aye. Danfoth controlled Arnst as much as he could, and when he could not stop him he bought silence."

"And if they were not silent?"

"Then I suspect Danfoth killed them. But he is cleverer than I gave him credit for and I cannot tie him to it. If he is backed into a corner he will simply blame Arnst."

"So Darvin killed for revenge?"

"Partly, I think. Arnst's rejection of the dead gods and what he did to Fara must have been like blood to a warmount for Darvin. But I have seen his writings. He was a man obsessed. He believed the world to be falling apart, that the dead gods were ready to be reborn, and he thought Rufra in thrall to a hedging. His daughter may have been ill treated and even killed because of Arnst, but Darvin saw him as a symptom. I think, at the end, he saw Rufra as the disease."

"There is often a strange logic to the mad, and it would make sense for him to betray Rufra to Tomas."

I scratched my head and hissed at the pain in my bruised shoulders.

"Would it?" I stared into the smoky air of the tent. "If you had seen what Darvin wrote in that book, there was no logic to it. How he appeared sane is beyond me, and I cannot see him as a spy. He barely hid his killings, took foolish risks like the death of the priest in Gwyre. He must simply have killed her for admiring Rufra. A spy would have had to be careful, and I cannot marry that with Darvin. Rufra's spy, Hallan, was a careful man, and he ended up nailed to the gates of Gwyre. I should have seen it, Darvin's madness, I should have looked harder."

"A fractured mind is not mirrored in a face, Girton." I stood, testing how my club foot took my weight. "It hurts?"

"Always, Master."

"I mean does it hurt more than it does normally," she said. Usually she would have made a joke, called me a fool, but there was a still a distance between us.

"Will you fight with us, Master?"

She shook her head. "I am not strong enough, not yet. And neither are you, really." I opened my mouth to protest, but she held up a hand. "I am not saying I will try to stop you going. I do not think I could, and Rufra may need you."

"There is one thing that worries me, Master."

"What is that?"

"Nywulf."

"What about him?"

"He has not been seen for two days, and he was not at Rufra's blessing."

"You think he could be the spy?" She could not hide her surprise, and I laughed quietly.

"No, I cannot imagine that –" we shared a smile "– but I wish I knew what was important enough to take him away from Rufra. I wish I knew where he had been."

"I have been to Gwyre," came the reply from behind me, and I turned. Nywulf was a black figure framed in the door to the tent. More figures moved behind him. "Gwyre was important enough to take me away from Rufra."

He moved further into the tent, looking old, grey and tired as if life had become an unbearable weight on his shoulders. On one side of him appeared Crast and on the other stood Neliu. Both held crossbows. One was aimed at me, one at my master.

Behind Nywulf was Ossowin, the man who had been headman of Gwyre. He smiled at me and, because I knew what to look for now, I saw the same madness in his eye that I had failed to see in Darvin. By Ossowin stood a child, a young girl whose frightened eyes and round face I recognised from a burning house full of dead men where I had brought black birds from my mouth and where nothing would ever live again.

"Merela," said Nywulf quietly, "step away from Girton, please."

"What is this about, Nywulf," she said.

Nywulf pointed to a corner of the tent.

"You are fast, Merela Karn, but you are not faster than a crossbow bolt. Stand over there, please." My master took slow steps away from me, Neliu's crossbow following her.

"What is this about, Nywulf?" she repeated.

"Betrayal," he said simply. He turned to the girl and pointed at me. "Is this the man with birds in his mouth?"

She nodded shyly, bringing her fist up to her mouth and sucking on it. Her face was streaked with dirt.

"Girton is no traitor," said my master.

"Girton is a sorcerer!" shouted Nywulf, and then his voice became dangerously quiet again. "There can be no greater betrayal."

"You take the word of a little girl on this?" she said.

"He has my word, filth," spat Ossowin. He looked close to mania, a strange and savage joy in his eyes.

Nywulf turned to him.

"I have told you not to speak," he said, every word vicious. He turned away from the man. "And no, I do not simply take anyone's word. That is why I have been to Gwyre. That is why I skinned my knuckles moving the wreckage of the building Girton fought in to find the souring beneath it." He transferred his gaze from my master to me. "How could you, Girton?" I felt the pain behind his words. "After what happened to his son, this will break Rufra's heart."

I stared at the floor. Crast covered my master with his Crossbow and Neliu stepped forward with ropes, binding me as tight as the silence in the room.

"It was not Girton she saw," said my master quietly. "It was me."

"I am not a fool," said Nywulf quietly. "You were here, ill and close to death in your bed."

"No," she said, "that was all a ruse. I was well and followed you to Gwyre. When Girton went to the house he was knocked out and I took his place. You do not believe me? A jester trains in mimicry; it is all about shape." She changed – her posture, the way she stood and moved: everything about her became different – and it felt as though I looked into a pool and saw a version of myself staring back. Different, but in the dark, in a burning building surrounded by the chaos of battle, I am not sure I would have known it was not me. "Are you sure who you saw now, little girl?"

The little girl looked wide-eyed from me to my master and then burst into tears.

"Enough of your assassin tricks," said Nywulf.

"If you do not believe me, Heartblade, the healer we brought guessed my secret and I had to kill him," she said. "You will find his body sucked dry of life in the copse behind this tent."

Nywulf gazed at her thoughtfully.

"Crast, bind her too." As Crast advanced, Neliu moved away from me and took up her crossbow. "If you make a move on Crast, Merela, I will put a bolt through your boy, you understand?" My master nodded and seemed to deflate as Crast bound her hands and then pushed her down into a chair and tied her to it. I tested my own bonds – subtly, by flexing my muscles and trying to move my wrists – but the knots were depressingly professional. Nywulf watched as Crast tied my master and then sent him outside to make sure there were no witnesses to see me led to a separate tent. While we waited he knelt by the little girl. "Return to your tent, and you must tell no one of what you have seen. Do you understand?" She nodded. "Good," he said gently and ruffled her hair. "You have done the right thing. The king will be proud." He watched her leave and then turned to Ossowin. "And you . . ."

"I need no reward," he said. "It is enough to see that creature brought to justice." He pointed at me. "I told you, did I not? I told you that you would see me again, Girton Club-Foot? Now—"

Nywulf plunged his blade into the man's chest before he could say any more. Then he put his hand on Ossowin's shoulder and pushed him back, pulling the blade from him. Ossowin staggered back two steps and then fell over the bed, sprawling on it, his mouth opening and closing as he gasped for air.

"I told you not to speak," said Nywulf as the light went out of the man's eyes, "and I meant it."

Crast returned. He stared at the dead man for a second.

"It is clear," he said.

"Just let us go, Nywulf," said my master quietly. "We will leave and never be heard of again. Just let us go."

"I cannot," he said. "I do not doubt your word, Merela Karn, but we cannot allow a sorcerer to live."

"It will hurt Rufra," she said, trying to use the only leverage she had on the old warrior. "To lose his friend will hurt him, and the truth will damage his reputation. It could destroy him."

"Aye," he said, "I know. That is why he must deal with it in public, in view of all. And for all your clever tricks we both know the truth. Rufra must send Girton to the Landsmen, and you too."

"You know what they will do to him?" she said.

"Yes," said Nywulf, "and were it up to me I would cut your throats here and now, but Rufra is the king – he must be seen to do justice. Think! What if any of this came back to haunt him later? The king who let a sorcerer go? Everything he may ever achieve would crumble. No, we must do this right." He took me by the arm, he was surprisingly gentle despite the bitterness of his words. "You, come with me. Crast, stay and guard Merela; she is too dangerous to be left alone."

"But I am to fight in the battle," Crast said, and I wondered at the foolishness of youth. He looked truly distraught at the idea of missing the battle with Tomas.

"And now you are not," snapped Nywulf. "Do as you are told. Neliu, help me with Girton." Neliu moved to my side. As I came between her and Nywulf she glanced at Crast and he made some sort of hand gesture to her. I did not understand what it meant, only that it meant something as it had the same weight of meaning as the assassin's signals my master and I often used. Nywulf pushed me from the tent and for the first time ever I was glad of the sigil cut into my chest and the way it numbed my emotions. But still I could not look at him, could not bear to see the hurt and disappointment in his eyes.

"Nywulf, will you do me one favour?"

"I owe you nothing," he said. I felt the touch of the Birthstorm on my skin, a spattering of cold rain as we passed through the night.

"Then do Rufra one favour."

"What?"

"Don't tell him about this until after the battle."

"Do you hope I will be killed and this will never come out?" he said.

"No." I stared at the ground. "I think that Rufra already carries enough pain onto the field and needs no more."

Nywulf nodded and pushed me ahead of him.

"I did not plan to tell him before anyway," he said, "but do not think it is for you. I serve only him." They hurried me, into a tent that smelled of old grass and the rancid fat used to oil armour and weapons. Nywulf tied me to a chair, the ropes tight enough to stop my blood, painful where they crossed and cut into my bare flesh. He stood and looked at me and for a moment I thought he would say something. He bit his lip. The pain I saw on his face was almost unbearable.

"Guard him well, Neliu," he said. Then he turned and left. He did not look back.

And that was it. I was lost. All was lost. The scarifying web of magic had caught me. The ties that bound me could not be loosened, and when I struggled it only served to constrict the web around me more tightly. I had fought armies, dodged assassins and toppled a king, but in the end it was my own actions that had brought me down. Now I sat in the dark with only judgment on the horizon. Neliu did not try to talk to me. No doubt she felt only disgust, a pity. I had felt a grudging friendship developing between us.

Pain started to rack me after about an hour. It began as simple discomfort caused by being unable to move but became a swelling, throbbing thing as the blood trying to move around my body met the resistance of the ropes holding me. My club foot was livid, a pulsing ball of agony that radiated a fiery twisting pain through my muscles and made me gasp. Neliu looked up the first time I let out a whimper, and that added anger to my pain. I had no wish to show her any weakness.

From very far away I heard a faint voice.

I could have helped.

No.

You could not.

You never have.

You do not help at all.

I shut the voice out, but even the thought of magic caused the sigil on my chest to add a new layer to my pain, a writhing agony, needles worming into my chest. I concentrated on breathing, on the steady out and in of air, pushing my mind away from the prison of my body and into another space where pain and worry could not touch me – they were still there, like cruel jailers poking at me with sharp sticks as I tried to sleep, but as I let myself fall upwards into a grey place they faded. Time ceased to have meaning; only the slow out and in of the air in my lungs was real, a hollow wheezing backed by the slow drumbeat of my pulse. All else was gone: all scent, all sight, all sound. At some point I became dimly aware of someone else in the room, low voices talking, and then I left the world entirely. Lofted up into the darkness while I searched myself within, felt the rhythm of my heart and knew that, given time, I could slow it, stop it. *The last iteration: the Assassin's Peace.* The pain of the Landsmen's questions? The humiliation of the blood gibbet? The awful prospect of seeing Rufra's face as he pronounced judgment on the friend who had betrayed him in a way no one else could? I could take the hand of Xus now and step away from it all. The slowing beat of my heart filled my ears.

One, my master.

Two, my master.

I heard a voice I had heard before, familiar and unfamiliar, welcoming and awe-inspiring, comforting and terrifying.

Three, my master.

Four, my master.

Five . . . my master.

"You would be welcome at my side."

I felt no terror; this voice I had known all my life. If anything all fear fled, all pain left me.

"Only hurt awaits outside my dark palace."

Six . . . my master . . .

Seven . . . my . . . master . . . Eight . . .

. . . my . . . master . . .?

"She would join us soon enough."

Cannot leave her. Will not.

"She would call you stubborn."

Aye. Stubborn.

"She would call you foolish."

That too. I will not leave her.

"Very well, best beloved. Very well."

Eight . . . my . . . master.

Nine, my master.

Ten.

Fire.

What agony I had felt before multiplied by two, three, ten, twenty, a hundred. Something vicious and cruel gnawing on my hands and feet, numbness receding like the tide to leave me high on burning sands of agony, bringing me back to the world. I leaned over in my chair. How? My hands were loose and I held them before me. How? Barely seeing them, barely recognising them as my own, I fell to the side. How? Whimpering as I hit the floor, saliva spilling from my mouth. What had happened? Keep quiet or Neliu will hear. Had the magic come for me again? Cut my ropes? I could not feel it, could not smell it. Had Xus himself set me free?

"Girton? Can you hear me?"

"Master?" I had gone so far and deep within that I saw the world as if from the bottom of a pool. Everything was out of focus, objects little more than blobs of colour floating in my vision.

"No, Girton. I am not your master."

"Rufra?" I said, my thoughts barely in this place. I floated somewhere in the past, on a cold field shrouded in mist. "Rufra always comes."

"Rufra is not coming." That voice, so cold. "Can you stand?"

I groaned, rolled onto my front. The fire in my hands and feet had lessened, become a dull ache. I clamped my hands between my biceps and my chest as I sat up, trying to warm them. I squinted as the figure dropped my stabswords on the floor in front of me.

"You need to leave here, Girton." I knew that voice.

"Neliu?"

"You have to leave."

"Need my master," I said.

"No." She pulled my armour down over my head, forcing me to wriggle into it. "Forget her and forget Rufra. Just leave. Go."

"Nywulf will never forgive you if—"

"Do not worry about Nywulf," she said. "He is lost. Just go."

I stood, still woozy. My armour seemed unbearably heavy. A coldness was seeping through me, but it was not due to the temperature. It was the coldness of horror.

"Why are you doing this, Neliu?"

"Crast made me promise to help you. He thinks you do not deserve what Tomas will do to you."

"What Tomas will do to me?" More of her words filtered through my subconscious. "Forget Nywulf?" Ice in my veins. "Rufra has lost the battle?"

"Not yet," she said, "but he will."

And then I understood. Understood everything. Understood how I had walked past, the traitors every day without ever thinking about it.

"You are the spies," I said, "you and Crast?"

"Just go, Girton, go."

"I thought you loved Rufra," I said.

"I do," she said, and for the first time that supercilious smile slipped, and I saw someone broken and damaged – but only for a moment. "We both do. Crast and I love everything about him. We understand what he tries for, admire him."

"Then why?"

"Tomas has our mother," she said simply. I took a deep breath.

"So you really are brother and sister?" she nodded. "Tell Rufra," I pleaded. "Just tell him. Even now it is not too late. He will forgive you. He will understand."

"No," she said quietly, "he will not understand –" her face was like ice, pale, cold and damp "– and he will not forgive. Not what we were part of. Not ever."

"What do you mean?" But as my senses returned so did my ability to think. "What could you have done that Rufra would never forgive?" I knew. There was only one thing

Rufra would never forgive. "Arnlath? His son? It was you? You poisoned his son."

"Go, Girton," she said, but she would not meet my eye. "Crast rides for the battlefield to finish this. Rufra will fall to his blade. Your king's fate is sealed, but you can live."

"Where is my master?"

"Unconscious, and you cannot save her. We must keep one of you for Tomas, or he will be angry."

"Let me past," I said, standing and stooping to pick up my blades from the floor.

"Only if you promise you will leave," she said.

"Let me past, Neliu." My voice was unyielding and unpitying. "And if you run you may avoid Rufra's justice. But I will not leave my master here and I will not let Crast kill my friend." I tightened my grip on my blades.

"Rufra would give you to the Landsmen," she said, almost begging me to see her point.

"Let me past, Neliu, and then run and hope Rufra or I never find you."

For a moment I thought she would move aside. Then she bit her lip and met my gaze, her eyes as hard and black as the enamel on her armour.

"I am sorry, Girton, but it has gone too far and I cannot do that."

She unsheathed her blades, longsword and stabsword, and took up the position of readiness.

Chapter 30

She is better than me.

From the moment our blades crossed I knew it.

Straight thrust at her throat. She counters with the third iteration, *the Meeting of Hands*. She looks lazy, slow, practised. Pushing my blade up and kicking out. *The Bow*, my midriff pulling away from the kick. A glint of her weapon to my right and have to throw myself to the floor to avoid the blade coming round at throat height. I roll away from her, building momentum and bringing out my knee, pushing hard as my knee hits the floor and rising just in time to ward off a furious attack from her. Left, right, left, left right, right, right, left, blades sparking as they block, edges dulling. We draw back, neither breathing too heavily, not yet. Measures have been taken and we both know the truth.

She is better than me.

"You can still run." A nod towards the tent door.

"Can I take my master?"

"No."

"Can I save my king?"

"No."

"Then I cannot run."

Leading with the left, making her expect a dummy from the right as it's my stronger hand. Feint a slash. She twitches but doesn't go for it and my thrust is blocked. Rather than strike with her blade she pushes forward with the same hand she blocked my strike with, punching me in the shoulder with the blunt guard of her stabsword and sending pain coursing through me, making my hand convulse.

My Conwy blade falling to the floor.

"You're out of practice. Pick it up." She is grinning, the thrill of the fight filling her with adrenalin that makes her skin glow. I bend to pick up my blade, all the while keeping my gaze on her.

Breathe out.

Breathe in.

Back to ready position and—

Eyeblink and she is there, body against mine, blade at my throat, razor edge cutting a stinging line across my skin. A smile on her face.

"The Speed-that-Defies-the-Eye," I said, barely able to breathe, barely able to think.

"Did you think you were the only one?" Her breath coming in gasps, her chest heaving against mine. "Nywulf was not my only teacher." I push, hard, against her shoulder while hooking my club foot around the back of her leg, sending her sprawling on the hard floor and following her down, stabswords bared like the fangs of a swordmouth, but I only wound the earth. When I turn she is at the other side of the tent, blades by her side, casually walking towards me.

"Get up." The air smells of honey and pepper; her feet leave golden trails in the muddy air. Pulling myself up, wiping at my nose – somehow it has become bloodied. The scars on my body dance and stretch like a net full of fish.

"How did Nywulf not notice?" I said.

"He is like everyone." Into the ready position, one blade raised, one blade low. "He sees what he wants to see." She waits, wanting me to attack, but I am tired and the world is blurred around the edges. The floor no longer feels solid.

"You are an assassin?"

"Was. My sorrowing is over, my old master lies dead in a ditch."

"The attack in the wood, the arrows? They were you?"

"We paid for the woman. Crast was the bowman."

She feints. I bat away her attack and she comes in harder, blades like snakes, trailers of light intersected with dark blocks. Our movements faster than the eye can follow, all instinct until we part again, now on opposite sides of the tent.

"Crast said he was not much use with a bow. He was right."

Blows exchanged. Blades sparking in the gloom.

"So your mother, that was a lie?"

She shook her head.

"My master fell a long way from here, my training unfinished. I returned to keep my family safe from the war."

She lunged, a perfect, beautiful move. Her blade stopped a finger's width from my chest and she was so quick I never even had the chance to block it. She stretched out her trailing hand, giving her that all-important extra bit of reach and the tip of her blade touched my armour. She smiled, letting me know she was better, emphatically. Letting me know she was toying with me.

"You seem to have finished your training," I said, my breath coming slowly, readying for the final thrust.

"Yes, I have," she said. "Run, Girton Club-Foot, and I promise, when my mother is safe I'll finish Tomas for you – avenge your master."

"No."

Her eyes were like chips of grey stone.

"I'll make his death slow."

"No."

A quick movement – stepping forward and to the side, the flat of her blade coming down and slapping my hand, making me drop my left stabsword and leaving my hand numb. I attacked with my Conwy, putting my all into it, dancing a bright streak across the floor. She did nothing but parry, countered with nothing but lazy defences, only ever raising one blade against mine. Her skill was astounding, and I wondered, for a moment, if I could have beaten her had I kept up my training. What would it have been like if we fought here with me fully practised and the magic loose?

Beautiful.

It would have been beautiful.

"Enough!" And she struck. Dropping her weapon and darting through the web woven by my Conwy blade, bringing forward her hand, fingers stiffened, the Final Message; a hard hit to the nerve centre in the neck that causes the entire body to cramp and then go limp. I felt it as a lightning-quick wave of pain through my body, and then I was falling backwards, the air knocked out of me as I hit the floor.

Neliu picked up my Conwy blade.

"I promise you, Girton, that Tomas will die, and he'll die with this." She held up my blade and played the light up and down the blade, reflecting it into my eyes. "But first, you have to die." With all my muscles paralysed and the reflected light in my eyes she was not much more than a blur holding a shining object. I tried to move, to say something, to beg her to let my master loose, but I had nothing. There was a warmth at my crotch where my bladder had let go. The blur of Neliu moved nearer. "It didn't have to be this way," she said.

A storm hit her.

Silent and so fast it seemed as if Neliu was simply plucked out of the world, but I heard the grunt as she was hit. Then the metal-on-metal clangour of combat. No talking, only the dance of blades.

The Final Message began to wear off, and I could move my head, focus my eyes, feel shame at having pissed myself, see my master and Neliu blade to blade. I had only ever seen my master fight another assassin once, at Maniyadoc Castle, and that had been less a fight, more a dance, a ritualised piece of theatre to decide who should have the right of the kill. This was entirely different. In the castle my master had been serene, but not now. Now she was a fury, her face twisted into a grimace. She had given up her usual two-bladed style for a dagger in one hand and a shield on the arm she had been forced to cut. She pushed Neliu back. When Neliu struck, my master countered. Their feet moved forward, back, no clever moves, no finesse, the iterations abandoned for speed and anger. There was nothing fancy or artful in what they did. Theirs was a fight of fury, of desperate attack and desperate defence. The shield gave my master an advantage, and she pressed it, pushing Neliu back, using it to disrupt her counters. Neliu tried to find her way around the shield, blades scything out and cracking against the metal, and still my master came forward. Never had I seen her work so recklessly against a skilled opponent. Always she had told me, "Take your time if you must . . . Wear them down," but now she applied the opposite strategy – an almost brutal straightforwardness, and it was working well for her.

But the moment I realised why she had adopted such a strategy, so did Neliu.

And then, of course, the fight was all but over.

My master was still recovering. She had been ill and she was weak. Now my sight was better I could see she was also hurt. Fresh blood covered the side of her face and an ugly lump had risen under the hair. Her expression wasn't simply furious, it was also strained. The shield helped her, but I could see the tightness in her muscles as she fought against the drain it was on her strength.

As my master's fury started to subside Neliu's retreat slowed and stopped. When the end came it came quickly, as it always did. The shield slipped and Neliu kicked at the edge of it, sending my master spinning. Neliu dived in with her blade, cutting across the back of my master's leg and making her cry out. With a kick Neliu sent her sprawling onto her face in front of the tent entrance.

Though it seemed our deaths were now assured, I felt sad that Neliu's hamstringing of my master had ended her effectiveness as an assassin. Neliu stood in the centre of the tent, breathing hard, her blades held at her sides and a rapturous smile on her face.

"Both Girton Club-Foot and Merela Karn beaten by my blade. It is a pity there will only be Crast, Tomas and Neander to tell about this." She glanced from me to my master. "I'll keep her for Tomas, but I promised Crast I would spare you Tomas's attention, Girton, and I keep my promises." She took a step towards me and then paused.

A quiet voice spoke one word.

"Stop."

Neliu turned.

In the door of the tent stood Areth.

"Dead gods," hissed Neliu, "is there anyone else out there waiting to come in and die? If so bring them all now and save me some time."

"It was you?" said Areth, and her head tilted to one side. "You killed my son?"

"You heard that?" Neliu looked confused.

"I have done nothing but listen for his name since he died. You wonder I hear it when it is spoken?"

Neliu's brow furrowed, as if trying to understand what she meant. Maybe she thought Areth had been standing outside the tent all the time, though the queen was panting and her legs were muddy from running.

"It is war, Areth," said Neliu. "People die."

"But you swore to protect us." She sounded confused, unable to understand the betrayal. "I liked you."

"Tomas has my mother," she said simply, and again she looked torn, her facade fracturing. "I'm sorry, Areth," she said, "but I had no choice in what I did, and I have no choice in what I must do now. It is a kindness really, considering what Tomas would do with you . . ." She took a step towards Areth.

I tried to move. Couldn't.

"No," said Areth. She shook her head and Neliu made her first mistake. She thought Areth was powerless, thought her only a pampered queen, but Areth was far more than that. "No," she said again.

The grass at her feet died.

The air froze, became solid and amber.

The world became quiet and then it became loud. That one whispered word filled my ears and my mind. "No" filled the ears of everyone in the tent, growing and ringing until it was unbearable.

Then Areth ap Vythr threw the black hammer.

She was not powerful, not a sorcerer by any real stretch, not like I was, and nor was she even a weak power like my master, Neliu or my dead lover Drusl. She was little more than a village wise woman really, but all her anger and fury and pain went into her casting. She thrust her hand forward, pushing out an explosion of darkness that hit Neliu. The black hammer threw her backwards onto me, carving half the skin from her face and denting her armour.

Quiet.

Areth staring at her hands, as if shocked by what she had done. My master trying to pull herself up. I can feel everyone's pain. It courses around the room. It resonates through us all.

Neliu groaned.

She wasn't dead.

Areth's casting hadn't been enough. She'd hurt Neliu but not killed her. My master was sorely wounded, and Areth was lost, caught in the horror of what she was. That left only me.

Neliu moved, breath bubbling wetly from her ruined face,

elbows digging into me as she forced herself up to find her blades.

But while I had lain there I had worked loose my only remaining weapon, the chain garrotte my master had given me as a present and I wore sewn into my clothes. I held it in my hand more for the comfort of having a weapon at the last than through any expectation of using it. I breathed deep, once, twice, and lunged forward, my legs barely worked and collapsed under me. I stretched out my arms. The garrotte slid over Neliu's blood-soaked head, caught around her throat.

Pull!

She fought, clawing at her throat then stretching back, trying to find my eyes with her gauntleted fingers. I leaned as far back as I could, pushing my knee against her back for leverage. Swaying from side to side as her hands clawed at my face, the air I sawed the little chain backwards and forwards, cutting through the flesh of her neck, rasping through the armour of her windpipe. Being rewarded by an explosion of blood from a severed artery. Even then I kept sawing, kept working the chain back and forth until my master crawled to me, hand over painful hand, dragging her bleeding legs behind her. Then her arm was on mine and she was urging me to stop.

"Enough, Girton. It is over," she said softly, then repeated it. "It is over, Girton, over."

"No," I said. The chain dropped, a bloody necklace around the wreck of Neliu's neck. Every inch of me ached. "It is not over, Master. Crast rides for the battle and he intends to kill Rufra."

I could see in my master's eyes what she was going to say. That we were finished here – exposed – and that nothing good could come from this for us, but it was Areth who spoke first.

"You are the king's champion, Girton Club-Foot," she said,

and there was all the weight of a queen behind her words. "If the king is in danger, you must ride."

I looked my master in the eye, my tired, battered, and for the first time I could ever remember, scared, master. But it was not herself she was scared for, it was me. And it was because she knew what I was going to say.

"I must ride, Master," I whispered. She held my gaze for a moment and then bowed her head before speaking so quietly only I could hear her.

"Yes," she said, "you must. And though it scores my heart to send you into such danger. I am proud of you for it."

Chapter 31

I rode.

On the horizon the Birthstorm began to breach, huge grey arms reaching out from the land ready to smash back down with wind, rain and burning light. I set Xus's head for the storm and told him to run, and he, great and strong and furious as any storm, ran as if to meet a long-lost mate, head out, antlers back, great muscles bunching and twisting beneath me as they powered us over the long grasses.

At first the sheer explosive speed of Xus brought with it such a strong rush of adrenalin that it banished the tiredness and pain the day had left me with, but that could only ever be temporary. Despite the urgency, despite the panic, the exhaustion started to tell. Rufra's army had over a day's riding on me. Crast also had a huge start, and I would not catch him before he joined the army. I could only hope I got there before the fighting started and Crast struck. If Rufra fell, everything he had built would be finished and his army would be massacred. Tomas and Neander would ride through the rest of Maniyadoc hunting down Rufra's supporters until none remained, the thankful would go back to begging and serving, the living would remain for ever stuck in whatever trade they followed and the blessed and the Landsmen would close their iron grip even tighter around the people of Maniyadoc and the Long Tides.

But for now all I could do was ride, and slowly the hypnotic rhythm of Xus's feet began to lull me into sleep. Sleeping in the saddle was one of the first skills my master taught me, and, as the adrenalin ebbed, my tired mind drifted back, and I became a child nodding off in the saddle as my master led Xus to our next job. The teeth of the Birthstorm, cold winds that bit through the metal and leather of my harlequin armour, seemed to withdraw and it was as if a warm cloak was placed around my shoulders: a cloak of black, darker than night – a familiar comfort. I rode Xus and felt sure that both he and I were protected by his namesake, Xus the unseen, god of death. I did not fear my mount would stumble, or that straggling Nonmen would stop us, or that the herds of feral pigs would attack. I rode through an otherworld, a semi-real place of shadows and distant voices. I rode for Goldenson Copse and I did not ride alone; I rode with death and we shared a destination, if not a purpose.

I was woken from my semi-doze by thunder as I approached Goldenson Hill, where the land rose gently before falling away to the copse and the shallow river valley that held the remains of an Age of Balance bridge. I urged Xus up the rise and heard a low, long rumble and scanned the towers of black cloud that loomed over the land. But it was not the thunder of storms that I heard, it was the thunder of battle, the meeting of shields as two great armies charged into each other. I reined Xus in at the top of the rise, his great lungs working like forge bellows as I surveyed the land below.

Tomas had arrayed his forces in the bend of the river, his camp train and tents set up around the base of the giant pillars which had once supported the stone structure that crossed Adallada's River, long since lost. A makeshift bridge of logs had been erected, wooden braces connecting jagged and broken stone teeth, but it appeared to be a tactically foolish place for Tomas to have set up. Of course that did not matter if, as Tomas and Neander thought, they could not fail to win. Tomas clearly intended to make it seem like he had won the old way, his opponent falling on the battlefield. He would claim he had felled Rufra himself and that he had been chosen by the dead gods. With the priests and the Landsmen to support his story that was how it would be remembered. No doubt after the battle Crast would quietly be disposed of, his body fed to the pigs and his involvement never mentioned. Even without Crast's intervention Tomas still had a far bigger army than Rufra's, his heavy cavalry swollen to half again as many by the Landsmen, and in the melee where the two armies met I saw a phalanx of green armour where more Landsmen fought. Tomas was stationed behind his troops, well out of bowshot, watching the fight, and my heart skipped a beat, a shard of hate interrupting the flow of blood as I recognised the colourful masked figure by him as Neander.

Aydor led Rufra's right against a collection of the Tired Lands' blessed. I counted many flags but was too far away to make out the devices, but there was no disguising the huge form of the man who would have been king as he laid about himself with my warhammer. There was a terrible joy in Aydor's movements, in his fury. Beside him I could just make out Captain Thian, methodical and careful, but Aydor had no care. He seemed born to the melee, and every swing of his hammer made a corpse. The sun glinted on his shoulderguards and from the enamel on his helmet – it seemed vanity and pride had not left him and he had dressed like a king to go into battle. I found myself wishing for a blade to find him, to create one problem less for Rufra. On Rufra's left, Danfoth and the followers of Arnst faced the Landsmen. Although Danfoth's people were badly equipped and organised, there were a lot of them and they fought as a huge, seething mass of black cloth. Where they did not have weapons, clawing hands pulled at shields, bodies offered themselves to the blade so those behind them could get at their opponents. In the centre was Rufra in his silver armour, the flying lizard standard snapping in the wind, right in the thick of the battle. I searched for Nywulf, finding him still alive and at Rufra's side, guarding the king's right, holding the bonemount aloft, while Gabran the Smith guarded the king's left.

Behind Rufra's infantry stood his archers, led by Bediri Outlander, dressed in the savage finery of the far borders. At their rear were Rufra's mount archers, led by Boros, and on the far left, furthest from me, stood the heavy cavalry on their mounts with Cearis at their head, calmly waiting for their moment.

Abruptly, and as if at some pre-agreed signal, the two sides stepped back, retreating from each other and leaving a tideline of corpses. Most of the dead on Rufra's side were in the black rags of Arnst's followers, while Tomas's dead wore armour of varying types. It was difficult to tell who, if anyone, had the advantage, and it did not appear the battle had been joined for more than an hour or so. I scanned the ranks of Rufra's army for Crast but could not see him, so turned my attention to the tents of the baggage train, hoping to find him where he could be more easily intercepted. Again I saw nothing.

A roar went up from Rufra's troops, dragging my attention back to the battlefield. Something had happened on Tomas's left flank and his withdrawal was in disarray, the wall of shields had fragmented. Rufra was quick to take advantage. Coloured flags were raised from his position, giving out orders. Bediri Outlander lifted an arm and a hail of arrows flew from the archers in Rufra's rear ranks, reaching for the sky as if desperate to escape before vanishing against the dark clouds of the looming Birthstorm, then falling, landing to a chorus of screams. Behind the arrows came Cearis ap Vythr and her heavy cavalry, galloping round the rear of Rufra's army to take advantage of Tomas's disarray. Even from my vantage point on the hill it felt like the ground was vibrating beneath me as her mounts thundered forward, gilded antlers down, Riders' spears at the ready to smash into Tomas's troops.

The Landsmen cavalry counter-charged, riding between the two armies. It was a brave thing to do as it left their flanks open to spears, and many were thrown from Rufra's side. I saw green Riders fall, but still they charged on, and I braced myself for the clash. But Cearis was no fool. She veered her Riders away. Her cavalry was too valuable, and one on one with Tomas and the Landsmen she knew that, at best, she would take heavy losses, and it was too early in the battle for Rufra to have his cavalry crippled. Behind Cearis thundered Boros with his lightly armoured mount archers, and now it was the turn of the Landsmen to veer away, and though they rode back to their lines at full gallop they still lost men to Boros's archers before a hastily assembled wall of shields and spears sent them cantering back to Rufra's lines.

With my knees I urged Xus forward and down into Rufra's baggage camp, all the time looking for signs of Crast but seeing nothing. Thunder rumbled, this time it was from the Birthstorm, and a fitful rain spattered down.

I spotted Crast.

He had removed his helmet, the better to be recognised, and was at the very rear of Rufra's lines. As the mettle-chanters started their howling for another round of fighting he pushed his way forward diagonally from behind Aydor's position to Rufra at the centre. I slid from Xus, running for the rear of Rufra's lines as the horns sounded and his army moved forward to attack again.

Another rumble of thunder was echoed by the crack of shields meeting, and the air filled with howling as the two armies released their aggression and fear. More troops joined the fray from behind me, adding their weight to the push against Tomas's forces and trapping my arms against the back of the woman in front of me. My legs were barely able to move, I was held helpless by the crush of bodies while danger advanced on my friend. It seemed I was mocked by fate, to be thrown into a seething crowd to save Rufra twice in almost as many days. All my life I had done my best to avoid crowds. I had been raised to live the lonely life of the assassin and to be enclosed by shifting masses of people was alien to me. But Rufra ruled through his people. He went to them and moved among them, and where he went danger followed and so I must go also. No matter how many people stood between us, I would get to him and I would defend him. Maybe this was not mockery, maybe fate simply forced me to acknowledge the direction in which my life headed.

"Let me through!" I shouted, and I cursed the leash cut into my chest. Had I waited just a little longer before I let my master cut me, there would have been no need for me to find myself stuck in a seething mass of men and woman once more. I could have used the magic to make myself heard. "I am Rufra's champion. Let me through!" But I was not the only one shouting, and by no means the loudest voice. The sensorama of battle was overwhelming – my nose filled with the stink of rust and rancid fat, open bowels and death, mud churned by feet and rain – and no one paid any attention to one more screaming warrior. I was smaller than most around me and even pushing myself up on my toes could barely see above the crowd. My club foot ached, hampering me, making it harder for me to get purchase on the churned ground. I pulled off my helmet, hoping someone would recognise my face, but no one was looking behind.

Arrows sailed down from above and the man to my right groaned, a shaft sprouting from the top of his head. I pushed his limp body aside, squeezing into the space he had left, forcing my way forward with my elbows, but the going was slow. I pulled myself up onto tiptoe again. Freezing rain lashed the heaving mass and just as quickly stopped. Was that Crast? Ahead of me? And past him could I see Rufra?

Yes!

It was Crast, and he was also having trouble getting forward, but his red hair made him far easier to recognise, and people moved aside when they saw him. He glanced over his shoulder and I saw alarm on his face as he recognised me. He fought his way forward with even more urgency.

I was shouting again, my voice now hoarse, and half the time I choked on my words. The one time my club foot would have helped, marking me out as Rufra's champion, no one could see my feet for the crush of people.

"Crast! Stop! Crast, you must stop," but he either could not hear me or did not care so I started calling to those around me. "You must stop Crast! He will kill the king!" But my words were lost. The sky was roaring with the pangs of the Birthstorm: thunder crashed and hail swept the battlefield, bouncing off the armour of the woman in front of me and stinging my eyes. All my senses were assailed as I fought my way forward through a sea of angry faces.

Crast!

There!

No, there!

At one point he was just ahead of me, and I made a desperate grab for his copper hair, falling backwards and almost going under the boots of those around me. Only a quick and unseen hand saved me and then the press of bodies pulled me away from Crast once more. I struggled, pushed forward and the currents within the tide of troops pulled me back towards my friend, I could see Rufra's back, the tiny plates of his armour sparkling with droplets of water. There was blood on his gauntlets, his sword arm rose and fell. By him was Nywulf, working methodically with a stabsword in his right hand and somehow holding the bonemount and his shield in his left, all their concentration to the front. Behind them Crast drew his blade and – as if fate required a stage for treachery – a gap opened around them.

Crast stood alone.

Rufra and Nywulf before him, unaware of the blade at their back.

And Girton Club-Foot – assassin, sorcerer, king's champion – was too far away to do anything. I could not even throw my blade because of the crush of men and women around me. Despite the thronging soldiers I was just as alone as Crast. Only he and I knew what he intended and only he and I knew I was about to fail to save my king and friend.

"Nywulf!" I said it as the Whisper-that-Flies-to-the-Ear, more in hope than anything, but the magic was not there, the sigil carved into my chest contracted. I found a wall of grey within that allowed no access to the black sea beyond and a searing pain shot through me, making me think I had been hit by one of the arrows that had been falling from the sky. A scream. As if in answer to my thought an arrow had pierced the shoulder of the man next to me, a mortal wound that had punctured his lung and would drown him in his own blood. He looked at me, as if confused that Xus had chosen him for his dark palace. The soldier's mouth opened, he coughed up blood and I remembered something my master had said, something Areth had said, *something terrible I had done*. The magic is in all of us. I grabbed the hand of the dying man, felt his life force as a sliver of silver, twisting and spinning against the darkness of Xus's keep as it swiftly ebbed. Some understanding passed between us. I saw a knowing in his eyes, and an agreement. His life was done, he knew it, but he would gladly give me what was left of it for his king. I grabbed the tail of his life, that small vanishing thread, and I used it to create the smallest of magics.

Then I spoke again.

The Whisper-that-Flies-to-the-Ear.

"Nywulf!"

He turned.

Saw Crast.

Saw the blade.

Saw me.

Understood.

The pain of Crast's betrayal was a scar on his face – and the anger a fire. All seemed to happen in slow motion. Nywulf pulled the man next to him across so his shield filled the position in the wall he had held and then pushed Rufra out of the path of the blade aimed at his back. Too slow! It plunged into Rufra's side and he fell back, blood gushing from him as Crast pulled the stabsword out to strike again. Crast's face was every bit as fanatical as Darvin's had been. Like Darvin he knew he was lost, but he had chosen to focus entirely on the death of Rufra. His blade came down again. Nywulf moved but Crast had been trained by Nywulf, trained by me. As Nywulf lifted his blade, he realised he would not be quick enough. He dropped his weapon and stepped in front of Crast's blade, letting it carve into his chest rather than his king's.

With a heave and a final shove of my elbows, I was through, my blade in my hand. I thrust it into Crast's back. It was a killing blow, through his ribs and into his heart. I tossed Crast to one side as Nywulf collapsed, the bonemount falling, and though I longed to catch the old warrior it was the bonemount I grabbed. To let it fall was to signal defeat. The troops around me reeled as they realised what had happened, and I felt the line start to waver. Bending, I used all my strength to pull Rufra to his feet. He hissed in pain. Once more I had to perform for a crowd. I must. My throat, raw from shouting, felt like I had been swallowing soured land. I gathered myself, coughed, spat on the ground and forced volume into my voice.

"The king lives!" A coughing fit. I fought to recover my voice. "The king is wounded but he lives!" I shouted it as loud as I could. A roar went up from the troops around us, taking up my cry.

"The king lives!"

I passed the bonemount to Gabran, and then Rufra, Nywulf and I were pulled away from the front line and I heard a second cry go up: "For the king! For Rufra!"

Horns sounded from Tomas's lines and they pressed their attack. The whole of Rufra's army was being forced back as we passed through it. All around went up shouts of "Hold! Hold!" but as Rufra and Nywulf were lain behind the lines I could feel panic and uncertainty in the air. Rufra could not hide the blood gushing from his side, and to see a warrior as feared as Nywulf brought down was the sort of shock that could lead to an army breaking.

A hand grabbed at the hem of my armour, pulling on it, and I turned. Nywulf beckoned and I knelt. He pulled me close, his face before mine. Blood everywhere: blood on my armour, blood on his hand, blood on his teeth as he tried to speak. With the last of his strength he hauled me even closer.

"Protect him," he said, and then let go, his life gone.

Rufra was stricken, staring from where he lay in the filth at the rear of his army's lines, his own pain forgotten.

"Nywulf," he said simply.

"Gone," I said.

"It is Goldenson Copse," he said, his voice dead. "It is my curse to lose here."

"No!" I crawled across the mud, my words fierce. "Nywulf gave his life to save yours, and you must not give up. How badly are you hurt?"

Tarris pushed me away, pulling at Rufra's armour to get at the wound. "Too badly to fight, Girton Club-Foot. Get him to my tent," he said to his acolytes. For a moment I saw gratitude on Rufra's face, as if he was glad of an excuse to walk away, to hide in the healer's tent, and I thought Nywulf's death had broken him.Then he looked to me. Closed his eyes, took a deep breath.

"No." Rufra's voice was strong, though filled with pain. "Bring my mount."

"King Rufra," began Tarris, "you cannot fight. If I do not treat the wound you will die."

"If I vanish from the fight we all die," he said. His troops were being forced further and further back, the rear ranks beginning to encroach on the baggage train. Balance, his mount, was brought, and with her came Xus, trotting happily by her side.

"Girton," said Rufra, "help me up." I lifted Rufra into the saddle and gave him his sword, then pulled myself into Xus's saddle by his side. He stood in his stirrups and I marvelled at his inner strength as he lifted his blade. "I live!" he shouted "Fight hard! I live!" He sat back down, beckoning me. "Girton –" his breath came quickly "– Tomas is readying his cavalry to charge, and if we are to break it will be that which does it. Find Cearis, ride with her. If the army sees my champion it will give them heart." He passed me his helmet with the flying lizard crest. "Wear this as my mark."

"I will." Before I spurred Xus away he grabbed my arm.

"And Girton . . ."

"Yes."

"Don't die."

"I'll do my best not to."

"Not enough." He grimaced, the pain momentarily overwhelming him, and for a moment I thought he would fall from his saddle. "You can't die, Girton, by royal decree."

"There have been enough traitors today," I said. "I would hate to add to them." He smiled sadly as Tarris helped him down from Balance and helped him towards the healers' tents.

I rode to join the cavalry.

Cearis had not needed Rufra's orders; she had already seen Tomas's cavalry readying and was busy tightening the girth of her saddle when I found her.

"Girton."

"Rufra wants his champion to be seen riding with you."

"Makes sense." She pointed at the armies. Rufra's troops

were now holding their position. "Tomas will send his cavalry against Danfoth and his followers."

"They will not break," I said. "There is a madness upon them."

"Tomas does not need them to break; a massacre will be demoralising enough after what happened to Rufra. And we need their numbers, so we will have to intercept his cavalry before they hit."

"And beat them," I said.

"We don't have the numbers to beat them." I could not hide my shock that she would speak as if we were already defeated. She pulled a saddle strap tight and her mount hissed. "We'll hold them, and when they are too deep in with us to retreat, Boros and the mount archers will hit them from behind." She bared her teeth at me. "They will beat them." Then she grabbed Xus's bridle, and despite the excitement in the air and the growling of the other mounts he let her. "You are no cavalry Rider, Girton."

"So what do I need to do?"

"Let Xus lead. He is war trained and up for the fight; you simply need to hang on and kill anything that comes close to you."

"That I can do," I said.

"I know." She grinned and pulled the visor down on her helmet. "Cavalry," she shouted, "for the king! To war!"

We rode.

I knew little of cavalry and had never ridden in battle formation before. As Xus drove himself along by Cearis's mount I found that the clawbeats of the mounts synchronised, and when I glanced to each side I found the other Riders were moving in time with me, rising and falling with the rhythm of their animals. The formation was so steady it seemed as if we stayed still and the world moved in a blur around us. It was how I imagined it must be to be part of the flocks of flying lizards that wheeled and turned in dizzying patterns in yearsdeath, many becoming one. I watched To'mas's cavalry rushing to meet us, marvelled at their discipline as they changed formation, first bunching up into an arrowhead to punch through the infantry, then, when their commander realised they could not beat us to Danfoth, opening up, like wings, into a long line. Our smaller formation changed also – I expected us to become an arrowhead to punch through their line, but instead we became two lines, the second far enough back to ensure that when the first contact came it did not simply crash into the first line and impale us on the antlers of their mounts.

The ground between the two forces was eaten up in moments. At the last I heard Cearis shout, "Brace!" and saw a Landsman opposite aim his spear at my heart; at the same time his mount lowered antlers – gilded in razor-sharp silver. The Riders around me crouched behind their shields and levelled their spears.

A single second of quiet, when everything held still. I felt the terror and the madness of what we were doing; riding two tonnes of angry, vicious animal with its own forest of razor-sharp spears straight at another just as big, just as angry.

And then we met, and the jarring impact drove all fear and thought away.

A spear came at me and I swayed in the saddle, feeling the point sweep past my right shoulder. The air filled with a noise like a thousand trees being battered by axes as the mounts' antlers locked and the creatures met, rearing and screaming and striking. The impact almost threw me from the saddle and all I could do was hang on as I rose into the air with Xus, the mount growling furiously and twisting his locked antlers in a test of strength against the other Rider's animal. Around me mounts struck out with clawed feet and metal spurs. The Rider by me let out a gurgling scream. I glanced to the side. One of her mount's antler's had snapped under the impact and hit her in the throat. She clawed at the horn jutting from her flesh, pulling it loose just as I regained my saddle and a spray of arterial blood coated Xus and I. The Landsman opposite leaned around the locked antlers of our mounts and swung at me with his sword. I was in no position to defend but the dying woman by me grabbed the sword arm of my attacker and let herself fall from her mount, dragging the other Rider down among the animals' churning feet. I drew my sword and as the two soldiers were trampled underfoot Xus let out an ear-shattering scream and twisted his head, breaking the neck of his opponent.

Behind me another rippling crack of antler against antler and more screams of mounts and Riders as blade and claw went to work. Another Landsman swung at me. I dodged his axe and struck back. He took my thrust on his shield and my sword scored a deep line across the white and green. As he lifted his axe for a return strike Xus drove his antlers into the side of the man's mount, the tip of one going straight through the Landsman's leg. He screamed as his mount fell, taking him down with it.

I felt panicky, scared; this wasn't like any fight I had been in before. Skill seemed to play little part in it – Axe! Dodge. Swing back – and my attacker was gone before I registered his face or struck a useful blow. The fight around me became fiercer and more confused, the mounts made it so much faster. There was no way of knowing where the next blow was coming from. Something hit my armour, pushing me forward into Xus's neck and only quick reactions on the part of Xus saved me from being impaled on his antlers. He put his head forward and swung his whole body round, bucking and wildly swinging his antlered head from side to side, creating space. He screamed his dominance, challenging the other mounts.

Chaos. A Rider fell. A sword bit. A mount screamed. A shield broke. The enemy's numbers started to tell. I found myself facing two Riders not one. A sword came at my head. I blocked. The other Rider swung at my exposed midriff. Xus bit through his armour, almost taking off his arm and shook his head from side to side, pulling the screaming man from his saddle. His mount ran rather than face Xus. My eyes watered from the astringent stink of mount piss, bull animals fought, spraying burning urine everywhere to mark territory. Another hammer blow into my side. I felt a rib crack and swung backwards with my sword, not seeing who I hit but feeling the sword bite and hearing a scream. We were losing. Again and again I was forced back. I started to understand the fighting a little better, manoeuvring Xus so that my fellow Riders were always at my back. Xus, having been stabled with them, knew which animals he trusted and which to attack. More and more I relied on my mount – and dead gods he was fearsome, unrivalled in fierceness to the point that opposing mounts were clearly loath to approach us. But even that would not be enough. Two Landsmen whipped their mounts into attacking Xus, trying to time their blows so I could not defend while avoiding Xus's antlers and snapping jaws. A third Rider spurred towards me and I thought all was lost.

The arrows hit.

Pinpoint strikes. Archery like I had never seen before. Arrows cutting through armour like knives through stewed flesh. Shouts and the pounding of mount feet coming nearer and then retreating, near and away, near and away. The hiss of arrows making me flinch. A sword blow, block and return it. Arrows. Then Tomas's forces were disengaging, galloping at full speed for their lines pursued by Rufra's mount archers. Boros's voice, screaming after them, "Where is he? Where is my brother? Is he here? Did he run back to your false king?" Then Cearis was by me, blood-streaked and breathing heavily.

"Come, Girton. Withdraw before they bring up their

archers." As we galloped back, a wave of elation went through me: we had survived.

"Look, Girton!" shouted Cearis. "Tomas's forces are withdrawing."

"It is done?" I said. "Is it over?"

"No." Cearis shook her head and she had no grin for me now. "This is just a lull, but we have held them. For now at least."

Chapter 32

The pause in the battle brought with it a strange and unnatural calm, though we were all glad of it. I sat with what remained of Rufra's Triangle Council outside the healers' wagon while they worked on the king. Dark clouds were our roof and cold winds were our walls.

"What happens if he dies?" said Aydor.

From somewhere distant came the grunting of pigs, hundreds of them.

"Why? Do you see your opportunity?" I spat on the floor but Aydor ignored me.

"He will not die," said Cearis softly. "I am sure of it and –" she glanced at me "– bickering will not help him. Tomas has withdrawn for now but he still has more troops than us. We must decide, if Rufra is sorely hurt, whether we stand here or withdraw to Castle Maniyadoc."

"He'll cut us to pieces if we retreat," said Gabran.

"My mount archers will protect you, don't worry," said Boros.

"It makes most sense," said Cearis, "to withdraw. Maniyadoc can stand a siege and—"

"No." We turned. Rufra was walking down the stairs from the wagon. He held his side and was clearly in pain, but his face was set. "If we withdraw, Tomas will have time to call the full might of the Landsmen to him, and what support we have among the blessed will slowly ebb away. It is not enough to hold Castle Maniyadoc; we must not let him leave here as victor. Too many will turn to him as king if we do."

"How do we win then?" said Cearis. "We are still outnumbered and have lost half our cavalry."

"As did Tomas," said Boros. "He may be wary about sending his cavalry back out again."

"Gabran," said Rufra, "how stands the infantry?"

"Well," he said, "and they will stand better for seeing you walk among them, but I worry about Danfoth's side of things."

The big Meredari stood. He radiated authority in a way he never had before. "My people will fight to the death. They have fought hard already for your king."

"He's your king too," said Boros, standing, angry.

"I do not doubt they will fight and die, Danfoth," said Gabran, "it is that they die too willingly. They won't even take scavenged armour – they say it is an affront to Xus."

"Death is a blessing," said the Meredari.

Before we could descend further into squabbling an infantryman ran up, falling to his knees before his king.

"King Rufra, Tomas stands before our army and requests to speak to you."

I felt something cold then, some inner sense of foreboding, a feeling something had been missed that should be obvious, but Rufra smiled.

"Then I shall speak to him," he said. "And maybe we can end this."

I stood.

"Rufra, do not trust him. Tomas tried to have you murdered, despite your agreement."

"He was desperate," said Rufra, and for a moment I could not believe he was so naive. And then I understood: no matter what it cost him he would save the lives of his people if he could.

I wanted to tell him not to be foolish, explain how Crast and Neliu had murdered his child on Tomas and Neander's orders, but I remembered the look on his face when he had spoken of Arnlath and what he had said he would do to Tomas if that was the case. I remembered a cage door shutting on a terrified woman I told myself I did not love. I saw a thousand flashes of my blade and wrong decisions. I remembered a cruel Landsman with a warhammer and my sword opening his throat, and I knew revenge had brought me no solace; it had been a bitter and empty thing. So I said nothing because he was my friend and he was a good man in a way I was not sure I could ever be. I nodded and made a secret vow that if Rufra died today I would exact vengeance for him and his child. And though I knew I would get no solace from it, I would make that vengeance long and slow.

"Very well," I said, moving aside and letting him pass.

"You do know it is me that is king, Girton?" He tried a smile through his pain, but it was a wan thing.

We walked down to find Tomas, looking magnificent atop his mount, waiting for us. He had always looked magnificent, had always looked like a king; so unlike Rufra who had to work to appear at all regal. Tomas had not come alone; Neander waited by him half a bowshot from our lines. I wondered what Tomas could have to say that he wanted all to hear. As we approached, Rufra did his best to walk tall and not to show the pain he felt from the wound to his side, but he could not hide it entirely. Tomas smiled when he noticed. I wished I could simply pick up a bow and put an arrow in his face then one in Neander's heart and end all this now, but it was not Rufra's way. He would win as he thought a king should or not at all.

"Rufra ap Vythr," said Neander quietly.

"Tomas ap Glyndier," said Rufra, as if it were the man on the mount who spoke and not the priest.

"A time back," shouted Neander, "Rufra offered single combat to end this foul war that strikes at Maniyadoc's heart and takes our children from us." Now I saw what they intended. We were lost. "Though King Tomas longed to take this honourable path, I advised him not to fight Rufra. But I made an error, because I lack honour, being only a humble priest." He looked up and down the silent lines of our army. Somewhere a mount growled, somewhere someone sobbed in pain. A flag cracked in the wind and the swelling Birthstorm let out a low grumble of thunder. "I regret that now," he said, and he managed to sound sad while still looking like the dog that got the liver. "Too many have died." Neander raised his voice. "King Tomas wants the killing to stop! He wants the war to stop!"

Tomas urged his mount a step forward.

"Under the laws of the high king," he said, "I say that only one king may stand in the lands of Maniyadoc and the Long Tides, and I call on the right of kings, combat until only one king stands."

Silence.

Tomas glanced at Rufra, then spoke again:

"You made the challenge, Rufra, and I have accepted." He gave him a nod. "I will wait in the centre of the field for an hour. Of course you do not have to come. If you are afraid of death you may simply forfeit your crown and no one else will have to die for you today." He turned his mount and trotted away, stopping midway between the two gathered armies. Neander followed, then passed his king and vanished into the army gathered opposite.

We returned to our lines, the eyes of Rufra's commanders on us.

"Dark Ungar take them both," I said as we walked. "They know you are hurt – that is the only reason they offer this. Let me fight him, let me finish him for you."

"You are not a king," said Rufra simply as we rejoined his army.

"You cannot fight him, Rufra," said Cearis. "He is a yellower of a man but he is still a great bladesman, and you are too hurt to take him on."

"As Girton says, he would not offer otherwise," said Rufra. He placed his hand on the hilt of his sword.

"You do not have to fight him," said Gabran. "No one seriously expects you to fight him sorely wounded."

"It is good of you to say that, Gabran –" Rufra tightened his sword belt "– though we both know it is not true. That is why Tomas made sure everyone heard his challenge."

"Let me fight him," I said again. "Let me put on your armour and put the visor down to hide my face. I will—"

"Fall over?" said Rufra with a smile. "You are a skilled fighter but more than a little smaller than I am, Girton. No. This is my battle. I must—"

"I take up the challenge of kings!" The roar came from our side of the battlefield, and if I had felt a cold worry before, now I became frozen to the spot.

Aydor strode out on to the field, warhammer in one hand, shield in the other. He was weaving and barely able to stand, so drunk he could hardly walk in a straight line.

I slid my blade from my scabbard.

"I knew he could not be trusted. I said he would betray you."

"He is a king," said Rufra. He sounded sad but put his hand on my arm. "It is his right."

"I can finish him before he gets near Tomas," I said. "Give me a bow, or I can catch him. He is slow and—"

"Stay your hand, Girton," said Cearis. "Aydor will never beat Tomas, but he may wound him, and that could help us."

"And what if he wins, Cearis?" I spat on the floor. "Dead gods damn him to the land, this has been his plan all along. That is why he has worked to make himself popular with the troops. If he wins here, everything will be lost and everyone will be in a worse position than if Rufra had simply walked away."

"Quiet," said Rufra. And though his voice was not loud

it was the command of a king. "You are too quick to judge, Girton. People can change."

"I wish that were true," I said. "But he is a monster, Rufra. He has never been anything else and never will be."

Tomas sat still on his mount as a swaying Aydor staggered to a halt in front of him.

"Go away, Aydor," he said. "This fight is not for you. When you swore fealty to Rufra you lost any claim to the crown."

"No," said Aydor, he seemed to have difficulty making words. Nywulf had warned him not to drink before a battle, but I wasn't surprised though his words had made no impression. "Rufra let me keep my claim," he said, "and refused to take my oath. I am still a king."

"Do you forget how many times we fought in the squire-yard?" said Tomas with a small, mocking smile. "And how you always ended up slinking away like a beaten dog?" He raised his voice. "In fact, in the end your mother forbade me from fighting you so you were not mocked!" Laughter from the troops on his side, but not from ours. Aydor had managed to weasel himself into a sort of popularity.

Aydor stared up at Tomas, the hilt of my warhammer held tight in his fist.

"Are you scared?" he said, and that shut Tomas's flapping mouth. "You've always said my bark is worse than my bite, Tomas, and I have few teeth now. Surely you're not afraid of being bitten?"

Laughter from our side. I glanced at Rufra, he looked tense.

"Very well." Tomas slid from his mount. "Let's get this over with quickly."

They circled, but not for long, Aydor made a foolish lunge with the warhammer and Tomas skipped out of the way, shaking his head as if disappointed. I found myself whispering under my breath, "Come on, come on." The only good outcome for us was for Aydor to wound Tomas and then die. But Aydor was Aydor, unpleasant and useless. He was so drunk, falling about the field, that it seemed unlikely he would do anything but demoralise our troops. This would be little more for Tomas than a warm-up, and he treated it as such, dancing around Aydor, making small cuts and dodging Aydor's clumsy blows with showy moves.

I do not know when I realised Aydor was not drunk. It was more a gradual dawning than a conscious thought. The way he handled the warhammer, how he fell about without ever truly being off balance, the way his eyes never left Tomas's face, the way, when he slipped, he always managed to right himself. Tomas did not see it; he felt he knew his opponent and underestimated him – it seemed everyone but me had.

Aydor slowed, breathing heavily, and it looked like his strength had drained to the point where he could barely lift the warhammer. He took a few clumsy swings that were barely above hip height, and Tomas laughed as he dodged nimbly out of the way. When he was far back enough to feel safe from Aydor's clumsy swings, he turned to our lines, giving us a mocking bow.

And Aydor moved.

He darted forward, dropping all pretence of being drunk. The hammer came round in a great arc. Tomas must have sensed something and turned – but he did not even have time to look surprised before the warhammer smashed into his chest, sending him flying back. A great cry of shock went up from both sides of the field. It was a killing blow, but Aydor did not leave it at that. All traces of drunkenness were gone as he stalked towards his prey. I could hear Tomas's laboured breathing, see him trying to crawl away as Aydor approached, raised the warhammer and then brought it down with a sickening crunch on Tomas's head.

Aydor screamed something wordless and angry into the sky.

And then, where there had been noise and blood and fury, there was only silence.

Aydor walked towards us, leaving the broken body of Tomas in the mud behind him. Both armies watched as if under a spell. This was betrayal, complete and utter betrayal. Aydor was far cleverer than even I had believed, or maybe he had simply learned patience enough to bide his time. He stopped. His huge, threatening, lumbering presence cast a shadow long enough to reach the feet of Rufra. My hand went to my blade.

"No," said Rufra, his grip tightening around my arm.

"He will—"

"No," said Rufra gently. "This war ends here." He sounded so calm. I wanted to rail at him, curse him for his trusting nature. I wanted to draw my weapon and run it through Aydor as he stood there, a grim smile on his blood-spattered face. I could kill him with one move, with a flick of my wrist send throwing knives into his throat.

Up and down the rows of the army I started to hear, "King Aydor, King Aydor," repeated again and again.

I could stop his heart with a touch to the right place on his body.

Some soldiers fell to their knees while others only watched, waited. Then Aydor took the last few steps and was standing right in front of us, the sun at his back and the clouds of the Birthstorm darkening the sky behind him. He looked every inch like one of the terrifying shatter-spirits of folklore. If I killed him now I would probably die too. He had the army behind him, I could feel it.

But it would be worth it.

Rufra did not let go of my arm.

"No," he said again. Wind caught the mousy-brown locks of his hair, blowing them into his face; half the strands were black, stuck together with dried blood.

"Rufra ap Vythr," said Aydor.

"Aydor ap Mennix," said Rufra, and his voice was thick with pain. The wound at his side was bleeding. Red spots marring the pristine white of his skirts.

"Under the laws of the high king," said Aydor loudly enough for all to hear, "I say that only one king may stand in the lands of Maniyadoc and the Long Tides, and I call on the right of kings, combat until only one king stands."

Rufra nodded and still, his hand did not leave my arm, his grip remained tight around tense muscles.

"Under the laws of the high king," said Rufra quietly, "I accept the challenge of kings." He glanced at me. A twitch and Aydor would be dead, but Rufra was my king and I had sworn an oath to obey him, and I had meant it. He commanded nothing and so I did nothing. I bowed my head. Rufra drew his sword, and even that movement was difficult for him, it etched pain onto his face. Aydor watched Rufra draw his blade, and when every eye was on him he lifted his warhammer, my warhammer, high.

We waited for the end. Aydor's muscles bunched and tensed, sweat stood out on his brow. It was obvious to all watching that he could finish this with one swing. Rufra could barely stand.

Aydor dropped the hammer in the mud.

Then he threw his shield to one side and fell to his knees, raising his head and baring his throat to Rufra in the old salute.

"I concede the fight," he said, his voice thick with emotion. "I concede the fight," he said again, louder. "In the name of the high king I recognise a greater warrior and a greater claim on the throne. I renounce my kingship and swear my weapons to you, Rufra ap Vythr. My king."

Rufra stared at him, then he lowered his blade, pushing the tip into the ground and taking a deep breath. When he spoke his words were audible to all.

"Aydor ap Mennix," he said, "you may have renounced the kingship of men, but I say you remain a king among them."

There was a moment's silence. Then a shout went up from somewhere in Tomas's lines.

"Rufra ap Vythr! Hail the king!"

And the shout was taken up by both armies: "Hail the king! Hail the king!" It filled the small valley, and at that moment the Birthstorm truly broke. Lightning quartered the sky and rain hurtled down from the heavens. And I was glad of the rain, thankful beyond reason, because I looked upon Aydor and saw a man changed, saw a man who had left behind the darkness of his past and become something else. A man who had chosen a different, and better, path.

And only I knew that the water running down my face was not rain, but tears, tears of fierce joy.

Epilogue

It may not be the truth that the Birthstorm broke the moment Aydor bowed to Rufra, but it is how I have always chosen to remember it, and it is as real to me as the black birds which wheel and turn far above.

The rain that night beat on the tents and caravans with the same fury that men and women had fought with earlier in the day. Yet you would not have known those men and women had been fighting each other if you had walked into anywhere that drink was being served. The Landsmen had left, taking the cursed priest Neander with them, and the soldiers from both armies mixed – warily at first, then with better humour, and though there were fights and even some deaths they were overlooked and, largely, peace reigned – as it would for many years under Rufra's rule.

I had moved through the drinking tents, pushing my way between drunk soldiers, smiling to calm hostility, scowling at those who wished to engage me in conversation, scanning for one man. I found him, unusually, alone. I had expected him to be surrounded by well-wishers, by soldiers toasting his actions, but that was not the case. He was sitting, his huge frame hunched over, his long hair touching the surface of the table where pools of spilled drinks dyed its ends a deep black. I stood behind him, my hands twitching for want of a blade.

"I thought you would be with the troops, celebrating being the hero of the day."

Aydor turned at my voice and shrugged.

"I threw away a kingdom today, Girton Club-Foot." He drew strange patterns in the moisture on the table. "It is not every day a man can say he threw away a kingdom, is it?"

"And now you regret it?"

Aydor shook his head and laughed quietly.

"No, that is the strange thing. I do not regret it at all. I feel like I have put down a great weight."

I nodded and walked away, feeling his eyes on me as I did. I took two cups of perry from the boy ladling out drinks and returned, putting a cup down in front of him and taking the seat beside him. I tried to speak, but it was as though a fire lizard nested in my chest, its venom burning me, closing up my throat and I had to cough to clear a passage for the words.

"I wondered, Aydor," I said, "if you would drink with me." He stared at the cup in front of him for a moment, not long, but it felt like a long time. Then he nodded and picked up the cup, took a sip. For a while we were silent.

"Sometimes," he said eventually, "I look at the things I have done and I do not know who I am."

"Aye," I said. "I know that feeling."

One, my master.

Two, my master.

"But I think I am in the right place, Girton Club-Foot."

"Yes." I nodded. "I think you are. We are."

He grinned then and sucked down the entire cupful of drink in one gulp.

"I shall get us another then," he said. "In fact, I think I may need two."

The Birthstorm was unusually savage that year. The rains washed away the blood and the bodies from the field at Goldenson Copse, and the next morning it was almost as if the battle had never happened. Tarris, the priest of Anwith, declared it a miracle though I imagine, if you lived downstream of the battle, you would have been less inclined to agree.

The Landsman's Leash carved into my flesh should have freed me of the strange dreams of hedging lords that had plagued me, but there was one more dream, and it happened when I returned to camp after I had stood by Rufra and watched, so proud of my friend, as he was acclaimed King of Maniyadoc and the Long Tides by all.

When I slept that night I dreamed of Dark Ungar, the worst of the hedging lords. He was the one who promised the most and, in turn, took the most. I felt him more than saw him. He offered me his hand, and though it smelled of sourings and yellow sand drifted from between his fingers I was drawn to him – only to do good. He offered me power and, even more tempting, knowledge. With it I could ensure Rufra's rule. I could take on Dark Ungar's mantle and Rufra would never have to dirty his hands. The life of the land would answer to me and through me to Rufra. Then I felt a calmness, as if a black and silent cloak had been wrapped around my shoulders, and a different hand took mine, a gentle, if cold, touch, and Dark Ungar's presence faded. I found a peaceful place within myself, felt that gentle hand upon my shoulder.

When I woke, pigments had been placed by my bed: black and white, and beneath them, folded carefully, was the soft material of Death's Jester's motley. I picked up the pigments, smelled the familiar scent of the animal fats used to bind them. In the other bed my master lay; she would never walk unaided again. Her eyes were open, bright and sparkling, watching me. I lifted the paint stick, stopped just before it touched my face. My master smiled, nodded at me, then closed her eyes and fell straight into a deep and peaceful sleep.

And I took on the mantle of my god, Xus the unseen, god of death.

Considering what was to come, maybe I should have put the paint stick down. Maybe I should have taken the hand of Dark Ungar and sacrificed myself for knowledge.

I could have saved so many that I would come to care about.

But I did not.

Acknowledgements

It doesn't seem like five minutes since I was writing the last one of these so I'll try not to repeat myself but it's probably a little bit inevitable. At least this version should be shorter.

The inestimable Ed Wilson for some high quality agenting and for sending *Age of Assassins* on a worldwide and multilingual adventure. My editor, Jenni Hill, whose gentle nudges in interesting directions are always welcome and my American editor, Lindsey Hall, who is round and about doing the same. Also, the rest of the wonderful team at Orbit: Joanna, Emily, James, and Nazia, my publicity officer, who has sent me off on some excellent adventures (and the unknown Orbit people I know are there but never meet. Oh! and Ellen and Nita in America.). I'd also like to thank Hugh the copyeditor, one of the unsung heroes of the literary world, who spends a lot of time making me look less stupid than I really are. Thank you, Hugh. I put a deliberate error in them for you, I thought you'd like it.

Matt, Fiona, Marcy and Richard for reading the early versions and offering their opinions which were, as always, useful and well thought out. (Even when you were clearly wrong.) Tim Payne for his technical assistance, thank you kindly.

My fellow 2017 debut authors who have gone a long way to making this year one that has been very funny and full of joy, so if you have enjoyed *Age of Assassins* and *Blood of Assassins* you could do worse than check out the books by Anna Stephens, Ed Mcdonald, Nicholas Eames, Anna Smith-

Spark, Melissa Caruso and the tidily bearded Lee James Harrison (1*ol*cy8l).

All the nice people who have asked me to come and witter on at their conventions, top work. Stephen J Poore who was kind enough to invite me up to Sheffield to do my first ever reading, there will be others, I am sure, but, Stephen, you will always be my first. Michael W. Everest who was kind enough to show me round the Facebook fantasy forums. A big thank you to everyone who reviewed *Age of Assassins* and liked it, and those who didn't like it, because the world would be very dull if we all liked the same stuff. Though, I suppose, it's unlikely you'll be reading this if you really hated it, but it's the thought that counts.

Lastly, Lindy, for being Lindy and Rook for being amusing, and sometimes even being quiet when I ask. And our families who go a long way to making life as pleasant as it currently is.

I am sure, by the time this has seen print, there will be a whole host more people I want to thank but that'll have to wait for *King of Assassins*. As ever, if you should be here but you're not, mea culpa.

RJ Barker
Leeds, July 2017

Look out for

KING OF ASSASSINS

Book Three of the Wounded Kingdom

by

RJ Barker

Many years of peace have passed in Maniyadoc, years of relative calm for the assassin Girton Club-Foot. Even the Forgetting Plague, which ravaged the rest of the kingdoms, seemed to pass them by. But now Rufra ap Vthyr eyes the vacant High-King's throne and will take his court to the capital, a rat's nest of intrigue and murder, where every enemy he has ever made will gather and the endgame of twenty years of politics and murder will be played out in his bid to become the King of all Kings.

Friends become enemies, enemies become friends, and the god of death, Xus the Unseen, stands closer than ever – casting his shadow over everything most dear to Girton.

extras

www.orbitbooks.net

about the author

RJ Barker lives in Leeds with his wife, son and a collection of questionable taxidermy, odd art, scary music and more books than they have room for. He grew up reading whatever he could get his hands on, and has always been "that one with the book in his pocket". Having played in a rock band before deciding he was a rubbish musician, RJ returned to his first love, fiction, to find he is rather better at that. As well as his debut epic fantasy novel, *Age of Assassins*, RJ has written short stories and historical scripts which have been performed across the country. He has the sort of flowing locks any cavalier would be proud of.

Find out more about RJ Barker and other Orbit authors by registering for the free monthly newsletter at www.orbitbooks.net.

if you enjoyed
BLOOD OF ASSASSINS

look out for

THE SHADOW OF WHAT WAS LOST

The Licanius Trilogy: Book One

by

James Islington

AS DESTINY CALLS, A JOURNEY BEGINS.

It has been twenty years since the god-like Augurs were overthrown and killed. Now, those who once served them – the Gifted – are spared only because they have accepted the rebellion's Four Tenets, vastly limiting their own powers.

As a young Gifted, Davian suffers the consequences of a war lost before he was even born. He and others like him are despised. But when Davian discovers he wields the forbidden powers of the Augurs, he sets in motion a chain of events that will change everything.

To the west, a young man whose fate is intertwined with Davian's wakes up in the forest, covered in blood and with no memory of who he is . . .

And in the far north, an ancient enemy long thought defeated, begins to stir.

CHAPTER 1

The blade traced a slow line of fire down his face.

He desperately tried to cry out, to jerk away, but the hand over his mouth prevented both. Steel filled his vision, gray and dirty. Warm blood trickled down the left side of his face, onto his neck, under his shirt.

There were only fragments after that.

Laughter. The hot stink of wine on his attacker's breath.

A lessening of the pain, and screams—not his own.

Voices, high-pitched with fear, begging.

Then silence. Darkness.

Davian's eyes snapped open.

The young man sat there for some time, heart pounding, breathing deeply to calm himself. Eventually he stirred from where he'd dozed off at his desk and rubbed at his face, absently tracing the raised scar that ran from the corner of his left eye down to his chin. It was pinkish white now, had healed years earlier. It still ached whenever the old memories threatened to surface, though.

He stood, stretching muscles stiff from disuse and grimacing as he looked outside. His small room high in the North Tower overlooked most of the school, and the windows below had all fallen dark. The courtyard torches flared and sputtered in their sockets, too, only barely clinging to life.

Another evening gone, then. He was running out of those much faster than he would like.

Davian sighed, then adjusted his lamp and began sifting

through the myriad books that were scattered haphazardly in front of him. He'd read them all, of course, most several times. None had provided him with any answers—but even so he took a seat, selected a tome at random, and tiredly began to thumb through it.

It was some time later that a sharp knock cut through the heavy silence of the night.

Davian flinched, then brushed a stray strand of curly black hair from his eyes and crossed to the door, opening it a sliver.

"Wirr," he said in vague surprise, swinging the door wide enough to let his blond-haired friend's athletic frame through. "What are you doing here?"

Wirr didn't move to enter, his usually cheerful expression uneasy, and Davian's stomach churned as he suddenly understood why the other boy had come.

Wirr gave a rueful nod when he saw Davian's reaction. "They found him, Dav. He's downstairs. They're waiting for us."

Davian swallowed. "They want to do it now?"

Wirr just nodded again.

Davian hesitated, but he knew that there was no point delaying. He took a deep breath, then extinguished his lamp and trailed after Wirr down the spiral staircase.

He shivered in the cool night air as they exited the tower and began crossing the dimly lit cobblestone courtyard. The school was housed in an enormous Darecian-era castle, though the original grandeur of the structure had been lost somewhat to the various motley additions and repairs of the past two thousand years. Davian had lived here all his life and knew every inch of the grounds—from the servants' quarters near the kitchen, to the squat keep where the Elders kept their rooms, to every well-worn step of the four distinctively hexagonal towers that jutted far into the sky.

Tonight that familiarity brought him little comfort. The high outer walls loomed ominously in the darkness.

"Do you know how they caught him?" he asked.

"He used Essence to light his campfire." Wirr shook his head, the motion barely visible against the dying torches on the wall. "Probably wasn't much more than a trickle, but there were Administrators on the road nearby. Their Finders went off, and . . ." He shrugged. "They turned him over to Talean a couple of hours ago, and Talean didn't want this drawn out any longer than it had to be. For everyone's sake."

"Won't make it any easier to watch," muttered Davian.

Wirr slowed his stride for a moment, glancing across at his friend. "There's still time to take Asha up on her offer to replace you," he observed quietly. "I know it's your turn, but . . . let's be honest, Administration only forces students to do this because it's a reminder that the same thing could happen to us. And it's not as if anyone thinks that's something you need right now. Nobody would blame you."

"No." Davian shook his head firmly. "I can handle it. And anyway, Leehim's the same age as her—she knows him better than we do. She shouldn't have to go through that."

"None of us should," murmured Wirr, but he nodded his acceptance and picked up the pace again.

They made their way through the eastern wing of the castle and finally came to Administrator Talean's office; the door was already open, lamplight spilling out into the hallway. Davian gave a cautious knock on the door frame as he peered in, and he and Wirr were beckoned inside by a somber-looking Elder Olin.

"Shut the door, boys," said the gray-haired man, forcing what he probably thought was a reassuring smile at them. "Everyone's here now."

Davian glanced around as Wirr closed the door behind them, examining the occupants of the small room. Elder Seandra was there, her diminutive form folded into a chair in the corner; the youngest of the school's teachers was normally all smiles but tonight her expression was weary, resigned.

Administrator Talean was present, too, of course, his blue cloak drawn tightly around his shoulders against the cold. He nodded to the boys in silent acknowledgment, looking grim. Davian nodded back, even after three years still vaguely surprised to see that the Administrator was taking no pleasure in these proceedings. It was sometimes hard to remember that Talean truly didn't hate the Gifted, unlike so many of his counterparts around Andarra.

Last of all, secured to a chair in the center of the room, was Leehim.

The boy was only one year behind Davian at fifteen, but the vulnerability of his position made him look much younger. Leehim's dark-brown hair hung limply over his eyes, and his head was bowed and motionless. At first Davian thought he must be unconscious.

Then he noticed Leehim's hands. Even tied firmly behind his back, they were trembling.

Talean sighed as the door clicked shut. "It seems we're ready, then," he said quietly. He exchanged glances with Elder Olin, then stepped in front of Leehim so that the boy could see him.

Everyone silently turned their attention to Leehim; the boy's gaze was now focused on Talean and though he was doing his best to hide it, Davian could see the abject fear in his eyes.

The Administrator took a deep breath.

"Leehim Perethar. Three nights ago you left the school without a Shackle and unbound by the Fourth Tenet. You violated the Treaty." He said the words formally, but there was compassion in his tone. "As a result, before these witnesses here, you are to be lawfully stripped of your ability to use Essence. After tonight you will not be welcome amongst the Gifted in Andarra—here, or anywhere else—without special dispensation from one of the Tols. Do you understand?"

Leehim nodded, and for a split second Davian thought this might go more easily than it usually did.

Then Leehim spoke, as everyone in his position did eventually.

"Please," he said, his gaze sweeping around the room, eyes pleading. "Please, don't do this. Don't make me a Shadow. I made a mistake. It won't happen again."

Elder Olin looked at him sadly as he stepped forward, a small black disc in his hand. "It's too late, lad."

Leehim stared at him for a moment as if not comprehending, then shook his head. "No. Wait. Just wait." The tears began to trickle down his cheeks, and he bucked helplessly at his restraints. Davian looked away as he continued imploringly. "Please. Elder Olin. I won't survive as a Shadow. Elder Seandra. Just wait. I—"

From the corner of his eye, Davian saw Elder Olin reach down and press the black disc against the skin on Leehim's neck.

He forced himself to turn back and watch as the boy stopped in midsentence. Only Leehim's eyes moved now; everything else was motionless. Paralyzed.

Elder Olin let go of the disc for a moment; it stuck to Leehim's neck as if affixed with glue. The Elder straightened, then looked over to Talean, who reluctantly nodded his confirmation.

The Elder leaned down again, this time touching a single finger to the disc.

"I'm sorry, Leehim," he murmured, closing his eyes.

A nimbus of light coalesced around Elder Olin's hand; after a moment the glow started inching along his extended finger and draining into the disc.

Leehim's entire body began to shake.

It was just a little at first, barely noticeable, but then

suddenly became violent as his muscles started to spasm. Talean gently put his hand on Leehim's shoulder, steadying the boy so his chair didn't topple.

Elder Olin removed his finger from the disc after a few more seconds, but Leehim continued to convulse. Bile rose in Davian's throat as dark lines began to creep outward from Leehim's eyes, ugly black veins crawling across his face and leaching the color from his skin. A disfigurement that would be with Leehim for the rest of his life.

Then the boy went limp, and it was over.

Talean made sure Leehim was breathing, then helped Elder Olin untie him. "Poor lad probably won't even remember getting caught," he said softly. He hesitated, then glanced over at Elder Seandra, who was still staring hollowly at Leehim's slumped form. "I'm sorry it came to this—I know you liked the lad. When he wakes up I'll give him some food and a few coins before I send him on his way."

Seandra was silent for a moment, then nodded. "Thank you, Administrator," she said quietly. "I appreciate that."

Davian looked up as Elder Olin finished what he was doing and came to stand in front of the boys.

"Are you all right?" he asked, the question clearly aimed at Davian more than Wirr.

Davian swallowed, emotions churning, but nodded. "Yes," he lied.

The Elder gave his shoulder a reassuring squeeze. "Thank you for being here tonight. I know it can't have been easy." He nodded to the door. "Now. Both of you should go and get some rest."

Davian and Wirr inclined their heads in assent, giving Leehim's limp form one last glance before exiting the Administrator's office.

Wirr rubbed his forehead tiredly as they walked. "Want some company for a few minutes? There's no chance I'm going straight to sleep after that."

Davian nodded. "You and me both."

They made their way back to the North Tower in thoughtful, troubled silence.

Once back in Davian's room both boys sat, neither speaking for a time.

Finally Wirr stirred, expression sympathetic as he looked across at his friend. "Are you really all right?"

Davian hesitated for a moment, still trying to sort through the maelstrom of emotions he'd been struggling with for the past several minutes. Eventually he just shrugged.

"At least I know what I have to look forward to," he said wryly, doing his best not to let his voice shake.

Wirr grimaced, then gave him a hard look. "Don't say that, Dav. There's still time."

"Still time?" Normally Davian would have forced a smile and taken the encouragement, but tonight it rang too false for him to let it go. "The Festival of Ravens is in three weeks, Wirr. Three weeks until the Trials, and if I can't use Essence before then, I end up the same way as Leehim. A Shadow." He shook his head, despair thick in his voice. "It's been three *years* since I got the El-cursed Mark, and I haven't been able to do so much as touch Essence since then. I'm not sure there's even anything left for me to try."

"That doesn't mean you should just give up," observed Wirr.

Davian hesitated, then looked at his friend in frustration. "Can you honestly tell me that you think I'm going to pass the Trials?"

Wirr stiffened. "Dav, that's hardly fair."

"Then you don't think I will?" pressed Davian.

Wirr scowled. "Fine." He composed himself, leaning forward and looking Davian in the eye. "I think you're going to pass the Trials."

His tone was full of conviction, but it didn't stop Davian

from seeing the dark, smoke-like tendrils escaping Wirr's mouth.

"Told you,' Davian said quietly.

Wirr glared at him, then sighed. "Fates, I hate that ability of yours sometimes," he said, shaking his head. "Look—I do believe there's a chance. And while there's a chance, you'd be foolish not to try everything you can. You know that."

Wirr wasn't lying this time, and Davian felt a stab of guilt at having put his friend in such an awkward position. He rubbed his forehead, exhaling heavily.

"Sorry. You're right. That wasn't fair," he admitted, taking a deep breath and forcing his swirling emotions to settle a little. "I know you're only trying to help. And I'm not giving up . . . I'm just running out of ideas. I've read every book on the Gift that we have, tried every mental technique. The Elders all say my academic understanding is flawless. I don't know what else I can do."

Wirr inclined his head. "Nothing to be sorry for, Dav. We'll think of something."

There was silence for a few moments, and Davian hesitated. "I know we've talked about this before . . . but maybe if I just told one of the Elders what I can see when someone's lying, they could help." He swallowed, unable to look Wirr in the eye. "Maybe we're wrong about how they would react. Maybe they know something we don't. It is different from being able to Read someone, you know."

Wirr considered the statement for a few seconds, then shook his head. "It's not different enough. Not to the Elders, and certainly not to Administration if they ever found out." He stared at his friend sympathetically. "Fates know I don't want to see you become a Shadow, Dav, but that's nothing compared to what would happen if anyone heard even a whisper of what you can do. If it even crosses their minds that you can Read someone, they'll call you an Augur—and the Treaty's pretty clear on what happens next. The Elders may love you, but in that scenario, they'd still turn you in to Administration in a heartbeat."

Davian scowled, but eventually nodded. They'd had this conversation many times, and it always ended the same way. Wirr was right, and they both knew it.

"Back to studying, then, I suppose," said Davian, glancing over at the jumble of books on his desk.

Wirr frowned as he followed Davian's gaze. "Did it ever occur to you that you're just pushing yourself too hard, Dav? I know you're worried, but exhaustion isn't going to help."

"I need to make use of what time I have," Davian observed, his tone dry.

"But if you ever want to use Essence, you need to sleep more than an hour or two each night, too. It's no wonder you can't do so much as light a candle; you're probably draining your Reserve just by staying awake for so long."

Davian gestured tiredly. He'd heard this theory from plenty of concerned people over the past few weeks, but it was the first time Wirr had brought it up. The trouble was, he knew it was true—when a Gifted pushed their body past its limits they instinctively drew Essence from their Reserve, using it to fuel their body in place of sleep. And if he was draining his Reserve to stay awake, his efforts to access the Essence contained within were doomed to failure.

Still, three years of keeping sensible hours had done nothing to solve his problem. Whatever prevented him from using the Gift, it ran deeper than a lack of sleep.

Wirr watched him for a few moments, then sighed, getting slowly to his feet. "Anyway—regardless of whether you plan to sleep, I certainly do. Elder Caen expects me to be able to identify the major motivations of at least half the Assembly, and I have a session with her tomorrow." He glanced out the window. "In a few hours, actually."

"You don't sleep *during* those extra lessons on politics? I just assumed that was why you took them." Davian summoned a weary smile to show he was joking. "You're right, though. Thanks for the company, Wirr. I'll see you at lunch."

Davian waited until Wirr had left, then reluctantly considered the title of the next book he had laid aside for study. *Principles of Draw and Regeneration*. He'd read it a few weeks earlier, but maybe he'd missed something. There had to be some reason he couldn't access Essence, something he hadn't understood.

The Elders thought it was a block, that he was subconsciously resisting his power because of his first experience with it, the day he'd received his scar. Davian was doubtful, though; that pain had long since faded. And he knew that if he really was an Augur, that fact in itself could well be causing the issue . . . but information on Andarra's former leaders was so hard to find, nowadays, that there was little point even thinking about the possibility.

Besides—perhaps it was simply technique. Perhaps if he read enough about the nature of the Gift, he could still gain sufficient insight to overcome the problem.

Despite his resolve, now that he was alone again he found the words on the cover blurring in front of him, and his jaws cracking open unbidden for a yawn. Perhaps Wirr was right about one thing. Exhaustion wasn't going to help.

Reluctantly he stood up, leaned over, and extinguished the lamp.

He settled into his bed, staring up into the darkness. His mind still churned. Despite his tiredness, despite the late hour, it was some time before he slept.